BISHOP

LAS VEGAS MAFIA SERIES

AMBER ALLEE

Cover Design: Graphics by Stacy
Editing: Kristen Portillo @ Your Editing Lounge
Formatting: Stacey Blake @ Champagne Book Design

Trigger Warnings:
This is a mafia book. If you are not one who likes action, killings, revenge, sex, and violence then this novel is not for you. This book is meant for audiences that are 18+ years old.

To the ones who have been hurt mercilessly by others.
Let Bishop be your revenge.

BISHOP

LAS VEGAS MAFIA SERIES

PROLOGUE

"MATTHEW, STOP! YOU'LL WAKE THE CHILDREN!" The sound of my mother's voice echoes through the halls awakening me from my sleep. Again.

It's been getting worse over the last few weeks and the twins are starting to run and hide when he comes home.

"You think I don't see how you prance around this house and in public trying to get attention?" Dad's voice is slurred which means he's drunk or drugged out again. "You're a whore!"

"Just go to bed, Matthew." I can hear the defeated tone in Mom's voice.

Every day Mom's light starts to dim a little more. She tries to not show it when she's around me or my sisters but I see it. The far-off look she gets while gazing out the window.

The sound of glass shattering reverberates off the walls as I peek out from the bedroom door. I look both ways before the final slam of the door shakes the paintings on the walls. Anger surges through me. We deserve so much better than this. I hate him and avoid his presence when I know he's here or coming home. Our guards relay to us when he is near and that is a small mercy. They probably hate his guts too and want to avoid confrontations like these.

Slowly, I make my way along the destructive path being mindful of the shards of glass on the rugs and tile to the kitchen area. I see Mom standing in front of the freezer with her back to me. The only light in the room is the bulb from the freezer door. As I take a step further in the room my foot crunches on some broken glass and my hiss gains her attention.

"Maddox, what are you doing up at this hour?" She hurries over to me with something in her hands. "You should be in bed, honey. You've got a big math test tomorrow." Her concern is a far cry from what my father shows us.

It's still dark throughout the house and when I reach my hand out to click the light switch on she tries to stop me. "Don't," she begs.

She knows what I'll find but this has to stop. We can't live like this anymore; we shouldn't have to.

"He's getting more and more out of control, Mom." I flip the switch and let my eyes adjust to the brightness of the room.

Mom stands there holding a bag of peas at her side sporting what I assume will be two black eyes in a few hours. They are puffy and swollen red, and she has what looks like a handprint around her exposed slender neck.

"We need to talk to Arturo or Bobby," I growl.

"Hop up here and let me check on your foot." She ignores my comment and nods over to the island. "I hope you'll still be able to play in your game this weekend."

I know why she doesn't agree with me. Contacting them would mean the others would learn what a monster my father is, and if they don't believe her, his actions will only worsen towards her— or maybe he'd turn it on one of us.

"Are you just going to ignore me?" It's an unfair question. My mom is the most selfless woman on this planet. There isn't anything she wouldn't do for me or my twin sisters, and that includes taking a beating from a man who claims to love her.

She pulls the medical kit from under the sink and comes back over to me. "Maddox, what do you want me to say?" Her eyes are so sad. This is not the fun-loving mom who plays ball with me or does tumbling with my sisters. She looks much older than her thirty-four years. "I've tried everything I can to make this stop."

"They'll help us. I know they will."

"You're fifteen, honey. Let me handle your father and you handle school, sports, and girls." She tries to lighten the mood but I don't find any of this amusing.

My dad is a Don in the mafia here in Las Vegas. He's part of the Five Families who run this town. I never thought of my dad as a villain until a year ago. Something changed. I overheard from some of his men that he was trying out new products and had taken a liking to them…a little too much and too often. The first time I witnessed my dad hit my mom was seven months ago. It shocked everyone in our household, including Dad. Thankfully the twins weren't around to watch it unfold.

Then came the paranoia and accusations against Mom. At first, she'd stood her ground and called out all the lies he spewed at her, but over time she'd had enough and packed us up. Some of his men helped her take us out of the city after another night of him coming home drugged out of his mind. Dad found us the next night and not only killed those men but beat Mom so badly that he put her in the hospital. The twins saw what a true monster he was that night and we have been his prisoners ever since.

I hate him. The more time passes the more my plan for our escape develops. We are not staying here much longer. If Bobby or Arturo won't help then I'll find another way.

"You deserve better. We all do," I let slip as I watch her clean up the blood on my foot.

"It's going to be okay. I've got some things in the works, but for now, we wait it out," she whispers as if the room is bugged.

"You may not survive if he continues like tonight." I hold the bag of peas up to the side of her face. She's swelling more and her cheek looks like she's storing marshmallows.

"Promise me you'll watch over your sisters. That you'll take them away from here as soon as you can if something happens," she rushes out. Her eyes are a little wild and I can hear the pleading and panic in her voice. "I want you to get away from him."

"I'll protect them with my life," I firmly swear.

"You're a good brother and son, Maddox," she says causing me to frown.

I'm not so sure I am, seeing the destruction on her face. A good son would stand up and take action against the one who purposely hurt his mother.

"Let me help you clean this mess up," I offer after she has bandaged my foot and helped me off the island.

It takes twenty minutes for us to sweep up all the glass so the twins don't come down here and hurt themselves.

"Get some sleep, honey," Mom says as we reach the top of the stairs. She has a different frozen bag now as we walk towards our rooms.

"I love you, Mom."

"I love you too." Her eyes fill with tears as her bottom lip starts to tremble. "I'm sorry, Maddox."

I pull her into a hug and hold her. She's our backbone and it breaks something inside of me to see her like this. Over her shoulder, I see a family picture of the five of us on the wall. One of the few that hasn't been destroyed over the last few months. From our smiles, you'd never know the hell we've been living in recently.

I watch Mom head into her room and close the door. She doesn't realize it but I've spent many nights listening to her sobs through that door. I feel a fire start to burn in my chest as I hear the beginnings of her muffled cries. Something settles into place and I take a deep breath letting it out slowly.

Things were about to change. I don't know what but we are not going to live like this anymore. What I do know is that I'm done watching the man who I share DNA with raise a hand to my mom and terrorize our family.

Tonight was the last time.

Even if I had to kill my own father to make it so.

CHAPTER ONE

Bishop

MY HAND COMES AROUND FROM BEHIND AND COVERS the guy's mouth. He wasn't expecting someone to be in the shadows waiting to pounce. His muffled rants do nothing but fuel me in my quest. I've had him in my sights for a while waiting to pull the trigger.

"How does it feel to be the prey and not the predator?" I ask as I maneuver him further away from the busy Strip of Las Vegas.

His body is shaking even as he tries to break free from my clutches. He can try all he wants but I'll never let go. He's the scum of the earth and deserves to die here in the gutter with the rats and trash.

"I think we should go for a little ride and get to know each other." My deep voice reverberates against the dumpster I snatched him at.

He screams out from under my hand but my grip on him keeps the noise from alerting others. It'd be so easy to snap his neck right now and have Davis, my computer genius, wipe all footage of this, but I don't. This man needs to feel the same fear he's instilled in others.

Mr. Daniel Nichols abuses children. He owns and runs a boys' baseball sporting league here in Vegas. I'd overheard his name pop up in passing a few months ago but everyone was too worried their kid would be kicked out of the program and possibly lose a chance at a scholarship if they spoke out about it. I have a deeply rooted need to exact revenge on those who use their station in life to mistreat or abuse the vulnerable. Mr. Nichols uses his power and ability to mistreat these kids because he can. Their parents send them to his league for the chance at a better life knowing he could potentially get a college to scout them. The more I looked into and watched this piece of shit around the boys, the more I wanted to get involved.

There are many different layers to abuse. I should know; having lived under the same roof with an abuser has given me an eye for picking up on the mannerisms of others. I grew up playing on competitive teams and had hard coaches at every level of baseball. Some were intense hard-ass coaches but never crossed a line from discipline to abuse.

I've witnessed this guy grab these kids by the back of their collars and drag them across the field to make a point. I've witnessed the bruises the boys have on their lower backs from being hit by something. I've also seen multiple kids with finger bruises around their necks and upper arms. The punishment runs he makes them do is extreme. I've watched the boys run snakes up and down the length of a football field until most of the team was throwing up all because a kid was late due to their parent's flat tire. Then he refused them water. And during out of town tournaments he withheld meals if the team wasn't winning.

Mr. Nichols loves to intimidate the players as well, making the emotional abuse he uses sometimes worse than the physical. These kids are barely teenagers and some haven't hit puberty, yet the things he says to them and calls them are inexcusable.

The parents who push back either get the players kicked out of the league or make it even harder for their child, and seeing how this might be the only ticket for some of these kids out of their situation to a better life, they bite their tongue.

"I had a dream of you last night, Nichols," I start. "You were doing your jogging warm-ups and as you passed first base, I clotheslined you."

He'd huddled the players around before practice last week and singled out the first baseman. All the players laughed and thought it was funny but it was a targeted attack on this kid. The player had an older sibling who was there watching the game and made a joke to cheer up his brother. The two siblings thought they were alone after the game, but Mr. Nichols has little spies reporting back every little detail so he can use it to keep the kids in line. According to my own little spy that practice almost killed the player.

But not on my watch.

The needle in my hand slowly sinks into his neck as I press my thumb down to plunge the sedative into his body. He struggles for a few moments then goes limp.

Perfect.

"Enjoy your little nap."

Now the fun can begin.

Mr. Nichols wakes abruptly, vaulting up to take in his surroundings after I empty an entire large orange water jug onto his previously prostrate body.

"What—"

I've had my men clear the field and surrounding areas so we can be alone for this show. My team has been with me for years; they know the drill and make sure that no one else will see what happens but us.

"Mr. Daniel Nichols, you don't know me but I surely have heard a lot about you over the last few months." I circle him as he sits on the first base side of the baseball field where he brings the players. I bought it a month ago and have a team in place to take over all the maintenance. "My name is Ox Bishop and I've become aware of the program you manage for the less fortunate families in our community. My community."

He doesn't say a word for a few moments as I come back around and stand over him. I make sure my face shows no emotion. He doesn't deserve any type of sympathy or concern for his well-being.

"Why am I here?" His voice shakes as he takes in the sheer size of me and all the men I have waiting along the field and bleachers.

"I'm glad you asked," I sneer and squat down to his level. "I'm going to put you through one of my little practices for the next two hours and see how you handle being treated like you treat your players." I let that sink in. "Sound fair?"

I don't give him a chance to respond before I connect the rope to the hip harness that's around his thighs and waist to the four-wheeler by home plate.

"What in the hell is going on? Who the fuck are you?" He moves to stand while tinkering with the harness.

I turn around and give him a look that would send chills down the devil's back.

"I already told you, and I don't like having to repeat myself, Mr. Nichols. I hear you're the same," I spit, repeating what I've heard him say to his players on multiple occasions.

Slinging a leg over the four-wheeler I turn the key to start the ignition. The engine roars to life and I can't help my menacing smile.

"We'll start the warmup slow," I give as the only warning before my wrist twists and the four-wheeler moves forward with a jolt.

Mr. Nichols is tugged off balance and loses his footing making him fall flat on his face. I drag him fifteen feet before I stop. He's screaming and I can see his hands and knees are scratched up.

"You might want to step it up to keep your skin on," I snap.

It's going to be a good night.

He tries to run even though he's strapped to a rope and harness, but my men all stand in front of the dugouts with their holsters showing the guns they're packing. It takes around ten minutes of starting and stopping before Mr. Nichols finally catches on to what is expected of him. He's covered in grass stains and his skin is torn up. I feel comforted knowing he's experiencing the same type of treatment he loves to dish out.

"Now that the warmup is over, let's work on our sprints," I announce as we make it another lap around the outfield.

"Please—" he begs and it's starting to make me mad.

I rush off the four-wheeler and bump my chest to his causing him to fold to the ground.

"When your players pleaded and begged, did you stop?"

He doesn't answer, still trying to catch his breath.

"Did you show any sympathy at all?"

I grab him by the front of his grass-stained shirt and haul him up to eye level to show how much stronger I am than him. He didn't have a problem exerting his power over kids so I take immense pleasure doing it to him.

"I will show you the same mercy you exacted on those kids." Tossing him away from me, he staggers back still pleading, but I refuse to listen. People who target the young or vulnerable are not going to be shown leniency.

Not on my watch.

After dragging him across the outfield for sprints we move to the fielding portion of tonight's events. My men close in and get into place as I move an exhausted Mr. Nichols to the first base position and I stand at home plate with a bat and ball.

"This should be self-explanatory, but just in case, field the ball then throw it to second base." I point over to where Thomas is positioned with his glove.

"I—I don't have a glove." He states the obvious.

I let out a chuckle. "Of course you don't. Use soft hands."

On several occasions, he'd made the players go without gloves and purposefully tried to drill the ball to hurt them. It wasn't a learning drill but one used to punish the players whose parents spoke up.

Not wasting any more time, I hammer ball after ball at him, not letting him have a chance to field them. Every ball that makes contact with his body is for every child he's ever punished or abused over the last five years. He'd been making money off these poor defenseless kids and abusing them for his own sick pleasure.

Once he collapses, I make my way out to him.

"How did you ever have a team if you can't even field a ground ball, Nichols?"

"Please, I'm sorry. I'll never coach again," he pleads. "I'll go away and never come back."

I look him dead in the eye and lean down, crowding his body.

"Oh, I know you'll never coach again after tonight because your body will be six feet under desert sand."

I meant what I said.

These things aren't going to happen on my watch.

Not in my town.

CHAPTER TWO

"ARE YOU GOING TO APPROVE THE SAMPSON LOAN?" Thomas comes into the office without knocking like always.

I'm researching my next location to build a strip mall to open more avenues to launder money. I've found check cashing places along with pawn shops, and title loans are excellent places to move a lot of cash under the radar. The casinos are the easiest way, but floating it out in other ways keeps the Feds and government off the trail.

I cut my eyes away from the computer when Thomas plops down in the chair across from my desk.

"Sampson? The name isn't registering in my brain. Who is it again?" I know all the big whales that are in Vegas and those who frequently visit.

He lets out a long sigh, trying to come across as irritated, but I know it's all in good fun. Thomas and I have a great working relationship and friendship outside of business. He has been my second-in-command for almost fifteen years and is like the brother I never had.

"Oliver Sampson, sixty-eight years old, owns the little sandwich and coffee shop on East Fremont Street, called Sampson's Sandwich Shop."

"Very original," I joke, giving him my full attention. "Why isn't one of the banks taking care of this?" I ask. The banks I own have dozens of managers in place so I don't receive these easy everyday loans.

"He didn't go to one of them. He brought it into EZ Cash," Thomas answers. It's one of our quick loan places where you walk in, ask for money, fill out a few papers then walk right back out with cash in hand, but the interest rate isn't exactly low. "Nancy thought you should make the call because of the guy's age and the amount he's asking for."

"Of course, she did," I grumble. Nancy has a heart of gold when it comes to the elderly. She'd stand out on the curb with stacks of my money and hand it out to every old person who walked by if she could. "Let me have the file and I'll swing by there on my way home."

"We going out tonight?"

I know what he's asking. Thomas loves when we go hunting. It's been a few weeks since Mr. Nichols had his *come to Jesus meeting* and I know he's itching for our next prey.

"Not tonight."

He nods and stands while fixing his cufflinks, looking like the ever-prominent banker and businessman that he is. I look down and see the same in my appearance. During the day I'm a businessman who owns banks, real estate, and lots of small businesses. When I'm clocked out I'm one of the Dons of the Five Families here in Las Vegas. The mafia is my family and we run this city with an iron fist. While the other Families deal with the more dangerous side of things, I handle all the money we make and turn it into legitimate profit that keeps the government off our coattails.

"Call if you decide to go out for a drink or to shoot some hoops."

"Will do."

After he leaves I finish up a few emails then lock everything up.

My secretary, Kristen, is already gone for the day since banks close at five and it's already close to six in the evening. My loyal team of men is waiting for me as I step out on the sidewalk to the waiting car. I might not get my hands dirty with the drugs and guns, but I'm still a big target of wise guys who would love to trade places with me.

"Mr. Bishop," Darren, my driver since I was twenty-one, greets, "where are we off to this evening?"

"Take me to East Fremont Street, a little place called Sampson's Sandwich Shop," I answer as we pull out into traffic.

"Mr. Oliver's place?" he asks.

"I believe so. Do you know him?"

"Oliver Sampson has been a staple in the community over in Fremont for almost fifty years. He and his dad opened the shop up."

Interesting.

I wonder what could be going on that he'd need a quick loan for.

Twenty minutes later we pull up to an outdated building within walking distance of the busy Fremont Street with all the casinos and entertainment. The location is excellent but the building looks to need a lot of work. The businesses on either side look to be in the same shape.

Before I open the door I can smell delicious freshly made bread. It makes me hungry and my mouth waters the closer I get to the counter.

"How can I help you, sir?" a kid who looks to be around eighteen asks.

"Never been here before, so what's the best sandwich to order?"

The kid's eyes light up. "Man, there are so many good options. The turkey is my favorite with our special sauce but Piper raves about the meatball sandwich. Mr. Sampson will tell you the teriyaki is the best."

I almost laugh at the enthusiasm. "How about I get one turkey and one meatball? Load it up for me."

"Yes, sir! Will this be for here or to go?"

I turn my head and see a small dining area off to the side of the store. A guy in a suit similar to mine sits at one of the tables alone, his eyes focused on the phone in front of him.

"I'll eat here. Is Mr. Sampson here by chance?"

"He'll be right back. Had to run an errand," the kid states.

"Perfect."

He rings me up and then tells me he'll bring it out when it's ready. I find my seat in the corner and keep watching out the window and at the counter. The foot traffic is steady it seems, with people moving about early evening. I imagine the weekends are extremely busy with tourists coming in for quick getaways.

"What took you so long?" The annoyance in a man's voice pulls my attention over to the suit from earlier.

A gorgeous woman who would give Jessica fucking Rabbit a run for her money with red, wavy hair comes out from the door behind the counter. She's wearing a knee-length, fifties-style dress with math problems on the entirety of it with a multiplication belt around her small waist. She's a walking equation and right up my sense of humor.

"Really, Piper? Is it possible to ever dress as an adult?" the guy chides and the hair on the back of my neck rises.

Piper looks down at her dress, confused. She slowly brushes her hands down the front as if trying to smooth any wrinkles looking uncomfortable instead of confident like she did when she first walked out.

"I'm a middle school math teacher, Trent. The kids love all the fun math outfits I have," she says defensively. She takes her seat sitting straight as an arrow. "Why did you want to meet here today? I thought we had plans later this evening?"

Trent finally sets his phone down on the table. His jaw locks into place and he narrows his eyes at her. "This isn't working for me anymore, Piper. We come from two different worlds and clearly, you are still living out your childhood while the rest of us are maturing into adulthood. I mean, you're about to be twenty-six years old for god's sake, and look where you are in life." He pauses for dramatic effect then continues. "You barely make any money being a teacher and work a second job for some old guy doing his books in a sandwich shop. My family is a pillar in this community and this relationship is not good for our image."

The kid who took my order comes out with my two sandwiches giving Trent a death glare, no doubt having heard him berate her. He doesn't pay me any mind as he sets the tray down on the table and heads back to where he came from.

"I can't believe you'd say something so horrible to me like that. I make the same salary every teacher in the state of Nevada makes. No, it's not six figures like you or your family, but I love teaching the students math. My god, Trent, your mother was a teacher for many years before she quit," she points out. "And I work here as a second job because I need the extra income to help with my parents' healthcare."

You don't owe this dipshit any explanation, sweetheart.

"That's neither here nor there." He waves her off, apparently not liking being called out for talking like a douche.

"How very shallow of you to even comment that I'm not good enough because I'm not in a certain tax bracket."

He shrugs like he just didn't insult her. I quickly send a text out to Wayne on my team to stop this jackass and get his info.

Just as the asshole is about to open his mouth again, the kid— who is bringing a drink over to me—pretends to trip and the entire drink empties on Trent. It's all over his suit and his phone is doused on the table. Piper hops up to miss the splash just in time, although, I'd pay for her dry-cleaning if a drop of liquid got on any inch of that work of art. The more I look over at the drenched pissant the more I like the teenage kid because I didn't even order that drink.

"Oh—how clumsy of me," the kid says. He looks over at me with wide eyes but there's a sparkle in them. "I'll get you a new drink, sir." He leaves as Trent fumes over his ruined clothes.

"Here you go." Piper offers a few napkins from the dispenser. "You might want to soak that when you get home."

He doesn't say another word but stands abruptly. My body goes tense waiting to see if he makes a move to retaliate against her. He makes the best decision of his life as he storms out the door ranting about the cost of his suit and that he's glad to be done with her.

The side of her lip quirks up as she bends over to wipe up some of the spill and the kid comes back with a mop and bucket.

"Rob, you can't do that again, okay?" Piper tries to sound scolding but there's a lightness to her tone.

"He had no right to speak to you like that. You are the best person I know, Piper, and you do so much for others. I can't believe you ever gave that idiot a shot."

"I understand what you're saying and feel the same, but still, it's not right," she tries again.

"Yes, ma'am."

A few minutes later Piper comes over to my table with a drink in hand. I playfully put my hands up in a surrender gesture.

"Don't worry, I come in peace." She laughs as she sets down my drink.

This close I can see she's even more beautiful. Even with her light makeup, she has a dusting of freckles that sweep across her cheeks and nose. She looks almost porcelain.

"Sorry you had to witness that. If there's anything we can get you please let me or Rob know."

I nod because my mouth is full of a meatball. I swallow quickly to speak so she doesn't walk away. "I'm actually here to see Mr. Sampson."

"You're not with some department that could shut us down because of what Rob did, are you? Clearly he tripped and lost his grip on the cup and—" I can hear the panic in her voice and hold a hand up to stop her.

"No, I'm nothing of the sort. That dipshit deserved a lot more with the way he spoke to you. It goes to show money can't buy class. Mr. Sampson and I have some business to discuss about numbers."

Her shoulders perk up.

"I do the books for Mr. Sampson and can help with most everything around here," she offers. "He should be back any minute. He recently took a fall and is a little bit slower getting around, but he's on the mend."

I motion with my free hand. "Here, have a seat."

After looking back at the counter she pulls the chair out from under the table and gracefully sits. "I'm Piper by the way." She extends her dainty right hand across the table.

"Maddox Bishop," I return and envelope hers with mine. Her skin is soft as if she bathes in moisturizer. Why I gave her my full name instead of Ox or Bishop puzzles me. Only my mom and sisters have ever called me by my full name.

"How long have you worked for Mr. Sampson?"

Piper leans back in her chair with a thoughtful expression. "Off and on for the past ten years. These last few years I've been helping regularly."

Just as I'm about to ask her more an older man comes from the back of the store with a walking cane in hand.

"Oh, Mr. Sampson, this is Mr. Bishop. He needs to speak with you," Piper informs Oliver as she gets up and goes over to the man.

He only takes his eyes away from me to whisper something to Piper. She nods then turns back to face me. "It was nice meeting you, Mr. Bishop." She ends our conversation and before I can correct her to call me by my first name she quickly walks toward the back of the store and out of sight.

Mr. Sampson hobbles over and takes a seat where Piper was a few minutes ago. "How can I help you, Mr. Bishop?" His tone isn't a pleasant one.

"I'm here to discuss your application for a quick loan you recently applied for."

His tense demeanor releases and I wonder why he's wound up. "Oh yes, I did. That sweet girl at the store said someone would get back to me soon."

"You have a nice place here; the food and service are excellent," I comment trying to open the discussion up.

"Thank you. I've been here since my father and I opened it almost forty-eight years ago."

"That's a long time for an establishment. Not many have lasted that long around here especially when the economy drops."

"My father taught me how to manage for the low times."

"Why do you need a twenty-five thousand dollar loan from me, Mr. Sampson, and not from a more traditional bank where the interest rate won't kill you?"

He turns his head to the left where the back rooms and Rob and Piper are located before he turns back to me. "Kids these days don't have any respect. I had to earn every penny by working hard, keeping my nose clean, and saving. The punks these days never have had to work hard for anything. These kids now just expect you to hand it over and if you don't comply they use force."

"Is that why you're using the cane?" I ask remembering Piper had mentioned him taking a fall.

"I don't want any more trouble, Mr. Bishop. I just want to keep the peace and continue on the way it's always been."

"If you pay, they will keep demanding more and more," I note. I've dealt with a lot of punks over the years taking things they didn't earn.

"I don't have too many more years left in me but I want to keep helping those two in the other room. They both work so hard it reminds me of myself at their age."

I nod my understanding as I sit back and listen.

"My Sally and I were never blessed with children so we put all our time and energy here. We've had some wonderful employees over the years but those two are special to us." He points over his shoulder. "I couldn't live with myself if something were to happen to one of them."

"Tell me who is demanding the money and I'll make it go away." I look him dead in the eyes.

Some punk taking advantage of the elderly is right up my alley.

"If it's not him then another kid will come along eventually and do the same. I've just gotten older and am unable to stand up to them like I used to."

"I can take care of this problem for you. Give me the details," I offer again.

Oliver lets out a heavy sigh, defeated. "A developer wants our properties so he can tear down our buildings and put in another casino. We've held out as a group, declining all the low offers because most of us have been here for so long and the location is prime. It wasn't until recently that Mr. Slater started sending a more physical approach."

"Slater? As in Victor Slater?" I question making sure I heard correctly. This isn't his territory and he has no business over here.

"That's what the letterhead said, Slater Enterprise."

Interesting.

"What's the name of the punk who roughed you up?"

"I don't know his name. He caught me off guard when I was locking up the backdoor to the alley before walking to my car. I'm only glad it was me and not Piper or Rob."

What a little coward to jump an elderly man.

"Listen, I don't want Piper or Rob to hear about any of this. The last thing I want is for them to get involved or hurt because they think they can stand up to these bullies on my behalf. I told them I tripped over a box by the dumpster."

"They'll be none the wiser," I agree.

We both sit for a minute in silence as a thought whirls around in my head. I want him to think about what I'm about to offer.

"You say you don't have any family to pass this place down to. So what are your plans for the business?"

I'm not in the restaurant or food service business but for some reason, this place settles something in my chest. The numbers are running through my head as I calculate the cost and possible profit on the return investment. The real estate alone is worth a fortune.

It just needs to be updated. It also helps so that I keep running into a certain redhead.

"I was hoping Piper might be interested in taking it over. I know she has a passion for working with kids, but Rob's really picking up his weight and I think they'd make the best team for this place and keep the memories alive."

I nod. "How'd you like a silent partner?" He's about to protest but I hold my hand up. "Hear me out."

Over the next five minutes, I go over what would be in the contract and what my role would actually be. He, Piper, and Rob will still have the majority stakes and profit. In the event things don't work out I'll sell my stake back to them for one hundred dollars. No strings attached to any of this.

"I want to keep your legacy around. It's good for the area and for business, not to mention this is one of the best sandwiches I've ever had."

"Can I sleep on it?"

"I'd be worried if you didn't," I say. "I'll have my attorney draw up the paperwork and have it sent over for you to review. I promise to be straightforward, no hidden loops."

"I know who you are, Mr. Bishop. You can't live in this city and own businesses and not know of you. You've really made a difference to so many people here. Even if no one gives you the credit you so deserve."

"How do you—" I stop talking for a moment. What I do has always been off the grid. My team and I work our asses off to stay off the radar.

"You forget I've been here all my life, Mr. Bishop. They might not know it's you directly but our community thanks you."

Not wanting to draw any more attention to the subject I stand and button my jacket to leave.

"I do what I can."

Walking out of the business I'm quickly met with Rob who grabs my elbow and I let him lead me to the side alley. I motion for my team to stand down. I'm trained for every surprise that might arise. I saw Rob a mile away as did my team.

"I want to help take down this asshole." He stops and turns to face me. He reminds me so much of myself as a kid with the weight of the world on his shoulders. He has a fire in his eyes like he's remarkably familiar with how harsh the world can be.

"Do you know who hurt Oliver?"

Rob nods his face serious. "He goes by the name Sully. Low-level punk trying to make a name for himself in the ranks."

"How old are you, Rob?" I take him in really looking at him.

"Nineteen," he states with finality but I know that's horseshit.

"Try again and don't ever lie to me." My shoulders roll back and my head tilts down toward his. My face has gone deathly serious to show I mean business.

Being called out isn't a good look on this kid.

"Fine, seventeen."

"Where do you live, Rob?"

A nervousness or embarrassment comes over him all of a sudden. "Here and there," he answers not looking me in the eyes. "Piper lets me stay with her."

"Let me deal with this and you oversee making sure Oliver doesn't have any more falls." I pull out a card and hand it to him. "Put this number in your phone and call me if something comes up," I say, giving him my direct cell phone number. "This situation is more of my caliber, Rob. You keep an eye on those two for me."

He nods. "I will."

I walk back to the car and place my cell to my ear once the car door is shut and Darren is pulling out on the streets. I only get a quick glance at Piper before she's out of view.

"Yeah," Thomas answers on the first ring.

"Head over to my place. We've got some research to do before going hunting."

"Be there in twenty."

CHAPTER THREE

Piper

"**M**s. Caldwell, Mrs. Roberts would like to speak with you during passing period," Becky, the secretary, calls out from the phone intercom.

"Ahhhhhh," the classroom echoes out as if I'm in trouble after being called down to the principal's office. It makes me chuckle because I was thinking the same thing in my head.

"Settle down and work on your problems. These will be on the final exam," I remind them.

Five minutes later the bell rings making the students scramble to collect their belongings and race to their next class. This is my off period so I pick up my lanyard full of keys, my folder of papers to make copies, and my cell phone. After closing my classroom door and making sure it's locked I pass the herd of kids meandering their way down the hall to the different rooms for next period.

"Good afternoon, Ms. Caldwell," Becky greets me when I step into the front office. It's always bustling with students, parents, and staff. "She said to go on in when you got here."

"Thank you, Ms. Becky." I smile, making my way around the counter and down the hall.

The last door on the right belongs to our principal, Mrs. Jackie

Roberts. She and my parents knew each other through church many decades ago. She's in her mid-sixties and should be retiring soon.

My parents had me when they were in their mid-forties. Mom had always said I was their little surprise miracle baby. She thought she was starting menopause the first four months of her pregnancy. When the doctor announced the result of her bloodwork, Dad burst out laughing thinking Dr. Bruce was joking. Mom and Dad had tried for fifteen years to have a baby but every month it never happened. When Mom turned thirty-nine she and Dad decided that it wasn't what God had wanted for their family and they focused on a new path for just a family of two. A few years later their path changed again and I was born.

"You wanted to see me, Mrs. Roberts," I say as I knock on her open door.

She's filling out some paperwork and stops when she hears my voice. "Yes, come in and have a seat. Leave the door open," Mrs. Roberts says not looking up. I do as she asks and take a seat across from her. "I just got off the phone with administration and it seems you've been selected for the Teacher of the Year Award for the entire district," she finally looks up and at me. "Again."

"Ohhh?" I'm confused. Is this a good thing or bad? I'm not even sure who selects the nominees for this award.

"Obviously, it looks excellent on Kennard Middle School but at the same time your peers might start to resent you for always taking the spotlight."

"I—I didn't sign up for this contest," I begin.

"It's not the point, Piper. Parents are always coming up here singing your praises and wanting their kids to be placed in your class. The school had to enact a policy that requesting a teacher wasn't allowed."

I'm still so confused about how this is my problem when I haven't done anything wrong.

"Okay?" I keep staring at her waiting for the punchline to this conversation. Is she getting on to me for being a beloved teacher or not happy that I won an award for this school?

"I can see this isn't penetrating." She actually looks mad that I'm not reacting and her tone is getting increasingly condescending. "When the new school year starts in August I want you to try and tone down everything."

Her eyes drop to my Albert Einstein E=MC² patterned dress. A lady across the street from my home, Irene, is a retired seamstress and makes all my math-themed dresses. When she found out I was a math teacher she'd brought over several dresses years ago and I find new ones on my doorstep every few weeks. I've tried to pay her for the dresses, especially because it's been such a hit with the students and parents over the years, but she refuses to take my money.

"Just come over and have a drink with me once in a while," Irene had said. So every Wednesday night we have a girls' evening where she tells me all the stories about making outfits and costumes for the shows here in Vegas or memories of her and her late husband through the years.

Not wanting to argue, I simply nod hoping the bell for the next class rings soon so I can get the hell out of her office.

"That will be all." Jackie turns back to her paperwork dismissing me.

Not wanting to spend another second in her presence, I quickly rise out of my chair and make a break for the door. Just as I'm almost past the threshold I hear her voice. It's like nails on a chalkboard. "Also, you'll need to make arrangements about that fish tank in your room. The custodians shouldn't be the ones to take care of or deal with those smelly things."

"They—" I snap to respond when I turn around to face her and can feel the sharp edge of my voice coming through. Clearing my throat, because I can't afford to lose this job, I simply say, "I'll make sure they are fully taken care of. All summer."

I've never had anyone look after my fish or the tank for that matter that wasn't paid by me for their time. I was told many years ago that having a fish tank was good for calming students. It gives them a space when they have too much stimulation. The students love them and have requested to take turns with duties to keep them fed. I have a variety of fish and always try to find the most unique ones at the fish store.

"Don't forget to get the expense reports done and in to me by the middle of June. I have to have those over to Edith in administration."

She's talking about all the receipts for the entire year's expense report. She always waits till the last minute to turn them in and has me do them but she signs off on them as if she's the one who did.

"Are you sure I'm the one you want to do it?" I ask hoping she'll give me an out. She had me do them last year and something just didn't feel right. The receipts were a mess and it seemed like things were missing or weren't correct. I did the best I could with all the items given to me but the feeling wasn't right in my gut.

"Piper, you are given a stipend for your work, and I'd think under your current circumstances that you'd want all the help you can get." Her snide remark makes me want to lash out but I stay quiet knowing that I've got bigger issues than this to deal with.

The stipend she's referring to is the one hundred dollars she gives me for doing her expense report. A report that takes me forever to do because she refuses to have a system in place to keep it organized. And it's cutting into my summer vacation away from this place and other opportunities to make money elsewhere.

"I'm just not sure I can pull it off this year with me working more hours at my second job," I say, still trying to find a way out of it.

"You should've given me more notice and waiting till the last week of school to inform me of this is truly unprofessional," she clips.

Knowing I'm not going to win this battle I wave the white flag. "I'll see what I can do." My shoulders slump in defeat.

When I took this job at Kennard Middle School I was so excited to know someone who knew my parents and the situation I was in. Turns out that those people are the ones who will take the most advantage of you because they make you feel like you owe them.

Walking out of the office after getting all the copies I need and back into the hallway, I wonder where I would've ended up if I hadn't come back to help with my parents. The bell signals the end of the period and so I shake off the *what-ifs* and focus on the here and now.

Hours later I pull up to the sandwich shop starving. I had an unexpected flat tire that couldn't be fixed, so I had them put on the spare donut from the trunk until I can afford to buy a new one when I get paid at the end of next month. Thankfully, Oliver lets us make a sandwich and eat for free when we're working. I'm just so blessed to have him in my life right now.

"I'm here!" I announce as I walk through the door and see Rob behind the counter helping a couple.

"You just missed the crowd," Rob says after ringing up the order.

"On a Monday?"

"Yep. They all had some badge thingy, so I guess they're here for a convention."

I slip into the back office and see the new receipts from today's deliveries in the correct tray. When I was younger and looking for a job, Oliver hired me to make sandwiches but quickly learned I had a knack for numbers and switched me over to help him with the books and keep him organized. The office was a total mess and it took the entire summer to straighten out but it runs like a well-oiled machine now. Everything has its place and is labeled just like my classroom and home.

After inputting the last receipt, I hop up from the chair and head back out into the shop to see if Rob needs a hand before I make myself a sandwich. I hear Rob talking in a hushed tone as I step out of the storage room and see him speaking with the man from yesterday.

Maddox clears his throat and Rob pops his head over at me.

"Hey, Piper, Mr. Bishop was stopping by to drop off some paperwork for Oliver."

"Oh, I can put it on his desk. He had a doctor's appointment I believe late this afternoon but should be here soon if you want to have a seat and sandwich while you wait," I offer.

Maddox is dressed in another dark tailored suit with a light blue button-down shirt. He looks like the type of man who is the life of the party but also has a dangerous vibe. His eyes are so alluring with a silvery glimmer to them, like he could undress me with just a stare. A shiver runs down my spine when he refuses to look away.

"I love your dress," Maddox says when he finally breaks eye contact, and his eyes rover over my body. "You must have a thing for numbers." His gaze tracks up and down my body before meeting my eyes again. I almost feel as if I should give a little twirl to give him the whole effect of the dress.

"I try to keep the students engaged in the classroom. They seem to like when I wear my math outfits." After Trent's harsh words yesterday, I feel like I have to explain myself.

Rob snickers pulling our gaze in his direction. "Piper, it's not the only reason they like you wearing your dresses and beg their parents to put them in your class."

I look down at my outfit not understanding what he's trying to say. "What?" My face scrunches not understanding.

"He means you look fucking hot and the material molds to every curve of your body."

My mouth drops open and my eyes widen at Maddox's brazen words.

"Mr. Bishop, that's not very appropriate," I try to chastise this grown man as I would one of my students.

"Maddox."

"Excuse me?" The man has just flustered me.

"My name is Maddox. Call me that."

"I think I might take a quick break before the dinner crowd

comes." Rob tosses his latex gloves into the nearby trash. "You got this for a few minutes?"

"Of course, Rob." I know he's been here for hours by himself. "I better not catch you smoking out there!" I call out as the door that leads to the alleyway is about to close.

The door closes and I realize it's just the two of us alone here.

"Would you like something to eat while you wait for Oliver?" I ask as I grab a pair of gloves.

"I'll have whatever you're having," he says and I raise an eyebrow. "Rob said you always make a sandwich when you come in after school."

"Rob needs to learn to keep his mouth shut," I mumble under my breath.

"What was that?"

"Do you want mayonnaise or mustard with your ham?" I correct with a sweet smile.

"You choose."

I set out to make the two sandwiches all the while I'm highly aware of Maddox's eyes following my every move.

"Do you want to join me?" Maddox motions to one of the tables.

"I really shouldn't since I'm covering for Rob and someone might come in," I say but he takes both of our meals and heads over to the empty area.

Not having much of a choice, I toss my gloves in the nearby trash and follow over to the table after grabbing two bottles of water from the cooler.

"So, you and Rob run this place when Oliver isn't able to?" he asks after we both start to eat.

"Oliver is always here; he just has had a rough week since his fall. Rob and I help where we're needed." I hope this isn't some audit or someone trying to find a reason to shut us down. "What exactly are you here for?"

"Oliver and I have an arrangement of sorts."

"Like?" I want to know what his intentions are.

"I'm here to ensure the business stays open and continues to run smoothly without any bumps."

"I can assure you that business is doing well and that the numbers don't lie. I'm incredibly good at the books. What exactly do you do?"

"I'm in banking and real estate," he says but doesn't elaborate.

"If you're thinking of franchising our shop Oliver won't allow it—"

Maddox raises a hand to stop me. "I'm not here to upset the business but to invest and make sure it continues to flourish as it has been for the last forty-plus years."

I nod, happy with his answer then pick up my sandwich and continue to eat. "How long have you been in banking?" I ask after my last bite.

"A long time. It's kind of a family business," he says.

"Oh, like your father was a banker and his was too?"

"Something like that. What about you? Did you always want to be a teacher?"

"Not really, I went to school with the hopes of working for NASA one day, but right after I graduated my parents were in an accident. I came home and got my teaching certificate to help with their recovery. I worked for Oliver in high school then picked up shifts when I came back to earn more money. I've been here for the last few years helping wherever he needs."

"Sorry about your parents. I hope they are recovered."

The front doorbell rings alerting us to customers coming in so I jump up from my seat. Oliver comes in with his cane right behind them and sees us. He gives me a warm smile as I approach.

"How was the appointment?" I ask.

"Everything is fine. Just taking a little longer because I'm getting old."

"Let me make you something. Mr. Bishop is here with some paperwork for you."

"Bring it back to the office when you can," he says then motions for Maddox to follow him.

They both walk back but not before Maddox places his large hand on my shoulder and runs it down the length of my arm. His touch sends tingles through my body. Honestly, everything about this man sends tingles through my body.

The bell rings again and a flood of people make their way into the shop just as Rob comes back from break. We work together as the masses of the dinner-time crowd come in. When the line starts to lighten up I realize the sun has set and my back is starting to ache. The business phone rings by the cash register next to Rob and I pray it's not a large order to be delivered right before we close up.

"It's for you." Rob's face looks worried as he reaches out for me to take the phone.

"Hello," I say when I place it to my ear.

"Ms. Caldwell, this is Nurse Tammy. We've been trying to reach you. Your mom fell during physical therapy."

"Oh my gosh, I'll be right there." I hang up in a rush. "It's Mom. I've got to go," I say to Rob as I run out of the back door to the shop, not stopping when he starts to ask a million questions.

Thankfully, I wear my car keys around my neck along with all my school keys. It takes me twenty minutes to pull up to the rehabilitation facility. I just hope she is okay and this doesn't set her recovery back further.

CHAPTER FOUR

A S OLIVER SIGNS ON THE LAST PAGE I HEAR HURRIED footsteps approaching. The door swings open and Rob comes in, worry written across his face. My mind immediately goes to Piper at the front of the shop. My men are positioned outside and down the street to make sure no threats can reach me, but with random customers coming in for food that makes it difficult to monitor.

"I need a ride," Rob says urgently.

"What's going on? Why, what happened?" Oliver braces his hands against the desk and lifts up to his feet.

"Piper, she—" Her name causes my own legs to push to standing.

"What's wrong?" My voice tightens. I look over his shoulder expecting to see her but don't. The entire shop is eerily quiet.

"She got a call, it must be bad," Rob continues but stops before he tells us the rest. "She just took off."

"Let's go," I say without thinking. We start towards the doorway.

"Take this." Oliver is holding Piper's purse out. Before I can reach it Rob snatches it out of his hand. "I'll close up here. Call me and let me know what's going on."

We walk out the front to my car. Chad sees us and opens my door before we reach it.

"Where to?" Darren asks from the front seat as Rob looks around the car.

I look over to Rob for the answer.

"Piper mentioned her mom so it's the rehabilitation hospital. They're over off of Valley View Boulevard."

Depending on which side of the highway it might not be in the best area. Rob gives Darren all the info while I calculate the risk of the area and what we might be facing.

"How long have they been at this treatment facility?" I ask as traffic causes us to stop at another light. "Is it for the car accident or a drug problem?" Piper had mentioned a car wreck but it sounded like it happened years ago.

"They were in a car accident a couple of years ago and need round-the-clock care to get better," Rob snips as if disgusted that I thought so poorly of these people despite not knowing them.

"My apologies, I was just trying to figure all this out."

Rob shakes his head. "It wouldn't matter if it was drugs or not though. Piper helps everyone out no matter their situation."

"Like you?" I infer. "Where are your parents, Rob?"

"They left me…" He trails off not meeting my eyes and instead looking out the window.

"They passed?"

"No, they packed up one day while I was at school and left." His eyes are full of hate and resentment.

"How long ago was this?"

"Few years ago. Piper caught me digging in the dumpster in the alleyway. She recognized me right away. She made me come into the shop and made me the biggest sandwich." He stares off like he is reliving the day. "She introduced me to Oliver and he gave me a job."

"So, Piper takes care of you."

"I can take care of myself now," he says, getting defensive.

"I'm just trying to understand." I raise my hands up.

"Piper took me in. I was staying at a shelter but one night I didn't make it in time before the cut-off and had to sleep out on the street. I got beat up bad that night. When I didn't show up to school and work she came looking for me and found me. She lets me stay in her spare bedroom as long as I go to school and make good grades."

"I see."

Darren and I make brief eye contact with each other.

"The food that's about to expire and get thrown out, she takes it a few streets over to a few of the homeless people living at the park and gives it to them. She's always trying to help others. She's the best person I know besides Oliver. I'll do anything for her," he confesses.

Darren pulls up to the facility and Rob hops out. He's about to close the door but stops.

"You aren't coming in?" he asks.

"I don't think she'd want a stranger in her business."

He nods. "Thanks for the ride." He doesn't wait for a response before shutting the door and hustling into the building.

Darren waits until he's secure inside before easing the car forward. "You want me to park the car and wait, sir?"

I shake my head. The more I hang around and learn about Piper the more I start to want things. Things I promised myself to never want.

Darren circles the parking lot, heading for the exit onto the street when something touches my leg. Looking down I notice Piper's purse Rob left behind.

"Circle back to the front." I sigh and lean my head against the headrest. Every time I try to do the right thing and put some distance between myself and this gorgeous woman the world has other plans.

Darren parks the car under the awning of the building. "Want me to take it in, sir?"

"I've got it."

Walking in, the lady at the front desk perks up from playing on her phone. "Can I help you, sir?" she purrs and it makes her come across as more constipated than sexy.

"I'm looking for Piper Caldwell. Her parents are here at this facility."

"I'm sorry, sir, but we can't give out information to people who aren't on the approved list."

"I just need to return her purse—" I start to say but hear her voice a short distance away.

"I don't understand how that's possible. I made the payment and the funds were clearly taken out." Her voice sounds tired and irritated.

"Ma'am, you'll have to contact the accounting department during business hours to get answers. I'm just letting you know that your parents' charts have been flagged because of insufficient funds."

"This is unbelievable," she argues rubbing her forehead.

"I found her," I tell the receptionist and ignore her protest as I make my way around her desk toward Piper.

She is looking down at something on her phone, unaware of her surroundings. She looks adorable in her Albert Einstein math dress and I just can't help myself from commenting.

"Excuse me, are you a math book?" I ask trying to keep a straight face and even tone.

Her head shoots up when she hears my voice, realizing she's not alone. "What?" She looks around, clearly shocked to see me.

"I asked if you were a math book," I repeat. I can tell she's trying to determine if she's missed something with my question. "Because you've got a lot of problems that I'm willing to solve."

Her eyebrows almost touch looking up at me. For a moment I think I've lost my charming touch toward women until she bursts out laughing. Her laugh is so infectious that I join in causing the medical staff to pause. Her face relaxes and it makes her even more beautiful. She holds onto the counter once she's settled down.

"I've never had someone tell me a math joke that wasn't under the age of thirteen." She chuckles as her gorgeous smile stays in place. "I really needed that, thank you."

"I've got more if you ever need to put that smile back on your face."

"I might need one every day if this kind of news keeps being thrown at me."

"Then your wish is my command." I reach into my pocket and pull out my phone. My other hand glides down her forearm to her wrist turning her palm upward and sliding my phone into her hand. "Are you good at adding numbers? Try adding yours to my contacts."

Her eyes glitter with such joy a bubble forms in my chest. Her laughter rings out and several staff members shush us. She's laughing so much her eyes are watering and her bright smile never falters. She's beautiful, inside and out.

"I really needed that," she says after getting herself under control. I don't think I've had a smile on my face this long since before I became a teenager. "Do you really want my number?"

"I'd love to have it," I say with a nod. After I press the code to unlock my phone, I open up the contact list and add her name. I could easily get her number in less than two minutes but this way she can feel a little more in control.

"I better not find my number on some bathroom stall, Mr. Bishop, or I'm coming after you." She winks at me as she hands me my phone back.

I take my time retrieving my phone making sure to have my fingers linger across her skin. Her hand trembles letting me know she's just as affected as I am.

"I'd never give your number out."

"What are you doing here? Not that I'm ungrateful for the distraction but this place doesn't look like your typical hangout spot."

That makes me laugh. This woman might be trouble for me and my rock-solid plans if I don't rein myself in.

"Rob needed a ride here and you forgot this in the office." I reach behind me to my waistband, avoiding my gun, and pull out her purse.

"Oh, thank you. I got the call and rushed out without thinking."

"Rob said your parents are here. Are they okay?" I ask looking around the place. It's not the best facility but not the worst either.

She follows my eyes and looks around. "It's better than the last place."

Just as she's about to say more, an announcement is made over the sound system. "Visiting hours will be ending in five minutes and will resume tomorrow morning at eight."

"I better grab Rob and say bye. Thank you again for bringing Rob and my purse, it was very thoughtful."

She walks the few steps separating us and wraps her arms around my midsection. At first, a foreign feeling of being touched jolts me, but her vanilla scent filters through my nose sending a calming balm through my system. My arms immediately engulf her, squeezing her tight. It's dangerous how perfectly she fits against me. My cheek settles against the top of her head and I hold onto her for as long as I can.

"Uh…"

My head snaps up at the noise and see Rob standing there shifting his weight on his feet.

"Oh, I'm sorry," Piper says then steps out of my reach. I want to snatch her back into the comfort of my grasp as her warmth leaves me.

"Don't be."

"I heard the announcement and wanted to come find you," Rob tells her.

"Thank you, Rob. I'll go and tell them bye." She turns to leave but stops when she passes him and turns back to us. "Thank you, Maddox, it means a lot to us."

She doesn't let me respond before she walks off and I'm left there staring after her like a love-sick fool. I do catch two male jackasses in white medical jackets watch her delectable ass sway as she heads down the hall and around the corner.

"Walk me out," I grit out to keep myself composed from pummeling the two doctors. I catch their eyes and from the glare I'm giving, they swiftly get back to work.

Darren isn't parked by the door so I walk with Rob over to where Piper's car is parked. He pulls out a key from his pocket and I notice the lean of the car.

"This is her car?" I ask looking at this scrap of metal.

"She had a really nice one last year but sold it to pay her parents' bill," Rob tells me as he looks the car over.

"She's driving on the spare," I state as I walk around the rest of the car to see if all four tires are jacked up.

"Piper said she had a flat but it was going to be too expensive to replace so she's waiting until she gets paid next month."

"She shouldn't be driving on this now, much less for a month."

"I know but—" Rob starts to say something but catches himself.

"What?"

"I—she wouldn't want me to tell others, but Piper tries to keep so much hidden so everyone won't worry about her." He's trying to protect her pride and their bond.

"I won't say a word to anyone."

I hold the door open for him to get in and watch as he tries to start this bucket of bolts. It takes three tries before it turns over. The dashboard lights up like a Christmas tree with the check engine light along with several maintenance icons. How this car can get them anywhere is beyond me.

"Get her home safe," I demand before closing the driver's door.

Darren sees me and pulls up behind Piper's car. Getting in, I rest my head back against the cushion.

"Where to, sir?" he asks as he pulls out onto the street.

When I turn back to look at the entrance I watch Piper emerge with her shoulders slumped and the saddest expression on her face.

Something starts to tug in my chest. "You know anything about fixing cars?"

He cuts his eyes over at me through the rearview mirror. "Not much, but I'm sure I know a guy who does."

"He's going to have to be discreet and fast. Think he can steal a car and bring it back before the morning?"

"I'm sure we can figure it out if that's what you want, sir."

I nod then text Thomas.

> Me: Up for some work tonight?
>
> Thomas: Always
>
> Me: It's not our usual hunting though.
>
> Thomas: If you're doing it, I'm game.
>
> Me: I'll remember you said that.

I toss my phone in the seat next to mine and close my eyes. This woman has me stealing cars and doing cheesy pickup lines.

"This is not what I thought you had in mind when you texted me," Thomas grumbles as we put the last lug nut on Piper's tire. We made sure to dirty up all four new tires to make them look like her old ones.

"So this isn't your cup of tea?" I say holding back a laugh.

"Who the hell drives this piece of shit car? I'm fairly sure the junkyard would reject it." Thomas is checking the pressure to make sure it's got the right amount of air. "There's no way some dude is going to believe this is the same car when he went to sleep last night. Which means this has *woman* written all over it. Who is she?"

"What does it matter who it's for?"

Thomas stands to his full height and his eyes zero in on me. I hold myself in place not giving anything away. My eyes narrow, challenging him.

"We don't keep things from each other so I'm willing to let this one slide for now."

I shrug as if I don't care and check my watch. We've been helping Justin, Darren's mechanic, fix all the major problems with Piper's car. Thomas and I hotwired it once we knew Piper had gone to bed and brought it over to his shop to start the work. We've been working on it for hours and Justin thinks the car is finally safe enough to drive on the road.

Thomas and I are driving across town back to Piper's house with Darren following us. It's going to be one interesting night if we get pulled over. I can see the headlines now, *Alleged Mafia Boss and Bank CEO Caught in Grand Theft Auto*. The car couldn't outrun a scooter much less a cop car.

"Did you hear back from Mr. Falcone about the China shipment?" Thomas asks as we wait for our light to turn green.

"I'm meeting with him later today," I respond and accelerate through the light.

"Hopefully we'll get some answers about what's taking so long."

The other Families have been waiting on a drug shipment to come in from their supplier in China. I don't touch that stuff but we do have some new equipment for surveillance and a few other tech pieces to try out that'll be in the same container.

I slow down when I turn onto Piper's street and look at our surroundings to make sure no one is out at four in the morning to see us. The last thing we need is for someone to witness what we're doing. Quietly we ease the car back into its original spot. Thomas comes around and we work to fix the wires under the steering wheel before gently closing the driver's door. The car already looks a hundred times better even with us roughing up the new tires.

"Never thought I'd see the day that you'd fall so head over hills for a chick that you'd steal her car," Thomas spouts as we get in the back of my car and Darren pulls away from the curb.

"Don't know what you're talking about. I'm just helping a friend."

"You're so full of shit. I watched you stand over Justin's shoulder making sure he was doing everything right." He starts to laugh, making me want to punch him in his smug face, but then it would give him the satisfaction of being right. "You are well and truly fucked, Ox."

I keep my demeanor steady, looking straight ahead, wondering if I'd deeply miss him if I killed him and then dumped his body in the desert. I keep quiet and he finally loses interest and plays on his phone while we head back to my estate. Glancing at Darren in the rearview mirror I see his smug expression staring back at me. He raises an eyebrow and I know my armor is cracking.

Shit, I am fucked.

CHAPTER FIVE

Piper

MADDOX: You must be a 90° angle. 'Cause you're looking right!

The last two weeks Maddox has sent me a text every morning with a funny math pickup line. We've had a few light conversations getting to know each other but nothing too deep since I'm always having to cut the calls short to work or go to bed just to get up early and start all over again. School has been out for a week and Rob and I are getting into our summer routine of working at the sandwich shop. He pulls the mid-morning shift and I take over and close most days. This year our summer is going to be cut short because the school board is changing the start date to the beginning of August instead of after Labor Day, which only gives me five full weeks of vacation. Excluding the time I am required to work on Mrs. Roberts' reports.

Today I'm heading up to the school to pick up the expense reports to turn in as soon as possible. The faster I can get this done, the faster I can start my summer and hopefully never have to do this again.

Walking into the building I see Becky behind the counter going over some paperwork.

"Good morning, Ms. Becky."

"Hello, Piper," she greets in her usual friendly way when she lifts her head. I'm pretty sure she's never had a bad day in her life or she's just really good at masking it.

"I'm here to grab Mrs. Roberts' expense receipts," I say leaning on the tall counter.

"Yes, she mentioned you'd be by sometime this week. She put the box on the table by the window in her office for you to grab."

"Great, thank you."

When I enter her office, I can tell she's gone for the summer. Rumors have always circulated that she's best friends with the school board members and they take off jet-setting for the summer. I've never paid it much mind because it's none of my business. The politics in the school system can be brutal and I have enough on my plate to not add to it.

I see the white box Becky was talking about but when I get closer I notice another box on the other side of the table. Not sure which one I'm supposed to take, I peek in the first box and see several receipts for a conference trip Jackie and the school counselor took. When I look in the other box it contains similar receipts. Not wanting to have to redo or extend getting the job done, I stack the two boxes on top of each other and carry them out.

"I think I've got them," I tell Becky as I come back up to the front counter.

"Alright, if I don't see you in the next two weeks you have a fantastic summer, Piper, and try not to overwork yourself."

"I'll do my best. Hopefully I can get all this organized and turned back in by next week." She gives me a sympathetic look and nods as I back out of the door and head for my car.

I start my car and love that it doesn't take several attempts. The air conditioning is working so much better too. Rob had borrowed it to have the oil changed two weeks ago and ever since then the car has run better than when I bought it last year. Rob swears he didn't spend any extra money on it but that the guy at the auto shop did replace a few parts he had lying around. He was even able to find a used tire to match my other ones to replace the donut. I keep asking him where this place is so I can go and thank the guy, but Rob said he isn't much of a people person. It seems a little suspicious but I let it slide. I want him to save his money so that he can start to build a future for himself. The world is so cruel and he's already been dealt a hard hand.

Now that I don't have to worry about the cost of buying a new tire I'm focusing on saving up for a repair guy to come out and look at our dryer. Rob thinks the heating element has gone out but is worried about it being an electrical issue from all the Google research he's done. I've been taking our laundry to this laundromat a little ways from our home for the past month.

After pulling down the one-way row, I park the car in the first slanted spot in the large parking lot. I get out, gather up our hampers, and make my way through the parking lot, letting cars go by as I step up onto the sidewalk at the door of the washateria. The place is empty except for one other lady using the machines in the back corner, which is probably why I was able to snag such a close spot. She's got her earbuds in and has her head in a book. The book has a discreet cover so I think it must be a spicy book. I know this because I buy the same type of books. Being a teacher, I'd be crucified if my employers knew what I liked to read.

I decide to use the front machines and give her some space. Rob and I don't have but two loads of laundry so it makes doing this quick and easy. We each have a set of chores we are responsible for. I do the laundry, cook, and wash dishes and he's in charge of taking out the trash, mowing the lawn, and killing all bugs and critters that happen to invade our space. He is also the person to go and check when strange noises come up.

It takes a little under two hours and as the timer on the dryer says there are ten minutes left before it's all done, I see three cars pull up to the curb right in front of the washateria. The middle car door opens and a tall man in a nice suit stands adjusting his cufflinks and jacket sleeves. His clothes look a little rumpled but he wears them so well. He's got sunglasses on but I'd be able to spot this man any-where. Maddox is the epitome of handsome. Movement behind him catches my eyes and a blonde stumbles out of the back of the car. He makes no move to help her as a man from the first car walks over to Maddox and initiates what looks like a tense conversation. The men are both posturing and Maddox is gesturing with his hands in stiff movements. The blonde adjusts her short dress that's ridden up her legs and takes a few steps toward the men before wrapping her arms around Maddox's waist. The picture is starting to form in my brain as to what is going on here. Clothes are pushed up and wrinkled and she's all over him like a koala. The conversation stops and they both look down at her. Maddox moves his hands where hers are wrapped around him.

I stand involuntarily and find myself inching closer to the floor-to-ceiling window to watch them. I know I don't have the best track record picking men to date but I thought we were build-ing something. Did I read too much into our interactions thinking we were moving toward a relationship?

I must've because the blonde bounces up as Maddox looks down and connects her red lips to his. A rock drops down to the bottom of my stomach and disgust starts to form in my chest. I should've known it was too good to be true. I mean, look where my life has ended up. The man Maddox was speaking to looks over his shoulder and sees something in the parking lot where all the cars are parked then looks towards the windows of the businesses of this shopping strip. He positions his sunglasses from his nose to the top of his head and our eyes connect before Maddox separates himself from the blonde. The man knocks his hand on Maddox's upper arm and continues to stare in my direction. Maddox whips his head in my direction as well and I take steps backward away from the window. Voices start getting loud outside the washateria but I've already turned my back, moving to the dryers to gather up the last of Rob's and my laundry to take home. I dump the clothes into the hampers, not caring to fold them. I'll do it at home. Right now I feel completely stupid because I thought Maddox and I were something more than what we actually were and it's a hard pill to swallow. It's no one's fault because we've only been having flirty texts and phone calls. I'm the one who thought we were moving in one direction and he was headed in the opposite.

The ding of the bell from the door chimes and I'm reaching to the very back of the dryer for the last lone sock when I hear his deep voice. "Why are you doing laundry here?" His words sound almost accusatory.

When I feel his presence at my back, my body jolts at the closeness and I bump my head to the top of the machine. "Am I not allowed to wash my clothes here? I didn't know this was a members-only washateria." I don't look up when I exit rubbing my sore head. I feel a mixture of shame for thinking we were more than we were and anger because he doesn't have the right to question me and what I do. Clearly, he's doing what and who he wants.

"That's not what I meant—" He stops abruptly. I continue to move around him gathering up my detergent and hampers ignoring him and avoiding looking at him. He clears his throat and starts again. "What I meant was, did something happen with yours at home? You never mentioned your machines being broken."

I sling my bag over my shoulder and stack my hampers inside one another crushing the freshly clean clothes before picking them up to move to the door.

"It was good to see you," I move around him trying to avoid brushing my body against his as he crowds me.

"Let me get that for you," he offers and leans in but I don't need his help.

"I've got it." I lean away from his outstretched arms, using my butt to open the door and head outside. It's not his fault I read more into our interactions but I feel so foolish and need to regroup.

There are now only two cars at the curb and the same man that was speaking to Maddox earlier is still standing there watching as we come out.

"Ma'am," he acknowledges.

I give a tight smile but continue walking between the two vehicles out to where my car is parked.

"Piper wait, I think there's been a misunderstanding." Maddox comes up beside me as I open the back door.

Once I shove everything in, I belatedly realize the amount of force I used to close the door when it shakes the entire car. Clearing my throat and taking a deep breath, I finally look up at him. His face is without his sunglasses now showing off his silvery eyes and worried lines mar his forehead.

"No misunderstanding, I get it. It was my mistake for reading too much into something," I begin and hold my hand up to stop his interruption. "I didn't realize you already had a girlfriend."

"I don't. Celine wasn't supposed to be here and overstepped today—"

"It's okay, you don't need to explain. I think a friendship is better anyway," I say hoping my face doesn't show the lie I'm telling.

A deep low growl has me taking a step back pressing me flush against the car. Maddox crowds me, placing both arms on either side of my shoulders, boxing me in.

"I don't want to be your friend," he says leaning down.

My heart plummets and my shoulders sag. It almost feels like I've been punched in the chest. This blow hurts. I don't have many friends because I've been focusing on my parents' accident and making enough money to cover all the bills.

Regrouping, because it's better not to let others see weakness, I straighten then push at his chest to give us both space.

It's time to go.

"It was good to see you again, Mr. Bishop," I say as my hand blindly searches behind my back for the door handle. As I open the door and turn to get in the car, I look over my shoulder not able to stop the petty remark swirling in my head. "Red really isn't a good look on you."

Thankfully, my car starts right away and instead of backing

out because my brain just might want to clip him, I put the car in drive and pull through the parking spot, thankful the lot is almost empty at this time of day. I don't even stay in the lines as I drive straight across the lot to the nearest exit. Once I've put some distance between us, I glance in the rearview mirror and see Maddox still standing there watching my car leave. His friend is beside him talking but he doesn't acknowledge him. When I reach the street, I let go of the breath I'd been holding onto for so long.

"You've always been on your own and not needed anyone. Rob and Oliver are the only attachments you need," I say to myself in the empty car. "Your wants and hopes are never going to happen. He will only break us."

CHAPTER SIX

Bishop

DAMN IT.

How in the hell did that just explode in front of my face so horribly?

"I think that went well," dumbass Thomas says walking up beside me as I watch Piper's car turn the corner. "You've got something on your mouth."

He points to my lips and my hand automatically swipes at them. Red lipstick rubs onto my fingers.

"Fuck!" I groan as my fingers shove through my hair.

"Yeah, I don't think red is your color either," Thomas reiterates what Piper said. He's just looking to get his ass kicked today. He looks back at where Piper's car just was and smirks. "Well, not the lipstick red anyways."

I know he's referring to Piper's red hair which makes me want to lash out even more for how things just went down. "You tell Tyler, that if he ever sends his daughter in his place for a meeting I'll ship her back in pieces to him," I threaten.

Tyler is who I've used for the construction of all my real estate buildings. We were supposed to have a meeting today and go over changing the layout of the next strip mall that I need to be built.

Instead, the bastard sent his daughter in his place. That bitch did nothing but paw at me the entire time I tried to have a business conversation. I normally don't have anyone ride in the car with me in case I get a phone call that can't wait and need to discuss more sensitive matters. Celine had already gotten in the backseat before I could tell her to hop in the last car. Thinking it was going to be a short ride over here, I let it slide even though Darren was giving me a wary look. I'll *never* make that mistake again.

"We're going to be late with meeting Mr. Dawson if we don't leave now," Thomas says.

Looking down at my watch I see he's right. Bobby called last night and wanted to meet up for a quick chat. "Let's go," I say and walk over to where Darren is standing watching over the parking lot. Even though I only require him to be my driver and have other men on my team for lookouts, he still watches over me.

We drive through the streets and make our way over to the other side of the highway outside the tourist area. Arriving at a hole-in-the-wall restaurant, Darren holds my door open as I exit the vehicle just when Bobby's team pulls up. We both nod at each other as we enter through the back door and make our way to a secluded table against the back wall away from the general public.

"How are things going?" Bobby asks as one of his men brings over drinks for us.

Arturo and Bobby taught me to always have your own men bring your drinks to you. We have enemies that aren't below poisoning our food or drinks while out in public.

"Things are good as usual," I say, but the scrutinizing way he's looking at me tells me he knows things aren't.

"I'm here to listen if you need to talk," he offers.

I owe Bobby and Arturo so much. After everything that happened with my father, they were the ones to pull my family out of the bad situation we had gotten into. They both stepped up and became father figures to me and my twin sisters. I'll never be able to pay back what they did for me but I do try every day to be a better man because of the second chance I was given.

I throw back my drink in one gulp, not making eye contact, and look down at the empty glass.

"I've met someone," I start. "She's different—special."

"Ahh, I see."

"I'm messing it up at every turn," I say, finally looking up. "It's like my brain, mouth, and actions can't get on the same page. Today she saw another woman kiss me. It was a big misunderstanding and she said something about just being friends." My hands fist in my hair and give a tug in frustration. "Sometimes I think I should just throw her over my shoulder and lock her away until we're on the same page."

"Good Lord, between Luca, Wyatt, and you, Arturo and I have our hands full when it comes to finding and keeping your future wives. Have Arturo and I not shown you boys by example how to find and treat a woman right? I know Arturo and I were hard on you boys growing up but it's not rocket science to maintain a loving and healthy relationship." Bobby shakes his head and downs the rest of his drink then waves a hand. "Tell me about her."

"She's amazing, lights up the room as soon as she walks in. Piper is a middle school math teacher and a whiz at numbers. She had dreams of working for NASA because she's so smart. She's caring and so generous with people. Not to mention a bombshell to look at."

"Sounds like she'd fit right in with Gemma and Kendall," he says, mentioning Luca and Wyatt's wives. I'm older than Arturo and Bobby's sons by a few years. We all grew up together in the mafia and get along great. "Invite her to the wedding and introduce her to everyone. Does she have parents?"

"She does, but they're in a rehab facility after an accident. Piper hasn't opened up much about it though."

"Why haven't you had Davis run a check on her?" He raises an eyebrow. Being in the mafia we're always having to watch our backs, making sure we aren't letting the wrong type of people into our circle. Loyalty is key if you want to stay out of prison or keep living.

"I want her to tell me all these things. I feel like I'd be devaluing our relationship if I did that."

Bobby's eyebrow arches again, "Really? Yet you've never had a problem in the past researching your next move. You're a very calculating person, Ox. It's nice to see you looking to settle down."

"I told you Piper is different. I want to get to know her from what she tells me and not what I can have my guys dig up."

"Does she know about the type of business and life you run?"

I shake my head. "Not yet. I want her to give me a chance and have our foundation set before we dive into the heavy stuff."

"Having a strong foundation is the key to every successful relationship but have you thought she may not be able to handle this lifestyle."

I have thought about it, but the moment the thought entered my mind I squashed it. "It won't matter because I'm not letting her go anywhere."

Bobby lets out a chuckle. "Maybe you did listen a little too much to Arturo and me on our life lessons. Just remember that she needs to be told and have the option to decide to stay or leave, Ox. I know you want her but she'll never be truly yours if she isn't given the choice."

"I just worry once she knows who I am she won't look at me the same or when she does she'll think I'm a monster," I confess one of my deepest fears and the main reason I've never tried to look for more in women.

"You are not *him*. You'll never be like *him*, Maddox," Bobby states firmly. "Look what you do to those who mistreat others. There's no way you could ever cross that line."

My head dips a little as my eyes find my hands on the table and I release a breath. "I know."

"Very well. Now tell me more about what you've found with

Victor strong-arming these shop owners." I welcome the change of subject.

"I've found that he's been placing these kids at the center of each of our areas trying to get the prime real estate to turn over their properties to him. He's offering pennies on the dollar for these locations and if the owners refuse he sends in these young punks to rough them up."

I show Bobby all the paperwork and the map of the areas. He finally sits back and places both hands on the table. "I've got a surprise meeting planned in two days for all five of us. I'm going to need your support."

"Of course," I say without hesitation. "Whatever you need, I'm there to help in any way."

"I don't want to give you all the information because I want your reaction to be authentic and not be accused of setting this up."

"No worries, just tell me when and where and I'll be there," I commit.

Moving the map back on top of the other papers we start to plot how to stop Victor Slater and his little gang of punks from moving any further into our areas.

"I've got some other avenues of our money stream I want to run by you before I bring it to the table," I say after we finish talking about Victor.

"Whatcha got in mind? The casinos and payday loans are doing well. I was looking over the report you sent yesterday."

"They're doing well but I think we need to expand more. I've got word that the ATM company, which eighty percent of the casinos here on The Strip use, is going under. We can funnel the cash through the ATM being dispensed and I'll take care of the interest charge for each transaction." I pull out the documents from my jacket pocket and place them on the table.

"How much are we talking in profit?" he asks.

"A lot, if my numbers are correct. The casinos need those ATMs to keep people spending money so they pay a pretty penny to the company to place them every so many feet throughout their establishments."

I start showing him the profit margin lines of the company that is currently being used and show how the owner is tanking his lucrative business down the shitter.

"How big of an undertaking will this be?"

"I've already made contact with a guy involved with the failing company and I think we'll be able to get everything for pennies on the dollar. All the new company will have to do is rebrand. The contracts will stay in place and we put our people in the key position to maintain the operation. I'll use three of my banks, run it through so I'm paid on that end, but The Family will get paid through the Connors portion on every machine."

"Get everything in order for the purchase of the company. I'll speak to Arturo on the way home but let's not bring this to the meeting yet," Bobby says as he strums his fingers on the table. "After the wedding, we'll present this officially and have our people put into place."

"Sounds good."

We both stand to leave and our men make a path for us to head back out the way we came.

"I know I don't say this enough but I'm proud of everything you do, Ox." Bobby stops me with a hand on my shoulder as we reach our vehicles at the back of the restaurant.

My chest tightens at his words. I never heard that growing up from my piece of shit father.

"Thanks," I choke out.

He and Arturo took me my mom and my sisters under their wing and promised to take care of us after everything that happened with my sperm donor. They were there pushing me to go to college knowing I'd want to continue to run my side of the business when I grew up. I owe them a lot and their approval means everything to me.

He nods tightly then moves around me and heads to his waiting car. I hop into mine and set out in a different direction.

> ME: Your smile is like the curve y=x^2, it brightens up my negatives.

I sit back, hoping Piper responds and I didn't completely screw this up. What I told Bobby earlier about tossing her over my shoulder and locking her away is on the very tips of my fingers if she tries to shut this down.

"She's going to friend-zone you," Thomas says from beside me as Darren drives us back to my house from the restaurant.

"Shut up," I growl hoping he's not right.

A thought from earlier pops into my brain and my fingers move along my phone. It rings two times before he picks up. "Hello," Rob answers, and I can hear people in the background. He must be working.

"Why is Piper going to a washateria to do laundry?" I respond, getting straight to the point.

"Man, our washer and dryer went out a while ago. I can't figure out if the heating element is out or if it's something else. Piper didn't want us to waste money on a part if it wasn't the right thing to fix it. We called some services to come out but they all wanted to charge an arm and leg just to assess it so she said she'd wait until we had some money to spare to repair them."

"Next time it's laundry day you take it to the place around the corner. Text me when you're there."

"Dude, I don't know the first thing about doing laundry. Plus, Piper and I split up the chores; like I take the trash out and she does the clothes. I do the mowing and she cooks. It'd be weird if all of a sudden I said I'd do it."

"Just find a reason and make it happen. I'll have someone there to do it for you, just make it happen."

"What'd you do to Piper?"

"The fuck?"

There's no way she called and told him what happened. Right?

"She just texted me wanting help setting up an online dating profile," he says and my blood starts to boil.

"You help her set that up and I'll wring your neck," I threaten and hang up, beyond annoyed.

There is no way on God's green earth I'm letting her set one of those up when I'm right here. I'm all she needs.

"Darren, take me over to Piper's house," I tell him.

"Don't you think you're coming off a little strong?" Thomas gives his two cents. "You might make it worse. And Red doesn't seem the type to like being told what to do."

"Apparently I haven't been forceful enough." I narrow my eyes at him. He has the entire team calling her that now. "She's trying to set up one of those online dating apps."

His shoulders shake as he tries but fails to keep his laugh in. "Should we contact Davis to track her movements? Maybe he can set you up a profile to be her date."

Now he's just making fun of me. I'd normally find this comical, but for some reason, it just pisses me off.

"I'm handling it now," I say as Darren pulls down her street.

As we approach her house, I see Piper out by the street speaking to an older lady. Darren parks the car and I hop out.

"Hello, ladies," I greet and see Piper's eyes widen in shock.

"What are you doing here?" She looks around. "How do you know where I live?

"I texted but you never responded. Thought I'd come in person instead of waiting."

"Isn't he a tall drink of water," the older lady standing next to Piper comments. I can't help but smile. As flustered as Piper is, a blush creeps up her cheeks. It's good to know I affect her the same way she does me.

Sticking out my hand I say, "Ox Bishop, ma'am."

The older woman slides her hand into mine as she winks. "Irene, handsome."

"Nice to meet you, Ms. Irene." I release her frail grip. Her hands are calloused which makes me think she's had a strenuous job throughout the years.

"How do you know *our* Piper?" she asks.

"We met at Oliver's shop. He's just become an investor in the business," Piper informs her.

"Oh, and investors now make house calls?" There's a gleam in her eyes and I can tell Ms. Irene's got a mischievous side to her.

"Ones that are trying to date a beautiful and intelligent woman do," I say looking right at Piper. "I've got a friend's wedding to attend and would like it if you'd be my date."

"I can't, I'm bus—"

"She'd love to, and I have the perfect dress for it," Irene interrupts even though I never said when the wedding was. It makes me chuckle at her attempt to dodge spending time with me.

"Irene!" Piper chastises. "I might be busy."

"Oh pish posh." Irene flops her hand dismissing Piper's words. "No one turns down a man like this, especially if he drives over here to invite you to something. Kids these days don't appreciate the effort in courting like we used to. They just hide behind their phones and avoid any type of face-to-face interaction."

"Thank you, Ms. Irene, I couldn't agree with you more."

She nods with a smirk before looking back over at my flustered cherry bomb. "Try not to look so sour, honey." She turns back to me. "When is this wedding?"

"This Saturday."

"Perfect. I must go and make sure everything is ready. The color is an emerald green so make sure to have a matching tie," she informs me and pats my arm.

"Yes, ma'am."

"See you tomorrow, honey, for our weekly meet-up and a try-on for the dress." Then Irene's gone across the street with Darren right beside her, helping her step up on the curb and into her fenced-in yard.

"Ms. Irene seems like a lovely woman," I comment the moment her front door closes. The smile on my face shines in victory.

"Maybe you should invite her instead," Piper says and turns on her heels to head for her front door. I follow closely behind. If I didn't know any better I'd think she had a jealous side to her and it pleases me to no end.

"I think a lot of things were said and misunderstood earlier," I say as she opens the screen door and spins around to face me.

"Oh, I heard you loud and clear." She crosses her arms over her chest pushing her breasts up.

"I said I didn't want to be your friend because I want to date you."

"Date me?" she questions like it's not even in the realm of possibility. "You were just kissing another woman not hours ago and now you want to date me?"

"Yes, us dating," I explain. "Food, movies, long walks on The Strip."

Her face looks as though I just told her milk comes from the moon.

"Why?"

"Why? Why not? Everything about you draws me in. We share a love for numbers and have the same sense of humor. You're so gorgeous. The thought of you dating someone that's not me makes me lose my mind. Especially those stupid dating apps." I mumble the last part trying to not show my temper.

"Is this a joke?" she asks quietly, and I think she meant it not to be heard.

"Would you please go to this wedding with me and afterward we can go out on the town or anywhere you want. I just want to hang out with you."

If Thomas could hear me now he'd be calling me the biggest

pussy after I've practically had to plead my case. I've never begged a woman for her time, ever.

"And you're not seeing anyone else?" Her eyes are narrowed on me.

"No, Celine was the daughter of the guy who does all my construction. He decided to not show but sent her instead, not giving me a heads-up. I'm not interested in her or anyone else who's not you. She'd been making advances throughout the entire meeting that I brushed off. She just happened to catch me off guard on the sidewalk."

She's regarding me and everything I'm telling her. Her fingers come up to rub her forehead in contemplation. "I have a lot of baggage attached to me right now, Maddox. I'm not sure you'll want to compete with it."

I place my hand on her jawline and caress her with my thumb across her cheek. She stills her hand and drops it from her head. "Then let me help you carry some of it; we can navigate this together."

She lets out a breath through her nose.

"Don't let me go all by myself and be attacked by the old ladies," I quickly say hoping to lighten the tension in the air.

"Okay, I'll go with you to the wedding on Saturday." She smiles up at me. "But only because those old ladies can get a little handsy and pinchy with their fingers."

I blow out a breath and pull my hand away placing them on my hips. "Well thank goodness you agreed; thought I was going to have to kidnap you," I say shaking my head in a joking manner.

"You what?" she asks with a laugh. If she only knew how close I am. This woman is making me do things I never thought I'd ever be doing.

The tension is gone between us and it feels electric like always when the two of us are near or talking over the phone. There's a spark when the two of us are together and it started that first evening when I went to see Oliver about his loan.

I shrug playing along. "A man's gotta do what a man's gotta do."

"Is that so?"

My phone pings, interrupting our playful time, alerting me of a text.

"I've got to go, but I'll call or text later," I say wanting to end our conversation on a high note.

"Okay."

Leaning down in her personal space I put my hands on her small waist and press my lips to her cheek feeling her soft skin against mine. Her eyes flutter shut and I'd love nothing more than to kick the door closed and have my way with her right now, but I know I can't. We have a little ways before we can take that step. She's not the only one carrying baggage around.

"Lock up after I leave," I say, forcing myself to pull away from her. This isn't the best neighborhood in the city but at least it's not the worst with crime.

"Has anyone ever accused you of being controlling?" she sasses.

"I've been called much worse, cherry bomb."

"Cherry bomb?" She reaches up to touch her hair thinking it has to do with the color.

"Yup, from the moment I saw you I knew you were a firecracker." Her cheeks pinken and I can't help the tightness in my chest. "Next time I text, text back." I give her a pointed look. "And stay away from those dating apps."

I swing around to walk back down the driveway to the car before she can comment and we have our first disagreement. I have a feeling this woman is going to challenge me at every turn and I'm going to love it.

"I'll respond when I feel like it, Mr. Bishop," she brazenly calls out as I approach the car where Darren and Thomas are standing watching our surroundings for any threats. "And dating apps aren't my thing."

When I slide into the car I see she's already gone into the house and closed both the screen and front door. Thomas hops in with Darren and pulls the car away from the curb.

"You've got a wildcat on your hands," Thomas says holding back a smirk. "I think she just might be your match, Ox."

"Remind me to whoop Rob's ass after I'm done kicking yours."

Rob set me up and I played right in his hands. I knew Piper wasn't the type to join a dating app, but with how today's events went I lost my rational mind. I have to give it to the kid though, I thought I was doing a good job masking my feelings for Piper but he saw right through it.

I chuckle thinking how I just moved up our timeline. I was going to give Piper a little longer before pressing for more, but this seems to work out better. She's not used to someone like me so I'll have to be a little more cautious to not scare her off, but the end result will still be the same. She doesn't know it yet but her life is about to get turned upside down.

"Where to, sir?" Darren asks.

I turn to Thomas. "Let's head home. I'm ready to hunt down Sully tonight and teach him and his crew a lesson."

CHAPTER SEVEN

Piper

J UST WHEN I THOUGHT THE DAY WAS GOING DOWN THE toilet Maddox comes in and saves it. I still need to keep my wits about me where he's concerned. A man like him can have the pick of the litter and why he'd want to pursue someone who has a mountain of issues she's dealing with is mind-boggling.

After locking the door, I walk back over to the couch and sit down with the two boxes of receipts and my laptop to try to make some headway on the principal's expense report. Hours later my head is throbbing and my eyes hurt from looking at a screen, but my mind is reeling from the discovery. One box is all the small least important invoices used when going to conferences and all the expenses used. The other box has a bunch of receipts that I'm sure Jackie wanted left out. There is so much wrong with this second box I'm not sure what to do with it. Some purchases shouldn't be covered by the funds of the school district at all.

There is also a huge rabbit hole I went down looking into the after-school care program. Several receipts were labeled for items bought to replace some damaged school resources and I had to look up the names of who signed off on buying those items. It's owned by the Assistant Superintendent, Rachelle Flores. A quick look on the State of Nevada business registrar's website showed she both owns and operates the business as a for-profit business. Isn't that a conflict of interest? Rachelle is getting paid already from the taxpayers' dollars but then double dipping by charging the parents to have their kids in the after-school care program.

Jackie, my principal, has receipts for meals for the two of them here in Las Vegas and out at a few of the educational conferences. The restaurants are extremely pricey and it makes me wonder if these luxury dinners and activities are the reasons we aren't getting the resources we need to help out in our classrooms.

Grabbing my phone I call my friend Belinda.

Belinda and I have been friends for a while. We both live very busy lives but try to keep in touch with each other as much as possible. We may not text or talk every day but we check in when we can. She's been a lifesaver when I get overwhelmed with my parents.

"Hey lady," she answers right away. "How are you doing?"

"I'm good. How's your summer going?"

"You know summers are crazy with the kids out," Belinda remarks about her two boys, Andy and Samuel. I taught Andy two years ago but met her the year prior at a PTA event. We hit it off right away. We don't get to hang out very much with her working all the time and wrangling two boys and me taking care of my parents and working two jobs but we try to meet up when we can. "What's going on with you so far? Enjoying some relaxation?"

"It feels like the summers always go by too fast," I say and she laughs in agreement. "Listen, I have some questions about some things I just found out and was wondering if you could give me some guidance on it?"

"Absolutely, whatcha got?"

I tell her over the next ten minutes what I've found so far and the more I say out loud the more questions continue to pile up. When I finish there is a long pause.

"Piper, this doesn't sound good if what you're saying is in front of you. I'm pretty sure that state and possibly federal funds are being abused. Depending on how deep this runs it could make the funds the school receives be taken away from the district and prison for those who abused it. In the PTA we are required to follow strict guidelines on what we spend and have to log every little thing and we are small potatoes compared to the educational department. This sounds like this isn't the only year this has been happening. Not to mention Rachelle, the assistant superintendent, owning the after-school program sounds like a huge conflict."

"I thought so but I was hoping this wasn't what kept unfolding," I blow out a breath. "What do I do with all of this?"

Belinda pauses for a moment. "You did last year's expenditures, right?"

My head starts to nod and I feel a lead weight sink in my stomach knowing where this is going. "Yeah," I say almost scared to admit it, "but I didn't know this was going on. The receipts last year were simple and straightforward like this one box. It's the second box that I'm starting to figure out now that I wasn't supposed to pick it up; it has all the incriminating evidence."

"I figured as much, Piper," she says. "You are not the type of person to be involved in something like this."

"Thank you." I rub my forehead trying to wipe away my pounding headache. "What do I do with all of this? Who do I talk with? I only have so long before I have to turn this back in to Jackie."

"You are going to have to gather up all the evidence you can. Make a list of everything you think is not on the up and up and go over to the administration office and start asking for a Public Records Request for every subject like emails for certain time frames or administrative charts and who is in charge and what their departments are. Ask for the past year's results of expenditures and budget. I'm very curious about Rachelle's involvement with the after-school program so make sure to get all the details of when she started and who approved that. Oh, and make sure you ask the lady to expedite it. They might charge for it to make it a priority but since we are working on a deadline we need it quick. Also, make sure you are documenting everything in a log to protect yourself, girl. This might get super messy if what you are onto runs deeper after the cat is out of the bag."

"This is not what I thought I was signing up for when Jackie told me to do this for her." Even I can hear the dread in my voice. I'm not sure I can balance one more thing on my plate right now.

"She probably has been doing this for years and got away with it hoping no one would ever find out."

My phone pings alerting me that I need to start getting ready for my shift at the sandwich shop. "I've got to go get ready to head to work. I'll call you tomorrow after I leave the administration office."

"You better. I need some excitement in my life that doesn't involve working my butt off or boys who fight every five minutes," she laughs.

"Bye."

"Later."

MADDOX: You have a fine body. Are you a Mathlete?

A laugh bursts out of me in the parking lot as I make my way into the building of our school district's administration office. I'm sweating and it's not from the Vegas heat. I've never been one to go looking for a fight but I feel like I can't let this go because now Jackie has involved me in this potential mess and I can't afford to lose my job over someone else's conniving schemes.

In front of me is a wall directory and as I read over all the departments I find the one I need. Summertime has limited hours, so it's taken me two days before I was able to come in and make this request. Walking in the designated door I see just a few people milling around.

"Hello, how may I help you today?" a lady with glasses sitting behind the large desk asks.

"Hi, I need to make a PRR on some things," I say and pull out my paper that lists all the information I need.

"Are you with the news media?" she asks skeptically, or maybe she's just being nosey.

I shake my head. "No, definitely not."

"Okay, fill out this form and list everything you need. If you need more than one inquiry please fill out a different form for each."

She hands me a clipboard and I find a seat by the wall where I fill out the forms for everything I need. It takes me around twenty minutes to finish and when I walk back up to the counter I see the lady scrolling on her phone. *Taxpayers' dollars at their finest.*

"All finished," I inform her to get her attention.

"It'll take a few days for me to gather up and find all these requests, but I'll call the number on the form when I'm done. Also, depending on the size of material you need there might be a charge to cover the cost of paper."

"You're the one doing the inquiries?"

"We run a skeleton crew during the summer and rotate the hours."

"Oh, I see," I say and smile. The last thing I want to do is piss off the person who is going to be giving me the answers I seek. "Okay, and thank you for helping me."

"Of course."

I turn around and retrace my steps out of the building back to my car. Tomorrow I'm going on a date with Maddox and Irene needs me to come over now to try on the beautiful dress she's lending me one more time since she made a few more adjustments.

Parking my car in the drive I watch Rob come out with one of our laundry baskets.

"Can I borrow the car for a little bit?" he asks. "I've got some errands to run but won't be gone too long."

"Of course. Whatcha doing with our laundry hamper? I washed the dirty clothes earlier this week."

He looks down at the hamper and then rubs the back of his

neck nervously. "Oh, well, um, I just need to rewash a few things that can't wait for next week," he rushes then moves to place the basket in the car.

"O-kaaay," I drag out hoping to get a little more of an explanation but he gives none.

"Thanks, Pipe. I won't be gone long. Do you want me to pick up dinner?"

I shake my head. "If you want to grab something for yourself you can but I'll just eat here."

"We don't have a lot here. Let me bring you something."

"I just don't want you spending your money on me when you're trying to save for a car for yourself."

Rob surprises me by pulling me in for a hug. "You've taken care of me for years. It's time to let others help you out a bit."

I squeeze him a little harder for his thoughtful words. "Be careful and call if something comes up and you need to be out longer."

"Yes, Mother." He laughs as he pulls away and opens the driver's doors. I can't help but worry about him. We are less than ten years apart in age but I still feel like a mother hen towards him.

I watch as he backs out of the driveway and drives down the street.

"You're going to be a good mama one day." The voice pulls me from watching the disappearing taillights. I turn and see Irene propped up on her fence watching me.

"I don't know about that," I say and make my way over to her. "Some days I can barely take care of myself," I admit out loud.

"I'd say you've done a fantastic job with that young man." She points down the street where Rob had just been. "Not many young people who have gone through what you have and sacrificed so much would take on the responsibility of a teenager."

"I just hope I'm helping him build the skills to survive this cruel life," I say.

"I'd say that boy is the luckiest kid on the planet to have you in his corner."

I smile at her compliment as I make my way inside her house. Irene's home is decorated with photos of her life with her husband over the years. She's got quilts she's made my hand hung over her sofa and sparkly dresses on mannequins staged in the corners throughout the house that she worked on with some of the big production shows over the years.

"The dress is hanging up in the hall bathroom, dear." Irene points down the hall. "I'm going to go make us a few drinks."

I nod and make my way towards the bathroom. When I walk in, the emerald dress is hanging from the top of the cabinet door. It looks so gorgeous on the hanger that I'm afraid to touch it. After washing my hands and drying them I set out to undress. It takes me a few minutes to figure out the best way to pull on the silky material but when I finally zip up the side and look in the mirror I realize that Irene did more than adjust the waistline. The entire top of the dress is different. It's got no sleeves and curves around my full breast in a sweetheart shape exposing a lot more skin than I've ever shown.

Completely shocked I open the door slightly I peek my head out. "Irene?"

"Yes, dear."

"I don't think this is going to work." My voice is more of a panicked plea and has gone up an octave.

"Really? I thought I wrote those measurements down even though I usually don't need to," she says more to herself. "Come out and let me have a look at you."

"I'm not sure it's appropriate."

"Is there a nip slip problem?"

"A what?"

"Just come out and let me have a look. It's not like I haven't ever worked with naked people before, honey." I take one more look in the mirror then back at the hallway debating on whether I should brave it. In the end, Irene calls me out. "Stop being a chicken and let me see what I've done."

Walking into the living room I've got my hands crossed over the exposed skin. Irene stands from her chair and pulls her glasses down from where they were sitting on the top of her head.

"Oh, I see what it is, mmhmm," she says and walks over to me. "Turn please."

I do as she says waiting for her to mention all the material missing from the top of the dress. She touches something at the center of my back and I feel a release.

"There," she states then walks back around to the front of me. She takes my hands, completely ignoring my horrified expression, and moves them away from my chest. "Honey, you can't wear a bra that shows straps," she says like it's the most ludicrous thing she's ever seen. "In fact, I think going without one is best." Somewhere in my shocked state she plucks the bra from underneath the material and tosses it on the sofa. She takes a step back and looks me up and down. My arms immediately start to cross and she latches onto both to keep them at their sides. "Beautiful." She points over to the corner of the room where a full-length mirror stands. "Go have a look."

My body moves on command and I walk over to the corner of the room. The person staring back at me is not someone I recognize at all. I've never worn anything so beautiful in my life and the material chills my skin with how silky it caresses it. I move closer to the reflection and my leg pops out revealing more than half of my thigh. My head whips over to where Irene is standing watching me.

"Irene! You cut it almost to my hip," I squeal in surprise at how much leg is showing.

"Make sure to shave all the way up, dear." She chuckles like she's having a private joke with herself all the while I'm over here with my jaw on the floor. This is not the same dress I tried on for her earlier this week. "Oh, I almost forgot." She snaps her fingers and walks over to the coffee table. "Your boyfriend had this dropped off earlier today after I spoke with him."

"He's not my—you talked to Maddox? How do you have his number?"

She waves her hand in the air dismissing the questions. "A woman can't reveal all her secrets."

"Oh, really."

She opens the shoe box and takes out a crystal-encrusted high heel. As she hands it to me I see the signature red bottom sole. "Are you kidding me?" I say as I hold it in my hands like it's a bomb. "These probably cost more than I make in an entire month on my teacher's salary." I gasp at the realization that Maddox and I come from two completely different worlds.

"Don't do that," Irene snaps.

My head swings over to her. "What?"

"I know what you're thinking and this man is the luckiest person to have you on his arm. It doesn't matter what he does or how much is in his bank account as long as his intentions are pure."

I frown when I realize I've let myself feel inadequate. I've always tried to not put myself down or compare my situation with others.

You get the hand you are dealt and you make do of it in the best possible way with a smile on your face because it could always be worse.

I nod. "You're right, sorry."

"Try them on silly girl." She picks up the other shoe from the box and hands it over to me as I carefully sit down on the sofa trying not to reveal any private parts.

The shoes fit like they were molded for my feet. Irene helps me up and walks with me over to the mirror again and I can't help the wetness in the corners of my eyes.

"You look spectacular, Piper," she praises.

I can't even form words at the moment as I take it all in. My red hair against the emerald green dress looks so beautiful together.

"I don't think I need to adjust any areas; just make sure to not wear any panties," Irene says looking at my backside.

"What?" I burst out a laugh at her random command.

She takes her finger and follows my panty line to my hip. "Leave the granny panties at home for the night."

"Irene!" I gasp. "I can't go without any panties," I whisper the last part as if we're in a crowded restaurant.

"Why not? Women do it all the time," she states and gives me a confident look.

"I don't even want to know how you know that."

"You can't work in the entertainment business for decades like me and not have seen or heard every little thing, honey."

She's got me there but I'm still unsure about going without underwear. "I'll take your word for it," I say and focus back on the mirror.

Irene spends the next thirty minutes talking about how to style my hair and make-up for the wedding tomorrow before I head back home. By the time I close the door, the clock shows that I've been over with Irene for the last three hours and Rob has just pulled into the drive.

"Piper!" he calls when he enters the house.

"Just changing clothes." I pull up a pair of sweatpants and head out into the living room. "Did you get all your errands done?" I ask when I see he's in the kitchen putting down a bag.

"I did," he says as he plates the food and hands me a burger and fries.

"Thank you for getting me something," I tell him as we walk over to the couch and take a seat.

"I'd never leave you out, Pipe." He gives me a look. "You do so much for me, it's the least I can do for you."

"Rob, you don't have to feel like you owe me. I'm just glad I was able to help you out when you needed it and that it's all worked out for you. I want you to have the best life," I say sincerely as I place my hand on his.

"Love you, Pipe."

"Love you too, kiddo."

We scroll through the TV trying to find a movie to watch.

"Oh, by the way, the laundry place had some kind of raffle thing to win a new washer and dryer set," Rob says watching the screen.

"Really?"

"Yeah, I signed us up since we could use it."

"You sure it wasn't some gimmick to gather stolen identification or something?"

He shrugs his shoulders still not looking over at me. "Guess we'll find out."

"You didn't give out any private info right?" I start to panic slightly.

"Nah, just the basic email, phone number. Stuff like that."

His cheeks pinken and I'm wondering what he is trying to avoid and why he won't look over at me. I'll let it go for now but something is definitely up with him. Maybe he met a girl there or something.

"So you are really going on a date with Bishop?" he asks a few moments later. It's still weird to me that Maddox gets referred to by several different names. I've heard people call him Ox or by his last name, Bishop, but I'm the only one so far that refers to him by his first name.

"I'm just his wedding date tomorrow," I say casually.

"You sure about that because every time I catch him looking at you it's like he wants to devour you as his next meal."

"Rob!" I gasp and smack him in the shoulder with the back of my hand lightly. "He does not."

"O-kaaay," he draws out. "If you say so."

"You think I shouldn't?" I ask.

"I think that as long as he treats you with respect I don't mind you being with him. He seems like a good guy."

We settle in on the movie and I can't help the smile forming or the butterflies in my stomach thinking about Maddox and spending time with him tomorrow.

CHAPTER EIGHT

Bishop

"I'M SORRY, I'M SORRY!" SULLY CRIES FROM THE BINDINGS that have him hanging from the hook on the wall.

"Did you stop when the store owners pleaded for mercy?" I bite back.

"I'll leave them alone! Promise!" He's missing several teeth now with a busted nose and his eyes are swelling.

"Not good enough. Should've never touched the elderly in the first place," I punctuate each word with a body jab.

He groans with each blow. "Swear!"

I deliver a final blow, a right hook across his face, and hear the crack in Sully's jaw. We've been at this all morning since picking him up with several of his flunkies. He didn't hold out long once the first bone in his leg snapped. He started singing like a canary about strong-arming the owners for Victor Slater to gain their real estate.

Victor is one of the five mafia bosses here in Las Vegas. We each have our own areas of the city and each deals in different avenues to make money. He's always been a sleazeball in my book, but I tolerate him because it's part of the business. Arturo Falcone and Bobby Dawson, who have been like fathers to me, can't stand him and after today I can see why. I mainly deal with the money laundering aspect of the business and rarely have to concern myself with the likes of him.

"Wedding starts in two hours," Thomas calls over my shoulder as he levels one of Sully's men.

We're on the outskirts of the city at one of my abandoned warehouses. It's where we take people to get answers. Usually, it's me and Thomas, and I have my team stay outside and wait for instructions, but since we picked up nine hoodrats, we needed a little help coercing them to talk. I decided a divide-and-conquer technique was best.

I stand and check the watch on my wrist. "Drive them sixty miles out in the desert and strip them of all clothes and shoes. Let's see if they make it back to town." I deliver my instructions to Nate. Sully will never make it with his broken leg.

"Sir." He nods and turns to relay the message to the other team.

"Why sixty?" Thomas asks handing me a damp rag to wipe my hands with.

"That's how many stitches Oliver Sampson had to get after that loser worked him over."

"I love how you always have a lesson with every punishment." Thomas laughs then looks down at his white shirt and the droplets of blood there. "Dammit, I was trying not to ruin another shirt," he huffs.

"Who wears white when going hunting? It's your dumbass's fault," I say and roll my eyes. "Is everything in place that Bobby asked for?"

"It's all ready and will be at the church waiting. Did he say why we needed to bring all our tactical gear and vans?"

I shake my head. "Said we'd find out soon enough."

"You stay out late with the group the other night?" he asks.

"Nah, I went to the chapel and watched the ceremony then went back home before we went out to find these guys," I say as I point my thumb over to the nine men we picked up early this morning.

Two nights ago, Bobby's son, Wyatt, and the new head of the

Chapman Organization, Kendall, tied the knot in secret. Kendall had been hidden away for the last sixteen years and only stumbled upon finding out about her true family just recently. She's taken her rightful place as the Head of her family and found love for Bobby's son. The wedding is supposed to be today but apparently, they couldn't wait to get married and I received a call telling me to get my ass down to the chapel. I watched as Elvis married them, and I have to say it was fun watching them tie the knot. I started to wonder if I could make a marriage work. I already know *who* my bride would be if I took that step.

"You sure bringing your woman to this is safe since you don't know all the details going down?" he asks as we make the walk out of the warehouse and to the waiting cars. It seems today's wedding is a planned farce to draw something or someone out.

"She'll be fine with me, plus Bobby wants me to introduce her to everyone," I say as Darren opens the backdoor of the car.

"I just find it weird that your first date is going to a wedding where the couple is already hitched and something could potentially happen. What happens if shit hits the fan and bullets start flying? Why not take her to the game tonight and show her the VIP treatment?"

I stay quiet, not wanting to voice that the real reason was to show her off to my family. They may not be my blood but Bobby and Arturo have been a part of my life since I was born and their approval means a lot to me.

The next twenty minutes are filled with silence as Darren takes us back to the house. When we pull through the gates, Thomas heads over to his car while I make my way up the steps to the front doors.

"Am I coming back here or meeting at the church?" Thomas yells out before I cross the threshold.

I contemplate for a brief second. "Church. I don't want to overwhelm Piper when I pick her up."

"You do know you're going to have to tell her eventually about who you really are, right?"

"When the time is right I will," I answer.

"Okay but just know women don't like things hidden from them."

"When did you become the relationship guru?" I ask with a chuckle.

"I've watched a movie or two." He laughs along with me. "I'm not just a pretty face, you know."

I wave him off and close the door, making my way up the stairs to the master bedroom to get ready for my date.

Date.

I don't think I've been on one of those since my college days fifteen years ago. The guys and I usually meet women at the bars or restaurants we go to.

After I wash off the dried blood and rinse it down the drain I scrub and wash my body and hair to rid me of the last few hours. I trim down the stubble on my face and make sure every part of my body is in pristine condition. Looking back at the mirror I take inventory of my body. I know I'm a good-looking fucker. I train daily, sometimes twice a day, to stay in tip-top shape. Being the head of my mafia family I have enemies along with Bobby and Arturo who are out to take what we have, which is why I have people who work with me to be ready for an attack in every situation. I've got scars scattered across my torso; some are faint but a few are really noticeable. Those I wear like a badge of honor. Those are the ones that made me who I am today and why I punish those who prey on the weak.

My phone chimes and I see Darren giving me an hour countdown for the wedding. I can't be late for this occasion or Bobby will kick my ass, so I rush to put on my suit with the emerald tie Ms. Irene told me to wear. I smile thinking about the conversation Darren told me about when he dropped off Piper's shoes with Irene yesterday. The woman is feisty and I can imagine she was a handful in her younger days.

"Sir," Darren says as I come down the stairs towards the front door where he is positioned. I've got men stationed all around the property who work in shifts to keep an eye on things in case someone thinks it's a good idea to breach our walls. "Nate and the others are on their way back and will come straight to the church ready for your call. Thomas is already there in position waiting with the others until you arrive."

"Thank you, Darren," I say as we step out into the heat. We both climb in the car and head towards Piper's place.

The closer we get to her place the more my knee bounces. Darren already has the air turned down to the coldest setting but I still feel sweat forming in my hairline. I haven't felt this nervous since I lost my virginity at sixteen to the prom queen who was two years older than me.

"Thought you might need these, sir." Darren passes back a bouquet of sunflowers mixed in with bright red roses. The arrangement looks like a firecracker explosion and my lips curve into a smile.

"Thank you, Darren. I think she'll love them," I say. "I'm a little nervous," I admit.

"You'll do just fine, sir. Mr. Dawson thought you might need a little help remembering so he texted me yesterday to pick them up for you."

My body relaxes back into the seat as we pull down Piper's street. Bobby has been looking out for me since I was a teenager and I couldn't be more appreciative that I've got someone like him and his wife, Mary, in my corner.

Darren parks the car and I stare out the window at her house. I hope she's ready for me because once she's met The Family, there's no going back. Not that I'd give her the opportunity. As I knock on the door I can hear Irene yelling then a moment later the door swings open.

"Don't you look nice. Come in, handsome. She's just grabbing her purse," Irene says and ushers me into the living room off the entryway. "Aren't those beautiful," she points at the bouquet as the sound of clicking comes from down the hall.

"Thank—" My words dry up in my mouth as Piper comes into view. She looks like a goddess in her emerald dress which shows off her beauty. I try to swallow to wet my mouth but it has the opposite effect.

My eyes follow down her gorgeous face to her naked neck and exposed chest. The cut of the dress accentuates her large breasts and dips down just where I'd love for my tongue to explore. Her tiny waist is cinched tight showing the curves of her hips. It's when I continue down that I have to lower the bouquet of flowers to hide my ever-growing dick in my suit pants. I watch as her left leg breaches through the slit in the gown and my fingers ache to trace her silky smooth thigh. The crystal-studded heels finish off the look and I can see those puppies wrapped around my head in the near future.

She looks like a walking wet dream.

"I take it you approve, Mr. Bishop?" Irene's voice brings me out of my stupor and I clear my throat to gain some sort of control, not only over my body but my thoughts as well.

"You look stunning, Piper." I gaze into her eyes. She has on little makeup because she doesn't need it to bring out her beauty. Her hair is pulled over to one side that's draped down her chest with curls and pinned at the neck with a crystal that matches her shoes.

Her cheeks pinken at the compliment. "Thank you."

"These are for you." I hand over the flowers once I believe I've got my body under control.

"They're beautiful," she says and brings them up to her nose to inhale. "You didn't need to spend the extra money on them but thank you."

I place my now free hands on her exposed upper arms, wanting to feel her skin on mine. "I'd spend my entire bank account on you if it meant I got to see you smile like this again."

Her body moves in a little closer to me like a magnet pulling mine to hers as well.

"I'll go and put them in water so you two kids can get going," Irene says breaking the bubble. "Let's get a picture first," she offers and I can't get the phone out of my pants pocket fast enough.

I've never been one to like having my picture taken but I make sure to have Irene take as many as possible over the next few minutes. The feel of Piper in my arms settles something within me. Like a piece of a puzzle snapping into place.

"We better get going," Piper says in a breathy tone as she looks up at me through her long lashes. I nod but don't make a move to leave. Instead, I tighten my grip on her hip. I'm tempted to bail on this wedding and take Piper back to my house and lock us up for the next year.

"I'll go and put the flowers in a vase and lock up behind myself. You guys get going." Irene comes over to us with my phone in her outstretched hand. I take the device from her and manage not to scroll through the photos like a little kid. Irene swipes the bouquet from Piper and shoos us out the door.

I help Piper down the steps and driveway toward my car with Darren keeping a lookout. He turns when he hears us approaching and stops. My instincts kick in and I pull Piper closer to my body, even though we're already locked next to each other. I know what he sees and I want to lay him out across the hood of the car, but he nods respectfully with a, "Ma'am," then turns back to watch the road.

Opening the back door of the car I help her in and make sure the bottom of the dress clears the door. I make my way around the vehicle passing Darren and ask, "All clear?"

"Yes, sir. No trouble in sight."

"I need to hear you say that you'll protect her if something doesn't go as planned." I look him straight in the eyes.

Darren lifts his shades to look back at me. He has always been a soldier since Bobby appointed him to my team. "I will lay my life down for her from this day forward, sir."

I nod knowing he does what he says. "Let's get going then," I say and make my way to the other side beside Piper.

"Do you always have a driver take you everywhere?" Piper asks once the car starts to move.

I turn to face her and give her all my attention. "Most days, yes, especially when I go to events," I answer. "Does that bother you?"

She gazes up to the front seat and then back to me. "I guess not. I've just never had someone drive me around all day except for my parents, but when I was able to drive that stopped. This gives off *Pretty Woman* but without the hooker part." She lets out a laugh and I have no idea what she's talking about but Darren's shoulders shake showing he gets the joke. *Note to self: find out what Pretty Woman is.*

It doesn't take Darren long before he's pulling up to Our Lady of Las Vegas Catholic Church. I see Thomas and several of our team standing by the front of the church waiting for us to arrive. When Darren comes to a stop at the steps, Thomas is there opening my door.

"Wait until I come around to open your door," I tell Piper and squeeze her hand that I haven't let go since being in the car.

Hopping out, I button my suit jacket as Thomas continues to survey the parking lot, always on alert.

"Are we in place and set up?" I ask as I leisurely make my way around the trunk of the car to Piper's side.

"Everyone is in place and Bobby has been notified. We are ready when he decides to pull the trigger."

"Good," I say and open Piper's door. I lean down and offer my hand to help her out but to also shield her until she rights her dress.

I hear a soft groan and shoot my eyes over my shoulder at Thomas. He quickly averts his eyes from my woman while mumbling, "Sorry, sir." I lead Piper up a few steps but swing my free hand back catching Thomas in the stomach for his inappropriate noises.

"Oof—" He doubles over not expecting it and his breath comes rushing out.

We're going to have one hell of a match in the ring tomorrow morning for our workout.

"Is he okay?" Piper looks back at Thomas concerned.

"He's fine. Probably ate something that didn't agree with him," I comment and swing my arm around her waist, settling my hand on her hip possessively.

Piper fits right in with everyone walking up the steps and through the double doors of the church. All the women are dressed alike on the arms of their men but none can hold a candle to Piper. She stands out like a shining star. As we stand in the line to sign the book I see Victor Slater in a tux walk in carrying a large manila envelope with a few of his men at his side. He sees me and comes right over.

"Bishop," he greets with a handshake. "There is something I'll want to show you in a few hours so if you could make yourself available."

"I'll see what I can do," I say noncommittally.

Victor cuts his eyes over to Piper for the first time and gives her a creepy wink. I swallow a growl and turn us away from him, succinctly ending the conversation.

We get up to the front of the line and I sign *Maddox and Piper Bishop* in the guestbook and love how it looks. Piper is too caught up in all the decorations around the church to notice as I lay the pen back down and move us to the sanctuary. The sanctuary is decked out with white and baby blue-dipped roses. Lantern lights hang from the exposed wood of the ceiling and there are dozens and dozens of pews on each side of the large middle aisle decorated with giant clear vases with tall flower arrangements. The center aisle has a sheer baby blue runner leading to the bottom marble step of the pulpit. A lattice covered in greenery with white roses and flowers dipped in blue is the backdrop. Candles line the outer edges of the four marble steps that lead up to the podium, and the natural lighting gives it an intimate ambiance.

I see my friend, Arturo's son, Luca, at the front of the groom's seating section in a tux. Several of his men line the wall keeping watch because his wife is there seated talking animatedly. I guide Piper through the crowd and over to meet my friend. We get stopped no fewer than twenty times with men paying their respect to me as one of the Mafia Dons.

"Luca," I greet with a handshake and half hug, then turn to his wife who stands to greet me. "Gemma, beautiful as ever," I say and lean down to kiss her cheek.

"Thank you, Ox," she says and blushes.

Gemma didn't grow up in the mafia and had a hard introduction to The Family. She was reserved at first but has since come out of her shell.

"Ox, good to see you, man," Luca says then spots Piper next to me. I'm not one to bring a woman around, so the shock that this gorgeous woman is next to me is clear on his face. "Who do we have here?"

I wrap my arm around her waist and pull her into my side. "This is Piper. Piper this is my friend, Luca, and his wife, Gemma."

"It's nice to meet you, Piper." Luca greets her the same way I greeted his wife, with a kiss on the cheek.

In our culture, we live by certain rules and formalities. One is showing the utmost respect to the wives. Me being the head of one organization makes Piper like royalty just like Gemma is the wife of the next in line to take over for the Falcone Family. We value our women and they are to be shown that, even though my father was a piece of shit who didn't abide by it.

"Hi, I'm Gemma and it's so nice to meet you." Gemma brushes past Luca and pulls Piper into a hug. "I love your dress! You look absolutely stunning."

"Thank you," Piper says blushing slightly. "I love your necklace."

Gemma touches the necklace. "Oh, thank you. My father-in-law bought it for me when I gave birth to our son, Dante."

Gemma was almost kidnapped and killed months ago at the end of her pregnancy by a lunatic who wanted to take out the

Falcone Family. They were able to capture and kill Enzo Perez but he was just the Patsy taking orders from a bigger threat. We are all on high alert for who the main culprit is behind the scenes. Enzo was killed right before he gave the name leaving us to wonder who wants to shake the hierarchy here in Vegas.

"Come and sit with me." Gemma grabs Piper's hand, not giving her a chance to decline, and pulls her out of my grip. She takes her over to her seat and they start chatting right away. We've got our men surrounding the room watching for any type of threat so I'm more at ease with her away from my side.

"I think she's going to fit in just fine." Luca nudges me as I watch Gemma share her love for teaching kids like Piper. I can't help my smile as both women talk as if they've known each other a long time instead of only a few minutes.

"I think so too."

Luca taps my elbow and we take a few steps away from the women. "Pop or Bobby give you any more details going down today?" Luca asks in a hushed voice. "Wyatt's been avoiding my calls, the prick."

I shake my head. "Just to be on alert and have my men ready. Wyatt has probably been told to keep it under wraps and they know he'd spill it all if you called."

"I didn't want to bring Gemma without knowing all the details but Pop said we needed to show out. He agreed to keep Ma home with the baby since we all went to the actual wedding the other night."

"I don't think your dad or Bobby would put our women in harm's way."

"There are too many people here to witness anything too."

Just then Arturo and Bobby walk in and are swarmed like I was with men vying for their attention. They nod and shake a few hands before coming straight over to us.

"Where's Mary?" I ask Bobby when they reach us and we exchange handshakes.

"She's in the room designated for Wyatt," Bobby says as he looks over the crowd.

"Saw Victor earlier working the crowd when I came in," I tell them and they both narrow their eyes.

"Really? Did he say anything to you?" Bobby asks.

"Said that he had something to show me in a few hours and to make myself available."

Both Bobby and Arturo share a look but don't elaborate on anything.

"Did you bring your woman?" Bobby asks looking over at Gemma and Piper.

"Piper," I call over where she and Gemma are still talking. She looks up from her conversation and smiles. I hold out my hand. "Come and meet a few people."

She and Gemma both stand and make their way over to us. I know the entire room is watching the interaction and wondering who the new redheaded bombshell in our group is.

"Good to see you, Bobby," Gemma greets first as he leans down and kisses her cheek.

"Adele brought that handsome baby boy over to see us the other day. Just a heads up, she's going to try and see if she can keep him from time to time."

Gemma chuckles. "At this rate, Luca and I aren't going to see Dante until he's eighteen between Adele and Mary."

"Not to spoil anything but Adele brought her contractor over and she and Mary have already picked out the rooms to turn into a nursery and playroom." Bobby winks as we all know Adele and Mary always get what they want no matter what Arturo and Bobby say.

Gemma moves over to Arturo and gives him a hug and a kiss on the cheek while Bobby turns his attention to Piper.

"Piper, I'd like you to meet Bobby Dawson," I introduce.

"It's nice to meet you, Mr. Dawson," Piper says formally then holds out her hand for him to shake.

Bobby takes her hand in his then leans down and kisses her

cheek. "Ox told me and my wife, Mary, a little about you but he never mentioned just how beautiful you are." She blushes at the compliment. "This here is my best friend, Arturo Falcone."

Arturo greets her the same way as Bobby. "Nice to meet you as well, Mr. Falcone."

"Call me Arturo, dear. I hear you're also in education," he says.

"Yes, sir, I teach math at Kennard Middle School."

"It's nice to know our future generations will be well educated with two certified teachers and a well-rounded businesswoman coming into The Family," Arturo states with a nod over to Bobby.

"Oh," Piper says surprised by his words and I know she wants to correct him about what he is implying but she seems to decide not to. Her eyes look over to me and widen slightly as if waiting for me to correct him but I just smirk and let the statement stand.

She doesn't know this but both Bobby and Arturo have already accepted her into The Family. The moment they kissed her on the cheek she was given their approval. I'm sure both men have already run their own background checks and looked into her past not only for the sake of our business world but for me as well.

The lights dim signaling that the ceremony is about to begin and people start to take their seats and quiet down.

"We'll all get together soon and get to know each other better after the newlyweds get back from their honeymoon," Bobby says. "I must go and take my spot, dear. It was a pleasure, and if you ever need anything please come to me."

"Same," Arturo agrees.

They both walk out the side door of the church with men at their backs, and Luca and I lead our women over to our seats where our men are positioned in the rows in front and behind our pew. Luca sits on the end closest to the center aisle with Gemma at his side then Piper is seated beside her with me ending our group. One of each of our men sits down and blocks others from sitting in our section.

Soft music starts to play and I think this is about the time I should confess a few things. Leaning over I reach my arm around the top of her shoulders and pull her into my body. "I feel like I should tell you there isn't going to be a wedding today," I whisper cryptically in her ear.

Her face scrunches in confusion. "What? Why?" She looks around as if my secret is the craziest thing to say.

"They were married two days ago in a little chapel on The Strip."

"Why?"

I shrug. "Couldn't wait, I guess." It's not a full lie but it's the easiest answer I can give her at the moment.

"How do you know—"

Gracie, the groom's sister, and Harper, Kendall's best friend, come in from a door behind the pulpit and stand at the top step. They both are wearing their bride's maids dresses in full makeup and hair.

"Thank you all for being here for Wyatt and Kendall's big day. We are so excited to celebrate their union and bring our families together. Unfortunately, the couple couldn't wait to start their journey and decided to jump the gun. They were married a few days ago and have since left for their honeymoon. We'd like for you all to watch their nuptials as it was videoed and then we will continue on with the reception afterward to celebrate as planned. Please enjoy and we hope to see you all at the venue after this."

Gracie and Harper return the way they came in and two screens come down from the ceiling. Piper looks over at me in shock and I just wink as the video starts. The company who made the video had to have worked tirelessly to create this in two short days because it is done so beautifully. When I'm caught in one of the shots, I feel a pinch on my outer thigh and almost jump.

"You didn't mention that you were there," Piper whispers cutting her eyes to me. "Why did you need a date if it already happened?"

I grab her fingers and kiss her knuckles then lean in and brush my lips to her ear. "Because I wanted to show you off and for you to meet part of my family."

The video lasts around fifteen minutes, and then a man from the church comes over to stand where Gracie vacated. "If you all will join us at the reception in honor of our newlyweds to celebrate their union."

The lights brighten and the congregation starts to stand. Our men immediately are up and standing around us from all sides. Luca gives me a look then helps Gemma stand and I follow suit.

"The video turned out so good don't ya think," Gemma gushes and looks over at Piper.

"I'm not sure what just happened. Is this like a new thing now? To get married before and not show up?"

We all chuckle. "No, this was a first, for all of us," I say.

Movement catches my eye and I turn to the side of the church. Arturo starts to wave us over. Luca and I hurry over leaving Piper and Gemma at our seats with our men.

"Everything okay?" I ask when we approach. The color of his skin has turned a shade lighter.

"We've got a problem," he admits and looks around.

"What is it?" Luca jumps in.

"They've taken Mary."

CHAPTER NINE

Bishop

"WHAT DO YOU MEAN, *THEY'VE TAKEN MARY?*" I REPEAT. "Where were her guards?"

"Most were incapacitated; the others are dead," Arturo states. "Bobby has tried to contact Kendall and her team but we can't get through."

"You need to tell us *now* what we are dealing with," I say and continue to look over at Piper as if she might disappear.

"Send our girls home for protection then we can talk." He rubs his forehead from side to side. "We only have a short window to make this work if we want to keep everyone safe."

I waste no time leaving the huddle and walk over to Piper as she and Gemma are chatting up a storm.

"I have to go and deal with something that needs my attention right away. I'm sorry we can't continue on to the reception but this can't wait," I say urgently hoping she understands.

"Oh, no worries." She nods and gives me a smile that doesn't reach her eyes. I feel like I've taken a swift kick to the chest disappointing her. My chest aches and I swear to myself I will avoid ever seeing her like this again.

"I wouldn't be leaving if it wasn't so very important." I reach for her hand. "Please believe me."

She waves it off. "Go do what you need to and I'll call Rob or catch a cab home."

Before I can speak Gemma interjects, "Gosh no, I have a feeling my husband is getting the same call and will be leaving as well. Why not ride together so we can exchange numbers and plan a girls' night out for when Kendall comes back and we can all hang out?"

I'm so thankful for Gemma and how she makes everyone feel so accepted.

"Darren is right outside and will take you home," I tell them then turning back to Piper. "I'm going to swing by after I'm done and we are going to finish our first date without any interruptions."

"How romantic," Gemma swoons at us. "We are going to go on a double date soon. Especially since Dante keeps getting taken from us."

"Baby, let's not overwhelm them too much so early." Luca wraps his arms around her waist. "I'll be home later. Keep this sexy little dress on until I get there."

"Depends on how long I have to wait," Gemma sasses making Luca growl. I love the banter they share; it reminds me so much of Piper and me. "Which guard is going with me?"

"Ernesto will be," Luca informs her. I've heard Luca's men teasing Ernesto about Gemma's nickname for him since he took over her guard duty.

"Okay, be careful."

"Always," he says then presses his lips to hers.

Both Piper and I turn to let them have a moment.

"I'll call you when I'm done," I say. "Let me walk you out to the car."

I know if I don't there's a good chance she'll go and try to make different arrangements and I need peace of mind after hearing Mary has been taken.

Luca and I both walk as casually as possible to the front of the church and down to the waiting cars. Darren will take the women with Luca's guards driving in the SUV behind them. Darren already has the door open as we approach and gives a nod. I help Piper with her dress then slip my lips over hers before backing away from the door and closing it.

"Keep a watch out; Mary was taken right under Bobby's nose," I inform Darren.

His face shows a second of shock before he masks it. "Yes, sir."

Once Luca has settled Gemma in, we back away from the vehicle and watch the cars leave the property before turning and hurriedly walking back into the church, bypassing the sanctuary toward the offices.

"What happened?" I ask the room as Thomas comes over to me from the wall where he was standing and hands me a gym bag consisting of a change of clothes, a vest, and a bomber jacket. Both vest and jacket are loaded down with guns and knives ready for battle. I switch out of my suit and into my apparel at the same time Luca finishes changing into his. I've got on a brown baseball jersey with jeans and my ball cap.

"Victor's men were able to get the upper hand on the guards and overpower Mary," Arturo states. "He is the one who has been hiring men to try and take out our family. We had suspected it for some time but had no evidence. He's been trying to sway Kendall over to his side with false evidence, but she saw right through it and came to Bobby and me. We were hoping he'd make the move before she and Wyatt got married and it looks like he's set his plan into motion today. We think his goal is to create a wedge between The Family and vote to wipe out an entire organization."

"He'd need a majority vote," I say and then it dawns on me. "Me, he thought I'd be convinced to vote with him."

"Exactly. He doesn't know how close you are to myself and Bobby," Arturo says.

"Let's go then and get Mary back," Luca pipes in ready for battle.

"Victor is taking them to pick up some surprise evidence he planted at one of Bobby's safe houses. Then the plan is for Kendall's team, which will include all of us and our men, to meet up with them at the final destination. We wait for the signal then attack full force."

We all nod and file out of the room into the back lot behind the church where all three of our organizations' teams are waiting.

"We need to fit as many men as possible in four vans with as many guns and ammo as we can. We don't know what we are walking into or where Victor is taking Kendall after the pick up so we need to be prepared for anything. All three teams are wearing the same brown shirts to differentiate between our men and Victor's guys. Kendall's team is also in brown. Shoot to kill but be mindful because we have Kendall and Mary there and don't want them in the crossfire. We want Victor alive if possible; he's got a lot to answer for."

I look over to Thomas who is also listening to Arturo.

"Make sure the team knows and is ready," I instruct him.

"Yes, sir," he responds. "Let's go hunting."

We knock our knuckles and I walk over to Bobby and Arturo along with Wyatt who has joined the group as they speak to each other. It's the first I've seen Bobby since he met Piper and I can see the fury vibrating off him.

"We're going to get her back," I say to him and Wyatt. "He won't hurt her."

"He is going to pay dearly for this," Bobby says as he continues to check his phone. A ping alerts of a text message. "It's time. They've picked up the package from the safe house and are on the road. Let's get a move on."

We pile as many of our men will fit into the four vans and make our way to the meet-up where we will join Victor and Kendall. Victor will think we are part of Kendall's crew and wait for a signal before going in on our assault. We drive for what feels like hours before we pull into a warehouse off the beaten path. Kendall and her immediate crew get out and Liam, her second-in-command, signals for the rest to stay put until needed. Victor meets her at the doors and I can hear Wyatt growling, wanting to barge out of the van towards them.

"Patience," Bobby chastises his son. "We wait for the signal from Frankie."

It takes a little under an hour before Frankie, Kendall's guard, walks out of the first SUV and speaks with the men there. The doors to the other SUV open and they all file out to walk around as if they're doing perimeter checks before they find an area to take up watch, surrounding Victor's men and the building. We are the last van to unload and carefully follow the same path but we are the ones who get closest to the doors.

Victor's men walk amongst us in their all-black attire and don't even realize we've infiltrated their lines, thinking we are all part of Kendall's crew.

"Start taking out the men with knives," I say into the mic at my neck. My team all have earpieces to listen to my commands.

As a guard who isn't one of ours walks by, I cover his mouth and sink my sharpest blade into his neck while wrestling him to the ground. His arms flail but after a few moments, he stills. My earpiece sounds with echoing responses. "Down."

Not hearing a call for help from any of Victor's men I turn to Bobby, Arturo, and Wyatt. "First wall breached," I say giving them the go-ahead for the next team to go in.

The closer we get in the warehouse the louder the shouting can be heard by the offices.

"I'm not waiting any longer," Bobby speaks into his mic as he takes out his gun. Arturo does the same and the entire warehouse lights up with gunfire. Victor's men are caught off guard and go down before they can return fire.

Bobby, Arturo, and Wyatt all head in the direction of the offices shooting men as they go. Thomas and I cover them and set up a block to not allow anyone to enter after them. Bobby needs to focus on finding Mary and not having to worry about if someone will hit him from behind with a bullet or knife.

Gunfire continues to ring out for several minutes until the warehouse goes completely silent. There's a slight fog of smoke and I turn toward Thomas. "Make sure no one is left alive. I'm going to check on Bobby and Arturo."

He nods and I hear him instruct some of our team to stand guard and for others to do a sweep of the large area.

I carefully head toward the sound of voices and clear every room before making my way in to assess the situation. It looks as though they've got it all under control. With Victor secured and a dead woman on the floor in front of a desk.

"Aren't bankers required to wear suits and ties to work?" Wyatt jokes, finally getting a good look at my attire. I guess he was so focused on getting to Kendall that he didn't pay attention earlier.

"And how do you not have a single drop of blood on you from the ambush outside?" Luca questions. He's wearing all dark colors but I can see he's got blood splatter on his pants, gloves, and shoes.

"First, I've got a hot date tonight, and second, you boys need to learn to work smarter, not harder."

They both roll their eyes. Over the years I've perfected the ability to make things a bloody mess and how to keep things pristine as well.

"Is it the woman you brought as your date to the fake wedding today?" Luca asks. "Gemma seemed to love her."

"Yeah, probably not the best first date but I'm hoping the game tonight will make up for it," I admit. "So how are we going to play this?" I point over to Victor as I pull up a seat next to Arturo.

"Let me get Mary settled first." Bobby ushers Mary out but not before grabbing Kendall and thanking her for saving his wife's life.

"I'm so sorry you had to choose, my sweet girl," Mary cries while cupping Kendall's cheek with her hand.

"It was never a choice, Mary. I was never going to let something happen to you. You were always safe with me." Mary engulfs her in the biggest hug and kisses her cheek before leaving with Bobby.

A few minutes later Bobby returns and tells Victor how he was set up and fell right for the trap he and Arturo had set. After a back and forth Victor sees he's now backed into a corner and starts making threats, not realizing that all of his men are being eliminated as we speak.

"Let's get the ball rolling shall we?" Arturo calls out. "I vote for the removal of Victor Slater and his organization from The Family. Total wipe out."

"I vote for removal and wipe out," I quickly agree looking down at my watch and seeing that I'm going to be cutting it close.

"I vote for removal," Bobby states. "And total wipe out."

The room turns to Kendall for the last vote even though it's not needed.

"I vote for the removal also," she confirms.

Arturo bangs his hand on the table like a gavel in a courtroom.

Judge.

Jury.

Executioner.

"Well, my time is up. You guys have a nice night since this is a personal matter," I say as I stand. "Make sure to make the bastard suffer. We can go over all his assets at the next meeting." I shake all of their hands then head out the door and back down the hall to where my team is standing watch.

Thomas leaves the line of men and falls into step with me as we all walk out of the warehouse.

"Load up most of our men and let's go. Leave a few for support until everyone has cleared out of the building."

Thomas follows orders and speaks quickly into the mic. The rest of the men load up into our designated van and we pull out of the property.

I reach into my back pocket and check my phone before dialing Darren wanting to check on Piper.

"Sir," he answers right away.

"She got home safely?" I ask.

"Yes sir, Mrs. Falcone ended up riding with us over to Ms. Caldwell's house then transferred to her car with her guards."

"How was the drive over? Was she upset?"

"Mrs. Falcone and Ms. Caldwell spoke the entire ride home. They seemed to be hitting it off pretty well. They did exchange phone numbers and planned to meet up soon."

I smirk at how well she's fitting right in with The Family.

"Are you still in the area?"

"I'm down a few houses. Mrs. Irene spotted me when she walked over to Ms. Caldwell's house. She approached after leaving the house."

"How was that?"

"She was all smiles but did tell me to inform you that a man who picks up their date is supposed to deliver that date and not send a hired hand to do a gentleman's job, sir." I can hear the amusement in his voice.

"Ms. Irene likes tradition," I say laughing. "Make sure to send a nice gift for all the work she did for Piper's dress. Let her know I appreciate her."

"Yes, sir."

"I'm going to get cleaned up and then Thomas and I will relieve you from your post."

"Yes, sir."

I hang up with him and then text Piper.

> ME: Are you the center of a circle? Because my thoughts are always revolving around you.

Not giving her a chance to respond, I dial her number.

"Hello," she greets with a giggle.

"Hey, beautiful."

"You know, I think you have some of the best pickup lines out there. How are you still single with all your smooth swag?"

"It's been hard. I've had to beat 'em off with a stick, but I've been waiting for the right woman to come along and I think I might have found her."

"Did you fix that problem?" she asks, not acknowledging what I just said.

"Sure did. Just finished and headed back to the house. Can you be ready to go in about an hour or so?"

"You sure you're not too tired or want to reschedule?"

"Not a chance, cherry bomb. We are hanging out the rest of the evening."

"What should I wear?"

"Going to the Ace's baseball game so wear shorts and a tank."

Wyatt told me all about his and Kendall's date to a hockey game. I gave him my tickets and with Piper loving baseball I think this will be a good one for us. I originally thought about dinner and a movie but we wouldn't be able to talk if we did that and I'd like to get to know more about her.

"That I can do. See you soon," she says then hangs up.

An hour later I pass Darren's waiting vehicle and pull up to Piper's house. Thomas and the team are in a separate car giving us some space. It can be overwhelming at first if you're not used to having people always around and the last thing I want is to scare her off because she feels suffocated.

Piper steps out of the house before I can even exit my car and I'm regretting my choice of clothes for her. Maybe we *should* go to a movie so I can hide her from others. She looks sexy as hell in a plain white tank that highlights her large tits with short denim shorts that show off her long toned legs. She's wearing a pair of platform white sneakers and she changed her hair to a high pony-tail that exposes her neck.

I meet her at the front of my car. "You look gorgeous," I start but can't help myself. "Next time wait for me to come get you."

"Why?"

She doesn't need to know it's a security thing and I want to have the area secured to make sure some idiot isn't lurking around looking for trouble.

"I'm trying to be a gentleman." I raise my hand and brush my thumb across her cheek.

She smiles as she rolls her eyes. "If you say so."

I lead her around to the passenger side and open her door to help her in but also so I can get a good look at her ass. I have to bite my lip to keep the groan in. It's going to take every ounce of control to be a gentleman tonight.

We fall into easy conversation. "How has your summer been so far?"

"It's good. I love when I get to sleep in," she tells me. "I still have a few things I have to complete before I'm officially on summer break but I'm hoping to finish it up next week." Her demeanor changes slightly and I can tell it's something she doesn't like doing.

"Like what?"

"Oh, it's something my principal has me roped in on. I compile all the invoices of her expenditures for the entire school year to turn in to the administration."

"Why can't she do it? Seems a bit lazy to me."

She snorts. "And have Jackie Roberts actually do her job?" she feigns astonishment. "I guess she thinks it's beneath her." She shrugs. "I get a small stipend for it but this time it's turning into a nightmare."

"How so?" I ask as we get closer to the stadium.

"I think I found something that may be concerning." She stops for a second and then turns to me. We're at a stoplight letting fans cross the street into the stadium.

"What'd you find?" Now I'm intrigued.

She shakes her head as if to clear her thoughts. "I don't want to say until I get all the facts first. I'm not much for gossip and I'd hate to say something that turned out to not be true."

"I like that you're logical but just know I won't go spreading what you say. You can confide in me if you need to," I offer. I want her to come to me with everything. I want to be the person she tells her every thought to.

"Thanks. Depending on what comes back I might need some advice on how to proceed."

There are so many questions I want to ask but we pull up to the VIP garage and I roll down my window to show my badge to the security guy at the gate. Once we pull through we park the car in my designated spot while Thomas does the same.

"Are you a ticket holder?" Piper asks as we get out.

"I'm an investor."

"Oh, wow."

I take her hand and we go through a set of doors where we are then ushered to a bank of elevators.

"I have a suite where we can watch the game or we can go sit in seats down by home plate," I offer.

"What do you usually prefer?"

"It's not what I prefer, it's where you want to watch the game," I say. "We can start at one area then move to the other if you want."

She thinks for a minute as the doors open. "Seats, maybe?"

"Sounds perfect. We need to get some gear; can't be here and not support our home team."

We walk over to a shop that's crowded with fans and to the wall of jerseys and hats.

"Which jersey do you like?" I ask looking over at the wall. I don't think I thought this through. Having the last name of a man on her back that isn't mine doesn't sit right with me.

"I'm always torn on jerseys with players' names on them. Players get traded so often that I hate to buy something and then they go to another team and I'm stuck with a shirt with a guy who doesn't even play for my team anymore. I think the team jersey without a player name or number is always the safe bet."

"Practical, I like it." And I'm relieved.

She walks over and looks over the selection. When she finally reaches out to hold up one of the red and black shirts she pulls the price tag up and quickly puts it back on the rack.

"I really don't need a jersey," she tries to play off.

"It's my treat, and besides I can't come to a game and not support a team I'm an investor in." I can see the wheels turning in her head. "How about we get these," I say and hold up the one she picked out. I grab the one in her size and then one in mine. Thomas comes over and takes the clothes and the matching hats that I'd already snagged and heads off to pay for it all.

I take Piper out of the store and into the bustling open hallway that shows the field before she can argue. Thankfully it doesn't take Thomas too long before he's handing me the bag full of merchandise.

"Thank you," Piper says to both Thomas and me. It amazes me how gracious she is about receiving anything. It makes me want to buy her everything. "My dad used to bring me here when I was a teenager," she says as she pulls the jersey on over her tank then works the hat onto her head and pulls her ponytail through the back.

One of the many things we talked about over the phone was our shared love of baseball. She grew up playing softball until she graduated high school and I did the same with baseball. I could've pursued it in college but I wanted to fast-track my education as quickly as possible.

"Oh, I love baseball," Piper says while we chat late after one of her shifts at the sandwich shop. "I used to sneak in with a friend from high school."

"Now that is a story I want to hear about," I say, pleasantly surprised that she'd do something like that.

She starts to giggle. "My friend, Jason, and I would wait outside the stadium, and as people started leaving early for whatever reason we'd ask for their ticket stubs. We'd say that it was for a school project."

"I can't believe you did that and it worked." I refrain from grilling her about this Jason kid and leave it for another day.

"Yeah, once we were in we'd wait and watch for empty seats then try to get as close to the field as possible."

"Wish me and my buddies would've thought of that." This woman has so many layers to her and I can't wait to uncover each one. Every time we talk I find out that she's not as Pollyanna as I thought when I met her.

"It was great until they went digital with everything," she sighs with disappointment. "I had to wait and go with my dad after that."

"Well, we can go anytime you want now. I've got the best tickets to all sporting events," I boast.

"What position did you play?" she asks.

"I was a shortstop mainly but would switch over to second when needed."

"Why didn't you play in college?"

I think back to that time and a shiver runs down my spine at the memories.

"It was a difficult time for my family. Going to class and graduating was the priority so that I could take over the family business," I explain. "Why didn't you?"

"I guess I wanted to experience the whole college thing and not be tied down to practices. Plus, I'm not sure I was good enough to get a scholarship in Florida."

"You sell yourself short, cherry bomb. I bet you were good enough."

We make our way down a special escalator to the lower-level seats and out of a tunnel. The field is now eye level as if we could walk right onto it. I see the field security and he nods and lets us pass as I guide Piper with our hands interlocked to the front row of seats next to the field. We are right on the first base dugout and have one of the best views of the entire field. An usher comes right over and asks for our food order.

"I'll take a hotdog, fries, and beer," Piper requests and I do the same.

"Never took you for a beer type of girl. I figured you'd order wine or a fruity drink," I tease.

"I guess we are all full of surprises." She wags her brows while giggling. *She certainly is.*

"Please rise and remove your hats as we honor America with our National Anthem," an announcer calls over the speakers and the entire stadium stands.

The song starts as a male sings into the microphone and Piper squeals beside me. She grabs ahold of my jersey and practically bounces on her feet.

"Oh. My. Gosh! That's Axel Cross!" she calls out then removes her hand from my shirt and cups her cheeks.

"Who?" I ask confused as to why she'd react like this.

"Axel Cross, the musician," she explains as if I'm supposed to know who he is. She finally turns her eyes back to me and an emotion I've never felt in my entire life roars as I watch her cheeks blush.

Jealousy.

"He's the hottest man on the radio right now. He's got five songs that have taken over the music charts for the past four months," she says as if that is going to explain why she's fangirling so hard. I glance around the stadium and I can see other women in the same state as Piper. At least I'm not the only male that has to put up with this shit.

The anthem thankfully ends and the cheering and screams that follow him off the field and into the dugout could bust an eardrum. Our food arrives and I've never been so happy.

"These seats are fantastic. You're so lucky to be able to be this close whenever you want," Piper comments as the players take the field.

"Where did you and your dad usually sit?"

She points to the outfield. "At the very top in the nosebleed section."

We settle in with our food and as the innings pass by I've got my arm around her seat and she's placed her hand on my thigh. Eventually, we start talking about the players' statistics as they come up to bat. She really is a numbers girl and I love having someone to talk with about it and not feel like it's going to go over her head. I'm in such a relaxed state no one would ever think I'd been in an ambush just a few hours before. By the time, the sixth inning comes around an idea occurs to me and even though I hate where my mind is going I tamp it down by thinking of the big picture. I quickly text Thomas what I want and to make it happen. Once I get a confirmation I make my move.

"Let's go up to the suite for a little bit. I've got something to show you." I stand and help her up.

We go up the steps and into the tunnel and right to an elevator. We quickly arrive at our floor and walk out into an elegant hall. Down to the right is my personal suite. I often let Luca and Wyatt use it when they want a guys' night out. One of my guys is standing outside the door and quickly opens it for us. As we walk in I see Thomas to the side of the room along with some of my other team. The suite is filled with a handful of men I've never seen until today.

"Mr. Bishop, thank you for offering us the use of your suite," a man in jeans and a polo comes over. "I'm Shawn, Axel's manager."

"My pleasure," I shake his outstretched hand. I watch as Piper's eyes widen when recognition hits her as to who Shawn is linked to. She looks around the suite at every person to see if he's really here.

"Let me introduce you."

We walk through the set of glass doors that lead out to a balcony of cushioned chairs overlooking the field. It's not as good as being down right by the field but it's still an awesome view of the game.

"Axel, meet Ox Bishop. This is his suite," the man who I've already forgotten his name says.

Axel stands from the seat where he'd been watching the game and comes over. Piper's hand that I've been holding this entire time tightens around mine significantly.

"That's Axel Cross," she whispers but it's not quiet at all. Her free hand comes up to my forearm holding onto me with a death grip as if to hold herself up.

"Hey, man, thanks for the invite and use of your suite," Axel says and holds out his hand.

"Absolutely," I shake his hand with my free one. "This is my woman, Piper."

"Nice to meet you, darlin'." He looks down at her and gives her a smile.

My instincts want to gut him, but I just grit my teeth and watch this play out. *You're playing the long game and are trying to make up for having to bail earlier.*

"Would you like me to take some photos?" Thomas offers from out of nowhere.

The fucker.

Piper nods because words are suddenly too difficult. At first, we take a group photo of the three of us but then Thomas apparently wants his ass kicked even harder when he suggests, "Why don't the two of you get one now." He points at Axel and Piper. My eyes flash over to him and if looks could kill he'd be dust. Retribution is promised as he stands there smiling back at me.

I step away from the two of them and stand next to Thomas.

"I'm going to kill you," I whisper through clenched teeth but with a smile still on my face. No one the wiser.

"You'll thank me later," he responds without looking at me. The amusement on his face is clear so I focus back on Piper and this pecker who had all the women swooning in the stadium. My fingers ball into fists as he wraps an arm around her waist for the pictures. After a few moments, Thomas says he's finished and I walk back over and stand behind Piper as she and Axel discuss his upcoming tour. I wrap my arms around her, settling them on her lower stomach, and she relaxes into me. I feel a sense of calm as her fingers strum against my forearms.

After a few minutes of them talking and laughing because apparently my woman can charm every man within a five-mile radius, the manager from Axel's team comes over.

"I guess that's my cue that we're leaving," Axel says. "Thanks again for the suite," he looks over at me and then back to Piper. "Nice to meet you, darlin'. I'm going to have my team reach out and set something up for those kids. I'm always looking for ways to help youth out. Also, I'll get Shawn to give you our card with our phone number to get you some tickets for when we're coming into town for you and your friends." He winks down at her.

Before the growl ever leaves my throat they all exit the suite leaving us standing in the same spot with a business card left in Piper's hand. I guess I was so in my head fuming and thinking of ways to torture this guy that I missed the conversation about them helping kids. Of course, my woman is advocating for children in need when all the while I'm worried about her gushing over some famous musician.

Piper turns in my arms so her heavy breasts are against my chest. Her eyes meet mine and she has the biggest smile on her face. "That was the most incredible experience I've ever had," she beams. I'm almost pissed until she continues, "Thank you so much for making it happen! No one has ever done something so thoughtful like that for me, ever."

The sincerity and appreciation in her voice do something in my soul. My chest puffs out a little knowing that I've given her something that no one else ever has.

She pushes up on the tips of her toes and my head bends down automatically like it's something we do every day. I quickly turn my hat backward to not have any obstacles in our way as our lips press against each other and it sends tingles down my spine. My arms tighten around her and pull her into my body not leaving a millimeter of space between us. My tongue coaxes her lips and they open giving me access to her mouth. We both stand there for minutes exploring each other's mouths as my hands roam her body. She's not shy about being in public as I pick her up and place her on the island inside the suite where food is usually placed. I do notice that Thomas has left the room and placed the glass windows to block out prying eyes from seeing in.

My lips leave her mouth and work their way down her jaw to her ear. I find her sweet spot just below the lobe and she shivers when I suckle it. She removes my cap and runs her nails through my hair making my dick jump against the zipper of my jeans. Her thighs wrap around my waist as my mouth descends from her neck to her chest.

"Maddox," she moans and it sends me into overdrive. My hands shuck off her jersey so that I can pull her tank up and devour her tits, but a loud thump on the suite door gets our attention. We both straighten realizing where we are and look around. Outside the suite, the game is over and people are making their way out of the stadium. "Think we made the kiss cam?" Piper asks and we both start laughing.

"I got a little carried away," I say looking down at her.

Her lips are swollen from our kissing and she's flushed.

"I think we both did."

I help her off the island and do my best to adjust my cock in my jeans. I grab my cap and put it back on while she pulls down her shorts which rode up her thighs giving me a peek of her lower lips in a sheer thong. My fingers twitch at the thought of touching her there. My dick pulses and I have to give it a tight squeeze for relief hoping it will help calm it down. The last thing I need is for my men to see me walking around with a hardon.

"Need help with that?" I hear her say with amusement in her tone. When I glance over at her she has a mischievous smile across her beautiful face.

"I like how you aren't shy about expressing what you want," I say.

"What do you mean?"

"Most women dance around affection or try to come across as innocent when sex is brought up, but you aren't."

"I'm twenty-six years old. I've had sex as I'm sure you have too. Wait, how old *are* you?"

The question makes me chuckle. "Just turned thirty-five," I say.

Her eyes go wide. "Really?" She pauses as if to process that tidbit of information and I don't like that this might seem like an obstacle for her to accept us.

"Is that going to be a problem?" I've never thought about the age difference but I'm not going to let it be an issue here. Nine years is a little bit of a gap but not enough for it to be a deal breaker.

"I mean as long as you don't start bringing your walker or wheel an oxygen tank around with us on dates I think it'll be okay." She giggles and the tension in my shoulders relaxes. She shrugs one shoulder adjusting her hat. "My parents weren't shy about being affectionate around me. They believed you show the person you care about how you feel and to not be ashamed about it." She walks over to me and places her hands on my upper arms. "I thought it was gross when they'd kiss or I'd catch them making out on the couch when I was younger but I'm thankful they didn't hold back. I see now that it's a healthy way for kids to understand how to express emotions in front of others. It isn't a bad or naughty thing. So many children only see the fights or aggression from their parents and not the loving side. At least that's what I've experienced teaching students. If they aren't getting it at home then they will seek it out in other avenues like online, or worse, they'll think those toxic relationships are normal."

She doesn't know how right she is.

"Will you tell me what happened to your parents?"

I can tell the question is a mood killer when her arms sag and she tries to take a step back from me. Her walls are going up but I refuse to let her put any distance between us. I want her to be able to tell me any and everything. For her to come to me with any issue good or bad.

"I guess." She avoids my eyes and looks around. "But not here."

CHAPTER TEN

Piper

WE PULL THROUGH A MASSIVE GATE AND UP A TREE-lined driveway to an estate. My phone chimes from an incoming text message.

"Everything okay?" Maddox asks from behind the wheel as he pulls around the circular drive leading to the front door.

"Just Rob wanting to make sure I'm doing okay."

We both exit the car and walk up the steps to the front door.

"He's a good kid," Maddox says as we walk into the foyer of the two-story mansion.

I smile at his comment. "He's the best." I take in the marble columns and floor. The walls are cream-colored with accents of brown throughout the room. "You have a very beautiful home, Maddox."

"Thank you. It was my family's home that's now mine, I guess." He looks around as if inspecting it for the first time with his hands on his hips.

"You never mention your family. Are you estranged?" I watch as he chews on the inside of his cheek. Maybe it's too personal to bring up; it is technically only our first date even though we've been talking for almost a month. I get the hint when he still hasn't said anything for a minute or two. "Sorry, it's none of my business."

"No, it's just…" He pauses again. "It's not something I talk about often."

"We don't have to. It's not like we have to tell all our deep dark secrets on the first date," I tease.

He comes over the few steps that separate us and pulls me flush to his body.

"I want to know every little detail about you, good and bad." He kisses the tip of my nose.

"Are you able to do the same?" I ask.

This man has many secrets he keeps hidden. Nobody walks around with a team of security without reason. Money is a powerful thing and invites problems but with as many people as Maddox has surrounding him…

The way he was greeted at the wedding today was too formal, too traditional, to be some investor. I can't put my finger on it yet but I'm sure he is hiding a lot behind those alluring eyes.

"Careful what you ask for Piper. Once you go down certain paths there's no turning back," he says cryptically. "Let's start with you first then we can dive into my family."

He leads me through the house, pointing out the formal dining room, living rooms, and the enormous kitchen. He shows me his office, the indoor pool that flows to the outdoor pool, and there's a bowling alley next door with an attached arcade that features just about every game imaginable. A kid's dreamland. He shows me a virtual golf room to practice his swing before going up the stairs to the second floor. The first room he shows me I'm in love with. He has a ginormous media room. The screen is massive and the chairs are oversized sofas. I immediately take a seat in the center of the room claiming the sofa. It's like I'm lounged out on a cloud.

"I'm assuming the tour is officially over now." Maddox laughs as he grabs a few beers from the full fridge on the wall in the corner where snacks are also located then plops down beside me.

"How do you ever leave this house? There's no reason to step off this property because you have everything here that you could want," I say and take a drink from the bottle.

"It gets a little boring after a while, but maybe if you're here with me all the time I'd think differently."

"Careful what you say, Stud." I throw his words back at him from earlier.

"Stud?" His eyebrow shoots up as he tilts his head back and swallows a few gulps from his drink.

"You called me cherry bomb so I think it's only fair to have a nickname for you as well. I'm still trying to figure out which ones fit you best; you already get called Ox or Bishop, but I want my own that no one else gets," I say as he rolls his eyes playfully. "Maybe Stud Muffin or Honey Bun—" He starts to tickle me and I squeal as he pins me down. "Okay, okay I give!" He finally stops and we both catch our breath. "So no nicknames involving food," I can't help but add.

"You are going to be the death of me," he says while chuckling. "Now tell me about what happened to your parents."

The playful atmosphere is immediately sucked from the room as I crisscross my legs and turn to face him.

"A few years ago I was getting ready to graduate college when I received a call from Spring Valley Hospital informing me that my parents had been in an accident. They said it was bad and that I should come as soon as possible. After I got off the phone I booked a redeye flight that same day. When I made it to the hospital both my parents had slipped into a coma and the outcome wasn't looking good. An officer had come by the next morning and told me that my parents were traveling down Highway 15 when an eighteen-wheeler crossed the median, went through the barricade, and slammed into their car." I paused to try and block the memories of the pictures of the scene I was shown. "They think the driver fell asleep at the wheel but he died at the scene. My parents both suffer from Traumatic Brain Injuries or TBIs. My mom broke her spine and is bedridden and needs assistance round the clock to function. My dad can be in a wheelchair but he isn't verbal and he doesn't know where or who he is just like Mom. They just stare off as if no one is in the room. The doctors say that where they are right now is the best to hope for their quality of life. Dad can breathe on his own but that is as far as it goes. Mom needs oxygen occasionally. The doctors don't expect their bodies to hold up long-term. There is so much we don't know about the brain but when they run the gambit of tests every six months their bodies continue to show decline. My mom's more so than my dad. I think it has to do with being stuck in a bed all day, but who knows?"

"I'm so sorry about your parents, Piper." Maddox pulls me onto his lap and holds me close. I lay my head on his shoulder and just breathe him in. I can't even cry because I drained those tear tanks years ago when all this was happening. "Is there any other medicine or doctor that could come in and help?"

I know he's trying to be helpful; most are when they hear what happened.

"No, I've researched and asked every question imaginable. All I can do for them now is make sure they are comfortable, safe, and well cared for."

"Do you like the facility they're at? I could call around—"

"Thank you but this place is the best I can afford at the moment."

"That's why you work all these jobs," he concludes. "To pay for their treatment and living. Does insurance cover most of it?"

I scoff. "The insurance company only pays a fraction of what the bills cost. In fact, I had to move Mom and Dad from the original rehab facility because the care there was so bad and they both kept getting infections from not being changed or repositioned. It was horrible. I feel like I'm constantly fighting with them to pay their portion every month. They expect us to pay on time every month to keep it updated but they sure do like to drag their feet when having to pay out on their side."

Every dime I make goes to pay something. The money I make

working at the sandwich shop all goes to the rehab facility for my parents. My teaching salary pays for my mortgage, electricity, water, and groceries, and what little is left goes to the rest of the rehab bill that's left over. I try to put away a few dollars to cover when the car breaks or something stops working at the house.

"So you stayed here and became a teacher instead of pursuing your dream?" he asks as he pulls me back a little to see my face.

"I did. They were the best parents in the world and I'd do it all over again if I had to."

"I'd like to go and meet them the next time you go up there," he says and I jolt back, shocked.

"Why?"

"Because they're important to you and I want to meet the people who raised such an amazing woman."

"That's so sweet but please don't feel like you have to," I offer letting him off the hook.

He kisses my forehead and I think I swoon even harder for this guy.

"Tell me how you met Rob. He told me a little bit but I'd like to hear your side," he says and I tell him about finding him digging through a dumpster.

We spend the next hour or so talking when a yawn catches me.

"We should get some sleep," he suggests and makes a move to stand but I stop him.

"Not a chance," I say and raise my eyebrows. "Tell me about your family, even if it's the watered-down version," I say because he's been avoiding the subject all night by putting the focus on me.

He settles on his back, putting his arms behind his head, and looking up at the ceiling. "So my father is dead. He was killed when I was sixteen—"

"That's horrible, Maddox. I'm so sorry," I say. I lay across his body with my head on his chest and he places an arm at my back holding me in place. I can feel his heart beating against my cheek.

"Bobby and Arturo took me under their wing. They'd known

my father for years and filled his shoes when it happened. When I graduated high school I went to college and got my degree in economics and business. Once that was completed, I came home to run the family business."

"What about your mom?"

"She and my twin sisters, who are in their final year of college now, live in New York."

"Are you close with them?"

"There's a twelve-year age gap between us, so growing up I didn't really have much time with them between school and baseball. I've been more active in their life in the last ten years or so. We talk once a week and I try to go see them as often as I can, which is every couple of months. They prefer New York and hardly come back here to visit."

"As an older brother, I bet you have your hands full with not one but two sisters, and twins at that," I chuckle.

"Definitely keeps me and their team on edge sometimes."

"Teams?"

"Security. Being wealthy can put the people around me at risk. It's why you see Darren and Thomas with me a lot," he answers.

I yawn again, not meaning to, and Maddox takes that as his way of ending the conversation. He picks me up bridal style and cradles me to his chest. We walk out of the room and instead of going down the stairs out to the car so I can head home, he walks in the opposite direction down a long hall to the double doors at the end. He maneuvers to open one door and strides into the massive room. A huge bed sits as the focal point in the center of the room against the wall with large floor-to-ceiling windows on either side. He doesn't take me to the bed but through another door into the bathroom where he sits me down on one of the long vanities.

"Let me get you something to sleep in," he offers and walks off to the side by the walk-in shower that I assume must be the closet. A few moments later, he comes back with an old vintage-looking shirt. "This should work."

"No bottoms?" I ask raising an eyebrow in question.

"I'll keep you warm enough."

He heads over to a smaller door where the toilet is and closes it. I take this as my chance to change. I pull off all my clothes and slip the butter-soft shirt over my head. The hem hits mid-thigh. While I neatly fold my clothes, he comes out in only boxers and stares at me as he pulls out a new toothbrush from under the sink. He hands it to me, but I'm gobsmacked staring at his body. He's the epitome of a Greek God. When I've touched his arms and chest I knew he worked out and was in shape, but seeing how every muscle is defined and sculpted makes my mouth water. When we both finish, Maddox takes my hand and tugs me to the bedroom.

"Which side do you sleep on?" he asks as we stand at the foot of the bed.

"I don't have a side. I sleep in the middle so I won't roll off and the monsters under the bed can't reach me," I joke.

He looks over at the closed bedroom door and pauses for a moment as if he's considering something, then he turns back to me and picks me up as if I weigh nothing.

"I'll keep the monster away," he says then tosses me onto the middle of the bed.

Maddox follows me to the mattress as I pull the comforter and sheets down. "What time do you have to be at work in the morning or are you off on Sundays?" I slide between the sheets and the feel of the luxurious softness of them gives me goosebumps.

"I make my own hours," he answers as he leans over me. "What about you?"

"I don't work at the shop until Monday afternoon."

He gets a wicked smile on his face. "Good to know we still have a day and a half left on our date."

"Wait, what?"

"You're mine until Monday afternoon."

"Oh, really? What if I thought this date was one of the worst and wanted to head home?"

He moves on top of me using his weight to hold me down. "I guess I'd have to find ways to convince you to stay then." He kisses my neck and I lose all train of thought. Just when I think he's going to make his move he lifts his head and stares back at me. "Let's get some rest. It's been a long day." The smirk on his face tells me that he knows what he's doing and I narrow my eyes at him. "Don't worry, I plan to devour you for the next day and a half but that'll take hours and I want you well rested. And I'm trying to be a gentleman and not take advantage."

It's so sweet that he wants to take this slow but he's got my hormones in a tizzy. "Ever think I might want to be taken advantage of," I tease as I trail my hand down his hard torso to the band on his boxers. I can feel his hard length growing. He quickly grabs my hand before I can take ahold of it and maneuvers us so I'm turned on my side with my back to his front. He's got one arm underneath my pillow and the other across my middle.

"Get some rest, cherry bomb. You're gonna need it," he whispers as his lips brush against my ear causing me to shiver.

The day's activities start to weigh on me as the lights turn off and my body relaxes into Maddox.

"Night, sugar booger," I chuckle still working on a good nickname for him when I feel a pop on my butt.

I feel him shake his head and can't believe how this day went. I'm finding that I'm glad he didn't give up when I tried to put a stop to this. My eyes start to get heavy as I lean more into him and let myself fall asleep feeling secure.

The next morning I'm awakened by the smell of food and coffee. Maddox is sitting on the edge of the bed with a tray of assorted breakfast foods and a carafe of coffee. I sit up as he types something on his phone and the shades lift, brightening the room with the morning sun.

"Morning," he greets.

"Morning. What time is it?" I mumble, my voice thick with sleep.

"Just after nine."

"Really?" I can't remember a time I've slept so late.

"Yeah, I didn't want you eating cold food so I thought I'd bring it up here to coax you awake."

"You didn't have to go to the trouble of doing this, but thank you," I say and grab a croissant. I don't usually eat breakfast because I'm either running out the door to get to work or we don't have any breakfast food in the house. "What do you have planned today?"

"Thought we could hang around the house today." He pours us both a cup of coffee and hands one to me.

"Sounds good but I'm going to need to run home and grab a shower and clothes."

"No need. I had Darren pick you up a few things for today and tomorrow before your shift." He sips his hot drink.

"Well, aren't you just so thoughtful," I say playfully.

"I aim to please. I'll let you take your first shower," he offers when we finish our food and coffee.

"You don't want to conserve water and shower together?" I know I'm teasing but it's so fun watching him try to be this 'gentleman.'

He groans and rubs his hand over his face. "I think you test every restraint I have, Piper."

"Just think of how boring your life would be if I didn't challenge it." I give him a sweet smile as I turn towards the bathroom.

"Very soon you're going to find out the full force of me," he tosses over his shoulder as he walks out of the bedroom with the tray in hand.

When I walk into the bathroom I see a stack of new clothes where I'd left the ones I wore yesterday. There are shirts, bras, panties, and a swimsuit lined up on the counter. As I inspect them, I find they are all my sizes, and I have to wonder if he broke into my house and took a peek in my closet to know what my sizes are. After taking one of the best showers of my life with the water spouts hitting me from all directions, I towel off and pull on a pair of shorts and a shirt just when Maddox appears. He's sweaty and his shirt is drenched.

"Did you jump in the pool?"

He chuckles as he pulls the shirt over his head. "I lifted some weights to give you time to finish."

He doesn't wait for my reply and starts tossing his clothes off. My eyes are fixated on his body like I'm a starving woman. His penis is long and the more I stare the harder and longer it gets. When he's standing there fully naked, staring back at me not ashamed one bit, he gives me a wink and turns to walk into the steaming shower. My body heats and it has nothing to do with the temperature of the room but with the man who is watching me as he lathers his body. My head wobbles and I think it best if I walk out to the bedroom and wait until he's finished. By the time I'm done making the bed and putting on my shoes, Maddox walks out in a pair of black athletic shorts and a shirt.

"What did you have in mind today?" I ask.

A wicked grin forms on his face. "That's a loaded question, babe, but I thought I'd show you around the house and property. Maybe play a few games in the arcade or bowling alley."

After we both pocket our phones, we head out and he shows me the rest of the house. During the day the house and property look even more opulent sitting on several acres.

"Down the way are Bobby and Wyatt's houses," he points out when we are leaning up on the rail of the second-story balcony. "Arturo, his wife Adele, Luca, and Gemma live over there in those houses." He points in another direction.

"You all live close by. Must be nice to have your friends so close."

"They're my family," he corrects with a smile. "Let's go and see how your bowling skills are."

"I don't think you realize how competitive I am when it comes to playing games," I tease.

"Is there truly any other way to play than that?"

"Okay, but don't start crying for your mama when you lose," I taunt playfully.

After hours of bowling and playing games in the arcade, and after Maddox grills us some burgers for lunch, we settle into the media room for a movie with popcorn and drinks.

"How do you maintain this property," I ask noticing how neat and tidy every room is. We cleaned up our mess after lunch but the floors and counters shine so much we could've eaten off them. I couldn't imagine having to clean a place this massive; I've yet to see a single speck of dust.

"I have a crew that maintains the entire place. There's always someone here doing something but I wanted it to be just us today." I nod trying not to let the thoughts of how much different we are and that we come from two totally different worlds invade my mind. "Stop what you're thinking." He taps my temple. "I'm just like any other guy."

He doesn't know how wrong he is, but I feel my cheeks warm at him being able to read my thoughts. A hand tugs on my ankle and I go from sitting on my butt to on my back with Maddox hovering over me.

"It's just you and me," he says as he leans down and kisses my jaw. The movie has started but I have no idea which one we picked at this point. He works a path up to my ear then across my cheek to my mouth. "You are so beautiful."

My heart kicks at my chest and I can't help but melt. "You're such a charmer," I say but he pulls back.

"I mean it, Piper. You're the first woman I've ever pursued or even wanted a relationship with. This isn't me trying to sell you lines to get my dick wet." He levels me with his eyes. "Although I like where this is going." He bounces his eyebrow and then bucks his hips against the apex of my thighs. "It's why I'm trying to take things slow and not mess this up. To build a long and lasting foundation and to earn your trust."

"To be a gentleman," I repeat the words he's been telling me for the last few days. I smile at him trying to impress me and show effort. I reach up and cup his cheek. "I'm glad you and I are on the same page then. I was worried that this," I point back and forth between us, "was just something for you to pass the time, but I can see that you want more than that. I just worry that everything I have going on with both jobs and my parents' care, that you'll feel put on the back burner or neglected because I can't always give you my full attention."

"Let me worry about that and you just keep being you." He kisses the tip of my nose, and I fall a little more for this man.

I tilt my chin up and capture his lips. My eyes close and all I can think about is how good his body feels against me. Our mouths open and our tongues massage each other. My hands find their way under his shirt exploring his warm skin. He deepens the kiss as our bodies find a rhythm. I grab his shirt and pull it over his head. His mouth stops its assault on mine and he sits up, taking me with him. He moves me to straddle his thighs as he reaches for my shirt. I help pull it off and toss it behind me somewhere as I feel the clasps of my bra release and my breasts fall free from their confines.

"I've dreamed of these tits," he mumbles running a thumb over my nipples causing them to peak. I release a moan as he brings his head forward to take one in his mouth. He tweaks the other between his thumb and forefinger sending a spasm straight to my core. My fingers find the back of his neck and I clutch his hair as the sensations overwhelm me. He sucks and nips at my breast before switching to the other one and giving it the same treatment. My panties are a wet mess as my breathing picks up. "I bet I can make you come like this." His words are muffled with his mouth full of my flesh. My hips move in sync with his sucking, knocking against his bulging dick through the thin athletic material of his shorts.

"Maddox," I moan his name like a prayer, close to erupting with an orgasm I didn't even know was possible with just my breasts being played with. I feel his hand slide up my thigh and inside the leg of my shorts. His fingers thrum against my panties and I cry out at the pleasure. My thighs try to close but I'm straddling his thigh making me open and ripe for the taking. He pushes the offending material to the side and brushes up along my clit making my body shiver. I suck in a breath and tighten my hold on his neck.

"You're so wet and sensitive to my touch," he says as he licks my nipples before plunging a finger into my dripping channel.

"Ahh," I call out as his finger rubbing up against the walls of my vagina throws me closer to the edge. "I'm so close," I pant.

"I know you are. The way you clamp down on me is incredible. Think of how my cock is going to feel inside you." He grabs me around the back of the neck where his lips are touching my ear. "I'm going to fuck you so good and hard that you won't be able to think about anything else but me for a week." His teeth clamp down on my ear as his finger curls inside of me and I feel his thumb rub on my clit.

My body seizes as my muscles lock and I fall over the ledge in his arms. I shout his name but it sounds so far away as my body floats like a cloud. It feels like I'm being touched by a feather as the moments pass by. When my mind and body sync I'm wrapped in Maddox's arms, my head against his shoulder while he rubs my back.

"Mmm." I slowly blink back to reality. "You sure know how to show a girl a good time," I giggle and snuggle in closer, loving the feel of our naked chests touching.

"Only for you, cherry bomb," he whispers.

I let my fingers trace up his torso until I reach his nipple, they circle the hard pebble, then pinch. His deep moan sends tingles down my spine as I kiss his neck. His fingers dig into my hips as I continue to play with his body.

"I want to make you come," I say into his ear.

Goosebumps spread down his neck and across the top of his shoulder.

"The first time I come with you is going to be in that tight pussy," he grits as I rock my hips in his lap.

My already wet panties soak even more at his words and I want that too. I place both hands on his naked shoulders and then push off to a standing position in front of him. I'm only in my shorts and panties so I guide my hands to the button and release them. Maddox watches as I shimmy the denim down my legs, and his heated eyes could set the world on fire.

When I touch the band of my panties I hear a tsking from him. "I'll take care of those," he says as he swings his legs off the couch and stands. He relieves himself of his shorts and boxers, standing there naked as the day he was born. My eyes roam over this sculpted man making me want to touch every inch of his body.

He kneels on the carpet in front of me, his nose and mouth right at my entrance. His fingertips caress my legs from ankle to hip. As they grab the band to my panties he ever so slowly peels them down my thighs, and I reach out to balance my hands on his shoulders. Once I step out of them his face comes forward and plants itself in the apex of my thighs. I hear him inhale and almost crumble at the action, but when I feel the tip of his tongue touch my clit, my knees buckle and my head lolls to the side.

"Let's lay you down so you don't hurt yourself," Maddox says as he guides me to the floor.

Once I'm on my back, I watch him take my right leg in his hand and start kissing his way upward exposing all of me to him. He's going painfully slow and my breathing picks up as the anticipation builds. His lips reach my clit and he starts to devour my entrance. No more are the slow, sensual movements but a man who feasts like he hasn't eaten for weeks. His tongue dips into my channel as his thumb rubs circles on my clit. He moves back and forth between the two as I grow wetter. My heart is pounding and I feel a heated flush blanket my flesh as my second orgasm starts to rush through me, but it halts right when I'm about to fall over the edge. My eyes come back into focus as I gaze up at Maddox.

"What? Wait, please," I plead, wanting to chase that high as he sits back and licks his lips.

"We come together this time," he states as he squeezes his dick hovering over my body. I'd agree to shave my head if it meant achieving the reward I know will rock my world.

Maddox lays over my body and braces on one arm as he guides his long, hard cock to my entrance. He slides it back and forth through my wet lips and the feeling sends me spiraling. His dick bumps my clit a few times causing a moan to escape. I stare up at his beautiful face thinking this can't be real when he enters me to the hilt in one smooth thrust. My body tenses at the force but also with the large intrusion into such a small space. Maddox dips down and covers his mouth over mine, his tongue taking charge as he waits for me to relax. In the back of my head, there is a small thought about protection, but it's squashed when I move my hands to his back as he starts to move inside me. The slight pain quickly turns to pleasure as his dick knocks into my G-spot.

"You feel amazing," he says when he pulls our lips apart and looks down at me. My orgasm starts to build again with each thrust and the gasps and moans become increasingly louder. He dips his head lower and consumes my nipple, sucking and biting. "That's right, get loud." Maddox grabs the back of my left knee pulling it up higher on his hip causing him to go even deeper. His pelvis rubs my clit with each passing and I feel dizzy. The sound of skin slapping drowns out the movie in the background as he speeds up.

"I'm close," I pant not able to control my own body.

He moans as my walls tighten. "Hold it a little longer," he grits. His back is sweaty and slick, and I do my best to hold on as he drills me so deliciously. "Not ready—" My body can't take much more as it starts to shatter. "Shit. Now, come now," he commands as the last of my restraint breaks and I burst into a million pieces. My sex pulses to my heartbeat and my body jolts as it releases the best orgasm I've ever had. Maddox has his head buried in my neck and

I feel his dick spasming inside of me. He rocks his hips in me for a minute as I feel our combined release trickle out of me.

Once we both catch our breath, Maddox lifts back up to his arms bracing above me. His hands frame my face as he smiles down at me. "You okay?" he asks.

I nod returning his smile. "Yeah, that was good—"

"Just good?" He feigns shock.

I start to giggle and feel more of our release seep out. I'm going to need to clean up soon.

"I thought it was amazing. Out of this world even," I stroke his ego but it really was the best. Never has a partner ever made me come so hard and twice during a sexual experience.

"That's more like it. I thought being a teacher you'd have better descriptive words in your vocabulary," he jokes.

"I'm a math teacher, not an English one," I counter.

"Touché." He chuckles. "Then you should say something like you are the square to my root." We both burst out laughing for a few moments before he shifts and falls completely out of me. "Let's get cleaned up."

Maddox swiftly rises and then bends down to help me up. He leads me to his room and through to the bathroom. I head straight for the toilet as fluid starts to run down my inner thigh but he stops me.

"I've got it." He grabs my hand and walks me over to the sink. He turns on the faucet and runs a cloth through it.

"I can—" I try to say but he stops me.

"Let me."

I watch as a man who has dozens of people working for him and are at his beck and call takes his time to attend to me as if I am the most important person in the world. When he's finished he tosses the rag in a hamper.

"I'm clean by the way. I know we didn't discuss protection or medical earlier but…" I trail off. Is it possible to ruin a moment that was so beautiful? "I never did what just happened." I try to convey but it's coming out frustratingly worse. "Condoms. I've always used condoms with others. This was my first time…"

His eyes crinkle trying not to laugh at my fumbles. "I'm glad we can be each other's firsts. I'm clean as well." He informs me and I release a breath I didn't realize I was holding. "Want to head back and watch that movie?" I nod and watch as he goes into his closet before coming out in new boxers and a plain shirt. Maddox raises my arms and helps me into a second shirt but not before coping a feel of my breast. "You feel okay?"

"I'm good," I say. I feel a heavenly ache with each step I take, and he must read my mind again because the smirk on his face is a dead ringer that he knows my thoughts.

We go back to the movie and tuck in on the soft couches. Maddox doesn't allow a centimeter between us, keeping his hands on me at all times. I find it hard to focus on the movie being stimulated by each touch. When the movie is over we head down to the kitchen for dinner.

"Where do you see yourself in five years?" Maddox asks as we eat the spaghetti we made together. It took us a little longer to make than normal since we couldn't keep our hands to ourselves.

"Five years?" I think it over. "I haven't really thought about it since I came home from college to help my parents out." I chew for a few moments running thoughts and ideas around. "What about you?"

He shrugs. "The same as now I guess. Maybe married to a hot redhead," he casually says then winks.

"Kids?"

His fork stops halfway to his mouth. "I never really thought I'd want them. If you'd asked me six months ago I'd say no without hesitation, but recently I'm coming around to the thought. My mom would love for me to already have a van full of them."

"I always wanted a big family," I comment sadly. "Growing up an only child with older parents was hard. My parents were great, don't get me wrong, but I was alone a lot and my parents didn't fit in with the younger parents in my grade. I always said that when I had kids I'd have as many as I could so they wouldn't be alone if something happened to me."

"Are we talking three or four? Or like a football team because I'm already up there in age so we better get started right now depending on your answer."

I laugh at his reply. This man is so not the same person I first thought he was when we met at the sandwich shop. He's still staring at me with a raised eyebrow and straight face waiting for an answer when I finally finish. My eyes widen when I realize he's not joking.

"Maddox, you can't just dive right into the deep end with something like that. We've only known each other barely a month and just had our first date and now you're suggesting we start having babies? We're missing a lot of steps in between."

"Like what? We don't have to go by other's standards. We can do our own thing and those that say different can fuck off. No one should dictate what we want or how we choose to live."

"Let's slow our roll, MadDog," I tease. "I like that idea for later, but right now let's just get to know each other. I mean your loud snoring might be a deal breaker after spending more time with you."

Maddox stands abruptly and stalks around the small kitchen table. I'm frozen by the sudden movements so when he picks me up bridal style my fork falls to the floor below. I squeal as he heads for the door that leads to the backyard.

"I don't snore," he insists but the corner of his mouth kicks up slightly.

"You do," I counter even though he doesn't. "It sounds like a loud whale mating call. I might need to invest in earplugs or a sound machine."

He grunts and then stops. I'd been so focused on his face that I didn't even realize we were in the backyard by the pool.

"Last chance. Take it back." His eyes narrow but hold excitement in them.

"I woke up thinking I was at a Harley Davidson convention—"

One minute I'm in his arms and the next I'm sailing through the air before plunging into cool water. I surface with a sputter only to find Maddox nowhere in sight. It's short-lived because an arm bands around my waist as he swims up from the bottom, and his lips connect with mine, not giving me a chance to say a word. I'm breathless when we finally pull apart, and he's got a mischievous glint in his eyes.

"Still think I snore?"

I huff out a breath and roll my eyes toward the sky. "I guess it's not that bad," I taunt.

His arms tighten around me and I'm dunked under the water.

"Is this a new waterboarding technique?" I spit water in his face and wrap my arms around his neck, locking my ankles at his back.

"This is me going easy on you, cherry bomb." He kisses the tip of my nose. "I'm much scarier to everyone else."

"What if I couldn't swim?"

"Don't worry, I'd save you."

CHAPTER ELEVEN

Piper

THURSDAY ROLLS AROUND WAY TOO SOON AS THE WEEK flies by like they always do during the summer. July starts next week and then we have to report back on school duty at the end of it. I just dropped off Jackie's expense report and both boxes of receipts with the front office. I emailed her this morning that I was done and sent her the report of the one box I think I was supposed to log and then sent another one that covered both boxes. She hasn't responded but I didn't figure she would. I did scan copies of all the items in both boxes to keep for my records though.

I'm now driving over to the administrative office to pick up the paperwork I asked for with my Public Records Request before I help out a shift at the sandwich shop. I close most evenings and Maddox seems to come by right before closing. He sits and watches me as I run through the place shutting everything down. He tried to help me Monday after we'd spent the weekend together but it almost turned into a playful food fight, so he now is only allowed to sit at the table by the front door and watch.

This past weekend was one of the best I've had in a long time. I've never had a partner I've connected with on just about every level. We talked about the financial world and what he looks for in new real estate ventures and then we laughed over stupid things we did in college. We ate, drank, and had amazing sex. I've watched him the last few days when he pulls up and gets out. His face is always so serious, almost harsh, but when he steps through the door and is with me, it's like he's a different person. He's more relaxed and softer.

My phone rings through the speakers in my car pulling me out of my thoughts. I hesitate to answer an unknown number but I always worry it has to do with something with my parents so I slide my finger across the screen.

"Hello?"

"Hi, is this Piper Caldwell?" My heart picks up speed.

I swallow thickly. "Yeah, this is she."

"This is Nancy and I'm the property manager over at Dirty Laundry Washateria. I'm calling because a Rob Smith listed you on the form he filled out for our contest."

"Oh, okay," I vaguely remember Rob and I talking about him entering something last week.

"We pulled your form from the bucket and we're happy to tell you that you won a brand new washer and dryer."

My car comes to a stop at a light and I look around for someone to jump in front of my car and yell, "Just kidding!"

"Are you still there, Ms. Caldwell?" the lady asks as I wait for the punchline.

"Yes, I'm still here, and thank you for this opportunity but I'm not able to subscribe or sign up for any type of monthly offer that comes along with it," I say because nothing in life is ever free.

"Oh no, honey, this is a no-strings-attached contest. The washer and dryer are legit and all you had to do was fill out that form to enter." I can hear a low voice talking in the background as Nancy pauses. "We do a yearly give back to customers who use our facilities."

The light changes and I think about pulling over because the excitement building up inside of me has me wanting to jump up and shout. I've never won anything in my life like this before. It's surreal.

"Oh my gosh, I can't believe this. Thank you so much," I say, my voice going up a few octaves.

I hear a chuckle. "You are most welcome, dear. Now let's set up a delivery date. We'll make sure to have everything working perfectly before the men leave."

We decide to have the delivery tomorrow morning and I couldn't be happier since that was when I was going to do our laundry at the washateria.

I call Rob right away as I park the car at the administration building. "We won!" I squeal. "I'll never doubt you again."

I hear Rob laugh over the line. "That's great and all but could you be more specific?"

"The form you filled out about the laundry contest. We won. I just got off the phone with the property manager and they are being delivered to the house tomorrow morning."

"Wow," he says but has a hesitant tone. "I didn't see that coming so soon," his voice is borderline sarcastic.

"You okay? What's going on?"

He's quiet for a few beats. "No, no I'm fine. I'm just shocked is all."

I hear a bell in the background. "Where are you?" I ask because it doesn't sound like any timers from the sandwich shop.

"I'm hanging with some friends before my shift," he answers and I hear his name being yelled. "I've got to go. See you later today."

"Okay, bye."

We hang up and I look at the phone. Rob has been gone a lot this summer, especially in the mornings. I try to give him some space and let him grow as a person but I think we need to have a day with just the two of us. We've both been working so hard this year and maybe I can find extra money for us in the budget to go do an escape room or some other activity before he starts his last year.

When I walk into the administration building I know where to go this time and the same lady that helped me when I came the first time is at the counter again.

"Hi, I'm here to pick up the PRR I asked for last week. I got a call that it was ready," I tell her.

She asks for my name then her eyes widen. "You've caused quite a ruckus the last few days."

"Really, why?" I notice her badge turn towards me this time and see her name is Megan.

"I had to get some help looking for a few things that were flagged. Upper management wasn't too happy at some of the requests," she leans over to whisper. "I'm also supposed to tell you that any other request will have a charge since this one was so large."

She points over to the wall and I see five medium-sized boxes stacked against it.

"Those are all for me?" I'm shocked. I was thinking it was only going to be a handful of pages. Not this monstrosity.

"Yep. I had some fun reading through some of the papers while all the others printed," she says. "Not that it's any of my business but I think it's commendable for someone to finally expose all the dirty little secrets happening around here." The more Megan talks the more I see she's going to be a good source of information if I need to dive even further.

"Is there a dolly to help me get them out to my car?" I ask worried about throwing my back out trying to carry and load all these boxes.

"Yeah, let me help you." She goes off down the hall and comes back a few moments later wheeling a dolly behind her. We slide the boxes onto the cart and she comes with me to open the doors out to my car. After we put the last one in and close the trunk she goes to leave but stops. "Next time ask for the conflict of interest form with family members working together."

"Are they not allowed to work in the same district?"

"Oh you can, it's just that it's supposed to be documented and those family members aren't allowed to report directly to each other," she informs me. "You'll see a lot of communication in the emails you requested. They go as high up as the members on the school board."

"Really?"

"The school district has a good ol' boy-small town mentality to it."

"How do you know all this?" I ask hoping to find out as much as possible. Maybe it'll help my research.

"These walls talk. And when you get a bunch of catty women together they all spill the tea. I've heard all types of things from the administration that shouldn't be happening. I don't even have kids so it doesn't affect me, but I do know that some things going on aren't right." A car pulls up beside us. "I've got to go but take this." She pulls a folded piece of paper out of her back pocket and hands it to me. She doesn't say another word as she turns, pulling the dolly behind her.

I decide to wait until I get home before opening the note. In the car, I call Belinda right away.

"Hey, lady!" she greets.

"Hey," I reply. "You are never going to believe what I just picked up. Five boxes full of papers full of the things I asked for from the school district."

"Holy crap! I was not expecting all of that."

"I know and the lady at the front desk told me even more," I say and fill her in on my conversation with Megan.

"Let's have a girls' night and drink some wine and go through all the boxes tonight," Belinda suggests.

"Sounds good. I get home around nine from my shift," I say.

"I'll bring the snacks and drinks since you're providing the entertainment." We both laugh before ending the call.

It's nice to have someone I can lean on even though we aren't super close. Belinda has a busy life with her family and we try to keep in touch with each other as much as time will allow. She isn't one who has to hear from me every day or she gets her feelings hurt. We have a friendship that understands that life is chaos and we do our best to stay in touch, even if a month goes by.

When I get home I unload all the heavy boxes in the living

room before going to get ready for my shift at the sandwich shop. I text Maddox letting him know that he doesn't have to swing by this evening since I've got plans after work.

> Maddox: What kind of plans?
>
> Me: Hanging out with my friend Belinda.
>
> Maddox: Where at?
>
> Me: Wouldn't you like to know? 😄
>
> Maddox: Not funny, and yes, I would.
>
> Me: 🍷 and 🥨

I change clothes and tidy up my bedroom before I hear my phone ping with another text. I finish the last bit of cleaning when it goes off again. I grab my phone on the charger and see Maddox has sent a few more texts.

> Maddox: What does that even mean?
>
> Maddox: PIPER!

The bubbles are waving and I can see he's typing another one.

> Me: We're just hanging out and having wine at my house. Calm down, MadDog!

The bubbles stop and so do his texts.

> Me: I'll call you tomorrow!

He doesn't respond and for a moment I worry about upsetting him but I'm crunched for time to get to my shift. When I arrive, Rob is there with one of our summer helpers. Oliver likes to hire high school kids in the summer to help with the tourist crowd that comes during these two months.

"Hey, how's it going?" I ask as I come in and check on everyone.

"Good so far," Rob says. Our other worker, Holly, just nods. She's super shy but a hard worker.

I nod and let them know to come get me if they need to. I've got a stack of invoices and statements to input for the month. Not to mention supplies to order. I work the next few hours getting all the numbers calculated in my spreadsheet before I stretch out my stiff back. The numbers are looking good for this quarter and I think Oliver is going to be pleased with the uptick of cash flow.

Walking out to see if Holly needs anything since Rob ended his shift almost an hour ago, I see a familiar face lounging at his designated table. I nod over at Holly who is ringing up a customer before taking a seat across the table.

"You didn't have to come tonight," I say as he puts his phone down and I lay my hand on top of his. Touching each other when we are in close proximity is becoming an addiction. "That's why I texted earlier."

He shrugs as his eyes roam over me. "I was in the neighborhood."

"Oh, really?" I start to laugh at the lie knowing his office is not even close to here. "You sure do a lot of business in this area. Might need to open a new office around here."

"Not a bad idea." He laces our fingers and then kisses my knuckles. "Wanted to come get my kiss since we aren't *hanging* out tonight."

"Don't sound so Bitter Betty," I tease. "Pouting isn't a good look on you, and plus, we've been together since Saturday."

He blows out an adorably playful breath. "Fine."

"Gemma texted me earlier about all of us hanging out sometime this weekend."

"Yeah, Luca called to let me know Gemma already has the weekend planned out and we are included in it."

The chime of the clock alerts us that it's closing time. I rise from my seat and lean over the table next to his ear. "If you wait until I'm done before you leave I'll give you one hell of a kiss to hold you over for tomorrow," I promise.

His eyes turn smoldering. "I'll hold you to it."

I saunter away from the table and get to work helping Holly close the shop down. She's done most of the closing chores when I start to count the cash register. I'm back in the office closing the safe when I hear Holly call out that she's finished.

"Okay," I yell back wanting to watch her walk to her car before I do the final walk-through and turn the lights off.

When I turn I see Maddox standing in the doorway. "I had Darren walk her to her car," he states. His suit jacket is missing and his sleeves are rolled up at his forearms, the top few buttons undone. He looks edible.

"That was very nice of you," I say allowing my eyes to roam over him.

He stalks the rest of the distance between us then plucks me up onto the desk before caging me in. "I think I was promised a kiss."

I reach up and cup the back of his neck guiding his lips down to mine. Once our lips touch Maddox takes control. This man knows how to kiss and he doesn't leave one inch in my mouth untouched by his tongue. His hands fist in my hair making my head tilt back allowing him to deepen the kiss. I moan and reach for his belt. Once it's unbuckled I work on the clasp of his suit pants. The outline of his dick is evident as I slowly work the zipper down. My hands come up to his chest and push to move him back. He gives me a step back and I surprise him when I slide down off the desk and onto the rug. Maddox groans from above me when I glance up.

"I've pictured this in my head for weeks." He cups my cheek.

My hands push down his pants and the band of his boxers letting his erection bounce free. He's long and hard when I pucker my lips and kiss the tip of his penis. Another groan leaves his chest and this time his hands return to fisting my hair. My tongue lavishes the head and trails down the underside along the vein to his balls. He grips my hair tighter as I work my way back up and wrap my mouth around him. My head bobs up and down as I work in a steady rhythm and his hips thrust causing his dick to hit the back of my throat triggering my gag reflex. He eases up slightly but continues to drive in and out, grunting with every thrust.

"You going to swallow, cherry bomb?" He moans looking down into my eyes. I'm planted in place as his hands hold me there not giving me room to nod. A flood of wetness gushes from between my legs making a mess of my panties. "You'll take every drop in that pretty little mouth," he demands and starts to pick up his pace. My hands are on the back of his thighs holding on as he uses me. My jaw is getting sore from how wide I have to hold it open to accommodate his girth so I gently reach over and cup his balls in my hand massaging them while I bare my teeth and allow them to lightly run over the flesh as it glides through my mouth. "Ah, fuck," Maddox pants as his dick jerks in my mouth and I feel his thick cum spurting into the back of my throat. I swallow as fast as I can trying to keep up. After a few moments, he slips from my mouth and his heavy breathing regulates. I sit back on my heels and watch this powerful man try to collect himself.

"Think that kiss will hold you over until tomorrow?" I ask playfully as I use my thumb to wipe the corners of my mouth.

Maddox doesn't say a word as he bends down reaching under my arms and picks me up from the floor. He lays me across the desk on my back and starts to bunch up my thin maxi dress.

"My turn."

Once he has my dress situated above my hips Maddox rips my panties off. He wastes no time diving into my wet mound. His tongue targets my clit as his finger works my opening, and I'm already on edge after hearing all the noises I was able to cause my man to make.

"Don't stop," I pant as little shards of light take over my vision. I'm hit with a surge of vibrations and my body falls further over the edge.

Before I can come down I feel my body flipped over and Maddox notches the head of his dick at my entrance. "Hold on tight, honey," he says right before he drives into me. My vagina was already spasming and when he enters me, my walls make for an even tighter fit. "My, God, you're so tight." He starts to move in quick steady strokes as he pistons into me. He places one hand on the back of my neck and the other is gripping my hip, holding me in place as he takes what he wants from me. As I'm coming down from my first orgasm the next one starts to build and I know this one is going to shatter me. "This pussy fits me like a glove," he grits leaning over my back next to my ear. His breathing is as labored as mine and I push back into him, meeting him at every thrust. My walls grow even tighter letting me know that he's close. The hand at my neck moves. "Suck," he commands. My mouth opens immediately and two fingers enter my mouth. I suck and twirl my tongue around them just as I did his dick earlier. After a few moments, he pops them out and moves them under me to torture my clit. My body is overwhelmed by sensation as he lays more of his weight on top of me trying to get as deep as he can. His scent floods my nose as his tongue licks up my neck. He nips at my ear and my body explodes. I'm riding the high and off in the distance I hear him shout my name.

I'm not sure how long my body lies limp on the desk until I feel him move off. I stay still for a little bit trying to get my bearings about me. My eyes are closed and my breath comes out in spurts.

"Fuck, I can't get enough of you," I hear him comment then feel something soft against my most sensitive parts. It makes me smile and I slowly start to open my eyes.

"Hey!" I yell when a stinging sensation bounces off my exposed butt cheek.

"You make me lose all my control, cherry bomb." Maddox leans down and gently helps me to a standing position.

"You say that like it's a bad thing." I feel drunk on sex as I focus on him and he helps right my maxi dress. My arms go around his neck and he holds me flush against his chest.

"Being with you could never be a bad thing." He pecks my lips. My phone beeps with a text and he sighs. "I don't like us leaving like this."

"Like what?" I ask when his face turns serious.

"Like we only meet up to have sex. That's not what I want for our relationship. I don't want you to think that's all I come around for."

Be still my heart.

A small smile lifts my lips and my stomach starts to flutter. "I don't feel that way at all. I do love the spontaneous sex that just happened but you've already shown me that we are trying for something more."

He nods and his lips match mine. "Good." He kisses me and holds me even tighter. "Let's get you out of here so you aren't out all night." There's a hint of sarcasm in his voice so I decide to put him out of his misery.

"We're just hanging out at my house." I turn from his arms to gather up my purse and phone.

"You're not going to a bar or club?" He eyes me suspiciously.

"Belinda is married and has two teenagers. We aren't going clubbing," I giggle. "We got some paperwork to look over. Remember me telling you about that expense report I did for my principal?" He nods. "We think that there's something fishy with it. So we're just going over some documents to see if it's true."

His left eye twitches as his body seems to relax slightly. "Let me know if you need any help looking things over. My business donates a lot of money to the schools around here. I'd hate for donors to be putting money towards one thing only for it to be pocketed for something else."

"I'll let you know. It's just me trying to understand why Principal Jackie's receipts aren't making sense. It's probably nothing."

We turn off the lights in the shop as we make our way to the main area, and I do a quick double-check of Holly's closing to make sure everything has been done correctly. When it looks as though everything is in order, I give Maddox a nod. "Ready?"

"Yeah." He nods and follows me to the back door that leads out to the alley. Once I lock the door behind me Maddox checks the handle. "You should park out in front and leave through there." His comment has me looking up at him, and he's looking up and down the parking area where the employees of all the shops enter and exit the businesses. "It doesn't seem safe for you to be back here by yourself this late."

I have to agree with him but know that there's nothing I can do to fix the time or streets in this city. "The parking out front isn't the best and we need those spots for customers. Plus the dumpster is back here."

He shrugs and continues to watch our surroundings. When we reach my car he opens my door after I unlock it. "Want to have lunch tomorrow?" he asks after I toss my purse in the passenger seat.

"I'll be home," I say then remember. "Oh, I forgot to tell you. I won a washer and dryer!" I can't contain the excitement in my voice.

"Really?"

"Well, Rob actually won. He signed up for some contest and we were selected. It's so wild to even believe it. I've never won anything, ever."

"That's incredible." His voice is soft and his face is so relaxed making him look younger than a man in his thirties.

"They're coming tomorrow around lunch."

"I'll bring lunch over while you wait for them to show," he offers.

"If you're not too busy," I say. Being a teacher the summers are ours but I know his working hours are during the day.

"Never too busy for you." He leans down and kisses my forehead. "Better get going so you're not keeping your friend waiting."

I lean up on my tiptoes and plant a kiss on his lips. I'm getting addicted to touching him and I don't know if that's a good thing or not. I've never been in this type of territory before and don't want to jump too quickly into moving faster than we should.

"See you tomorrow, MadDog," I tease the nickname I think works perfectly with him.

A growl leaves his throat and before I can duck into the car he pulls me in for one more kiss. I feel like we're teenagers sneaking around with the butterflies I get when he touches me instead of two grown adults with a ton of responsibilities.

"Get going before I make you stand up your friend."

I pull back and turn to bend down only to feel a zing against my butt from his hand. A squeal leaves my lips as I move quickly into the car. Maddox closes the door and waits there until I back up from the parking spot. I see his driver, Darren, parked on the curb with the lights on waiting for him just as my phone buzzes and I see Belinda calling. I swipe to answer and place it on speaker as I pull up to a red light.

"Hey, are you home?" she asks.

"On my way; should be there in about five."

"Okay, I'll head on over."

"Sounds good."

Let the girls' night begin!

CHAPTER TWELVE

Piper

WE ARE ELBOW-DEEP IN THE FIRST BOX OF DOCUMENTS when we realize we've stumbled on an enormous land mine.

"I think we might need to uncork the wine," Belinda suggests as she reads over the document in front of her.

"What does it say?" I ask as I continue to read my own paper.

"It confirms that the assistant superintendent and the superintendent, Barry Carver, do own and run the after-school care out of Jackie's school. This is absolutely crazy, Piper. He is a silent partner and that's why he's not listed on any of the state forms. We need to start separating the documents into piles and then we'll be able to deep dive into each one. I can tell you right now that the last five papers I've read already fall into a federal violation."

"Are you serious?" I ask feeling my stomach sink. This is not what I wanted to be involved in. "Do you think we should pursue this? I'm a little out of my league here."

"Piper, if this continues to go on the school district has the potential to lose federal funding. Our kids will suffer because the ones in charge are abusing the system for their own personal gain." Her love of students and their education is one of the many reasons

Belinda and I became so close. She has always championed for the kids even when she didn't have help. "Look, this email shows Rachelle and Barry using the school system to run background checks on employees of the after-school program, Discovery Ink."

She hands over the paper and I read the communication between the two of them. I think we're going to be in for a long night.

"Let's start to categorize the piles," I say. "What do you think we should label each stack?"

"Well, so far we have the after-school program, Discovery Ink, then I think we should combine all the nepotism findings together. Those are going to be difficult at first until we know for sure who is connected to who. Let's mark with a sticky note if anything looks off or names to come back at a later date in a stack over here." She points over to the side.

Megan's note from earlier had a list of names of all the nepo employees and who they were related to. It also listed some other topics to look into in the district.

Two hours in and Rob finally comes home after being out with friends. He politely greets Belinda and then heads off to his room to get some sleep. We decide to take a break, have a glass of wine, and chat.

"Jessica won't stop calling me after I told her to leave me and my family alone," Belinda says with a huff after topping off my glass.

"Really?" I'm shocked.

Jessica McClain and I are in the same pod together and team-teach. She teaches our students language arts and I teach math. She and I keep our distance because I think she's a mentally unstable woman who likes to create drama to fuel her life. She has a daughter who I believe terrorizes the entire family into doing what she wants. I'm friendly and help when needed if it involves school or classes but I steer clear and use the excuse that I've got a second job or my parents to not be sucked into her drama.

"Her daughter, Jenny, has her sights on Andy and won't leave him alone. I told Jessica to tell Jenny to stay away or I'd get the police involved. Andy has a sweet girl he's talking to and they are just the cutest."

A shiver runs down my spine. "I've heard rumors that she can be a piece of work so make sure to keep an eye out," I inform her. "I heard Jessica last year had to retain an attorney because Jenny was being accused of keying a boy's car because he wouldn't take her to homecoming."

"Oh my gosh!" Her eyes bulge. "Ugh, I hate that they are in the same grade and have two more years left. Hopefully, she'll move on over the summer."

We finish off another glass of wine and then get back to the boxes of documents. It isn't until Belinda's phone rings that we realize it's after two in the morning. My back has started to ache and is stiff from being in the same position for hours.

"Sorry to make you worry, honey," Belinda says into the phone. "We'll wrap this up and I'll be home soon." She hangs up and turns to me stretching out her arms. "Boy, time flies when you're having fun."

I giggle and look at our paper piles and empty boxes.

"I didn't mean for you to be out so late," I confess. "Are you going to be okay to drive home?"

We both stand and groan as the blood rushes to our unused limbs.

"I'll be just fine." She waves me off and looks down at our progress. "Being on the PTA, I know some ins and outs about the process of rules and standards on some of the compliances that we have to follow and this seems to violate some major issues. Not to mention ethically it's wrong."

"I was so afraid of that," I admit.

"I've written down some more PRR that I think we need—"

"I did too." I bend down and grab my notepad. "There are more questions that keep coming up the more I read over some of these emails and documents."

"Let's make a few more PRR requests and while we wait for

those, let's finish up the last box we have and figure out our next move. I'm free all next week after eight."

"I can do that."

"Do you get to sleep in?" she asks as she gathers her belongings.

"Not really. I have some people coming to deliver a washer and dryer," I say and move the stacks over to sit on a bookshelf in the corner out of the way. "Do you know anyone who needs the set I have? It stopped working a few weeks ago and I didn't know what was wrong with it."

"Why didn't you call me? Joseph could've come and fixed it when he got off work," Belinda chastises. "You didn't need to buy a new set. I know you've been trying to save money."

My cheeks heat. "I didn't want to burden him. You guys work so hard and have the boys to take care of. The new set was free. Rob won them in some contest so it was sort of a blessing," I tell her. "If Joseph can fix them he can have the other set to sell or keep."

"I'm sure he can fix it." Her eyes soften. "You have to start leaning on your friends, Piper. Let us help you when you need it."

"I will," I assure her as the tiredness of the day catches up to me and I let out a big yawn.

"Okay, I'll call you sometime tomorrow and we'll come up with a plan." She helps stack the last of the papers. "I think we need to contact one of your people at the teacher's union to help us with this. They might know the correct steps to take if this reveals any more surprises."

"I was just thinking about that," I say as we walk out to her car. "Drive safe and text me when you get home."

"I will, bye."

"Bye."

I watch her back out of the driveway and head down the street before I walk back into the house and lock up. I place the cork back on the wine bottle and put the glasses in the sink. Once I know the house is straightened, I head for the bedroom and fall right into bed. As soon as my head hits the pillow sleep takes me under.

"We have a delivery for a Piper Caldwell," the man states at my front door when I open it.

I've been up for several hours and just got back from the administration building filling out more PRR. Megan was there and she had a sly smile when I approached the desk. To my shock, she'd already filled out a form in my name.

"You'll need to add this to your request," she whispered as I handed over the other ones.

"Thank you?" I say more like a question because I'm not sure what she's requesting will help with what Belinda and I are looking for but I'll take the help where I can.

"Yes, that's me," I say to the man who has a box truck blocking the driveway. As I'm about to let the man in and show him where they are going to be put Maddox pulls up. "Hey," I greet as he makes his way over. This casual look is becoming my favorite way to see him, well, besides naked. He's wearing a black pair of athletic shorts and a tee with sneakers. The delivery guy takes a step back and I notice his posture straightens.

"Hey baby," he greets with a lip lock ignoring the guy next to us. When we break apart, he steps back and gives me a once-over. I'm wearing tight black yoga pants and a black tank along with my white sneakers and a ball cap. He snaps his head over to the delivery man and then back to me.

"They just got here." Why I feel like I have to explain, I don't know.

"Why don't you take lunch in and I'll show the guys where to take everything," he offers then hands over the plastic bag that smells heavenly.

"Do you even know where my laundry room is?"

"I'm sure I can figure it out." He pats my butt and tries to send me on my way but I remember something and turn toward the delivery guy.

"Are you able to take my other washer and dryer away?"

"Yes, ma'am, we can if you need us to." His eyes try to stay on me but flick over to Maddox briefly. I wonder if they think he's the man of the house and makes all the decisions.

"Well, do you think it's possible to take them over to a house not far from here?" I ask.

"Uh—"

"It's just that I was blessed and I'm hoping to pay it forward." He has a nervous expression on his face and his eyebrows start to rise. I feel like I'm about to be turned down so I up my ante. "I can pay a little bit or give a good tip," I try to lay it on thick. I'm hoping to save Joseph and Belinda from having to come over and load and unload the heavy equipment. These guys look like they are bodybuilders for a living and are a lot younger than he is.

"I'm sure they will be more than happy to deliver it to wherever you need," Maddox speaks up wrapping an arm around my shoulders, pulling me in close to his body. "Why don't you go and write down the address on some paper so they'll know where to take it."

"Oh, thank you," I say and he kisses my forehead.

I take the food to the kitchen and my stomach rumbles as I take all the boxes of Chinese out and place them on the table. I can hear Maddox's voice instructing the guys but can't make out what he's telling them. I find my grocery list pad and scribble Belinda's address on it. Ripping the page off I head to the laundry room. Maddox is standing in the doorway watching them closely.

"Here's the address," I say as I tap his back.

He turns and takes the paper from my fingers then hands it over to a guy who's sweating bullets as he unhooks the tubes from behind my old appliances. The guy takes the note and places it in his front pocket, nods, and turns back to the tools he's holding. There are three huge men in my small laundry room trying to move around and it's almost comical.

"Let's go and eat while they switch them out," Maddox says as he ushers me into the kitchen with his hand on my lower back and we take a seat at the small table. We are divvying out the boxes when he asks, "Who are you giving the appliances to?"

"My friend, Belinda."

"Is she the one you hung out with last night?"

"Mmhmm," I hum as I chew my food.

"All finished, Ms. Caldwell." One of the men installing the washer and dryer comes in the doorway of the kitchen. He's got papers in his hands. "These are the manuals for both and here is a card if anything should stop working. I believe they have a five-year warranty."

"Really? That's great…and fast!" I spring up from my chair. "Would you and your team like a drink before you go? That was really fast," I comment again.

"No, ma'am, we'll be on our way unless you have any questions?"

"I think I'm good. Thank you so much for delivering those to my friend," I say genuinely.

"Our pleasure, ma'am," he responds with a nod.

"I'll walk them out." Maddox stands and ushers the three men out of the house. A few minutes later the screen door opens and he returns. "You ready for this weekend with Gemma and Luca?"

"I think," I say nodding. "She told me only to bring my driver's license and asked me for all my clothing and shoe sizes. Do you know what she's planning?"

"I have no clue but knowing her she's probably got everything organized down to the minute."

"That's the teacher in her. Organization is key when you teach; some of us are a little more OCD than others." I giggle and wave my hand around the kitchen. Everything has a place and is labeled.

"Does this mean I'm not allowed to leave wet towels or clothes on the floor when we live together?" He opens the pantry door and sees for himself how everything is lined up and grouped together, even as sparse as it is.

My heart starts to race at his comment. We are a long way from living together but it makes my stomach do a little dance knowing he's thinking of the future.

"Rob used to have that same problem and it only took about a week before he saw the error of his way."

"What made him start using the hamper?"

"I made him do his own laundry but snuck a red crayon in with his whites. He was mortified that he had to go to school wearing pink clothes and begged to never do it again." I bite my lower lip to stop the smile threatening to come out as Maddox rears his head back shocked. It was an extreme way to teach him and it cost me to replace a few undershirts and underwear but it got the message across.

"That's mighty evil of you, cherry bomb," he laughs.

I shrug one shoulder. "You'll never see his clothes on the floor though."

"You working tonight?" he asks changing the subject after his phone beeps and he checks it.

"Yeah, since I'm going to be off this weekend I thought I'd work today and cover most of tomorrow before we meet up with Gemma."

"I've got a few things to wrap up as well and may not have it finished by the time you get off tonight." He looks a little frustrated about it.

I walk over and slide my hand up his chest resting it on his pecs. "I love that you come by and see me every night but don't feel like you have to. I know there are a million other things you could be doing other than sitting in a sandwich shop watching me."

He tilts his head to the side and smirks. "I don't know, after last night I think I like the benefits of hanging around with you."

My hand goes to smack his chest but he catches it and brings it up to kiss my knuckles. I melt when his soft lips press gently against my fingers.

"I'm starting to think that's all you want me around for."

"This is just a fraction of what I want with you." His eyes heat as he leans down toward me. Just as our lips make contact the front door opens and quickly all I see is Maddox's back and an arm in a protective hold.

"Piper!" I hear Rob's voice call out from the other room.

"It's just Rob," I say when I try to move but his arm is firm. I almost laugh at Maddox for thinking someone would just barge into a person's house.

"I've got some news!"

Maddox releases me and I see his features relax as we walk over to the living room to greet Rob. He's hanging up his hoodie and tossing his keys in the bowl by the front door table.

"Hey, buddy, what's up?" I ask.

His face could light up the city at night and I can't contain the enjoy it brings me to know he's so happy.

"Well," he stops when he sees I'm not alone. "Oh, hey, Bishop, I didn't realize you'd be here," he greets Maddox.

"Brought Piper some lunch." They give each other a man-hug in greeting.

"There is plenty left over so go and grab some," I offer.

"Cool, thanks."

"What's the news that has you so excited?" I ask.

He cuts his eyes over at Maddox before looking back at me and rubs the back of his neck, a telltale sign that he's nervous. "I've been lying to you and I want to come clean," he starts and Maddox's body goes rigid.

"Oh—kay?" I tense waiting for the bomb to drop.

He rubs his hands together. "I haven't been hanging out every morning with my friends."

I nod impatiently hoping to move this along so we can find out a solution to whatever this revelation is. I'm not as tense as Maddox, but all my muscles are locked into place and I'm still as a statue.

"Where have you been going every morning this summer before work?" I cautiously ask.

"I've been taking extra classes and as long as I keep doing well I'm set to graduate in a few weeks before the school year begins."

It takes me a minute to process his words. Rob was already scheduled to graduate in December ahead of schedule because he'd gotten with his school counselor and took some advanced classes last year.

"Wait, what!" I say as it all sinks in. "Like finished, completely?"

"Yeah, can you believe it!"

My mouth hangs open. "This is so wonderful, Rob. I'm so proud of you," I gush and walk over to wrap my arms around this boy.

He squeezes me back so tight. "I never could've done this if it hadn't been for you," he says then buries his head in my shoulder. "Thank you."

"You did all the work, buddy, I just helped guide you along." My eyes start to water. "Why didn't you tell me you were taking classes this summer?"

His eyes soften. "You had a lot going on and I didn't want to add to the stress."

I shake my head. "Don't ever feel like you can't tell me anything. We're a team and for us to succeed we have to be honest, remember?"

He looks over my shoulder then lifts an eyebrow and says, "Yeah."

I remember Maddox is here and step back from Rob.

"Congrats, man." Maddox reaches his hand out for Rob which he takes. "We'll have a party to celebrate."

"Don't congratulate me yet. I still have a few weeks left."

"You'll do fine," I reassure him.

"Y'all heading out?" Rob asks.

I shake my head. "I'm about to head to work."

"Cool, can I catch a ride?"

"Of course," I say. At some point, we're going to need to get a second car.

Rob heads to the kitchen and I can hear him digging into the food.

"I gotta get going but I'll text you later." Maddox leans down and kisses my neck. It sends a shudder through my body.

"Kay," I mumble with a smile.

I watch him as he walks to his car and can't help but feel like my life is finally looking up.

CHAPTER THIRTEEN

"WHERE DO YOU HAVE HIM LOCATED?" I ask over the speaker in my car.

"He's at the strip club over off St. Louis Ave. The one Mr. Dawson has now taken over from Slater's assets," Thomas says.

"Send his location and I'll be there shortly."

"How'd it go with the delivery?" he asks before I can hang up.

I let out a sigh and rub my forehead. "It went good."

"Why don't I believe that? What happened?"

I bite the inside of my lip not wanting to talk about it but Thomas is like a dog on a bone and he's been a good sounding board helping me navigate through all this relationship shit.

"I—" I groan not wanting to admit what I did. "I almost beat the shit out of Billy on her front porch."

"What the hell? Why? He's the most loyal guard on the team." The surprise in Thomas' voice makes my reaction even worse. When it comes to Piper I lose my level head and react at the drop of a dime.

"He was talking with Piper when I drove up." I pause to gather my words.

"Annnnd?"

"And I didn't like it," I grit then blow out a disgusted sigh. "Are you happy? I didn't like that another man was talking to her."

The car goes completely silent and for a second I think we got disconnected but then his laughter bounces off every speaker in the car.

I. Hate. It.

"When"—Laugh—"Did"—Laugh—"You"—Laugh—"Become so jealous?" He starts to wheeze and at times like this, I wish I'd never met him. It's so much better to employ 'yes men' than let someone into your inner circle.

"I'm glad you can take great pleasure in my misery," I say as I approach a red light. "The team is going to think I'm a lunatic. Fuck!"

"What'd you do to him?"

"I sent her in with the food then berated him for talking to her," I say, frustrated that I've let my emotions out in front of others. The only time my team sees a different side of me is when I'm out hunting scum.

Another laugh comes through the speakers and my hands tighten on the steering wheel.

"Dude, I wish I'd been there this morning," he exclaims agitating me further. "This is classic. We need to get her some security cameras so I can watch with a bowl of popcorn you handing over your balls."

"Call me dude again and I'm going to knock your front teeth out when I see you in a few minutes." My jaw ticks as I try not to ram the vehicle in front of me.

Thomas must not care for his safety because yet another belly laugh rings out through the car. I immediately press the button on my steering wheel ending the call and making it silent again. He is such an asshole.

About ten minutes later I'm pulling up to the strip joint that my next victim is at. Darren is parked and standing by the trunk of his car waiting for me. Thomas is speaking to several of our team members off on the other side of the space. He sees my headlights and then waves off the team to disperse before coming over to where I'm at.

"Everything go okay this morning, sir," Darren asks holding my door for me as I exit my vehicle.

I hesitate for a moment thinking Thomas told Darren what happened but from his tone I can see he's asking genuinely. He should be the one I speak to about Piper instead of asshole Thomas. Darren is in his mid-fifties, probably has a lot more experience, and can give better advise.

"It went just fine," I respond as Thomas approaches. He tries to school his features but I know he's ready to burst out laughing. Thank God he's professional and knows when business needs to be conducted.

"The team is in place and Davis is on standby to wipe out the camera system," Thomas informs me as I round the car.

When I left Piper's house this afternoon, I went back home and worked on a few things my banks needed to have signed for federal purposes. I've been waiting for this call ever since I learned this piece of shit was part of the equation for a job I'd already cleaned up. Now I'm tying up the last strings that Slater ever had his hands in.

The three of us file inside the strip club and a heavy fog meets us as we walk a few steps into the building. There are four stages and three bar areas that take up the entirety of the room. The place is half full of people on a Thursday evening. Drinks and half-naked women are everywhere. The room is dark except for the stage lights as the women dance to the music over the speakers. We find a booth in the far corner away from the stage passing several of our team sitting around the room blending in but focused on our target. It's darker over here and out of sight. All these men are solely focused on the half-naked women on the stage or walking around serving drinks.

"What can I get you gentlemen tonight?" a waitress asks as soon as our asses hit the seats.

"We'll take a pitcher of beer and water for the table," Darren tells the lady.

"Coming right up, sugar. I'm Daisy if you need anything else." She wiggles her shoulders making her tits shake but I keep my eyes on the target. The entire team is dressed in black from the ballcap on our heads to our socks and shoes.

A short while later the pitchers are put down on the sticky table but no one touches them. We aren't here for that. The music changes and new talent rotates the stages as the men hoot and holler over the song. Our target sits in the front row knocking back drinks like he's dehydrated. He's got a wad of bills in his hand as he tosses them on stage when the dancer crawls on her hands and knees working the crowd. I take note that our men are very professional as they pretend to engage with the workers as they pass by but keep it in check.

An hour later our guy has run out of money and is drunk off his ass. The manager has already been over to his table and warned him to keep his hands to himself with the waitstaff.

"God, please let him be ready to leave," Thomas grumbles next to me. He hates strip clubs. I do too because most are like walking into a petri dish of germs and diseases.

"I think security is going to throw him out the next time he touches the waitress." Darren nods over to the big bald guy standing ten feet away from our target.

Five minutes later Thomas drops a stack of bills on the table for our waitress as we walk towards the entrance of the club. Our target being escorted out is our sign to head out and get the night started. I'm already pissed I'm not sitting at my usual table at the sandwich shop waiting for Piper to close the business and this guy is going to feel my displeasure. When we get outside, we pass the bouncer coming back in but we keep our heads down to avoid any unwanted attention. Bobby owns this place now and the employees should know to keep their mouths shut but we don't want to take any chances.

Our target is stumbling toward his car as we pick up our pace. From the corner of my eye, I see my team surrounding the area. Our van is in place as I approach.

"Hey, Trent!" I call out getting his attention as I advance on him.

He turns sluggishly and squints to try to see where my voice is calling from in the dark night. I sling an arm around his neck before he can register what's happening.

"D-do I know you, man?" he slurs.

"Oh, come on, buddy, you don't remember me?"

He tries to pull away, rocking to the side as we walk between cars. I can't believe Bobby would let his staff kick someone out to drive home drunk. I'll have to speak with him about that. The last thing I'd ever want is for an innocent life to be taken because some idiot thinks it's safe to drive drunk.

"Not really." He laughs like it's the funniest thing and follows along forcefully laughing as the van pulls up beside us. The door opens and he's in the van before he's realized what's happened.

I knock on the door and the vehicle drives out of the parking lot.

"Did you get them?" Thomas asks.

I dangle a set of keys in front of his face. "Child's play."

He swipes them as Billy comes over. He is part of our clean-up crew that only gets to come out to play when our prey has been dealt with. He's not usually seen out with us, which is why I thought he'd be perfect to be one of the delivery guys who set up Piper's washer and dryer.

"Take it to the usual place then meet us at the warehouse," I say then head over to my car. It's time to tie up all the loose ends that Victor Slater had in this world.

My blade zings through the air and across the room nicking the cheek of the man strung up on the pipe. I grab another knife from the metal table and examine where the next cut will be.

"Tell me, Randall, do you think you should've been let off and out in the public again for the third time? You killed a family of three this time and what do you do while waiting trial? We find you in a bar drunk off your ass ready to drive home."

I fling the knife with a quick flick of my wrist before he has the chance to answer and it lashes across the side of his neck. It isn't deep enough to cause any damage but he'll think he's about to bleed out. I've been skilled in knife play for over a decade. Besides hand-to-hand combat, I'm an expert when it involves hitting marks with sharp objects.

"I'm so-rry," he blubbers, but I don't care.

Randall Sullivan is a fifty-six-year-old man who has repeatedly been caught driving drunk but because he has a relative in the government he's always been given a slap on the wrist. This time he killed a family who was coming home from a vacation. He'd made bail after pleading not guilty. Our justice system is fucked up. How you can plead not guilty when you are the only person caught at the scene committing the crime? There are even videos of him crossing over the line and colliding with the family's vehicle.

"Does that bring the family back to life?"

He's a crying mess and my agitation starts to rev up. He doesn't care because if he did he wouldn't have been bragging about getting off again when he was at the bar last night.

"Pl-please," he begs.

"Don't worry, Randall, I'll make sure this will be a night you never forget," I say before tossing another knife clipping his ear. His wails are pitiful and Thomas has to turn around to keep from chuckling. "Hang tight, I've got a friend I need to speak with."

John picks up Trent and sets him down in the chair next to Randall. We let him watch as I skillfully worked on my first guest. I'd say Trent is completely sober by now and is scared shitless if the wet stain on the front of his pants and the horrid smell of urine say anything.

"Welcome to my humble abode, Trent," I greet as John secures his hands and feet to the chair then takes the gag out of his mouth.

He's breathing so hard that his chest rises and falls like he's just finished a marathon. "I-I think you have the wrong person," he stutters.

"Trent Smith, son of Catherine and Timothy Smith," I say. "You're in finance and work for a wealth management group." His eyes widen as I list off his details. "You also used to hang out with a beautiful redhead who works at a sandwich shop." I wag my eyebrows suggestively.

He nods. "Yeah, yeah Piper," he offers like he's helping solve a crime but it makes this even worse. "I can get you all her info, man."

"Are you close with, Piper?" I ask walking slowly up to him.

"Oh, yeah, for sure," he tries to play.

This arrogant asshole would serve up his own grandmother to a pack of wolves to save his ass. Not wanting to hear him spew anymore lies about my woman, I walk right behind him and yank a fist full of hair extending his neck backward.

"You are so full of fucking shit," I say gritting my teeth hard. "I was there the day at the shop when you ended things." His eyes flash in terror. "Rob spilt that drink all over you." I let that set in. "You're not good enough to lick the scum off the bottom of her shoes."

"I—"

"How pathetic are you? No real man would give information away about a woman. Especially one like Piper." I look over to Thomas who's been standing off to the side waiting for a chance to get in on the action tonight. "Would you rat to save face?" I turn Trent's head over in Thomas's direction.

He starts shaking his head. "It'd never pass through my lips."

"Me either," I say looking back down at Trent. I narrow my eyes and wonder what Piper was thinking when she said yes to dating this asshat.

"I'm sorry, I'm sorry," he pleads. "My family has money they will pay you if you release me." He begins to panic.

"Where'd you meet beautiful Piper at?" I question.

Trent's breathing is coming out in huffs working himself into a heart attack.

He looks startled at my question and I think maybe he's still a little drunk. "She—I, ugh, saw her working at the sandwich place."

"A random meeting?"

He nods as I come around to the front of him.

"You sure?" I eye him giving him the chance to come clean.

"Yeah, yeah," he pants trying to control his breathing.

"Huh, 'cause I heard from Sully that he had you go in there and get the layout of Mr. Sampson's store and the employee schedules," I reveal. "Said you used Piper as a way to get the info for him."

His face pales and beads of perspiration form on his forehead. Sully was a plethora of information before he died. He'd told us every detail about being involved with helping Victor Slater and who gave a helping hand. When Sully mentioned Trent my blood boiled.

"You lured an innocent woman into a dangerous situation, Trent." I circle him again and when I reach his side I throw my first punch at his kidney. He screams like a girl and goes lax in his restraints.

"I-I, he made me do it," he cries.

"He made you do it," I say slowly as I come back around to face him.

"I owed him some money and he said if I did this for him we'd call it even," he confesses.

"What'd you owe him? What is your life worth, Trent?"

His eyes widen and his body starts to shake in fear as he grasps the severity of the situation.

"Please, my family has money and they'll pay—"

"But they wouldn't pay Sully?" I question.

"I-I bought a bunch of cocaine from Sully and didn't want my parents to ask me what the money was for."

I shrug, bored with this entitled douche. "For a man with a college education and dealing with low-level thugs, you should've known that once you start doing favors and owing scum that it's never-ending. Your biggest mistake was involving my woman in it. She didn't deserve to be deceived or hurt by the likes of you."

I reach over to the table that houses the last of my blades and grab a glass bottle of scotch. I hate wasting it on this asshole but it must be done. I walk back over to Trent and start pouring it down the front of his clothes then walk over to Randall and repeat the same treatment. Both are yelling for help and struggling against their restraints.

"Enjoy the last few minutes of your lives," I say and pour some down their throats.

Thomas walks over with two syringes and injects them into both Randall and Trent's necks making them immediately slump over.

"Let's get them set up in the car," I say as I hand over the glass bottle.

My guys remove them from their bindings and carry their limp bodies over to the van.

I turn toward Billy. "Is the car ready?" I ask since he's just gotten here.

"Yes, sir."

We leave the warehouse and head out toward the opposite side of Las Vegas. We're four vehicles deep when we pull off on a side road out of view from the main road. As we exit our vehicles I see Randall's car parked up ahead.

"Do we have it rigged up?"

"Yes, sir, everything is ready to go," Billy states as other members of our team pull out and maneuver the two men toward the car.

Once we have Randall behind the wheel we make sure Trent is propped up in the passenger seat. Carefully, Thomas takes a few bottles of liquor in his gloved hands and empties them all over the front seat across the floorboard and on the two men before closing the door to the car.

Usually, when I go after the people who have harmed others I handle it myself or have Thomas come along, but for big jobs that require a little more finesse I have to bring in a large crew to make sure every detail is taken care of and no traces can come back on me or those close to me. Over the years I've acquired a team of men I can trust and who have the same goals to rid the world of those who hurt others for fun or game.

"We sure this is going to work the first time?" I ask. "It's not going to be as believable if we have to recreate it."

"We've tested the equipment out," Thomas says a little too giddy.

I nod as we walk over to the back of the van where there is a remote that looks like a gaming system control but on a larger scale. Thomas hands it over to me and shows me the basics. After I've got a handle on it, Billy is given the signal to start Randall's car and walks back over to where we are. It takes a few tries but then I figure out the method and have the car off and going.

It's late at night so not many cars are out on the road at this hour. Slowly I'm able to adjust the car after a few turns and then I decide we are ready to get this over with. I push the button to accelerate then use my fingers on the joystick to steer the car. Once I have the car lined up and headed toward the line of trees I press harder on the accelerator button and the car goes flying head-on into the trees. The crash is loud and over before it even began. Quickly we jump in the van and drive over to the wrecked car. Once we get out, Thomas and I walk over with our gloves on to inspect the guys. Both are unresponsive as we look around at the scene.

"Get that remote out of the car and all the wires that go with it. I don't want Detective Bryce to have any reason to suspect foul play when the call is made," I say. "Make it look clean then sweep our tracks."

A string of, "Yes, sir," rings out from our guys as Thomas and I walk to the back of the van. Thomas hands me our burner phone and it only rings twice before a rough voice comes over the line.

"Hello?"

"Got a wreck out on Highway 15 past 146. Gonna need you to handle it," I say. I can hear voices in the background. "Looks deadly."

"Shit. I just walked through the front door." He sighs heavily. "I'm on it."

He hangs up and I hand the phone back to Thomas who takes out the sim card and puts them into a baggie to be destroyed.

"You heading home?" he asks as we make our way to our cars.

"I've got a few things to wrap up before tomorrow at the office. Thought I'd stop by and finish it so I didn't get interrupted this weekend."

"Are you going to assign one of the guys to Red's detail or are you going to keep doing it yourself at night?"

I cut my eyes over to him. I didn't think he'd know that I'd been hanging around her neighborhood lately, but after this weekend I'm sure the word and pictures are going to get out about us. The last thing I need is for some idiot to think he can search her out or try to use her against me as a bargaining chip.

"I'll look over the team at the office," I say and he nods.

"Billy might be a good cho—" Before he can finish the sentence, I jab him in the mouth with my fist but he blocks most of the impact. Thomas bends at the waist laughing at my reaction.

"One of these times I'm going to forget we're friends," I say and walk off.

"You make it too easy, Ox," Thomas calls out still laughing as I get in the car.

I check my messages to make sure I didn't miss any calls for texts from Piper. It's three in the morning but I schedule a delayed text for when she wakes up.

    Me: You are sweeter than 3.1415

When I finish I turn the car back toward the city to the office. I've got around twelve hours before I get the entire weekend with her and I don't want any loose ties to interrupt our plans even though Luca and Gemma will be there for most of it.

I finally pull up to the building and see our night security walking the perimeter. I shoot off several more texts and before I can even walk through the door my phone is ringing.

"Hey, Mom," I answer on the second ring.

"Why are you up so late, Maddox?" my mom, who lives in New York and is always up bright and early, asks.

"Just had some work that held me up. Nothing to worry about." I never go into detail with her even though she knows what goes on here.

"I always worry about you."

"How are the twins?" I say changing the subject.

She lets out a sigh. "Normal college girls. They are with their roommates in the Hamptons for the next week." I vaguely remember getting a briefing about them leaving earlier this week. "Are you coming out to visit soon?" I can hear the hope in her voice.

"I'll try to get out there before the summer is up and the twins start back in school."

"You know if you slowed down a little you might be able to find a good woman." Here she goes. "I've met a few young ladies who I think you might like—"

"I've met someone, Mom," I say cutting her off before she can finish her sentence.

"Really? Or are you just saying that to stop me from nagging you?"

I have to chuckle because I have lied and told her this before to get her off my back.

"Her name is Piper and she's a math teacher," I tell her.

"I bet the two of you love discussing numbers." She lets out a little chuckle. "Piper is a pretty name. Tell me about her."

Over the next few minutes, I tell my mom all about Piper as I stare out my office window at the city lights.

"Have you told her about what you do and who you are?"

"Not yet, but soon." I exhale a breath and rub my face. "I want her to get to know me first before I have to tell her the truth."

"It might not be as bad as you think, Maddox."

My mom doesn't know that I seek revenge on those who prey on the weak or vulnerable. She only knows that I've taken my rightful seat at the table where my dead father once sat.

"We'll see," I say.

"Bring her with you when you come for a visit. I'd love to meet her," she says after a pause in the conversation.

"I'll try," I say not committing to any plans because if I do and end up not following through Mom will never let me live it down.

"Has Bobby or Arturo met her?"

"They have. I took her to Wyatt's wedding and she got to meet most of The Family. This weekend we are going out with Luca and his wife, Gemma."

"Mary sent me some pictures. Kendall and Wyatt look so happy and in love. I know I bug you about settling down and getting married but I just want you to be happy and to have someone by your side to share this life with, Maddox. I don't want you to have any regrets when you get older and wish you'd chosen a different path or made different decisions."

"I know, Mom."

"Well, I'll leave it alone for now but I'm always a call away if you need me, honey."

I hesitate for a second before I ask, "Do you regret leaving Vegas?"

The other end of the phone goes silent for a bit.

"I don't think I regret it but I do miss you and my best friends. Mary and Adele come and see me but it's not like being able to jump in the car and drive down the street like it used to be. Especially since Adele has a beautiful grandbaby to love on," she gushes. "I feel like I've missed so much of your adult life with us being so far away but the memories there are hard for me."

"So, are you saying a grandbaby will make you come back?" I tease.

"Maddox Anthony Bishop! Are y'all pregnant and you are just now telling me? Why didn't you start the call with it? I'm going to tan your hide," she's practically screaming into the phone. Off in the background, I hear her telling someone she's fine and that they aren't needed. I'm sure I'll get a message about this from her security team in the next five minutes.

"Piper isn't pregnant," I say leaving off the *yet* part to try and calm her down. "Once I lock her down I don't think it'll take long. I'm not getting any younger."

"Between you and your sisters I'm going to be put on medication," she huffs under her breath and I can just picture her rubbing her forehead like she used to when I was in high school and we were pushing our limits. "Just enjoy each other and take it slow. There's no rush."

"Says the person who had a fifteen-year-old by the time she was my age."

"That was different times. You have the chance to carve out a different path and set the future for a healthy and stable relationship. You've seen what not to do in a relationship and marriage and so you know to do things differently."

My biggest fear in life is turning out to be like the man who shares half of my DNA. The thought of him leaves a bad taste in my mouth and I can't stomach any mention of him.

"I've got a few things left to finish up before falling into bed," I say trying to wrap up the call, my mood turning foul as thoughts start to swirl of that asshole.

"You do know that these late nights aren't going to work when you get married and start your family, right? No woman is going to put up with her man being out at crazy hours while she's at home wondering what you're doing."

I pinch the bridge of my nose, partly because I'm tired but also because she's right and I'm not sure how I'm going to justify being out late helping to rid this world of evil people.

"I'm trying to work out all those details before we move our relationship any further."

"Okay, honey, call me in a few days. Send me some pictures

of you and Piper from this weekend so I don't have to stalk her through social media." She laughs and it starts to break up the tension that's put me on edge.

"I'll make sure the team snaps a few just for you," I say.

"Love you, Maddox."

"Love you too, Mom."

The call ends and my mind tries to flick back to the last few years before the asshole died. I squash it down not wanting to relive what happened and what I had to do to release my family from his clutches.

Looking down at my desk where the papers I need to go over and sign are waiting for me, I quickly sign them and organize each into their designated folders for Kristen, my secretary, to send out before the end of business today. I type her an email giving her instructions for each one and to contact Thomas with any questions; that I'm not to be disturbed for any reason. After I've cleaned off everything and locked it all away I check my watch. It's just after six in the morning. If I go home now I'll be able to get a few hours of sleep before I need to pick up Piper and start our weekend. I text Darren to let him know I'll be home shortly and what we'll need for this weekend before I lock my office and head out to my car.

On the drive home, I swing down Piper's street and see my guy set up in one of our cars watching her house. I give a nod as I slowly drive by making sure there aren't any disturbances. Once I hit the highway the activities of the day start to wear on me. Falling into bed and waking up refreshed is just what I need to cleanse this evening off.

CHAPTER FOURTEEN

"DO WE KNOW WHAT THE PLANS ARE THIS WEEKEND? Gemma's been very vague about the details," Piper asks beside me as we drive toward The Strip. "I'm so confused as to why she said not to bring anything with us."

"I'm not entirely sure of all the details. I spoke with Luca earlier today and he didn't have a clue what she was planning. The good thing is if we need to make a quick getaway we aren't far from home."

She giggles. "I hope she doesn't get upset I still brought a small bag of things."

"She won't be. Gemma is a really good person."

Gemma booked us both penthouses at the newest hotel and casino on The Strip, Allure. As we arrive, the valet greets us and helps Piper out of the car.

"This place is phenomenal! Look at all the gold," she says admiring the detail as we walk through the lobby to the check-in desk.

"Can I help you, sir?" the man in a crisp suit behind the desk asks.

"Reservation for Bishop," I answer and show my ID.

"Yes, yes," the man says then snaps his fingers bringing another employee over. "Mr. and Mrs. Bishop, thank you so much for joining us this weekend. Daniel will help you with any baggage and if there is anything we can assist you with please let us know." The way Mrs. Bishop rolls off his tongue thumps something in my chest and I feel a sense of calm wash over me.

I glance over to Piper and see she's about to correct him so I quickly respond. "We will," and lead Piper over to where Daniel is standing with our room keys.

"Should we tell them I'm not the Mrs.?" she whispers as we approach the young man.

I wrap my arm around her waist pulling her into me. "Not a chance," I say into her ear. She shivers and I can't help but love that I have such an effect on her.

"Do you have any more luggage I can grab, sir?" Daniel interrupts and I push our two bags over for him to take.

We follow him to a set of private elevators off to the side of the lobby where a man in a black suit is standing. Daniel introduces us to the security as we wait for the doors to open.

"There will be a guard here twenty-four hours a day for the entirety of your stay," Daniel informs us as he scans our keycard over the panel. "If you need assistance with anything use the phone in the kitchen to call for someone to help you."

"Thank you, Daniel," Piper says with a polite smile and I have to fight to not narrow my eyes at the young guy. He blushes at her and on instinct, I block his view of her and press my lips to hers.

The ding of the bell alerting us that we've arrived at the top floor is the only thing that stops me from pushing her up against the wall and showing this pimply kid who she belongs to. As we walk the few steps off the elevator, we head left to the double doors away from where Luca and Gemma are staying when their door swings open. Gemma comes out in only a robe with Luca not far behind looking disheveled.

"You made it!" she greets Piper with a hug then does the same with me as I kiss her cheek. "This is going to be the best weekend to have some adult fun and relaxation."

"I can see you've started partying early," I comment to Luca who has the first three buttons missing from his shirt.

He shrugs but doesn't stop the knowing smile. "What else are you supposed to be doing when you're kid-free?" Gemma knocks her elbow into his ribs and he makes out like she did some damage with her poke.

"I've got us a section reserved at the pool to hang out at until dinner," Gemma says ignoring Luca's theatrics.

"Oh, umm, I didn't bring a swimsuit," Piper says looking over to me. "In fact, I'm a little confused as to why you said to not bring anything with us this weekend."

"You'll see. Let me show you why." Gemma smiles, grabs her hand, and drags her across the hall to their door. Luca and I follow behind.

When we walk in, the entire living area looks like a department store setup. There's a section for shoes, dresses, suits, shorts, pants, and every accessory imaginable.

"I met this lovely woman at a school event I was helping out at and she wanted to thank me for all the help I was doing for her child. She's in school to become a fashion designer and loves to make clothes so I reached out and let her know this weekend would be perfect to send over some clothes. She really went over the top, don't you think?"

"So that is why you asked for our measurements and sizes."

"Yep."

"These are so beautiful," Piper lightly touches a few of the sparkly dresses. "My neighbor across the street from me made clothes for the big production show here on The Strip for decades. Irene is retired now but she's so talented and has a gift for creating beautiful pieces like these. If this lady ever needs help or advice I'm sure she'd love to give it her."

"I know, she really does a good job. I bet she'd love to chat her ear off," Gemma says as she picks up a few swimsuits from the coffee table. "Go and try these on and we'll head to the pool to get our drink on. Shoo boys, we'll come and get you when we are ready to head down." Gemma waves us out as she hands us our swim trunks and points to the door. Luca steals a kiss and then we head out to our penthouse. Daniel is still standing by the double door with our key in hand.

"You can set the bags in the bedroom, Daniel," I say to him as he opens the door. The space is large enough to be two large apartments combined into one. Everything is over the top and high-end. I walk over to the bar and pour Luca and myself some drinks before walking back over to the living room.

"Please don't hesitate to call down if you need anything," Daniel says after I've tipped him. I nod and he takes his leave.

"Everything going okay with business lately?" Luca asks as he sits down on the sofa and props his legs on the coffee table. I raise an eyebrow and look around the room. "I had our men sweep the room right before we got here. No bugs to worry about and there will be someone stationed outside our rooms and the elevator downstairs to make sure we're not bothered."

I nod. "No complaints since Slater took a leave of absence. You?"

"Dad and I are looking into a few new avenues Kendall suggested with a product but things have been quiet for a change."

"They still on their honeymoon?"

"Yeah, I think they get back next week sometime. Bobby and Liam have been holding down the fort." Luca drains the amber liquid from the glass and sets it on the table. "You ready to lock Piper down?"

"I want to," I admit.

"Buuut—" I finish off the rest of my drink and stare at the wall. "You can be happy, Ox. I'm proof of that. If she is the one, then make it happen. Don't waste your time with the what-ifs. Life is too short, especially with what we do."

Right before I open my mouth, the door to the room opens and both women walk in but my only focus is my red-headed beauty in a sheer cover-up and a barely there bikini underneath.

"Abso-fucking-lutely not, babygirl." Luca jumps up from the sofa and heads toward his wife and I follow suit to Piper.

"You're not even dressed yet," Piper says as I get within reach of her.

My mouth dries up when I take all of her in. Her bikini is sage green to match her eyes and she's wearing platform sandals.

"You look gorgeous," I grip her hip and pull her into me.

I can hear Luca demanding Gemma go and change but I tune it out.

"Thanks." Piper blushes as I take her hand and twirl her slowly around to get the entire effect. Half of her ass cheeks are on display and I groan. I stop her with her back against my chest and lean down to her ear. My eyes get an eye full of her tits and I back her up and hold her to me. My dick is so hard it's painful.

"I love your body so fucking much but you have to promise to stay close to me when you wear this today." I'll never be one to tell her what she can and can't wear but I'll be damned if she doesn't have me beside her the entire time to make sure everyone knows that she belongs to me.

She pushes back into me creating friction where I need it the most. "I'll do my best but can't promise."

"Give us about five minutes then we'll be ready to head down." Luca gains our attention. I turn my head and look over my shoulder and see he's got her over his shoulder and storming toward the door.

"Five? Man, I thought you'd last at least a little longer than that," I joke as he's about to walk through the door.

"You learn to adjust when you become parents. Just wait until you and Piper start spitting out kids and then come talk to me," Luca says as he leaves.

Piper and I both burst out laughing as we hear Luca and Gemma still arguing down the hall. Once the door closes, the air in the room changes.

"Five minutes isn't even going to take the edge off," I say and look down at her.

"Then you'll have to wait until later tonight I guess," she says as she looks around the penthouse at all the decor.

"I'll make it work," I say then pounce.

I grab her hips, picking her up and making her wrap her legs around my waist. I walk us over to the dining room table and set her on the edge, wedging my body between her thighs. Reaching for the hem of her cover-up I slide it up her body skimming my fingers against her soft skin. The ties to her top unravel when I tug the strings, making it float off her breasts.

"So beautiful," I say as I lean down with my mouth and take a nipple in, swirling my tongue around the hardened peak. My fingers play with the other as Piper pushes her tits further against me. I switch sides giving the other the same treatment as I thrust my clothes-covered dick into the apex of her thighs. Her breathing is labored and I love that I can make her fall apart like this. "Can you come this way, cherry bomb?" She moans in response. Her head has dropped back and her elbows are all that is keeping her upright. I move my hands to the sides of her bikini bottoms and release the ties making the material fall limp to the table. "Watch me," I call out as I bend down to my knees.

Taking my hands beneath her knees I pull her further to the edge of the table and plunge my mouth to her dripping wet core. You'd think she just stepped out of the pool with the mess she has for me.

"Oh, Maddox," she hums and runs her fingers through my hair pulling me even closer to her.

I start to nip at her clit then swirl my tongue through her pussy. Her hips come off the table but I hold her in place. I suck on her pulsing pearl until I feel her legs start to shake. She's close. Reaching down I release the button and zipper of my pants to make room for my hard dick. Just as she's about to come I rise from the floor. Her eyes open and before she can protest I slam my cock into her wet hole. She comes immediately throbbing around my dick, squeezing the life out of me. I pull back to the tip then thrust back in again. I set that rhythm prolonging her orgasm. Leaning over her I place my hand to the back of her head to cushion it from the hard table. My other hand is anchoring her leg around my hip as I drive in deep and hard.

"That's it, take all of me," I pant as I pound even harder making the table propel forward with each ram. My dick has been on edge since the moment she walked into this room nearly naked and I start to feel the tingle at the bottom of my spine but I don't let up my pace. She moves her hips, meeting me at my pace, egging me on. "I can't go twenty-four hours without this tight pussy wrapped around me." Piper glides her hands from my shoulder and neck down to my pecs and tugs on my nipples. "Shit," that almost does me in. I've never had someone play with my nipples before and I think I love it.

I grab her wrists and slam them over her head trying to stave off my orgasm. My hips piston into her as her moans and little grunts fill the room. Her walls tighten even more around my dick as we move faster. My right hand comes off her wrist and collars her neck not putting any pressure on her throat but letting her know I'm in charge. Her pupils dilate with the anticipation of another orgasm. My heart is thumping so hard against my chest it might burst as I look into her eyes. I know it's crazy fast for us but I know she's the one for me. She's it. The realization of my feelings hits me hard at the same time as both our bodies explode. We never break eye contact and I feel it deep in my bones that this woman is my everything.

Overwhelmed at the realization I lay my head down on her chest calming my breaths and heart rate. We're a sweaty mess on the table but I don't give a shit. I feel her soft dainty hand draw circles on my back as we lie there.

"That was intense," she says after a few moments.

I pop my head up and rest my chin on her breastbone.

"Good or bad?" I ask schooling my face. The last thing I want is for her to read my thoughts and run for the hills because she's not ready to move our relationship at the pace I'm already at.

She gives me her bewitching smile. "Definitely good, Maddox."

"Well, you can plug my solution into your equation anytime."

There is a short pause before our laughter erupts.

"I don't think I've ever met someone like you before, Maddox."

"I *am* one of a kind."

"You sure are."

A knock interrupts our moment followed by the shout of Luca's voice. "Meet us down at the pool."

My dick gets removed from the comforts of its favorite place as I help Piper off the table. I help her tie all the strings back into place and make sure she's covered before walking over to the sofa and grabbing the swim trunks on the coffee table. I glide them up my thighs watching Piper bend over picking up her sheer cover-up. I grunt knowing I could easily bend her over and have another go if we had the time.

"I can't believe the table got moved all the way to the wall," she mentions as she looks back over at me as I pull on my t-shirt.

I glance over and see how far it is from the original spot. "The moving table was the last thing on my mind, cherry bomb."

She smiles and shakes her head then pats her hair to try and tame the wild locks.

"I guess we should head down to the pool. Should we grab some towels?"

"I'm sure they'll provide them for us."

I swipe the keycard from the entryway table and hold the door for Piper to exit. I see one of Luca's men standing guard by the elevator and we exchange a nod.

"They sure don't slouch on extra security everywhere," she comments as the guy holds the door for us. I swipe my key and we descend to the lobby.

When we arrive, I see several of my team blending in and give subtle nods as we walk down the path following the signs to the pool area. When we get to the entrance, I give our name and room number. They escort us over to a private area where we see Luca and Gemma lounging in chairs sipping on drinks.

"Gemma, you changed?" Piper notices but misses the smirk on Luca's face. I didn't notice what she was wearing when the women came into the room, only what my woman was in. She's now in a one-piece swimsuit with a sheer mesh across her midsection.

"This guy," Gemma points in the direction of her husband, "decided to rip it in half so I had to change."

"There is never going to be a day where I allow anyone else to see what belongs to me, babygirl," Luca says with a smug face. "Plus, when you start drinking your clothes seem to go missing. At least this way it'll be more difficult to lose a one piece."

Gemma maturely sticks her tongue out at Luca setting off a round of giggles from the women.

"Let's get some sunblock on before you burn," I suggest and lead Piper over to the covered cabana.

After I lather her up within an inch of her life, our waiter comes over to get our drink orders.

"I think I'll go take a dip before he comes back with our drinks," Piper says and Gemma follows right behind her.

Luca and I watch as the women step into the pool until their shoulders are covered where they stay close talking about something.

"It's crazy to think five years ago we were hanging out at resort pools doing completely different activities than we are now," Luca comments. Five years ago we were fucking everything with a skirt and partying hard.

"Didn't think I'd ever be able to have something stable like this," I say. "Especially not after everything with my sperm donor."

"What changed your mind?" he asks.

I look out to where Piper is and smile. The waiter comes over just as four guys break off from their group and tread water over to where our women are floating and having a good time. My eyes narrow and I hear Luca growl under his breath.

"Can't fucking take her anywhere," he hisses as we eat up the pavement toward the pool.

"You beauties staying all weekend?" we hear one of the dead men ask as we descend the pool stairs. There are four of them who all look like college frat boys.

"We're from here," Gemma answers in a friendly tone. "How about you all?"

"We—"

"Were just leaving," I spit and circle my woman's waist offering her the drink she ordered.

"No harm, man. We didn't know they were taken," the long-haired one says with both his hands up in surrender.

"The enormous rock on her left hand didn't say it?" Luca hisses then positions Gemma even further away from the guys.

"She doesn't have one," the idiot blond points out and my muscles lock into place. I can see some of Luca's and my team get into position to step in if this turns ugly. Not that we'd need the help.

Two of the four have started to float further back from us sensing the imminent eruption.

"She's mine." I grit my teeth.

"Leave it, Gary. Let's go get another drink," the smart one with glasses suggests.

The four boys leave and I watch as two of my men get in the water to put up a barrier around us.

"Down, MadDog, they were just being friendly," Piper says playfully with a wink as she sucks her fruity frozen drink.

"Friendly my ass," I mumble as she giggles.

"Now why would I want some college frat boy who can't even hold a conversation about physics." She wraps her arms around my neck and pulls me down to kiss me. "I mean you must be the square root of a hundred because you're definitely a solid ten."

My free arm pulls her up and she wraps her legs around my middle. I'm starting to think this is our favorite position. "Damn straight I am," I say and give her ass a squeeze.

"We should've gone to our home on the beach for the week-end," Luca tells Gemma. "At least we wouldn't have had to deal with other people."

"You have a beach house?" Piper asks.

"In San Diego," Gemma tells her. "I went to college out there and Luca has a business there."

"I bet it's beautiful," Piper smiles.

"We could do a girls' getaway and stay there for the weekend." Gemma offers. "My girlfriend, Bianca, would love to get away soon."

"I'm not sure I can get away so easy. Coordinating time off is tough but to leave the city is really difficult with my parents always needing something at their facility."

"Maybe if we give enough time in advance we can make arrange-ments. The flight is very short when we use our jets if we need to come back on a moment's notice," Gemma offers again and I can see the moment that it registers in Piper's head that she thinks she's out of her league here with us.

Piper just nods and I can tell she's about to shut down. The music starts to get loud as a new DJ comes on at the pool and starts engaging with everyone. We order more drinks and food as the pool doubles in occupancy. We play volleyball and float on pool rafts as the day goes on having a great time. We stop every couple of hours to reapply sunblock, and thankfully Thomas sent over two large hats for our women to help shield the sun from burning them. By the time the sun starts to set our girls are drunk and giggly. We barely manage to pull them from the pool to the cabana without incident.

"I don't think we're going out tonight," I say after we gather our belongings and turn to our women who are passed out on the lounge chairs, both with their mouths open.

"We can carry their items, sir," one of Luca's men says as he approaches.

"Thank you, Ernesto," Luca says then hands all of our stuff over to him.

We can't help but chuckle at our ladies sprawled out. Bending down I sweep Piper into my arms and carry her bridal style with our men surrounding us.

When we make it up to the hallway to our rooms I turn to Luca. "See you for breakfast?"

"I just love you so much, babe," Gemma slurs with her eyes still closed. Luca shakes his head, not in the least bit upset at his drunk wife. "Best husband ever."

"Was thinking of getting in a workout before, want to join?" he responds to me when Gemma quiets down. "This one won't wake up till late morning I bet."

"Text me when you get ready to head out."

We part ways and I walk into our suite after Dustin, one of Luca's men, opens the door for me. I walk us into the master bedroom and settle Piper down on the soft bed. If her chest wasn't rising and falling and if she wasn't making the most adorable noises I'd think she was dead. After removing her bikini I lift her slightly to pull the covers up over her. Making sure she's not going to roll off the bed, I walk to the bathroom to take a piss. Someone from my team put all our toiletries out for us so I brush my teeth and strip out of my swim trunks. I walk out to the living area and deadbolt the door before making my way back to the bed, turning off all the lights as I go. Sliding under the cool sheets, I position Piper on my chest wondering if she'll love me like Gemma loves Luca.

Piper

"Have y'all moved in together yet?"

I had just swallowed the last bite of my chicken when Gemma asks the table and I start to choke, shocked at her question. Maddox taps my back a few times but I signal that I'm fine. After reaching for my glass of water and taking a swig I say, "We've only known each other a short time."

"That doesn't matter. Luca and I got engaged then two days later got married. Wyatt and Kendall knew each other for less than a month, I think. When you know, you know."

I look over to Maddox for help but he just smiles at me without saying a word.

"Well, I think that's great for all of you but I think we might need a little more time," I say gently.

"You could think of it as a trial run before tying the knot," she continues.

"Baby, let them be. We don't need to play matchmaker this weekend," Luca butts in and I'm thankful since Maddox has lost the ability to talk.

"It doesn't sound so bad," Maddox finally speaks up and I give him a confused look.

I lift my glass to my nose to check to make sure it's not alcohol. After drinking at the pool yesterday I've decided to stick with water for the rest of the weekend.

"You haven't even met my parents yet," I say even though it has nothing to do with this conversation but I'm at a loss here being put on the spot.

"I thought we were meeting them on the way home tomorrow?"

"We are, but—"

"We should table this discussion for another time and stop trying to push things on their relationship, babygirl." Luca comes to the rescue and I think he might be my favorite person of all time.

"Sorry if I overstepped, but I do think you should consider it," Gemma says then glares over at Luca, who in turn brings her hand up to his mouth and kisses her knuckles.

I feel a hand on my exposed thigh and turn my focus from the married couple to Maddox. He winks and the tension I was feeling a few seconds ago melts. I place my hand on his and wonder how I got so lucky to have a man like this in my life.

"Are we ready to head to the club?" Gemma interrupts.

I watch Luca run a hand over his face. "Aren't you tired from all the activity we did earlier today? You sure you want to go out to a club?"

I have to keep from chuckling. I'm finding that poor Luca only wants alone time with his wife but he married a ball of energy who likes to go and explore which is the opposite of him.

Once we got up this morning we had brunch. Then Gemma planned for us to take a helicopter ride all over Las Vegas doing touristy things. We flew over Hoover Dam and then the Grand Canyon before circling The Strip. I'd never been on a helicopter before so it was the coolest thing I think I've ever done.

"How often do we have opportunities to hang out with friends and chill without Dante? I'd like to take advantage of this before you knock me up again. If you guys don't want to go, Piper and I will be just fine and we can meet you back at the room in a few hours."

I know she's trying to rile her husband up and I love seeing the back and forth between them. It reminds me so much of Maddox and myself.

"I wouldn't mind taking you back up to the room and fucking you out of this dress, cherry bomb," Maddox leans over and whispers. I can feel the heat in my cheeks as he inches his hand up my dress.

This man is a machine in the sex department. I woke up this morning to him coming from the gym and we took advantage of the shelf in the luxury shower before we went to brunch. Then again after we came back from the helicopter ride before we met up here for dinner. We actually used the bed that time.

"Are we ready?" Luca is saying as he helps Gemma up.

I'm gathering my purse when a commotion gains our attention.

"Ox!" we hear shouted across the restaurant. "Ox!"

A woman in barely any clothes walks through the crowded room bobbing between the tables to ours in the far back corner. A line of men in black and dark gray suits all stand at once and block her path before she comes within thirty feet of us.

"Ox! I thought you were going to call," she almost yells as she unsuccessfully tries to dodge the wall of men. "We had the best night together; you said we were going to hook up again. Excuse me," she tries to tell the men in front of her but they don't budge. "Ox!" she calls again and this time two men start to escort her towards the front of the restaurant.

Three sets of eyes from our table turn to Maddox who hasn't let go of my upper thigh and my heart drops to the bottom of my stomach. My hand tries to pry his off of my skin so I can stand up but he keeps me rooted in my chair. Maddox uses his free hand on my chin so that I'm looking at him in his beautiful silver eyes.

"This is going to make me sound like a fuckboy but I have no idea who she is," he says looking right into my eyes. "Before I met you I hooked up with a lot of random women and partied but that all stopped a couple of months before I met you. You have no reason to believe me but it's true. I haven't touched anyone else since you and I met."

This is where the fork in the road lies in every relationship. Do I believe what he is saying and we continue to build trust until it's broken or do I let my insecurities sink in and think the worst?

I force my way to standing, breaking all contact with him, and catch a glance over at Gemma who is glaring her narrowed eyes at Maddox. Luca has a neutral expression, not giving anything away, watching how this is going to play out. Maddox stays seated with his hands in tight fists.

I give him my best smile. "Let's head to the club," I say and reach for his hand. "Then I expect you to fulfill the promise you whispered."

His hardened features relax and that cocky smile comes back. "As you wish, cherry bomb."

He stands, wrapping his arms around my body and pulling me flush to his hard chest. He leans down and covers my mouth with his in an obscene public display. I feel his hands move from my back and cup my butt cheeks giving them a hard squeeze.

"Thank you for believing me," he mumbles against my lips when we break away breathless. He pulls back slightly and stares at me. "I'm falling for you, Piper."

I suck in a breath, shocked at his words. "Maddox..." I start to tell him it's too soon but realize I can't because I feel the same.

"I just wanted you to know in case my actions weren't saying it loud enough."

I grip the back of his neck pulling him down where our noses are almost touching. "Take me back to the room," I tell him. I can see the fire in his eyes and I'm sure mine are reflecting the same.

A throat clears popping the bubble around us and the noise from the restaurant comes rushing back.

"We'll meet you at the club," Maddox lifts his head to where Luca and Gemma are standing on the other side of the table at the same time he starts to walk us around the chairs.

I vaguely see a wall of men with their backs blocking out the other patrons of the restaurant as we make our way out and into the large hallway of the hotel. Maddox guides us through the lobby and over to the guarded elevator. When we enter he scans the keycard and we ascend. Not a word is spoken as he crowds me against the wall. The doors open and I'm whisked out and down the hall to our room. A man is there opening our door for us and when we enter Maddox kicks the door shut and deadbolts the locks before turning around. I'm standing in the middle of the living room watching as he leans up against the door staring back at me.

"I lied downstairs," Maddox says and my heart starts to beat faster.

"What?"

"I said I was falling but I'm already there. I know it feels like it's too soon but I don't fucking care. I feel how I feel." He pushes off the door and stalks towards me, eating up the space between us. "It's okay if you don't feel the same right now," he continues then stops right in front of me before placing both hands on the fabric at my chest. I swallow hoping to wet my dry mouth. "My love will be enough for the both of us till then."

His hands separate downward in a harsh tug ripping my dress down the middle and pouring my breast out, leaving me only in my heels and sheer black panties. Damp panties. The dress is in scraps on the floor as he picks me up and walks me toward the bedroom.

"There are so many things I want to do to you right now but I think nice and slow is what we need," he says as he slowly bends down and lays us across the comforter.

Placing slow wet kisses down my neck, he proceeds to make his way down my chest into the valley of my breast toward my bellybutton. He continues his path to the top of my pubic area and stops. Maddox lifts his chin and our eyes connect. Fire. His eyes are filled with lust and promises. I watch as he uses his tongue over the wet spot my core has created. With a hum, he starts licking me, twirling his tongue, and making sure to cover every inch of me.

"Ah," I moan when his nose bumps my clit.

"My woman needs more?"

"Yes, please, Maddox," I beg.

His fingers shred my panties and his mouth is back on me in an instant. I feel his finger rim my opening and then push in, dragging against my sweet spot making my legs close around his head. The feeling rocks me with such pleasure I don't even notice Maddox using his free hand and shoulder to pry my legs back down.

"Easy baby," he says as his tongue flicks my clit.

Just as I'm about to scream out, the sensation is gone and Maddox is standing ripping his suit off, causing the buttons to scatter around the room in his haste. Once he's completely naked, he reaches down under my butt, picks me up, and places me in the center of the massive bed. Crawling back over my body, Maddox positions himself at my entrance with one hand on his dick and the other at my head.

"I love you, Piper," he states, and before I can make a sound he enters me to the hilt.

His body lays on mine as he takes most of his weight on his forearms. Slowly he starts to pull out and push back in. My legs encase his hips and I start to move but he pins me down with his lower half. "Nah, baby, you just lay there and let me do all the work," he says then begins a leisurely pace.

Maddox bends his head and presses his lips to mine, consuming every inch of my being. I feel the build-up deep in the pit of my stomach as tingles spike through my body. My fingers thread through his hair holding him to me. Our eyes never look away from one another as if we are looking into each other's souls.

"This is so crazy, Maddox, but I love you too," I say just above a whisper, the words choking me up. My eyes water at their gravity.

His eyes move back and forth from both of my eyes searching for something. "You do?" he halts his hips mid-thrust.

"I do." I smile. "I love you, Maddox Bishop."

He smiles back and it makes him look so much younger. He pins me with his lips against mine like a hungry animal. His hips start to move again and I feel him expanding inside of me.

"Was gonna draw this out all night but you always seem to change my plans, cherry bomb," he admits then picks up his pace. "Gonna make you so happy," he says between thrusts. "You're never gonna leave me." Thrust, thrust. "Fill you with all my babies." Thrust, thrust. "Love you forever." Thrust, thrust.

My body splinters into a million pieces as my orgasm tears through me. I scream out his name as he splashes my walls with his cum. I'm panting as I come back down from the high and my eyes focus back on Maddox.

"You're the best thing to ever happen to me," he says. The sincerity behind his words stirs in my chest pulling it tight and making my heart thump hard against it.

"I feel the same way." I smile up at him. "You're definitely someone I didn't know I needed but I am so glad I found you."

He moves slightly, his dick falling from me as he repositions us so he's got me across his chest engulfed in his strong arms.

"Do you still want to head to the club?" he asks, stroking my back with his fingertips.

I turn my head into his chest shaking it. "You just wore me out and I don't want to put clothes back on after you've gotten me so sweaty. Plus, you shredded the dress."

His fingers crawl up my skin and lace through my hair positioning my head to look up at him.

"Then I guess we better go clean you up in the shower before we fall asleep," he tells me, a mischievous grin on his handsome face.

"Oh no. You are not going to get me to go another round. My vagina is closed for the evening. I know when to wave the white flag."

"I can kiss it and make it better," he coaxes as he lifts me off the bed and walks us through to the bathroom.

"Kissing leads to other things," I say. "One more round and you'll put me into a coma."

"All I hear is a challenge, cherry bomb," he counters as he turns on the shower, and steam immediately starts to fill the room.

"You are impossible." I roll my eyes trying to sound chastising.

"But you love me."

I pause and a thrill courses through my body sending goosebumps down my arms. "Yes, I do."

CHAPTER FIFTEEN

Piper

"I THINK WE NEED TO CONTACT AN ATTORNEY OR SOMEONE who knows how to handle a situation like this," Belinda suggests as I read her the latest email from my principal, Jackie. "The union all the teachers belong to offers attorney assistance, right?"

I nod still trying to process how best to navigate this new development. I received an email from Jackie this morning stating that I needed to halt all public records inquiries and to basically mind my own business. It was very colorful and not professional at all. I've definitely ruffled some feathers. What really concerns me is that she knew I was asking for records, which tells me that people are talking about my inquiries and it's spreading throughout all the departments. If I hadn't just collected the newest batch of records I might be inclined to leave it be, but now Belinda and I are certain that all the school board members are into some shady dealings. They seem to be getting kickbacks and using corrupt measures through the school system.

I look up the number of my representative and dial it.

"Hello, this is Teresa how can I help you today?"

"Hi, my name is Piper Caldwell, and I think I might need some representation," I say into the phone.

"Okay, let's get some information and I'll have one of our people contact you shortly," Teresa says. She takes down all my details then we hang up.

"I think we just uncovered the biggest scandal this town has seen in a while. I mean it's not Tupac big but this is up there. If the media gets ahold of this, it'll shake some big names. The entire board will have to be replaced, not to mention all of the top administration personnel in the district," Belinda says not looking up from the pages she's zoned in on.

"This really wasn't what I wanted to be involved with. I've got so much going on right now as it is." I start to rub my forehead. Being in the limelight is not something that calls to me. I prefer to keep my head down, do my job, then collect a paycheck.

"I know, honey, but think of all the kids that are affected by this if someone doesn't speak up and bring all this to light."

She's right. It's the kids that will suffer when the federal government comes in and decides to stop the funding after what the people in power have done and are doing.

My phone rings and it's my rep from the educational association. She has an opening to see me in about an hour so Belinda and I jump on taking it. After we hang up, Belinda and I gather our notes and a good chunk of documents to prove our findings.

An hour and a half later we are sitting across from Tracey. My hands are damp with sweat and my stomach wants to empty with every exhale. How in the hell did I pull the short stick when drama comes to town? I already have so much going on that I'm not sure my mental state can handle any more hits.

"Can you tell me what it is that you found or what you've come across that might involve the school district in corruption?"

"Well, for starters the assistant superintendent, Rachelle Flores, is an owner in the after-school care program that is for profit. She runs it with a silent partner Barry Carver who also happens to be the superintendent. They opened Discovery Ink and are charging the parents to attend."

"We aren't against starting businesses, but it seems a little deceiving that no one knew that they owned it and are making money off of it." Belinda chimes in. "I've asked several of my parent friends if they knew who owned it and they were shocked that this would be allowed since the taxpayers are already paying them a salary. It seems shady as hell."

"Rachelle also uses the school district's resources to run the background checks on the employees of the after-school program. Plus she uses the district's emailing system to contact her after-school program for their employees and all communication. That's how we found out that Barry is the silent partner. They only pay a fraction of the rental fees that the school demands of other non-profit organizations, which seems like special treatment because of who they are," I say.

"I see." Tracey is writing everything down on a notepad and hasn't lifted her eyes to us once. "What else?"

"Rachelle pays her nephew from the federal funds the school gets to translate documents from English to Spanish. He has no background or experience with that language but he sure gets paid a hefty amount."

"Really? Her nephew? Is he a current student?"

"No, he graduated a few years ago. Nepotism apparently runs rampant throughout the school district with no conflict of interest forms being filled out. The athletic director lets his wife have meet-ups using the high school gym for her weightlifting business. The superintendent, Barry Carver, employed his daughter-in-law to be the district lead counselor without even finishing her degree and she answers to him directly. Brad Rollings who is on the school board just helped vote his wife into a lead role in administration at the high school."

"Tell her about Donald Tucker," Belinda nudges.

Tracey has already flipped her notepad paper three times, writing so fast I'm worried she's going to injure her wrist.

"Donald Tucker is a school board member who owns a construction company. We have documents that show he used his company to do several of the big jobs for the district."

"Was this before he was elected to be on the board?" Tracey asks finally looking up at us.

"No, he's been on the board for over ten years. These contracts are within the last few years."

Tracey starts back writing everything we're saying nodding her head with each point we make. We spend the entire hour telling her everything we have and she copies all of the documents we brought with us. We are planning to meet up later in the week to give her the rest of the papers to back up our findings.

"This is crazy," Tracey finally says when she pushes our copies to us. "I've never had something like this come up before. Especially with the principal having the proof so open for someone to find."

"Trust me this is not something I ever wanted to come across. I did her expense reports last year and thought something wasn't right but I couldn't put my finger on it," I say.

"How will you approach the district? Or will you contact someone from the state first?" Belinda asks.

Tracey pushes her glasses up to rest above her forehead. "First we need to get all the facts and supporting documents in order. I'm going to have to speak with some of my colleagues and see what the best route to take moving forward is."

After a few more minutes, Belinda and I leave. I feel a weight lifted off my shoulders now that someone else can initiate the appropriate action and take it off my hands.

"Are you ready for the school year to begin?"

"I guess. This summer went by way too fast," I say.

"Of course it did. You're working like crazy and have a hot new man in your life." She laughs and nudges my arm with her elbow. "Remember to enjoy this time in your life, Piper. It goes by way too quickly."

I nod, agreeing. The moments Maddox and I get to spend

together are so special. He makes me feel things I never thought I'd have.

"I hate that they shorten our time off to start a new calendar year early. I loved that we didn't start our school year until after Labor Day but now we're beginning around the first of August," I gripe.

"I'm not a fan either, especially now that we really know who serves on the board," she says as we load up in her car and head out of the parking lot. "Everything going good with you and that hunk of yours?"

I can't help but smile. "Yeah, we're good." I look out the side window not wanting her to see my heated cheeks. "He met my parents last week."

"After the weekend getaway?"

"Mmhmm."

She lets out a half giggle half squeal. "I'm so happy for you, Piper. You of all people deserve to find someone who can make your toes curl." We both have a good laugh. "What was his reaction to seeing them?"

I turn to face her as she pulls into a drive-thru to order us some drinks to take back home.

"We don't have to go tonight to see them if you've got some things you need to catch up on with work," I offer, giving him a chance to back out.

Having to be in charge of both of your parents is hard and a huge undertaking. I don't expect everyone to understand or feel obliged to help. Maddox reaches out and takes my hand as we walk into the facility. I was able to get my parents' rooms next to each other in this place so it makes it easier to locate them and spend more time when I come to visit.

We turn down the hall and I take a deep breath before turning the knob to Mom's room.

"Hey," Maddox says and stops me. "It's going to be okay. I'm here to help with all this too. We're a team remember?"

I nod but don't voice that I've never had help when it comes to their care. It's always been on my shoulders and my responsibility. The thought of someone else helping seems foreign.

We enter the room and the stark white walls remind me of a hospital as does the smell of disinfectant. Mom is asleep and according to the nurse's report I received earlier in the day her vitals were up and down. She looks even smaller than just a few days ago and they've put an oxygen mask over her nose and mouth.

We walk over to her bed and I place my hand on her cold and frail one. The sound of beeping shows her stats at a normal range and I'm thankful she's not in any distress.

"They loved you very much," Maddox says drawing my attention over to where he's looking at the picture frames I'd put up around her room. He's looking at one when the three of us went to the beach.

"I think that's why I went to Florida for college. I fell in love with the weather and beaches there," I say and walk over to him.

We stay there for a few more minutes and then go find Dad down the hall because he wasn't in his room. They have a recreational room at the end with tables and chairs for others to do puzzles or games. Over on the other side, they have recliners and TVs to watch movies or the news. We find Dad in a recliner staring at the TV.

"Hey, Dad," I greet squatting down to his level. "I'd like for you to meet Maddox." I place a hand on his forearm but he doesn't respond. He doesn't even flinch when I touch him. He just stares straight ahead. "Mom is doing good and her vitals are steady."

It's always hard to hold a one-way conversation, so I usually just ramble through most of it, but today, with Maddox here, I feel a tug of emotions as I open this part of my life up for him to see. No one sees this side of my life. Rob has been here fewer than a handful of times because it's not something I want to subject him to. So having Maddox here watching this has me wanting to shield myself from any potential judgment or pity.

"It's nice to finally meet you, Mr. Caldwell." Maddox leans down and places his hand inside of my dad's. He gives his hand a slight shake and then pulls a chair up next to Dad's recliner. "Piper has told me

about your love of sports and I couldn't agree with you more that base-
ball is a much superior game than football."

I listen to the love of my life talk with my dad as though it's an
everyday occurrence and I feel a burning in my nose and eyes. Quietly,
I excuse myself, claiming to need to speak with a nurse and leave before
I erupt into tears as my emotions flood through me.

I find a bathroom and give myself a few minutes to calm down
before checking in at the desk for updates on my dad. After getting a
pleasant report, I head back down to the rec room and find Maddox still
talking with him. My heart clutches as I hear him speak about things
I've told him that my dad and I used to do.

And I didn't think I could love this man any more than I already did.

She reaches over the console and gives my hand a squeeze.

"I don't know how you do it, but you're my hero because I don't
know if I'd be as strong as you have been over the last few years, gir-
lie," she says and her words mean a lot. "You've had to take on more
than one person your age should ever have to handle. Most would've
crumbled by now but you keep fighting and standing strong."

"Some days I don't feel that way," I admit.

"A village is not just for when you have kids but to enjoy during
your entire life. Having people to share the ups and downs in every
aspect of your life is crucial."

"I'm starting to see that," I say as our drinks get handed to us
and we head back to my house. "How are Andy and Samuel?" I ask
about her sons.

"Good. Samuel is at soccer camp until next week, and loving
being away for two weeks from Joseph and me. Andy and his little
girlfriend are attached at the hip. Joseph had the talk after we came
home from the store and caught them in his room. They weren't
doing anything but I think it was time."

"I can't imagine having to have a conversation like that with my
kids. I was mortified when Mom sat me down and told me about
getting my period when I was twelve."

Belinda laughs out loud. "I think I'd be just as horrified to give the sex talk but I told Joseph it was his responsibility to talk with both of our kids because he's a guy and it might not be so bad coming from him instead of their mom."

"Sounds fair," I agree.

We pull up to my drive and I gather up all my things to hop out.

"You and that hunk of yours got plans before you start back to school next week?" she asks putting the car in park.

"He mentioned going to see his mom and sisters in New York and wanted to take me along."

"That sounds very official and serious," she jokes.

"I know. I'm not sure if we're there yet though. We come from completely different circles, you know."

"Don't let fear and insecurities hold you back from experiencing wonderful things in your life. The biggest regret is looking back on a situation and wishing you'd done something you were too scared to do at the time. Ride the coattails and you might be surprised how it turns out."

I nod thinking about what she's saying. "You sound like you're talking from experience."

"Honey, I've got at least ten years on you and there are some things I wish I'd done differently or jumped off the deep end for. That's why I can say this." She winks as her phone starts to ring.

"I'll call you later," I say then exit the car.

As I walk up to the house, I think about whether I'm brave enough to jump in the deep end or if I should stay in the safe confines of the structured box I've created over the last few years.

Dating Maddox feels like jumping into the deep end for sure. I just hope I don't drown.

CHAPTER SIXTEEN

Piper

WE ARE TWO WEEKS INTO THE NEW SCHOOL YEAR AND
I think this might be the best one since I started
teaching. I've got a great group of students eager to
learn that aren't too rowdy. The other teachers in my pod are excited
and refreshed from the summer—all except one, Jessica McClain.
She's been very cold and snippy with me ever since we came back. It
makes it hard to work well as a group because everyone has noticed
it, but we are pushing through ignoring her attitude.

*We just had our last team-building activity of the day with our
pod teachers before lunch and I'm ready to ask for a new pod. Jessica
is becoming unbearable to be around. All she has done since the day
started was bitch about my friend, Belinda, and how she's ruining her
daughter's life. Normally I'd stay out of the drama, especially when it
involves Jessica, but she's spouting off things that are simply not true.
Jessica knows I'm friends with Belinda and I think she's trying to needle me into a reaction.*

*"…and the boy, Andy, just won't leave her alone. He calls at all
hours of the night and just won't stop. Jenny's told him that she's not
interested in him but he's not taking her seriously," Jessica whines to our*

other pod teacher, Sandy, and I've had enough of her bullshit. Sandy isn't a big fan of Jessica's either but she's too polite to tell her that.

"Jessica, that is a flat-out lie and you need to stop," I pipe up before I can stop myself. "I've witnessed your daughter stalking Andy and his girlfriend multiple times over the summer. I've also heard the voice messages she leaves from other phone numbers because Andy has her blocked on his phone and all social media."

"Excuse me? You don't know what you're talking about. Jenny has told me all about it," she defends sounding astonished that I'd speak out against something she'd say.

"I do too and Belinda is going to take action against her and you just like that parent did last year when Jenny tried to pull this on another boy in their grade."

Jessica huffs, mad that I've called her out. "You need to mind your business and stay out of mine, Piper. This doesn't involve you at all."

"Then stop spreading lies and misinformation," I suggest.

"Don't you think it's inappropriate to be friends with parents? You don't even have kids and you and Belinda hang out."

"What does not having kids have to do with being friends? That makes no sense at all." I roll my eyes as our school counselor comes back on stage to give a chat about the new guidelines regarding testing this year.

Maddox and I are still seeing each other almost every night and he comes with me regularly to see my parents. I received a phone call three weeks ago from my parents' insurance company letting me know that they were eligible to be sent to a new rehab facility with state-of-the-art medical staff and care. I was floored when they listed all the benefits that came with moving them. I had the poor woman on the other line repeat our entire conversation three times after it set in. The great news is that I won't be paying out of pocket for this facility like the one they were in. Insurance is going to cover every expense including tests, doctors' visits, rehab, and trial testing if it becomes available.

I'd called Maddox crying so hard from the relief being lifted off my shoulders that none of my words made any sense. He'd sent his business partner, Thomas, over to check on me until he could make it there. Twenty minutes later Maddox stormed through the front door like his ass was on fire wanting to know what was going on. Poor Thomas just stood there not having a clue how to handle me and bolted out the door when he showed up. After finally calming down, I explained everything and he held me, rubbing my back and soothing my soul.

I can't believe how life has a way of turning around when you least expect it.

"Ms. Caldwell, are you in the room?" I hear the speaker on the phone call out to me as I file the last of my papers.

"I'm here, Becky," I call out from across the room.

"Mrs. Roberts would like to see you in her office immediately."

"Okay, I'll be right there, thank you."

Walking to the door, I give my classroom one last look to make sure I have everything in order for my next class to start in thirty minutes. Once the door closes, I give the handle a jiggle to make sure the lock is in place and then head down the hall toward the office.

Ms. Becky is seated in her regular spot with a welcoming smile.

"Good afternoon, Ms. Becky," I greet as I walk by and tap a finger on the front office desk.

"I'm loving this glow you have, Piper. Happiness is a good look on you."

"Thank you," I say and round the corner to Jackie's door.

I rap my knuckles on the wood when I see she's on a phone call. Her head pops up and I hear her say, "She's walking in now. Yes, okay, I'll call you after. Bye." She waves me in and gestures for me to have a seat across from her as she hangs up the phone.

For some reason, an unease comes over the room as she stares at me for a moment. The temperature feels as if it's dropped twenty degrees. Jackie's eyes narrow and then she picks up a pen and taps the cap on a folder with my name on it.

"Ms. Caldwell, it has been brought to my attention that you have conducted yourself in an unsavory manner," she begins and the hairs on the back of my neck rise. "I've been told by a fellow peer that you have been involved in several instances that involve a minor in this district."

It's like time stands still when she stops talking. Is this a joke? My brain is misfiring and I don't even know how to comprehend what she is saying to me. Unsavory manner? What is that supposed to mean?

"I'm sorry…what?"

"You are being accused of having an inappropriate relationship with a student, Ms. Caldwell. I need you to tell me about the relationship you have with a Rob Lewis."

"Rob?"

What does Rob have to do with anything? He graduated a week before this school year began and has been working full-time at the sandwich shop with Oliver. White noise sounds through my ears as she continues to ask me questions.

"Yes, a Rob Lewis. Do you know him?" She looks down at a piece of paper before looking back at me expectantly.

"Of course I know Rob. I had him in my class years ago and we also work together at my second job at the sandwich shop."

"I see." Jackie tuts then writes down something on her notepad. "What about Andy and Samuel Garcia?"

"I taught Andy about two years ago. I'm friends with his mother, Belinda, and their dad, Joseph."

"Friends? Were you friends before or after you taught Andy?"

My mind is reeling and I can't concentrate on timelines or anything for that matter. I've never been in trouble a day in my life. Why is she asking me about all of this? What is going on?

"Do I need to speak with an attorney or my representative from the teacher's union?"

Jackie tosses her pen on the desk. "Only if you feel as if you did something wrong, Piper," she hisses. "These are just a few questions the district wants answers to clear up from the inquiry. I see no reason to get more people involved than necessary. Just answer a few more questions and that's all I need."

I nod because I don't know what to do. I haven't done anything wrong or inappropriate with a student.

She picks the pen back up. "Friends before or after teaching Andy?"

My hand comes up to rub my forehead. I try to think back to when Belinda and I met.

"We met the year before he was in eighth grade. She was helping at an event the PTA was putting on. We worked a booth together. The next school year Andy was placed in my class, I believe."

"I see. Did you give Andy any special treatment or grades that he didn't earn or deserve?"

I can't even believe I'm being asked these questions. Why is any of this being brought up?

"Never," I say defensively. "I give every student the same treatment whether I know the parents or not."

"Uh huh."

I'm starting to feel a burning in my stomach and my temper is about to start showing. Why is she acting like this towards me? I've never stepped out of line in all the years I've worked here.

"Do you give students gifts?"

"Gifts? Like what?"

What the hell?

"Ms. Caldwell, this will go much quicker if you just cooperate."

"Why don't you just ask directly what you're searching for instead of beating around the bush? Just say it," I blurt out tired of this fishing game.

"Very well, did you buy Andy and Samuel Garcia a washer and dryer?"

"What in the hell does giving a friend an old used-up washer and dryer have to do with teaching? I gave something to an adult friend, not their kids. And it was broken!"

My mind is reeling trying to figure out what all of this has to do with my job.

"So you admit to giving this gift."

The dots start to connect and the person who is behind all of this is revealed. The only person on this planet who knew about the washer and dryer was one of my team teachers, Jessica McClain. Even though I haven't spoken with Belinda this week because she's been busy, I had heard she and Jessica had a falling out last week over Jessica's stalker of a daughter. I always tried to stay out of their business because Jessica and I had to work together every day. Belinda had come up to the school to drop off several gift baskets from the PTA and I was asking how the machines were working. Jessica was standing not too far from us and started asking questions and being nosy.

That jealous bitch.

When the school year started I thought Jessica was a little frosty toward me but thought she just wasn't happy because I had called her out on her bullshit when we were doing our training several weeks ago. This jealous bitch is trying to mess with me over being friends with Belinda.

"What I do on my own time with my friends outside of these four walls has nothing to do with my teaching career. Who I spend time with also doesn't concern you," I tell her, my volume rising and I can hear the venom coming out with every word. My adrenaline is pumping fast. "Jessica McClain needs to grow up and learn to keep my name out of her mouth."

My body can't sit still any longer so I go to stand.

"Sit down, Ms. Caldwell," Jackie hisses standing and placing her hands on the desk, but my energy is matching hers.

"I won't sit here and be accused or labeled something I'm not," I say pointing my finger right at her. This bitch has awakened something in me I didn't know existed.

"In that case, Ms. Caldwell, you are hereby placed on administration leave until further notice when the investigation is concluded. You are not to come on any district property unless given written permission from Mitch Connors, the school district's attorney. I suggest you take your belongings with you. This process may take some time."

"Why are you doing this to me? I've never done anything ever to warrant this." My voice breaks as my emotions start to take over.

Jackie sits back down in her chair and taps her finger on the desk. "You've poked your nose where it doesn't belong, Piper. And I told you in that email to leave well enough alone," she says cryptically.

"What's that supposed to mean?"

"It means that you need a cooling off period until you learn to mind your own business," she narrows her eyes. "There is already a substitute teacher in your room to take over for the rest of the day. Please exit the property without making a scene. It will only make the case worse for you."

She picks up the phone dismissing me like I'm some nuisance or annoying child. Turning on my heels, I walk to the closed door and open it. Never in my life have I ever bucked the system and I usually believe in doing the right thing, but the little devil on my shoulder wins out and I use every bit of strength I have and jerk her door shut sending a loud booming sound echoing off the walls of the entire office. As I round the corner, the staff are all standing watching as I storm out of the room and into the hallway toward my classroom.

My legs are wobbly and my eyes are swimming with unshed tears but I refuse to show any type of weakness in front of these evil people.

No good deed goes unpunished, that's for sure.

By the time I make it to my classroom the door is wedged open and an older woman, maybe in her fifties, is writing her name on my whiteboard.

"Oh, hello," she greets as she caps her marker.

"Hi," I grit. I know none of this is her fault and she probably has no idea what's happening right now but I can't even muster any emotion.

Moving around the room, I grab a few empty boxes and start to pack the essentials that I'll need until further notice. As selfish and petty as it is, I don't want someone else to use and have access to the things and materials I've worked so hard to build over the years to make the kids love my class. It takes a lot for teachers to build up resources, especially when you're on a budget. Not every teacher has a two-person income to help finance a lot of extras to spruce up their rooms but over time we collect items to make our rooms into the perfect setting for the students to feel comfortable learning in.

I write a quick letter to my student Kyle to feed the fish every day until I return. Mr. Wayne, our weekend janitor, feeds them on the weekends for me and I pay him ten dollars a week. He is having a hard time with his mother passing away and all the funeral expenses so he was more than happy to accept my offer. One time I came in and he was having a full conversation with the fish and it was the most excitement we'd seen him have in a while.

Looking around the classroom I've spent the last several years pouring my blood sweat and tears into has me wanting to smash everything to the ground. I've always done what was expected of me. I've always followed the rules and stayed out of trouble. Never ruffled any feathers and always volunteered when no one else would. And it was all for what? So some entitled bitch who can't control her daughter can come and make false claims against me to hurt someone else.

Fuck. That. Shit.

The bell for the passing period rings and I know it's time to go. I can't let the students see me like this. As I make my way out of the room with three boxes full of my stuff on a rolling cart, I have this bittersweet feeling coursing through me. Would I even want to come back when this *'investigation'* is over? Just as I'm pulling the rolling cart through the doorway I see Jessica standing outside her classroom watching me. Her face is blank but I see the flicker of triumph in her eyes. I must still have a little fire left from earlier because I waste no time marching across the hall and right up to her. Students are passing us not even knowing the storm brewing around them.

"Going somewhere?" Jessica moves her eyes from me to the rolling cart that houses my three boxes.

Big mistake bitch, because I advance on her getting right in her face and taking her by surprise. "I know it was you who went to Jackie." Our noses are almost touching and that spark that was in her eye just a minute ago is now gone replaced with fear. "You might think this is some kind of game or petty payback that has nothing to do with me but you've fucked with the wrong person."

She tries to take a step back but she knocks into the lockers. "I don't know w-what you're talking about." Her voice is shaky feigning innocence.

"You know exactly what you did," I spit. "I'm going to make it my life's mission to ruin you and even then I'm going to keep going until there is nothing left but a hollow body. You should've kept my name out of your mouth because when I'm through with you there won't be a rock you can crawl under to hide or a job that will hire you." I'm not even sure if I can follow through with all these threats but my mouth and brain continue to give her a verbal ass-whooping. "You better watch your back because I'm coming for you now," I threaten and give her one last look before taking a step back. I grab the handle of the cart and walk down the hall to the front entrance of the school and out the door.

Fuck these assholes.

I'm not sure when I placed my boxes in my car or when I pulled out of the parking lot. I'm not even sure how I drove on the streets and made every turn or stop to end up sitting in my driveway, but I did. Both of my hands are gripping the steering wheel as my arms shake and tears are flowing down my face like a waterfall. I sob as I look out the windshield at my home. I can faintly hear my phone buzzing off in the background but all of the emotions I was trying to suppress erupt and just pour out of me.

How did the day turn out this way?

The space in the car starts to feel like it's closing in on me and the need to claw myself out takes hold. Somehow, I open the door and when I go to stand up out of the car my weak legs give out. I'm sure if someone were to pass by they'd think I was a lunatic out on the front lawn sprawled out having a meltdown. My knees throb where they hit the pavement and I hear my name being called off in the distance. Shortly, two hands box my face in.

"Oh dear, what has happened?" Irene says panicked. She tries to help me up but my body is so limp I don't think I have the strength to hold myself up to walk. I'm a blubbering mess not able to speak in full sentences as the last hour of events mount. "What do you need, sweetheart? Tell me what to do. Should I call an ambulance?" I shake my head as my phone continues to ring from my seat in the car. "How about Mr. Bishop or Rob, honey?" she tries again but my lifeless body slumps up against the car.

The heat is beating down on us but it's not drying my tears as they continue to flow out of me. My body is so numb I can't feel anything. The phone rings again and this time Irene leans over my prone form.

"Hello? No, this is Irene how can I help you?" She listens for a bit. "I'll have her call you when she's available." She hangs up and then comes to kneel down as best she can.

My heart is hurting so bad it might explode at the pain and realization of what has happened.

"Piper, sweetheart, I know that something bad has happened but we need to get you inside the house before we both have a heat-stroke. Help an old lady out, will ya?"

Irene goes to stand and reaches down for my hands. She starts to pull me up and it feels like they weigh two tons. After several attempts, I manage to stand on shaky legs and lean heavily on her as we stagger to the front door. Once inside, she helps me over to the couch and she makes her way to the kitchen opening and closing cabinets. I hear the sound of something being poured then a glass is right in front of my face. She forces me to take a drink and then sits next to me holding my hand. We sit there for what feels like hours or maybe it's just minutes, I have no clue. I continue to stare at the wall housing the TV getting lost in the black screen.

How is it possible that the lying word of someone else can ruin the lives of others? They open their mouth knowing what they are saying is going to cause another hurt and pain but they don't care.

The front door bursts open and Belinda comes barreling in and falls to her knees in front of me and Irene.

"I just left the high school. Andy called me from the bathroom telling me he'd gotten called into a meeting with the principal and an administrator questioning your relationship with him. He went with Joseph who met us up there."

"Oh my god!" I cry out and more tears rush out of my eyes.

"Those fucking idiots. I told him to not say a word and that I'd be there to get him quick. I had Joseph go and grab Samuel after we parted ways so I could come and find you. He got into a shouting match with the assistant principal for speaking to him without a parent present."

Sobs wail out of me hearing what Andy and Samuel were put through all because of Jessica.

"Th-they p-put me on administrative leave until further notice," I cry and cover my face with my hands.

"Whatever for, honey?" Irene asks horrified as she sits there listening to our conversation. Belinda looks just as confused.

"J-Jackie said that I was involved in an inappropriate relationship with students. She asked me about Rob then about Andy and

Samuel." I shudder saying those words. "Said I was giving gifts to Andy and Samuel."

"Gifts? Like what kind of fucking gifts?" Belinda is barely holding back her rage.

"The washer and dryer," I tell them then finish the rest of what happened with Jackie and how I confronted Jessica in the hallway.

"That fucking piece of shit bitch! I'm going to cut out her lying, jealous tongue for what she's done," she seethes.

"What can you do, Piper? Do we need to find you an attorney to clear this up? Surely the school district is going to do an investigation and see this for what it is." Irene gently rubs my forearm.

"I've been thinking about this and I think Jessica is only half the problem," I say looking at both of them. I've gotten my breathing under control and every word I speak isn't a stutter.

"Why do you think that?" Irene asks.

"Jackie was very cryptic about how I shouldn't have poked the bear and that she told me to leave well enough alone. I think this has to do with what we uncovered with all the open records."

Belinda's eyes widen. "You think they know what we found out?" I nod. "But how? The only people who really know are the two of us and your rep from the union, Tracey." Belinda's eyes start to move back and forth thinking intently. "What if Tracey or someone who she has helping her with what we found alerted the administration?"

"I'm behind and I don't like not knowing what's happened," Irene says in a clipped tone.

We spend the next twenty or so minutes telling her everything we found out. "I know corruption happens everywhere, I just didn't think it'd be so close to home," she mumbles processing everything we've just laid out for her. "There is a leak somewhere. Either from the union or in the open records department," she adds. "This feels like pure retaliation but they are being smart about it."

"Call Tracey right now and tell her what has happened and see what she says." Belinda looks around the room. "Keep it on speaker phone so we can record. Where is your phone?"

"I think it's still in the car. She fell out of the car when she got home and we left everything out there when we came in," Irene says.

"I'll go grab it." Belinda hops up and rushes out the door. She's back in less than a minute with my phone and purse. "Here you go."

She takes her spot on the floor she'd vacated and I tap the number to Tracey.

"Hello, this is Tracey. How can I help you?" she answers

"Tracey, this is Piper Caldwell," I say trying hard not to tremble.

"Hi, Piper. I was just about to go into a meeting with my boss regarding your findings. She's wanting all the documents you've gathered."

"I was just put on administrative leave because I'm being investigated for an inappropriate relationship with a student," I blurt out as Irene rubs my back.

We hear her gasp. "What are they basing this on?"

I tell her the conversation Jackie and I had along with the one Jessica and I shared by the lockers. Of course, I give her the watered-down version.

"This is retaliation bullshit, Tracey," Belinda pipes up, anger vibrating off her.

"This is crazy. Why would they do this?" Tracey asks before quickly adding, "Let me go and speak with my boss and I'll call you back."

After we hang up, Irene is the first to speak. "What are you thinking?"

"I don't know what to think. I keep thinking this is all some prank that's going to stop any minute. I don't understand how they can do this to me."

A knock on the front door reveals Joseph with Andy and Samuel in tow.

"Hi, Ms. Piper." Little Samuel comes over and gives me a hug like always. Andy stands next to his dad looking about as glum as the rest of the room.

"Sammy, tell Mom and Piper what happened before I got there to pick you up," Joseph instructs their youngest.

"Mr. Greenward and Coach Benson called me down from class and asked me if you had ever touched me inappropriately. Or if I ever slept over at your house."

All three of us women suck in an audible breath.

"What in the actual fuck?" Belinda, who I rarely ever hear cusses, especially around her kids, shouts.

"Mom, you—"

"They asked you if she touched you?" Belinda yells and he nods. "What did you tell them?"

"I said no and that I thought it was weird that they'd ask me that. Then they wanted to know if she ever hugged me. I said yes like she does all the kids—"

"They're trying to paint me as a monster. Some predator after kids." I start to sob again not able to hold back.

"I told them that you've only ever been nice to me. They wanted to know if you've been over to our house and if I was ever left alone with you there." Samuel starts to get upset and tears form in his eyes. "Ms. Piper, I told them that you've never crossed a line with me and that I would know when someone is trying to be inappropriate with me. They kept asking the same questions but in different scenarios." I'm sure this is very traumatizing for him too. "I asked to call Mom and Dad but they said they just had a few more questions and then I could go back to class. That's when I heard Dad out in the hall yelling for me."

"You did good, baby." Belinda goes over to him and gives him a big hug. My instincts want to do the same but I'm now terrified that it might be used against me. What the hell am I going to do?

"Samuel, honey, I saw that Piper had a few pieces of chocolate cake in the fridge. Why don't you go and have a piece while we talk for a minute," Irene suggests to him. He nods and goes into the other room.

"What did they ask you?" I look up to a very sad Andy.

He shifts from foot to foot. "Basically the same as what they did to Sammy. They wanted to know if I ever stayed over here or if you ever touched me without my consent in certain areas. It was Principal Watson and the football coach, Becker. He wanted to know if we ever talked about sex or if I was ever alone with you. I asked to use the restroom and called Mom. I didn't say a word except to tell them that you've never done anything like that with me. They kept pressing if you ever gave me special treatment when I was in your class. I said that you were actually harder on me."

The room snorts because at least that's true. Andy is the type of student who needs to be pushed and challenged with schoolwork to show his full potential.

"Thank you, Andy, for speaking up for me. I'm s-so very sorry they've dragged you into this mess." I broke down after that.

They all circle me, holding onto me giving me their strength.

"Do you want me to call Rob or Ox?" Belinda asks and I shake my head.

"Maddox just went out of town for a few days on business and Rob is working. I don't want to burden them with this." I frown. "I'm so embarrassed." I cover my face with my hands.

"They can't get away with this. They can't speak to our kids without a parent present," Joseph says as everyone sits down and grows quiet.

"We think it might be from all the open record requests," Belinda informs him.

His eyes widen. "Retaliation?"

"Think about it. Piper and I find out all their dirty secrets and start to investigate and then she gets put on ice. This screams intimidation. She's been 'Teacher of the Year' for years then all of a sudden she's a bad guy?"

"I fucking hate this city." Joseph threads his fingers through his hair. "It makes me want to move back to Texas with our family and get away from all this shit." He turns and looks right at me. "I'm so sorry they are doing this to you for shedding light on the corrupt bullshit system."

"Thank you for being so supportive," I say and give a weak smile.

"Well, what is our next move? We can't just sit here and not have a plan to fight back," Irene, who has been our silent strength this entire time, asks.

I haven't even thought that far ahead. I'm just focusing on my next breath. The room stays quiet as we all think about the next steps.

"You should start exposing them for all the parents and teachers to see. Maybe we can get enough traction that a news station will pick it up," Andy says from near the TV.

"How about writing a blog and uncovering everything we've found?" Belinda starts brainstorming. "We could post the documents to back up all the accusations. They couldn't deny any of it because all the material came from them." She looks around the room at everyone. "All the emails and paperwork is stamped with the district's seal. Plus, I have access to every parent in the district since I'm on the PTA board. There might be others who this has happened to or someone who knows something else but is too afraid to come forward. We could blow this thing wide open."

"Do we really want to bring more heat to Piper?" Joseph asks. "Think about all the hounding it will cause."

I nod, not wanting to be in the limelight. "Jackie was horrible to me. The accusation makes me look like I'm a monster. What if they start to say I was inappropriate with a minor for everyone to hear? We all know it's not true, but once it's out there even if it's not true people will always link those words to me."

"Let's wait and hear back from that Tracey lady before we make any decisions," Irene says patting my knee that's been bouncing out of control.

"I think that's a good start," Joseph chimes in. "Andy, I want you to go to school tomorrow and keep an ear out if anything is said. I don't want to involve Sammy in this since he doesn't understand the gravity of the situation, but he will tell us if anything is said. Belinda and I will be up at the school first thing making sure that bitch, Jessica, or her psycho daughter don't come within twenty yards of our boy." Husband and wife share a nod. "If we need to go to the police and take a restraining order out on her we will. We have enough I think with all the crazy texts she's sent over the last few weeks to at least make it known we aren't going to allow her to continue to hurt us or you, Piper."

"Okay," I agree. It's not much, but the knot in my chest that's squeezing me tight lets up slightly. "Thank y'all so much for this. I'm not sure I'd survive this if I didn't have all of you."

The group comes in, pulls me up on wobbly legs, and we hug each other.

"This is what family does," Belinda assures me.

"Exactly," Irene agrees.

"Don't worry, Ms. Piper, we've got your back," Andy says. "The students will stand behind you."

I just hope this all plays out like we hope.

CHAPTER SEVENTEEN

Piper

TWO DAYS LATER I'M SEATED AT A CONFERENCE TABLE WITH Tracey, my union representatives, and her boss, Laurie. Across from us is the superintendent, Barry Carver, and Mitch Connors, the school district's attorney.

Parents and students have been trying to reach out to me wanting to know why I'm not there teaching. Rumors are swirling and I'm sure Jessica is fueling them. Andy came home the next day letting us know Jessica's daughter, Jenny, was saying I had a sexual affair with a student. Andy embarrassed her in the crowded hallway calling her trash and sent her fleeing from the area. According to him, the students don't believe the gossip and are defending me.

"We think it's in the best interest for you and the district to part ways, Ms. Caldwell, after looking over the accusations coming forward and the investigation done so far by the district," Mitch says after a few minutes.

I continue to look over the pages they've provided, none of which seem to have an official answer as to what they found.

"I don't understand. Where are the findings that say if I've done something or not?" I ask when I turn to the last page again.

"The District feels as though the work environment has become questionable and that all parties would be better off not working together."

"It doesn't say what I've done exactly, though. It just states that I'm no longer needed," I argue.

"Ms. Caldwell, if you want to escalate this further please know that I'm sure things will not be favorable for you in the future. We are willing to sign off with a raving review for your future employment in other districts if you so choose to follow this career path. The district is also willing to offer you a three-month severance."

My head jerks back in confusion. This is crazy. The documents don't list anything to do with being inappropriate with a student or show any violations I've committed. Why are we even having a conversation at all if they can't even tell me what I've violated?

"So you basically want to fire me but don't have the grounds for it," I state. I flip to the third page and point to the tenth line down on their demands. "If I sign this then it states that I'm not allowed on any of this district's property indefinitely once I sign. What if I want to come to a graduation or football game? If I haven't done anything wrong then why do I have to stay away?" I flip to the next page and say, "And here states that I'm not allowed to speak with anyone involved in the investigation. Again, there aren't any details showing that you are investigating any situation. Or what for that matter."

"This doesn't seem to make any s—" Tracey starts to say just as confused as I am but her boss, Laurie, cuts her off looking right at me.

"Piper, I think this is something that you need to consider. This will allow you to find work elsewhere without any negative recourse, like blemishing your teacher certification."

My face scrunches as if I've eaten a handful of sour candy.

"And I think you're more worried about keeping up your relationship with the district than what is in the best interest of me!" I point at my chest. "They aren't even able to put into writing what *investigation* they are performing and you want me to sign off on it as if that is in the best interest of me?"

She sucks in a gasp then sits a little straighter in her chair. "Ms. Caldwell," Laurie's voice changes instantly almost chastising.

"I'm not signing this," I jam my finger down on the documents. "I know that I can stay on administrative leave until my contract expires in June if I need to. And unless there is reason to fire me, which you have clearly not proven, then I can ride it out on the couch eating bonbons all the while collecting a check."

Belinda, Irene, and I have done a lot of research the last two days going through every scenario they might come up with. We never thought they'd come here and have nothing but just wanting me gone, though.

I go to stand and look over the room. "You have the opportunity to make this right and we can move on with both parties happy but you are choosing to go down a road to save face," I seethe. "I'm not going to tuck tail like I've done something I didn't do," I grit then walk my ass out of the conference room and into the hallway.

Tracey catches up to me before I push the glass doors open leading to the parking lot.

"Piper, wait!" she calls then advances to me. "I didn't know Laurie was going to champion their side. I've only been working here a short time and there is definitely a lot of back-scratching going on with her and the district." She covers her mouth when she realized what she just said.

"I appreciate your help, Tracey," I offer even though I'm not sure I can trust her yet. I think she's starting to see what Belinda and I have thought about. The union is just there to keep the peace and not what is in the best interests of the teachers who pay for a service.

She nods, understanding I'm not going to let her in on my next move.

"I'll give you a call soon," she says then walks back the way she came out.

I take a deep breath and take the path to my car only to find the superintendent leaning against my car door. "You should take the separation agreement, Ms. Caldwell. I'm sure someone in your situation would not need any unforeseen events to happen," Barry Carver states.

"Are you threatening me?"

He pushes off my door and stands towering over me.

"I'm telling you to keep your nose out of our business and your trap shut. You have no idea the trouble we could make for you if you don't drop this and slither away."

I swallow hard. "I-I haven't done anything wrong. You can't—"

He crowds me up against the car beside mine and lowers his head so he's in my face. "I've been here for over fifteen years and can do whatever the fuck I want."

My legs start to buckle but somewhere deep inside I gather the strength to stay upright.

"Is everything okay over here?" a female voice asks, thankfully interrupting his tirade. When I look over I see Megan, the receptionist who gathers all our open records requests.

Barry straightens, and with a deadly glare never leaving mine, he walks back toward the administration building. When he gets to the doors I finally take a breath I didn't realize I was holding.

"Are you okay? I heard what he was saying and knew I needed to step in." She comes over to me and rubs my upper arm.

"I-I don't know," I answer honestly. "He…I was getting…" I look around making sure this isn't some kind of alternative world where men walk around threatening women.

"Let's get you in the car, okay? Do you think you can drive or do we need to call someone?" she asks as she helps open my car door.

"No, I think I can manage," I state as the cold air from the vents hits my face cooling off all the sweat.

"When you get home check your text messages," she says as she starts to close the door.

"Wait, why?" I put my hand out to stop the door.

She gives me a sly little smile. "Because I got that entire inter-action on video. Mr. Carver is a bad little boy."

She shuts the door and heads towards the building where she works. The entire ride home my phone is blowing up with texts but I don't look at them. I'm not even sure how I drove from one place to the other but when I pulled up in the drive I see Belinda's car parked outside and Irene in the window of my living room. Once I enter the house, I'm bombarded with questions from both women. Finally seeing the state I'm in, they guide me over to the sofa. They wait patiently while I tell them everything from beginning to end of how the meeting went. I pull the video up and the three of us watch Mr. Carver verbally attack and intimidate me. I wince as I watch myself cower when he boxed me in.

Irene gasps bringing her hand up to cover her mouth in shock. "I can't believe a man would do that to a woman half his size," she says shaking her head.

"That limp dick is no man," Belinda seethes next to me then changes her tone looking at me. "Are you okay, Piper? I know that must've been horrifying to experience."

I nod. "I think so. I still can't believe he did that. If Megan hadn't had that video I would've thought I made it up in my head."

"What do you want to do next?" she asks, and Irene nods, clearly wanting to know the same.

That's the million-dollar question. What do I want to do? I could hide away and lay low until this blows over and everyone moves on to the next scandal or I could stand my ground and defend myself against those who think it's okay to try and ruin innocent lives to cover up their dirty deeds.

"We fight back."

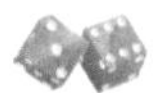

It's amazing what women can accomplish when they work together and have days of uninterrupted amounts of time on their hands.

With Maddox in Chicago doing business but coming home tomorrow, Belinda, Irene, and I have been busy laying out our next steps. We created a blog page and made sure to set it up just the way we wanted it to look. Irene admitted that she wasn't well versed with technology being close to eighty and not ever having to use it but she did know an attorney who we could trust to help look over all our material with the school district. She wanted us to make sure I wasn't breaking any laws or could be sued for releasing all these documents. Jolene couldn't believe what she was reading or seeing. She's not in educational law but was very excited to jump in and help read over our blogs to keep them precise and on track.

"Facts over feelings," she said after giving us a revised edit of our first blog to be posted. "I know this is super personal but you want to make sure this is more about the facts than the emotions you're having," she explained.

What she said made sense and after rereading our first entry, I took myself and my feelings out of the situation and it had an even more powerful statement behind it. She is writing up all of our findings in a legal capacity to turn over to the Department of Education here in Nevada.

We only launched the blog a few hours ago and it already has five thousand views and climbing. It explains what is coming and my story of how they are trying to push me out of my teaching job. Andy and his friends started posting about it on their social media and it's spreading like wildfire. Comments are pouring in and we are having a hard time trying to keep up with them. The first article is set to be released in a few hours. Belinda and I have the first three articles written and the evidence to back up our claims ready and scheduled to be published every other day at six in the evening. Jolene has checked and rechecked them to make sure there can't be any blowback from the district or the school board members because they are considered public figures.

"Has your man called?" Belinda asks from her seat on the sofa, laptop on her lap as she prepares for the emails to be sent out with our first article to all the parents in the district.

"Not today. Last night he said he was going to be really busy in meetings all day but he'd call as soon as he got back to the hotel tonight."

"When are you going to tell him about what happened to you? Joseph would be pissed if I didn't tell him," she says lowering her glasses down her nose and giving me a knowing look.

"There's nothing he can do from where he's at five states away. I'll tell him tomorrow night or the next day. He seemed a little stressed having to go to this meeting."

"He's a banker, right?" she asks.

"Yes, and he owns businesses," I say. I start to tell her more about those businesses but an alarm on her phone goes off.

"It's going live in five minutes," she squeals. "The emails will be sent out five minutes after that. Everyone who's been on the site has the option to sign up for alerts of new content so hopefully this will reach all the ones who have already been on the page today." I just nod as nerves start to sink in. "Hey," Belinda reaches out for my hand and gives it a squeeze, grounding me and taking my focus off my worries. "It's going to be okay. They can't hurt you any more than they already have."

The front door opens and we snap our heads in that direction. Irene comes in with bags full of things. I smell food in one of them but I also see fabric coming out of another.

"Thought we could eat since I know we skipped lunch earlier," she says heading to the kitchen. "Is Rob here? I brought enough for him."

"He is taking the closing shift this entire week," I answer. "I think he's met a girl and wants to save up to take her out."

"Well, isn't that nice," she says. "I'll leave his in the fridge for when he comes home." After a few minutes, she comes back with plates and wine glasses. "Thought we could drink and calm the nerves. I haven't been this riled up since right before getting married."

We all laugh as the pings from messages start to sound from the laptop.

"Here we go," Belinda cheers as the view counter starts to tick up showing a swarm of people visiting our page and reading the article.

I really hope we are able to shed light on this dark cloud the district has brought on the schools all in the name of greed and that this will have the outcome we want without getting bit in the ass.

CHAPTER EIGHTEEN

I DIDN'T WANT TO COME HERE AND BE A PART OF THIS conversation but I know it had to happen. When Arturo called and said he needed me, I was at his place in less than fifteen minutes. When he said he needed me to come to Chicago with him to have a sit down with Marco Gallo I knew I was headed out of state.

We rule Nevada and most all of the West Coast but our plans have always been to expand and get a foothold toward the East Coast. Marco Gallo rules Chicago with an iron fist and he was our way in. At first, Arturo and Marco had arranged for his son, Luca, to marry Marco's only daughter, Bianca, but when Luca up and left for an extended amount of time, he came back with a wife and a baby on the way. Marco had been furious and thought it was an insult from Arturo. A lot of back and forth and threats later, they agreed to have Bianca and Luca's second-in-command, Cassio, marry and bind the families together with that connection. Except Bianca and Cassio haven't gotten married yet and Marco is on a rampage. What he doesn't realize is that it's Bianca holding it up.

This meeting is to iron out the details and move the marriage forward…and soon. Arturo didn't want to bring Luca along with him thinking it would be in bad form so he called on me to join him and Bobby. Kendall and Wyatt are still in post-honeymoon bliss and didn't make the trip, though, we gave Marco her regrets for missing this meeting.

When we aren't meeting with Marco, Thomas and I have been scouting out the city to see the best areas where we can set up shop. Arturo and Bobby have been visiting several warehouses outside the city with his men getting the lay of the land.

Marco snaps his fingers and a new set of drugged-out women come slinking into the room. I skipped the meal for fear of getting food poisoning at this dingy place he brought us to tonight. It's not any better than the last several nights we've had to endure his presence.

"Come, come. Enjoy the women," he waves his hands to showcase them dancing on each other. I gag. A dumpster would be more sanitary than this place.

"We didn't come here for that, Marco, but night after night you keep pushing this," Arturo says, staring at him with disgust. "I don't touch anyone but my wife."

Marco makes a sour face and then turns his head my way but I cut off his words with the shake of my head.

"You have the world at your disposal and I'll never know why you don't partake in the drippings of our fruits," Marco taunts as he pulls one of the ladies in his lap and starts groping her.

My empty stomach feels the urge to heave so I stand and maneuver around the table trying to avoid knocking into drinks or the women lurking around.

"We're taking our leave. Enjoy the evening," I hear Bobby say.

I'm out on the sidewalk taking in the fresh air when both Bobby and Arturo come join me.

"If I didn't love my daughter so much I'd find another way to get a foothold in this territory," Arturo says talking about his son's wife, Gemma. Gemma is Bianca's best friend and made Arturo promise not to send her back under Marco's roof.

Our SUV pulls up and our team who's been surrounding us walks us to the vehicle. Darren drives after telling him to circle the city.

"What if we marry Cassio and Bianca and then put a hit out on him and his top associates?" I ask. "Make it look so messy there'd be no way it could have come from us."

Arturo leans back in his seat, thinking.

"We'd have to already be set up here for the takeover," Bobby says thoughtfully. "I'm sure there are a lot of people who want Marco gone but haven't succeeded yet."

"This won't be an easy feat," Arturo says. "We are going to need to find the right people in place for us to successfully rule both Vegas and Chicago."

"We could send ten men from each family here to start building our presence on the low. They can start recruiting men and building our army. The gangs here run rampant, some as young as twelve years old. We'd need to use a lot of force at first," I say pondering the best way to make this work.

"It might work," Bobby agrees.

"I've run some numbers and it's going to cost each Family around a hundred million if we want to do this right and rule this town," I tell them. "There is going to be a lot of bloodshed involved too. It helps that we've got four organizations coming in but it'll be messy before it's all over."

"That's a lot to put on the line not knowing the exact outcome," Bobby laments.

"It will be but the reward of having Chicago and the West Coast will strengthen our hold. Not to mention the return on investment will triple," I add. "The projected numbers look real good once we take over this city. The things we'll add here will boost the income and make us more powerful than those Families on the East Coast."

"Once we get back home we should get with Kendall, sit down, and go over what we want to do and then what we need to do to make it happen." Arturo nods his head. "I need a drink," he grumbles. "We are leaving tomorrow after lunch. I miss Adele."

"Fine by me," Bobby says.

"Darren, take us back to the hotel," I call out to him from the backseat.

"Yes, sir."

"How are things going with Piper? You haven't mentioned a proposal so I assume she's not there yet?" Bobby turns his head toward me.

"She's wanting to take things slow."

"But you're ready," Arturo chimes in.

"I've known for a while now."

"Gemma raves about her and I know Adele would like to meet her as well."

"Does she know who you are and what you do?" Bobby asks.

I shake my head. "I want to tell her but—"

Bobby rubs his forehead. "Where did we go wrong, Art?"

"Putting yourself out there is hard but not telling her and letting her fall in love with you before getting all the details is cruel. She has a right to know what she's walking into. Things in the dark always have a way of coming into the light," Arturo lectures.

"I know but—"

"No buts about it, Son. We helped raise you and we expect better than this. She deserves better than this. If you can't be honest with her then she isn't the one for you."

My hands pull into fists. She is the one for me. "I'm telling her when we get back." I grind my teeth hating to be treated like a child.

Arturo puts a gentle hand on my knee and gets my attention. "We are hard on you because we care," he says and the tension loosens. I know he's right and that they have the best of intentions for me. "You know we've said the same things to Luca and Wyatt. Lord knows you boys always do things the hard way."

We pull up to the hotel and head to our suites. After tossing my key on the table, I pull out my phone and see it's late. I'm sure Piper is already in bed, having to get up early and head to school for the day. I send a text message instead.

Maddox: My love for you is like dividing by zero, it cannot be defined.

Knowing she's asleep I strip out of my clothes and walk into the shower to rid myself of the smell of smoke from the nasty club Marco took us to. Sometime later, I crawl under the sheets and think about how I'm going to tell Piper all about who I am and what I actually do. Arturo and Bobby are right and I need to man up if I want a future with her. I'm just hoping the truth isn't going to send her running.

Our jet is delayed due to bad weather so we get back to Vegas late the following night. It feels like forever since I last saw Piper and I'm itching to get my hands on her. And tongue. And dick. We'd spoken briefly on the phone after the second delay and I told her to be at my house and naked waiting for me. She's seemed very distracted the last few phone calls we had and my mind raced to thinking she knows about me before I had the chance to tell her. She never alluded to knowing but something is off about her. I've had some of my team on standby at the ends of her street and they haven't reported anything out of the ordinary. They did mention her coming home from work early one afternoon but when I asked her about her day she'd mentioned not feeling well. She'd brushed it off and said that Irene and Belinda were there for her. I was tempted to call Rob to check on her so my team didn't have their cover blown but decided to wait until I got home to find out.

The house is dark when I come in with only a few lights on throughout. I pad my way up the stairs and a thrill comes over me. If I was a pussy I'd say it was butterflies at the thought of my woman naked in my bed asleep. The door is closed and I silently turn the knob. The moon is out tonight and the reflection coming in through the windows outlines her figure on the bed. I strip my clothes off and walk over to her side. My instincts tell me to wake her up and confess all of my truths, but looking down at her and seeing her in the flesh pushes those thoughts away. *Tomorrow.* I'll reveal it all tomorrow. Tonight I'm going to get my fill of her and pour all the love I have into her. Drown her in my love so she has no choice but to stay with me.

She moves onto her back and the sheet pulls down revealing her naked chest and I groan at the sight. She stirs with my noise. Her eyes barely open when she sees me. "Maddox," she says sleepily and her arm reaches out for me. "You're home."

I shudder at her calling this place home too. She's right where she belongs.

"I love you so much, Piper," I say tossing the sheets back and crawling on top of her.

"Love you too," she mumbles, still not fully awake.

I should let her sleep but my body has other plans. I latch onto her hard nipple and trail my fingers down the valley of her stomach to her pussy. Her body withers and she begins to moan. I love that I do this to her.

"I've missed you so much," I say then switch to the other nipple.

"Ah, I—" She stops talking when my fingers plunge into her hot, wet core. She's fully awake now and her hips are rocking with the motion of my fingers taking in all the pleasure. "I need to talk to you about something that happened," she pants but grinds down working towards that orgasm.

"We'll talk tomorrow," I mumble against her skin. "Let me have tonight to make up for being away."

Her legs lock into place and I know she going over the moment I feel her walls quiver. Her orgasm takes over and I quickly pull my fingers out and shove my dick in her pussy. She's so tight it feels like she's trying to push me out and I groan at the squeeze. Piper calls my name as I pound into her, chasing my own release and trying to prolong hers.

Hitching her thigh up higher on my waist, I change our angle and just when she's wrung from her first orgasm she calls out that another one is coming as I plunge in deep making her gasp.

"Maddox," she moans and grabs for my shoulders to hold on as I piston my hips trying to crawl inside her body to connect us forever.

"You like this angle?" I grit, sweat forming on my forehead. "You like taking it from your man?"

"Yes, yes," she chants as she pulls me down to her lips. "Give it to me."

My tongue invades her mouth and caresses hers. They dance as I feel pulsing in my balls. I pin her to the pillow with my lips and upper body. She's gasping with every thrust as her walls tighten around my throbbing cock.

"Need you to come, baby," I pant knowing my time is almost up and my load is going to erupt.

Not three more pumps and she's screaming my name. I follow right behind as I continue to drive into her making sure to empty my entire sack as I collapse on top of her. For a moment, it's only the sound of heavy breathing that fills the dark room.

"Welcome home, MadDog," she giggles as she runs her fingers through my damp hair.

"Next time you're coming with me," I say and use her bare tits as a pillow. "I'm an addict who can't quit you."

I finally roll over onto my back, taking her with me to lay on my chest. She plants her hand on my chest as my fingers flicker over the skin on her back.

"We need to talk—" she begins but I cut her off using my fingers to cover her lips.

"Not tonight. We'll talk tomorrow about everything."

I look down at her and the glow from the moon reveals some puffiness under her eyes, like she's been crying. Part of me wants to ask and talk now but at this moment I really just want to bask in us. We'll talk and then find a way to work it out.

Tomorrow.

CHAPTER NINETEEN

Piper

WE DON'T WAKE TILL ALMOST NOON THE NEXT DAY, exhausted from our nighttime activities. Though I'm sure mine is also from all the sleepless nights after being put on leave from my job. Maddox has been very attentive since we've been cooking lunch, his hands always finding a way to my skin.

"Did you want to come with me to see my parents today or do you have work to catch up on?" I lean back in my seat on the covered outside patio by the pool. My muscles have a sweet ache with every move of my body.

"Of course I'll go." He wipes his hands with a napkin and takes a long pull from his drink. "Did you take today off from work?" he asks as he reaches down to hitch my leg up between his, massaging my foot and calf.

I've been putting off this conversation until now hoping this won't change anything for us. Being labeled something as horrible as they are trying to make me out to be is hard to come back from. The blog has exploded locally amongst our little school circle. I have so many people commenting their support and wanting me to reveal more. Belinda has most of the PTA moms and dads making posts about wanting the school board to be transparent about all the documents. A lot of parents are calling for the administration to resign along with all of the school members involved in the schemes that are being run in the name of school funding.

There are a select few, however, who are riding around with pitchforks wanting to burn me at the stake. They're making up situations and smearing my name with no evidence to back it up trying to discredit me at every turn. Some of it is so outlandish there is no way a person would believe I'd be capable of such crimes and still be employed by the school district, let alone become Teacher of the Year that many times in a row. We believe that those trolls are either board members using fake accounts to spread false lies or their family members. Everything that has been released has had factual documentation to back up the claims.

Belinda and I released the most recent blog involving the board members. We gave a tease of what was to come by showing a few documents. The evidence backing up our claims took hours to upload onto the page so we decided to write a blog on each member involved to have their own. Brad Rollings has been on the board for the last six years and is an owner of a fitness gym but also runs a lawn business. The major issue with this is that the sitting President and Vice President, Ryan Jackson and Donald Tucker, approved Brad's company to be allotted the contract to service the school and install the turf. The amount of money that was given to him and continues to be given is exorbitant. Belinda and I called around to other districts of our size and the discrepancy is tens of thousands of dollars. Not to mention the installation on the football field was also outrageously overpriced. The school overpaid by a hundred thousand dollars to his company according to papers that were submitted by his company but were not initially released to us. Belinda got in touch with Megan, the receptionist helping us there at the building, and she was able to find the original receipt and sent it over to us. She was also able to find other companies who put in a bid for the lawn service and turf installation for half the cost, but they were never brought up at the school board meeting let alone voted on. In fact, nothing was ever voted on at any of the meetings but was automatically granted to Brad and his company.

Not only is this a huge conflict of interest, but they are padding the costs making hundreds of thousands of dollars that the kids are losing out on because of underhanded deals being made. All of that money is being put into the board's pockets or bank accounts.

"I've been off from work for a while," I say and his hands still on my leg. He opens his mouth to ask the questions I've been avoiding, but my phone starts to ring. I quickly scoop it up seeing the new facility where my parents are at. "Hello."

"Is this Piper Caldwell?" A woman's voice comes over the line.

"Yes, it is."

"I'm sorry but we need you to come up here to the building. Your mother has had a horrible reaction to something and she's not doing very well—"

My hand flies to my mouth, "Oh my god! Is she okay?" My hand starts to tremble against my ear.

"I'm not sure, ma'am, but we ask for you to get here as soon as you possibly can."

I don't wait to hear another word before I'm flying through the house and out to my car. Just as I'm about to climb in an arm circles me.

"What's going on, Piper? What's happened?"

"I-I don't know they said Mom had a horrible reaction to something and that I need to get there quick," I answer and see his eyes widen.

"You can't drive in this condition. Let me take you," he offers but I feel like we're wasting time talking.

"Fine but we need to go now," I urge.

"Of course, let's take my car." He leads me to one of his vehicles parked next to mine in the large garage.

He is on his phone giving out commands to someone as he pulls out and I watch out the tinted window, my legs bouncing.

"She'll be fine, Piper." Maddox lays his strong hand on my knee to try and calm me. Any other time it'd work, but I've got a sinking feeling in my gut.

Ever since I woke up today I've felt like something was going to happen. I just thought it was going to be me telling him about what the school was doing to me.

When we pull up to the facility, he leaves the car by the curb and races to catch up with me at the door. We speed walk in together to the nurses' desk. They see us coming and a woman with glasses waves us over. Her expression has my knees buckling.

"Ms. Caldwell, they are doing everything they can to stabilize her," the lady says as she heads down the hall with us on her tail.

"What happened?" I ask.

"I'm not in charge of her case so I'm not privy to the details, ma'am."

"You better go and find somebody that is then," Maddox barks.

We stop right outside her room and we see three nurses in there along with a doctor looking over paperwork.

"Ms. Caldwell, I'm Dr. Barkley," he says in greeting as we walk in. "It seems that your mother was given too much of one of her new medications and has had a reaction. We are closely monitoring her to make sure she remains stable until those meds are out of her system. We've got her intubated and sedated to give her body a chance to heal and recover."

"How is that possible? Don't you know how much to give a patient? How can you over-medicate if her chart and your system are being followed?" I've got my hands wrapped around hers. She feels cold and her skin looks grayer than it did a few days ago. She now has a tube down her throat and is on a breathing machine.

How could this happen? When we transferred my parents over here from the last place, the doctors were confident that this new drug might help Mom and improve some of the conditions that she was facing from being bedridden all day. They assured me that they'd seen tremendous results in other patients who recently started it that helped with their brainwaves.

"It seems that the new drug is only administered once a day for her but all the others are taken twice. We are looking into the matter but know that we will be doing a full investigation into the nurse that was assigned to your mother."

"Lot of good that's going to do her mother right now," Maddox spits. I can feel the anger rolling off him in waves.

"We understand and are here to do everything we can to make sure she is given the best care and that something like this will never happen again," the doctor acknowledges.

I can't listen to any more of this and drag the chair that's in the corner over to sit down. The doctor stays a little longer before leaving the room saying he'll be back shortly to continue to monitor her vitals.

A moment later I feel a warm hand placed on my shoulder. "I'm gonna step out in the hall to make a call then I'll be back. If you need me, I'll just be through the door. I'm not going far."

I nod then turn back to Mom. I hear the click of the door and fall apart. After everything that happened earlier this week, I didn't think I had any more tears left in my body but once again I'm proven wrong.

"Oh Mama," I cry and bury my face against her hip. "I'm so sorry this happened. I never wanted this for you or Dad. What am I supposed to do? What do I do to help you both? This wasn't supposed to be how you lived your life," I mumble as I soak the blanket. "Tell me what to do. Tell me how to fix this. I really need you right now." I continue to cry. Her body is slowly deteriorating after all these years. She doesn't even look like the person she was years ago. Is this really a life she'd want? Am I strong enough to say and do what I've only ever thought about in my head?

As time goes by the light filtering in through the window changes. When the sound of the door opens and Dr. Barkley walks in, her monitors are beeping more frequently and I know that it's not a good sign.

"I'm just going to check a few things," he informs me as he looks over at the monitor and checks her tubes.

I wipe my eyes and nose while I watch him work.

"I don't want her chest cracked," I state.

"Excuse me?" he asks and turns my way giving me his full attention.

"I don't want you or the nurses to crack her chest if she codes." My voice breaks at the end of my sentence. "Breaking her breast-bone is not an option for her."

"Ms. Caldwell, I know this is rough right now but are you sure about this?"

"I don't want you to do it. I've researched it many of times and I don't want that for her. I do want any other life-saving actions to be taken but not that one."

"I understand." He nods. "I'll put this in her chart right away. Please sign here and I'll let her team know." I walk over to the com-puter and sign the electronic pad attached to the desk mounted on the wall. "I'm really sorry that this happened to your mother." I nod and he turns to leave.

As he is walking out the door, Rob comes in out of breath with Belinda and Irene right behind him.

"Oh, honey, I'm so sorry." Irene crushes me with an embrace and I lean into it.

"Tell us what you need." Belinda places a hand on my shoul-der for comfort.

"I'm not sure. I think we are just in a waiting game. Her vitals are up and down. I think it's her heart that they're worried about."

"Pipe," Rob starts but I know he's never been good at express-ing his emotions, so he stops himself from saying anything.

I reach out my hand to him and give it a squeeze. I know what he wants to say and give him a nod in acknowledgment.

Maddox walks through the door with Thomas right behind him. They have bags in both of their arms. The smell of food makes my stomach grumble but eating is the last thing I want to do.

"Thought everyone might need a quick bite to eat." Maddox hands his bags over to Rob where he places them down on the counter. "I had Thomas run and get you a change of clothes," he says to me as Thomas steps up with an outreached hand.

"Thank you, Thomas." I offer a small smile.

"I'm sorry to hear about your mom," Thomas says then nods over to the hospital bed. "If you need anything I'll be around."

"Thank you."

He nods then takes his leave out the door but goes to stand across the hall against the wall watching as staff walks by.

"Let's make you a plate, dear." Irene and Rob start to plate the food and we all sit in silence barely tasting it.

After a while, Belinda is needed back at her home so I stand and stretch to thank her for being here. She leaves and the beeping from the machines is once again the only noise to fill the air in the room.

"Honey, why don't you go and visit your dad. Walk around for a little bit then come back. I'm sure sitting in that chair isn't good for you," Irene suggests. "We'll stay here and let you know if something changes."

I hadn't even thought about my dad this entire time and guilt settles in. How could I forget my dad?

I change clothes in Mom's attached bathroom and splash some cold water on my puffy face. When I come out, Maddox is waiting by the door looking down at his phone.

"I'll come with you, babe," he says then pockets his phone as I approach.

"You don't have to. He's only one floor up," I say, but he shakes his head keeping in step. "Thank you for calling my friends."

We enter the elevator and he presses the second floor button.

"Piper, I'm so sorry—"

I place my fingers over his mouth, stopping him from finishing. Shaking my head I say, "Not right now. I can't fall apart again."

He nods as the doors open and we arrive on our floor.

Outside Dad's room a man in the same type of suit as Thomas stands at attention.

"I don't want the full explanation right now, but is there something I need to know about all these men who stand around looking secret service?"

"It's…" he begins to say but stops. "Not right now, but we'll talk about all of this at a different time. Just know that there is nothing to worry about."

"Okay." I nod at the man by the door before walking into my dad's room.

His room has the shade down and a soft light in the corner gives off just enough illumination to show he's in bed. His normal routine has him eating early in the evening and in bed right around the time the sun goes down. Dad has always been an early riser and that is one thing the accident didn't take from him. He's up at a sharp five in the morning. I walk over to the dresser and mirror and see photos of Mom and him along with me mixed in. His nurse points out all of us every morning and tells him who each one is.

Slowly I walk over and stand by his bed watching his chest rise and fall. He snores with every breath and it reminds me of my childhood. Mom always complained that she never got a full night's rest because he was sawing logs. My fingers lightly graze the back of his hand needing to touch him. I feel like such a failure with their care and hope that one day I'll be able to forgive myself for not being able to do more.

I don't stay long because I don't want to wake him and mess up his routine, so I step quietly back over to the door where Maddox is perched. We walk out together and he grips my hand in his.

"I'm here," he assures me and it means the world even if I can't form the words to tell him right now.

We retrace our steps and as we come off the elevator Maddox's phone goes off.

"I need to take this real quick," he says and I nod.

"I'm going to grab a coffee before heading back. Want one?"

"That'd be great, babe," he says before stepping off to the side to answer his phone.

At the coffee machine, I grab a cup and start pushing the digital buttons for which one I want when a conversation nearby filters through my ears.

"Must be nice to have a rich boyfriend buy your way into this place. Can you believe he was able to jump her parents to the front of the line?" a female voice asks.

"Money can buy a lot of things," another female voice says.

"Yeah, but now Kelli is not going to be able to work in this state ever again," the first female says.

"That's because she didn't review the chart and made a mistake. A big one, and that poor old woman is suffering for it."

"I just don't like how people have been waiting forever to get on the list and because you have millions of dollars you can skip the lines. It's not fair."

"It's not our place to determine what is fair and what isn't. We are here to give the best care and are paid handsomely for it. If you have a problem with it then go see HR," the second female states.

My mind is reeling. Is she talking about me and my parents? The insurance company found this place for me, right? Would Maddox step in and get involved in this? Just as I'm coming around the corner, abandoning the coffee to face the voices and ask questions, an alarm sounds and Rob rushes into the hallway.

"Piper!"

A team of staff is making their way toward him and I know in my heart what is happening. My feet pick up and I rush into the room as the medical staff attaches the pads to her chest and another is squeezing a plastic-looking balloon over her mouth. In the distance, I faintly hear Thomas calling for Maddox.

"Clear!"

Everyone pulls their hands away and Dr. Barkley places the paddles against the pads on the sides of her chest. We hear a charge then a boom as Mom's chest shoots up off the bed. Her fragile little body looks broken and beaten after all these years of what she's endured. I'm standing there frozen as I watch them, waiting to see if her heartbeat starts on the monitor. After a few seconds of nothing hands are back on her.

"Charge again," Dr. Barkley says.

The rev of the machine fills the room and I hold my breath.

Please, please, I chant in my head not wanting to live in a place without her even though she's been gone for years.

"Clear!"

Hands pull back again as he places the pads in the same spot. The boom jolts her body again as he pulls the paddles back. The room is still as the anticipation of a steady beat never comes.

"Charge again," Dr. Barkley repeats but I've had enough.

Mom has had enough.

"NO!" I'm shaking my head as tears blur my vision and I walk over to her bedside. "No," I whisper. "She's had enough. She's had enough."

"Ms. Caldwell, we can keep trying—" he tries but I can't hear that and shake my head.

"It's okay, Mama, you can go now." I start to sob and lay my head on her middle with my arms around her. "I'm so sorry."

In the distance, I hear words being spoken about the time of death and sob harder. Loud voices are spoken but I tune them out. I feel hands on my back in comfort as the room becomes quiet again. The sound of footsteps heading out the door is the last thing I remember before I close my eyes and memories of me and Mom flood my mind. Years and years run like a reel of my time with her.

"Honey…" I'm brought out of my memories and pull back from Mom's body to look over at Irene.

She hands me some tissue as tears run down her cheeks. Rob is over in the corner silently crying and hugging himself. Maddox is sitting next to me, his head down, looking at the floor, but his hand is on my back. Movement has his head pop up and he looks warily at me.

"I-I'm so sorry, Piper. I—"

I nod because finding words for sympathy is always hard in times like these. I've learned that over the years since their car accident.

"It's okay." My head continues to nod even though I don't mean for it to. "Can I have a moment alone?" I ask and look around the room.

"Of course, dear," Irene says then walks over to Rob. She takes him into her arms and they lean on each other as they exit the room.

"I don't want to leave you alone," Maddox tries gently.

"I just need a minute. I'll be right out."

His eyes roam over my face searching for something but he only nods. He leans in and kisses my forehead before standing and walking out the door, not fully closing it. Once he's gone, I turn back to the bed. She looks like she's sleeping. Carefully I pull her gown into place making sure she's covered before pulling the covers up to her chest. Mom was always cold-natured when I was growing up—like me—and we'd have a blanket on hand at all times. I tuck a few strands of hair behind her ear and gently smooth down the rest of it. Leaning in, I kiss her forehead and hold my lips to her skin.

"I hope that I can make you proud, Mama," I say fighting back another wave of tears. "I love you so much and will miss you every day." With one last kiss to her head, I straighten up and take a step back from her.

Silently, I walk to the door and open it the rest of the way. My soul feels drained, as though I have nothing left to give. The first thing I see in the hall is Maddox with Dr. Barkley up against the wall. His fists have the doctor's white coat bunched at the neck.

"Maddox!" I shout and rush over. "Let him go," I say grabbing his upper arm to try and separate the two. I look around and see a wall of men blocking the view and not letting anyone pass as this unfolds. "Maddox, stop!"

Thomas comes over after hearing me and maneuvers his body to help separate them. He's talking in his friend's ear and Maddox is breathing rapidly. Dr. Barkley finally stands up tall after catching his breath and tries to fix his crumpled coat.

"Ms. Caldwell, we'll need you to tell us what arrangements you'd like—"

"You don't speak to her after what you did," Maddox spits and tries to take a step towards the doctor again but Thomas blocks his path. "I'll tell you what needs to be done."

Something stirs in my veins and the weight of everything that has happened boils to the top.

"That's enough," I say, but he doesn't hear me. He continues to go at Dr. Barkley.

I walk right up to him and pull his chin down to look at me. His eyes are wild and ready for a fight. I've worked with kids enough to know when they haze over and nothing is penetrating to get their attention.

"Did you pay to have my parents here?" I ask and am met with a glossy look.

"What?" His face jerks back confused at my question.

"It's all such a blur in my head when I got the phone call about this place, but it's all starting to connect."

"Why are you asking me about this, Piper? What's going on?" He tries to soften his stance but his muscles are tight and locked into place.

"I overheard some of the staff talking earlier."

Maddox's eyes shoot over Dr. Barkley's way and narrow. "It's been a long day and I think we should head home—"

"Okay, but answer me first."

"Piper, I don't know what you want me to say," he says avoiding the question.

"What I want you to say is the truth! I want you to tell me that you had nothing to do with arranging for my parents to come here. That my mom was killed because the insurance company picked a place that hires lazy nurses that don't know how to do her job." I start getting louder and a fire is lit inside me. I'm not sure if it's actually me saying all this because it's what I feel or if it is all the hurt and frustration over the past week and today is the tipping point.

"I thought this place was better—"

"How could you not have talked with me? Why did you go behind my back and do this?" Tears well up in my eyes.

"I thought I was helping—"

"By manipulating me?"

"I saw you struggling—"

"I'm not your responsibility and some charity case, Maddox! I don't need someone to come and save me!" I shout.

"Look, you're exhausted. Let's go home and talk, then we can make the arrangements for your mom—"

I throw my hands up in the air. "This right here is what I'm talking about. I don't need your help. I don't need anyone's help. Just because you were born with a gold spoon in your mouth doesn't give you the right to sweep in and bulldoze everything to get your way or manipulate the situation to fit your narrative."

My body is shaking. Rage is vibrating off me and I can't turn it off. I'm in fight-or-flight mode at this point.

"I thought I could help—"

"And look where that got me! My mom is dead!" I yell and point to the room that she's lying in. "Dead!"

I can see the hurt in his eyes after saying that and I hate myself for it. I feel an arm come around my shoulders and I go to elbow whoever it belongs to but it gets blocked.

"Pipe, that's enough," Rob says and I grab the front of his shirt, holding on for dear life. "It's going to be okay. We'll get through this." He pulls me in tight and wraps both arms around me. "We always do," he whispers in my ear.

"She's gone!" I wail and the flood gates open again. "She's gone!" I cry into his shirt.

"I know," he whispers.

"Do it now," I hear a growl at my back where I'm turned away from Maddox.

A small prick pinches at my upper arm and I struggle for Rob to release me. "Oww," I complain then break his hold, but my body is falling and I feel as though I'm diving into a fuzzy tunnel. I can see a bright light but it feels far away. Familiar strong arms come around me and I'm lifted. My head feels heavy and lobs back while my mouth turns dry.

"I'm so sorry, Piper."

The light starts to fade and it becomes dark.

CHAPTER TWENTY

Piper

I WAKE THE NEXT DAY ALONE IN MY BEDROOM. I GET UP AND stretch out my sore aching muscles and find it hard to breathe through my nose. Realizing why I feel like this is a punch to the gut and have to sit down on the edge of the bed. A wave of sadness hits me hard and I have to suck in a breath to keep from having a panic attack. Once I've got that under control, I walk to the bathroom, avoiding the mirror, and turn on the shower. I'm not sure how long I stand there but when the water turns ice cold I turn the knob to off.

I hear voices in the other room and flinch thinking how horrible I was last night. Sitting down on the bed, I try not to make a sound and feel like such a coward at the moment. Maddox probably wants nothing to do with me and I don't blame him after attacking him for only trying to help me. I've let my pride stand in the way a lot since coming back from college and having to care for my parents.

I send a text instead hoping to start a line of communication and see if I can salvage the damage I've done.

> Me: Why do plants hate math? Because it gives them square roots!

I wait for a few minutes, still listening to the muffled voices, my heart hoping he comes through the door. When he doesn't I type out another text.

> Me: I'm really sorry about last night and would like to talk if you're available.

I put my phone down and take a deep breath. Sitting around having a pity party is not being productive at all. I'm sure there is a list a mile long I need to do to get my mom situated.

Getting up, I slide into my house slippers and turn the knob on my door. Walking down the hall, I come into the living room where Rob and Belinda are on the couch drinking from mugs.

"Morning," I greet above a whisper.

They both turn.

"Oh my gosh, Piper. Come sit down. I've brought your favorite donuts and Rob has some coffee for you." Belinda stands and motions for me to sit down next to her. "I know this is a stupid question but how are you?"

I pause before answering. "I'm okay. It's hard to think about but I know that she wouldn't have wanted to continue to live like that. Her and Dad were so active before the crash and if she were in her right mind she'd have hated being that way."

"It's probably one of the hardest decisions you'll ever have to make, honey." Belinda places a hand on my knee and gives it a squeeze. "Do you think you should speak with an attorney about malpractice?"

Rob comes back in and hands me a steaming cup of coffee.

"Thank you," I say. "I don't have any ill will towards the facility because I do know accidents happen. I just hope that they can learn from this and take steps so that it doesn't ever happen again.

"What can we do to help with the arrangements? The rehab place called and was asking. I told them we'd call back in the next few hours," Rob explains.

"I'm not sure what we can do. I'll call in a few minutes and find out what the next steps are. I know that my parents wanted to be cremated."

Belinda has a notepad out writing everything down as I speak to the HR coordinator. We make all the plans to have her body sent over to the funeral home where she'll be cremated. After a few more calls, things are ironed out and my cup is empty. Rob refills all our cups and we sit in silence for a bit.

"Have you heard from Maddox?" I ask Rob as I check the screen on my phone for the thousandth time willing it to flash with a text from him. As the time passes I'm beginning to think he's avoiding me.

Rob shakes his head. "I tried calling right after I woke up but it went to voicemail."

"Oh." My mouth turns down in a frown.

"He was so distraught last night, Pipe. He's probably just giving you some space," he follows up. "It took a lot of convincing from Thomas and Darren to bring you back here."

I don't respond as I stare out the front window and think for a bit. Why hasn't he called or responded to my texts though? The silence stretches as we sit there.

"The blog is blowing up," Belinda speaks up after a while and I'm thankful to be pulled out of my thoughts.

"You both need to be careful. I've heard from several friends at the high school that if your name is mentioned, there's automatic punishment for the students," Rob warns. "But on the flip side, the students are saying a lot of staff is sweating bullets scared of what the next documents are going to reveal."

"Really?" I ask.

"The one last night about Brad Rollings has over a hundred thousand views. The comment section has fifteen hundred comments with stories about him and his *company*. It's weird that so many people are now willing to talk but only after someone else spoke up about it first," Belinda says.

"I really didn't think it'd be this big to be honest," I admit.

"Well, get ready because a friend of mine has a family member who works at the news station and wants an interview with you."

I shake my head. "I don't want any of this. I only wanted to bring to light the issues because I didn't want the kids to suffer because of the choices the adults were making to abuse the system."

"I don't think you have much of a choice at this point, Pipe," Rob says. "I think the district was hoping to sweep this under the rug like all the times before. I don't think they expected this to snowball like it has. It's only a matter of time before the state will get involved."

"Yeah, and I hope the little union person gets lumped into the fold with them," Belinda says heatedly.

Rob checks his watch and then stands. "I'm headed to work before meeting up with some suppliers later this evening."

"Everything going okay up there? I need to get caught up with the invoices," I say. "I haven't heard from Oliver in the last few days. Has he come by?"

"He didn't want me to tell you but he has pneumonia and is at home resting."

"What? Why didn't anyone say anything?"

"You've had a lot going on lately and we wanted to let you have some time away from having to worry about the shop."

"But that's not fair to everyone. We all need to pull our weight," I argue but he just shakes his head. "I feel horrible that I haven't even noticed that he's been sick." My heart hurts to know that I've been so consumed with myself that I haven't even thought about Oliver lately.

"Piper, it's okay to take time for yourself. You're always putting others first and it's time to change that for a bit," Belinda chimes in.

I throw my head back against the cushions and stare at the ceiling.

"I can't stay here like this or I'll go crazy. I need to be doing something," I say and look over at Rob and Belinda. "What time is your meeting with the suppliers? I can go and fill in until closing time."

"Pipe, you just lost your mom I think you might need a day or so," Rob says but I hold up my hand.

"I'll stay in the back office and work on the invoices. If Holly needs something I'll be there to help but I need this," I almost plead.

"Only if you're sure," he says.

"I'm sure."

I'm closing down the shop but I can't stop replaying how horrible I was to Maddox. Why did I have to yell and say those things? I need to make it right and try to explain better, to say how sorry I am for acting that way. I'll be lucky if he takes any of my calls now.

I let Holly leave early since we were so slow and I could use the silence to gather my thoughts from over the last few months. Maddox has been such a light and came into my life at just the right time when I needed him. Now I've pushed him away and I want to crawl into a hole and die. I'm at my breaking point with the school and losing my mom, and I can't bottle up these emotions anymore. As soon as I'm done here, I'm driving over to his house and we are going to talk. It's not like him not to communicate with me throughout the day.

Closing the fridge, I toss the bag of trash over my shoulder and walk to the back door. I wedge a brick against it to keep from getting locked out and make my way to the dumpster twenty feet away. Oliver had extra lights mounted to brighten the alleyway so it isn't a place for teens and the homeless to loiter.

Just as I swing the trash up to the open top I'm shoved into the metal dumpster and hit my head. I let out a cry reaching my hand to the throbbing pain when I'm pushed again. My legs give out but I'm yanked up by my shirt. My eyes swim and there are white dots in my vision.

"You little bitch," a man's voice hisses in my face. "You think you can expose us and get away with it? Nah, we aren't going to let a nobody ruin what we've got."

My head hurts and I'm reeling trying to make sense of what is happening.

"Please, stop," I plead sobbing as the pain gets worse. The side of my neck is wet. Something is trickling all the way down to my chest and I'm sure it's blood. I try to use my hands to push his chest but he's so strong I'm not even moving him. I try to claw at his hand but my fight is futile.

"I'm not stopping until you're dead. Can't have mouths running around town. I've worked too hard to have some woman take it all away. Consider this your early retirement."

I feel a hand clamp around my throat and I'm lifted from the ground. I can hear myself making gurgling sounds. My body feels weak and my chest burns trying to take in oxygen. My thoughts start to flash of Maddox and how much I love him and wish he was here. How much I regret my words that were said. How if only I had one minute to call I'd tell him how much he means to me and that I'm sorry.

As my eyes lower, I feel my body start to go limp when a loud bang echoes. It sounds so far away but for a split second, I think I hear Maddox's voice. Suddenly the pressure from my throat is gone and my body hits the ground heaving to suck air into my lungs.

The sound of thumps, slapping of skin, and grunts ring out down the alleyway. I can hear voices as my vision becomes less blurry. I see two figures wrestling on the pavement and hear hurried footsteps.

"Watch the knife!" a voice shouts out then a grunt sounds.

"Motherfucker!"

My eyes clear and I see Thomas standing off just beside the two grappling on the concrete. Darren is jogging over with his phone to his ear speaking with someone. A body is flipped and it draws my attention to the fight happening. I see Maddox stand, blood pooling from the side of his white dress shirt. He rears back and kicks the man in the torso. The man grunts heavily.

"Not so tough now are you, you sack of shit." Maddox's voice is deep and lethal. "Can't challenge a real man so you pick on defenseless women? Only scum come after the vulnerable." Maddox reaches behind him and pulls out a gun. My head pounds and my eyes can't focus. The sound of three loud pops and groans invade my ears making my head hurt worse and a whimper leaves my lips as my body collapses. Hurried steps resound on the pavement by me.

"Oh shit," I hear but it feels like I'm in a tunnel.

"Piper, baby, look at me. Come on, cherry bomb." I feel several hands touching me.

"She's got a pulse. Darren get the car."

"Put this on her head."

"God, look at her neck."

Tires screech and the sound of a siren are the last thing I remember before everything goes black.

CHAPTER TWENTY-ONE

Piper

MY EYES BLINK OPEN AND THE SMELL OF DISINFECTANT hits my nose. The lights are bright and the blurry room slowly comes into focus. I'm in a room with solid walls surrounding me and a glass wall in front showing the nurses' station. People are rushing by wearing scrubs calling out commands as I get my bearings. The glass door slides open and a woman comes in.

"I'm glad to see you awake, Ms. Caldwell," she says as she checks the machines next to my bed.

"What happened? How did I get here?" My voice comes out in a rasp and hurts as my hand reaches up to touch my head. I wince when my fingers make contact.

"You got a knot on your head from the fall it seems. You didn't need any stitches so that was good," she answers then types on the computer attached to the wall. I pull my fingers back and see a small amount of dried blood I didn't notice before. "The doctor said everything looked fine with your throat too when the scans came back. He'll be back around in a bit after he's checked on your boyfriend."

My boyfriend.

"Oh my gosh!" I rush to say with a wince as the memories come flooding back. "Is he okay? Did Maddox get hurt?" I make a move to remove the blankets across my lap.

The nurse comes over and holds my hand. "I'm not allowed to divulge personal information with non-family members but I can have someone from his room come over and see you."

"Yes, please, or I can go over there," I say and go to get up again but she holds me by the shoulder gently.

"We need you to stay put for a little bit longer to make sure you're stable enough to leave soon. We want to make sure you're strong enough and not going to fall over. We'll make sure you two are reunited soon. Drink some water in the meantime." She hands me a Styrofoam cup with a straw.

"O-okay," I relent.

It isn't too much longer from when she leaves that the door slides open again and a cop in uniform comes in with a notepad in hand.

"Ms. Caldwell?"

"Yes?" I whisper to ease the soreness still in my throat.

"I'm Detective Bryce, how are you feeling?"

"Fine, I think."

"That's good. I've got a few questions to ask about what happened earlier." He taps his pen on the pad in his hand. "Did you see Mr. Bishop kill Mr. Rollings?" I stare at him blankly trying to process the words he just said. "Was Mr. Rollings holding a weapon when Mr. Bishop attacked him?'

"I—wait, who was that man?"

The detective looks down at his notepad and says, "Brad Rollings. Do you know him?"

Brad Rollings? The school board member I just released an article about? Surely not.

The glass door slides open once again but with a little more force this time.

"Ms. Caldwell is in no position to be questioned at this time," a man wearing an expensive suit standing next to Thomas says.

They both come into the room and make a wall to block me from the detective.

"I'm just trying to get a statement for the report," Detective Bryce argues.

"Ms. Caldwell will only answer questions after she and I have a word. As her attorney on record, she has the right to consult with me before being interrogated by police officers. Especially since she's just had this most tragic event happen to her."

An attorney? I can't afford an attorney.

"Don't you find it a conflict of interest representing both parties in question, Saunders?"

"It's none of your business Mr. Bryce, and the next time you'll make sure I'm present before approaching my client," my attorney, I guess, sneers.

"It's Detective Bryce." The cop grits his teeth and then looks back over at me. "Here is my information. Call when you are ready to make a statement. I'm going to be around the hospital for a little while." He leaves, bumping Thomas in the shoulder. The look of rage on Thomas' face is like the one Maddox had in the alley.

"Hello, Ms. Caldwell," Saunders greets from beside me as I turn my attention away from Thomas to the man standing next to me. "I'm James Saunders and I'll be helping you navigate all the events that happened this evening."

"I—"

"It's okay. Take your time. Tonight must've been horrifying to experience. Did you know the guy who attacked you?"

I nod because the words about what happened aren't making it out of my mouth at the moment. Not only because it hurts but also because I think I might be in shock.

"I didn't realize it at the time but Detective Bryce said it was Brad Rollings. I've never met him in person but he's a school board member at the district I teach at," I finally say after wrapping my brain around all these events.

"What's a school board member doing attacking a teacher in an alley?" Thomas asks.

"I-I started exposing the board for their shady dealings and the favors they were giving within the district. It's why I was put on leave and not allowed to resume my job," I say and my hand reaches up to touch my tender throat.

"You were put on leave from the school?" I nod. "For what? When?"

I pause because right now I can't even remember what day it is.

"Right after Maddox left on his business trip," I answer, still trying to calculate the right date.

"Piper, you can't tell anyone what happened tonight." Thomas comes over and stands on the opposite side of the bed from Saunders.

"What? Why? I—he attacked me," I start to argue but Thomas holds a hand up.

"The cops and the justice system won't care. Right now they have a dead body and are blaming Maddox for it. They won't see it as self-defense with Maddox saving you," he argues.

"Why? If Maddox hadn't been there I'd be dead." My body starts to shake and my hand goes up around my throat at the memory of what Brad tried to do to me. "I need to go see him. He can't get in trouble for saving me," I say in a panic.

"What Thomas is trying to say," Saunders shoots a withering glare at Thomas before softening his features back at me, "is they are trying to pin charges on Maddox. Right now they only have you as a witness so they are going to be coming hard at you for details and answers. My contact in the department stated they've been waiting to pin something on Mr. Bishop for some time and this is their way in."

"They're going to try and use me and what happened to arrest Maddox?" I say sounding horrified. "I mean I'm sorry he's dead but he was going to kill me. He deserved more than those three bullets," I practically scream, straining my tender vocal cords. A beeping echoes around the room and my head starts to hurt. Mr. Saunders shoots a glare over at Thomas and he shuts his mouth. My body falls back against the bed needing some type of relief. I close my eyes willing for the room to stop spinning.

"Let's all calm down for a second." Saunders tries to soothe me by rubbing my upper arm. "We can come up with a plan and then move forward."

"Like what? That detective said he'll be around waiting for my statement," I say and open my eyes, the events of the day taking a toll on me. "I don't understand how this can be turned around and be used against a man who was trying to save the victim in all of this. It makes no sense."

"You could marry him, right?" My eyes which were just closing again pop open and I crack my neck, whipping my head in Thomas' direction causing me to whimper.

"Thomas," there's a warning in Saunders' voice.

"If they were married then Piper couldn't be questioned or forced to testify against her husband and give all of the details. Just the ones that led up to the attack," he argues smugly.

"What the hell?"

"Think like it's you saving Ox like he just saved you." Thomas looks pointedly at me.

Saunders lets out a heavy sigh and starts to rub his temples.

"Is that true?" I ask.

He starts to nod but says, "It's a little more complicated but yes a wife cannot testify against her husband."

"I need to see Maddox. Is he okay? Did he get hurt? Why is he getting looked at?" The last twenty-four hours have been so surreal and I need to talk with Maddox to help ground me.

"He has a few wounds from the scuffle," Saunders informs me. "The doctor is patching him up right now."

"I want to see him," I demand.

"Let me get a wheelchair so you won't get dizzy and fall," Thomas says on his way to the glass door. My eyes are playing games with me or I'm delirious because he looks like he's got a spring in his step that wasn't there when he walked in.

Once they have me secured, Thomas wheels me to the next room that is identical to the one I was in. The moment Maddox comes into view, my emotions get the best of me and I lose it. A sob comes out as I take him in propped up on the side of the bed. He's shirtless and the doctor is stitching up his side. The noise of my sob gets his attention and he tries to hop off the bed. Darren holds him down to keep him from coming to me. A growl leaves his throat and I feel awful for him.

This is all my fault.

When I'm close enough, I stand from the chair and reach out for him. He immediately engulfs me in his arms pulling me tight against his hard body. My body shakes from the relief I feel with his body touching mine. He's got me in a secure position holding me as tight as possible.

"I was so scared." My voice is muffled in the crook of his neck and my tears are soaking his skin.

"You're okay now," Maddox tries to soothe me, rubbing my back in circles.

"Mr. Bishop, if you could—"

"Beat it," he calls out and I hear a shuffle of feet then the sliding door closes.

I'm not sure how long we stay like that but as the time ticks my body starts to drift. I go lax as he sweeps my legs up cradling me. A throat is cleared and I realize that not everyone left the room.

"What's going on?" I hear him ask someone.

"The cop was trying to get her statement," Saunders answers.

The hold he has on me tightens and I burrow further into him needing the comfort after everything today.

"Why wasn't someone in the room watching her?" Maddox barks.

I finally get the energy to lift my head off his shoulder and look up at him. "They're going to try and arrest you," I tell him.

"It'll be—"

"We need to get married," I say in a rush going over what Thomas had said not even ten minutes ago.

"What?" He raises an eyebrow at me. "What are you talking about?"

"We need to be married so they can't use me against you for what happened tonight. That detective was asking questions that made it seem as if you were in the wrong for saving me."

"Babe…" he starts.

"It will solve a lot of your problems," Thomas pipes up from the other side of the room. "Think about it."

Maddox shoots a glare towards him. Thomas just shrugs and crosses his arms over his chest.

"You shouldn't have to suffer for trying to save me," I urge. "This is all my fault and I can't let you be punished for helping me."

"I'd do it a thousand times over again and again, but rushing to get married because you're scared isn't the right thing to do. We have Saunders to fight our battles," he tries to reassure me.

"I know but—" I pause for a second then realize, "Oh my gosh, never mind. I'm sorry," I say.

"For what? You didn't do anything wrong."

I sit up and try to move out of his embrace. "You don't want to marry me." I palm my forehead with my hand. Of course, he wouldn't want to be strapped down to someone like me. I was horrible to him last night and then got him all mixed up with the police now wanting to arrest him for trying to save me. I'll be lucky if he lets me still live in the same city as him after all I've put him through the last few days.

I move to get up and back away from him but he follows me and backs me up against the hospital room wall. "I'd marry you right here and right now if you let me," he growls bending down so we are at eye level with one another. "I wanted to tie you down right after meeting you," he says, his deep voice brooking no argument.

My heart flutters. "Really?" He nods. "So you aren't mad or avoiding me after last night?"

"Never."

"I tried calling and texting earlier but you never responded." My eyes slide down to the floor to avoid his.

"My phone was smashed," he says and uses his finger to gently turn my face to look back at him. "I was on my way to get a new one after I stopped and saw you first."

"We can make the marriage happen right now," Thomas voices breaking up our moment as he types something out on his phone. "Darren is registered to officiate it."

All eyes turn to Darren who's been silent this entire time. Thomas leaves the room and returns shortly with a form. "Fill this out and we can have you guys married here with Saunders present as a witness." He's smiling like the cat who ate the canary and I'm not sure why.

"Mr. Bishop, as your—" Saunders starts to speak.

"Were you serious about marrying me?" Maddox turns back to me after holding up his hand to stop Saunders from speaking. His eyes roam over my face.

I nod, without hesitation. "I love you so much and after tonight I know that more than ever. Most girls only dream of meeting their hero but I get to love mine."

He brushes a few wayward strands of hair out of my face. "I never thought I'd find someone I'd want to marry and spend the rest of my life with, but you came in and blew those thoughts out like a tornado. When I saw you almost die tonight, I thought they were going to have to bury me next to you. I don't want to spend another day without you tied to me in every way."

He leans down and our lips connect. He circles my body with his arms and presses me against him away from the wall.

"Mr. Bishop," a feminine voice calls out and Maddox barely lifts his lips from mine.

"What?" he growls.

"There is a detective that would like to speak with you," the same nurse that was in my room says from the door.

"Tell the doctor to get our discharge papers signed and ready. Then to come in here and finish with my stitches. And tell that cop to come back in twenty minutes," Maddox instructs and the nurse leaves closing the door. He looks over at me. "You really want to do this?"

"I'll do whatever you need," I say with conviction.

Maddox turns to Saunders who has the paperwork and is filling something out. "We good?"

"It all seems legit, but I must advise—"

"Darren, where do you want us?" Maddox ignores Saunders.

After Thomas pulls the curtain to block others from seeing in, we move to a small area in the corner. Thomas gave Maddox his undershirt and had the nurse bring a set of scrubs for me to wear instead of a hospital gown.

"I'll give you the wedding you deserve once everything dies down, cherry bomb," Maddox promises as Darren takes his place in front of us. If he's bothered by having to perform a shotgun wedding he doesn't show it. In fact, the smile on his face seems to have stayed there since we were informed he could officiate.

"As long as it's you across from me that's all I need for a wedding," I say.

He kisses both of my hands he's holding then nods over to Darren.

Seven minutes later Saunders is signing as a witness to our marriage license and we are officially married. He is going to meet some guy up at the courthouse and have them file it immediately. Maddox made it clear that it needed to be filed with today's date and the stamp better show it.

The doctor quickly finishes Maddox's stitches and I notice for the first time all the scars on his body. We are always so caught up in each other that I never noticed them before. After the doctor gives us our instructions and a lecture about me following up with my primary care physician in a week we are handed our papers to leave. As we are all walking down the hall the door to the elevator opens and Detective Bryce steps out and stops in front of us.

"I'm going to need a word with both of you," he demands.

Saunders steps between us. "You will have to contact me to gather any statements made. Mr. and Mrs. Bishop do not wish to speak on the issue until they have had a few days to heal from this traumatic ordeal."

"You mean Ms. Caldwell," the detective tries to correct Saunders.

"I mean Mr. and Mrs. Bishop. They are married in the eyes of the law of the state of Nevada and according to state laws they have martial privilege to keep from incriminating each other. Please call my office for any questions."

Saunders hands him a business card, and with promises to call him in a few days to check in for the both of us, Maddox ushers me onto the elevator along with his guys.

Once the doors close Thomas lets out a chuckle. "Well, I didn't see today ending like this when I woke up this morning. And you getting hitched definitely wasn't on my bingo card for the year."

With the last few hours weighing on us, the tension breaks and we all let out a laugh as we stride out of the hospital hand in hand with my heart a little lighter.

My brain can't handle any more for the night and needs a break.

Tomorrow we will deal with the fallout and what to do next.

Tomorrow we will come up with a plan and move forward.

CHAPTER TWENTY-TWO

Bishop

S HE'S SLEEPING NEXT TO ME AND HAS BEEN FOR THE LAST four hours. I can't take my eyes off her as I watch her chest rise and fall. The first hour I counted her breaths making sure her heart didn't stop. Mine did in the alley when I saw that bastard with his hands on her throat and I lost my ever-loving mind.

Brad Rollings.

He had some nerve thinking he could put his hands on my woman and continue living.

My phone vibrates and I see Thomas' name across the top in a text.

> Thomas: How's Red doing?

I take my eyes off her to respond.

> Me: Sleeping.
>
> Thomas: Davis was able to obtain the docs on the school board along with the others.

Davis does all the heavy lifting on the internet for all the mafia families. Thomas informed me of what Piper told him and Saunders about Brad being on the school board. Not wanting to pry into Piper's life and wanting to learn all about her on my own kept me from having Davis dig into her. I'll never make that mistake again. From now on, Davis is going to make her a priority. We immediately contacted him to dig deep into the entire board and administration. If they thought they could come after what is mine and live they are in for a rude awakening. I'll burn down every school before something like this ever happens again.

> Me: Have him send everything over to me and I'll look it over.
>
> Thomas: Sending now. Just skimming the docs these assholes are a piece of work.
>
> Me: Make sure he includes addresses and phone records between them all.
>
> Thomas: I'm still waiting for a thanks for getting you hitched. Fucker.
>
> Me: I should kick your ass for manipulating her.
>
> Thomas: Why? You've been looking for a way to tie her down. I just quickened the process.
>
> Me: Did you have to involve Bryce?
>
> Thomas: Made it seem more believable. Besides we pay that fucker too much not to use him when we want.

I'm not going to lie or deny that I've been trying to lock her down but I'll never admit it out loud. She's like a fragile vase that needs to be handled with care. Piper's been carrying the weight of the world and responsibilities of ten people. It was only a matter of time before the levee broke. When she blew up at me for manipulating her parents' situation at the rehab facility all the patchwork covering the cracks broke wide open. I knew she wasn't angry with me; she just didn't know how to not be the stable one that everyone always looked to when something tragic happened.

> Thomas: Besides this was much better than tampering with her birth control.

I don't respond, hoping he'll get the hint and go to bed.

> Thomas: Never mind on thanking me, I'll settle for naming your firstborn after me.
>
> Me: Shouldn't you be sleeping?

Thomas: Can't sleep.

Me either, I think.

Thomas: I keep thinking if we'd been caught by the light or if something held us up we wouldn't have made it in time.

My mind reels and the acid in my stomach threatens to come up at the thought of not getting to her in time but I block those out. I can't go there. The thought takes me back to the night of my father's death.

Thomas: The team might not know her well yet but they know she means a lot to you so they are just as upset about what happened to her. She'll never be put in that position again. Several have come forward to be on her duty.

Me: I need to tell her about The Family first.

Thomas: That would be helpful so she doesn't think she's being stalked.

Me: Asshole.

Thomas: I'll see you later this evening.

Me: Night.

I put my phone down on the nightstand and wrap myself around Piper to shake the memories of seeing her almost die. I don't know if I'll ever recover from those visions. When we wake up in a few hours we are going to discuss how our lives are going to look and there are going to be some decisions made on both our parts to move forward together.

The steady beat of her heart and the movement of her breathing calms me and my eyes grow heavy. I close my eyes and hold her tighter making sure she stays in place and has nowhere to go. Not even the devil himself can take her from me.

Sitting in the media room, we're cuddled up on the couch and I can't help but smirk at all the times this cushion has seen action the last few months. She loves to wind down and watch mindless

TV before bed and I can't help but watch her instead of the shows. The lights are dimmed and the screen is turned off. This room is like a comfort space for her and I'd build onto the house for her to have twenty of them if it meant she felt safe.

"Can you tell me what is going on with the school district and why they'd send a board member to kill you?" I ask.

She shivers even though my arms are tight around her and she's balled up between my legs laying on my chest with her head under my chin.

"I found some odd receipts when I was doing the principal's expenditures. I spoke with my friend Belinda who is on the PTA about it, and we started requesting some records to confirm what we thought was actually suspicious. We didn't know that those records would blow everything up and expose the administration and school board members."

"So this was the misunderstanding and the reason they put you on leave?"

"Yeah." She lifts her head to look up at me. "The more I uncover and expose the worse it seems to get."

"From now on I don't want you keeping me out of the loop. I was trying to give you space and let you handle the situation without getting involved but now, as your husband, I'm going to take care of everything," I say, my voice firm. This never would've gotten this far if I'd known. I've already gone over hundreds of documents Davis sent over in the early hours of the morning.

"I'll walk you through everything I have," she promises. "I need to get it all from the house." She gasps and sits straight up leaving the comfort of my arms. "I need to call Rob. They wouldn't hurt him would they?"

The panic in her eyes tugs at my heart. This woman was almost murdered last night and had just lost her mother the night before and she's still more worried about others than herself. Not once has she complained about her throat or head hurting even though it's evident.

"I've got a team watching his every move. He knows someone is guarding him and Oliver. I also have someone at your house packing up your things to move here," I reassure her making her tense shoulders slump. "I'm not taking any chances that someone else might come after you. If I'm honest, seeing you almost die has me not wanting you out of my sight for a while. Then you'll have your own team of security that will protect you when I can't be there."

"You killed Brad," she whispers.

I pull her back into our original position but move to cradle her head so she's looking up at me. My eyes burn into hers. "I'd kill everyone in this world if they tried to hurt you." I hold her gaze so she can feel the enormity of my words.

"Thank you for saving me, Maddox," she says and I can hear the tremble in her tone.

What she doesn't know is that Brad is still alive. Barely. He's at my warehouse under lock and key with Billy and a doctor keeping him breathing for now. I shot him three times but didn't go for the kill shot. It would be too easy to put a bullet in his brain. No, I want him to suffer for thinking he could seek her out to harm her. It's going to send a message to all those other fuckers who are involved.

"I'm so sorry I yelled at you at the rehab facility." She burrows her head in my neck as she lets out a sob. I pull her in and we rock for a bit letting her get out all the bottled-up emotions. "I don't like that you manipulated the situation and didn't discuss it with me first though."

"I'm sorry for not talking to you about it. I know how hard you work and was thinking I was doing it to take some stress off your shoulders. I'm here to help you in any way that I can. Let me be the one you lean on. We can do this together."

She nods. "I'm not used to having someone to rely on so please be patient with me."

"Always. Can you do the same for me?"

"Of course."

We sit there for a while in our thoughts and I'm making a

mental checklist of all the people involved who are against her. With everything that is in me, I promise to make them pay.

This should also be the moment to confess that I'm the head of my mafia Family but I think it might be a little too much for today. We need to get past this hurdle before I can throw another log into the flame.

CHAPTER TWENTY-THREE

Piper

MADDOX AND I ARE SITTING AT THE BREAKFAST TABLE in the kitchen eating when his spoon drops making a clinking noise. I'm startled when I look up at his face and see he's got this nervousness about him. Almost like a boy sitting outside the principal's office waiting to be called in for doing something wrong.

"Maddox?" I ask. "Are you okay?"

I go to reach out to touch the tops of his hands but he scoots his chair back from the table and starts to pace the length of the island.

"There's something I need to tell you," he starts running his hand through his hair then rubbing the back of his neck. "I've been meaning to have this conversation for a while now but something always comes up."

I push my plate of food away from me sensing the gravity of what he needs to get off his chest. My own nerves are starting to weigh in as he keeps his distance.

"O-kaaay. Umm, do you want to sit down here or on the sofa?"

He shakes his head looking around the room.

"I know I should've told you this sooner. Like when we first started seeing each other, but I didn't want it to sway your opinion of me, but now that we're married you're going to hear and see things that might make you see me in a different light."

I nod hoping he'll elaborate. He starts to pace again and I can't help but stand up and go over to him to halt his motions. "Stop pacing and look at me," I say and place both of my hands on the tops of his shoulders. "You can tell me anything."

"I hope you really mean that," he whispers and wraps his arms around me in a tight hug.

I give him a few minutes to compose himself then press on. "Now tell me." I lean back slightly and look up into his silvery eyes.

"I'm the Don of a mafia family," he confesses. His fingers dig into my hips holding me in place.

I stare for a minute, looking back and forth between his eyes thinking he was going to reveal that this isn't his first marriage or that he's got a child with a past partner or something. Not this. Well, that's not true, because I did see he was allegedly linked to the mafia in a search I'd done months ago but thought it was horseshit. I was expecting it to be maybe he spent some time in jail or something to that nature but not this. Not that he's a leader of organized crime.

"Yo—" I start to speak but my voice sounds scratchy so I clear it. "You're mafia?"

He nods then opens his mouth to comment but we hear footsteps enter the kitchen.

"Look who came for a visit?" I hear from behind me and turn to see Thomas with a woman who looks an awful lot like Maddox.

"Mom? What are you doing here?" Maddox asks still holding me in place as if I'd take off running if he let me go. Jokes on him because my legs are ready to give out.

"A little birdie called and told me that my son had gotten married and didn't bother to invite his mother." Maddox's mom shoots her hands to her hips and gives him the look that says, *don't mess with me.* Thomas' eyes widen and he slowly takes a step back ready to leave the room not wanting to be a part of her wrath.

"I—we—" It's almost comical to see this big strong man

struggle to form words against a woman who's the same size as me if the enormity of what he just revealed wasn't left unfinished.

"Well?" She stomps her toes and then drops her large bag that was resting on her shoulder.

"This is Piper?" he says it more as a question and I see Thomas sputter as he tries not to laugh.

"I hope it is since that's all you've talked about on the phone with me. I'd think I didn't raise you correctly if it were someone else." His mom comes farther into the kitchen closer to where we are standing by the island. "Hello, honey. I'm Susan but everyone calls me Susie."

She takes me into the biggest hug, reminding me of when my mom used to hug me. The thoughts of my mom chip away a little more of the wall of emotions I thought I had under control and I spring a leak. My stiff arms wrap around her middle and I hold on with everything I have. I sob on her shoulder as she holds me with one arm and pats the middle of my back with the other.

"Oh, honey, let it out," she coos. "Maddox go get me a tissue or wash cloth," I hear her say.

When I finally get myself together I jerk out of her hold. "I'm so sorry," I say. "It's been a rough few days."

"It's quite alright. Let's go sit down in the family room and chat," she offers and takes ahold of my hand to lead me toward the sofa.

"You must think I'm a basket case." I dab my eyes with a white cloth Maddox hands me. He's sitting on the coffee table while his mom and I are next to one another.

"Never honey," she starts but then her eyes look down and hone in on my neck. "What happened here?" she screeches then turns narrowed eyes toward Maddox.

"I was attacked by a man outside one of my jobs," I say, drawing her attention back to me. "Maddox saved me from almost dying. He got there just in time."

"Oh my goodness, how terrifying." She grabs both of my hands.

"It's the reason we got married so quickly. The cops are trying to pin the death on Maddox," I defend and hope this will somehow not look like such a shotgun wedding.

"Oh really?" she says then turns to her son. "And which officers were in charge of the case?"

"I was in the room next to hers at the hospital getting checked out when Thomas brought the idea up," Maddox defends.

"Is that so?" Susie clucks her tongue to the roof of her mouth. "Don't you run and hide mister!" Susie calls out and I watch as Thomas tries to flea out the front door but stops in his tracks. "You and I have some things to talk about."

"Yes, ma'am." Thomas nods then turns to head back toward the kitchen like a scolded child.

She turns back to me and softens her expression. "Now tell me all about you, honey."

"Oh, I um—"

"Mom, Piper and I were just having a really big discussion about my life and what I do—"

"Thank goodness you finally told her." Susie blows out a whistle of relief then she smiles back at me. "He was a nervous wreck about how you'd react. It was a shock to me as well but knowing he was only on the money laundering side instead of the drugs and guns side I felt a little better."

Her cheerfulness about the bomb I have yet to process is jarring.

"Money. Laundering?" I feel my mouth drop open. "I thought you were in banking?"

"I am, Piper. It's just—"

"You didn't tell her everything?" Susie interrupts.

"I had just told her about being the head of our Family right before you came through the door and surprised us, Mom."

"Well, this is a little awkward." She gives my hands a squeeze. "It's really not as bad as it sounds, dear."

My stomach starts to turn and the food we ate earlier rumbles.

"I think I need to go lie down for a minute," I say and stand. "I'm not feeling well."

Maddox stands as well. "Here, let me help you up the stairs."

I shake my head. "I just need a breather," I say then look down to where Susie is perched. "It was nice to meet you."

"We'll catch up once you've had some time to process this. His sisters are dying to speak with you. We can FaceTime later this evening."

Her smile is so genuine it's hard to deny her anything. "That would be nice."

I walk out of the room and into the hall leading toward the stairs knowing Maddox is right behind me. I turn once I get up on the first step. We still aren't eyelevel but it's close.

"Piper, I'm sorry about all this," he starts but I cup my hand over his mouth.

"I need a hot minute to think," I say. "Just give me a second to catch my breath and then we can finish our discussion from the kitchen."

"Yeah, okay."

I turn on my heels and hurry up the stairs to the bedroom. After throwing myself on the mattress, I pull the covers up over my head and turn my face into the pillow to scream. Once I have nothing left in me, I flip on my back and stare up at the ceiling.

How in the hell did my life get so complicated and what the hell am I going to do now?

After a grandfather clock from the hallway chimes for the fourth time I figure my hiding out is over and I need some answers. After using the restroom, I pad back down the stairs and find Susie in the kitchen along with a woman and man dressed in black and white attire.

"Piper, dear, would you like a snack before dinner?" Susie asks when she notices me in the doorway.

"I'm fine but thank you," I say as she comes toward me and hugs me again.

"I'm so glad my son met you," she says then pulls back.

"Did Maddox leave?" I ask.

"No, he and Thomas are down in the gym doing manly things." She giggles and it puts a smile on my face. "Can we go and talk for a bit?"

I nod and she leads me out to the covered patio overlooking the pool.

"This lifestyle isn't for everyone. I was so young when I met Matthew. I had Maddox not long after that. It was a whirlwind romance, one I thought would never end."

"Maddox told me he passed away when he was a teenager," I say and she nods in confirmation.

"I loved that man with everything in me," she begins and a sad frown mars her face. "He was a force to be reckoned with which was good considering the business he and the other Families were into."

"There are more mafia families?" I ask with wide eyes.

"Oh yes, dear. At first, there were the original five: Arturo Falcone, Bobby Dawson, Victor Slater, Nicolas Chapman, and Matthew Bishop. They divided up Las Vegas and agreed to certain rules and regulations. Once that was established the city ran smoothly with no problems. Each had a section and job to fulfill and everyone profited from it. Matthew's family had always been in banking and when he went to the west coast to expand, he met Arturo and Bobby. They became best friends. As the years went by, we had a family and everything was great." She pauses and then starts to fidget with her fingers. "Matthew was always an active man. He loved doing adrenaline activities looking for the next rush. At the time, I didn't realize he'd started doing drugs when he was opening nightclubs. He hid it well or maybe I was so busy with the twins I didn't realize my Matthew was just a shell of himself. He started going days without coming home and when he did he slept the entire time. Matthew wouldn't look at the children and started to miss Maddox's baseball games."

She has a faraway look over by the fireplace.

"I confronted him one night that he'd come home at two in the morning. He smelt like a brewery and his eyes were glazed over. He spoke to me as if I was a stranger." Absently she places her palm against her cheek. "It was the first time he'd ever laid a hurtful hand on me."

I suck in a gasp trying to imagine what that might look like.

"I'm so sorry, Susie," I say as her eyes focus back on me.

"I should've packed up the kids right then and left, but I didn't. I have no excuses that I didn't leave and I'll blame myself until the day I die for it."

"It's not your fault," I say but she shakes her head sadly.

"But it is, Piper. I stayed thinking he would never do it again but then the cycle continued and we fell into this loop. He would apologize and swear it would never happen again and I stayed because I didn't want to take the kids from their dad." She shakes her head to clear her thoughts. "I knew better and I was showing my kids that it was okay for him to treat us that way. It is never okay for that to happen no matter how sorry he was."

I have no idea what to say so I just hold her hands and listen as she unburdens this load.

"Maddox was my rock during that time and I was the adult. He'd patch me up or get me an ice pack, things a teenager never should do for their mom. I'll never forgive myself for not being the strong one and letting my fifteen-year-old son shoulder his parents' issues."

"You did your best, Susie," I try to console her as tears float down her cheeks.

"The night Matthew died was both the best and worst time of my life. That night I lost both my husband and my son," she confesses.

"I don't understand," I say. Did Maddox have a brother and they don't talk about him?

"Matthew came home again drugged out of his mind and it was a wonder he didn't kill someone driving under the influence. He never let his security team drive him anywhere. When he came through the kitchen I was getting some medicine for the twin who had caught a cold from their preschool. When he saw me he started in with accusations and paranoia. I went about ignoring him because the girls needed me, so I passed by him without a word and that set him off. His rage was out of control that night. He slammed me against the wall so hard it rattled my teeth. It jarred me for a bit and when I got my bearings I was on the floor and his fist nailed me square in the eye. It felt like my eyeball exploded. He was on top of me raining down blows then the next he was gone."

I'm on the edge of the seat leaning forward waiting for her to continue.

"With my one good eye, I was able to see blood everywhere. Lots and lots of blood. I heard the sound of running footsteps through the house and a figure caught my attention. I looked up to see Maddox with a gun in his hand pointing it over the top of me. My eyes followed and I screamed seeing Matthew sprawled on his back with several holes in his chest. I never even heard the gunshots. My son, my sixteen-year-old son, ended what I never could."

"You tried to leave, Mom." Maddox's voice jolts me and I whip my head over to the doorway. "You tried to leave but he found us, remember?" He makes his way over in his sweaty clothes and crouches down in front of us. "He didn't leave us any choice."

"But I was the parent and it should've been me that pulled the trigger, not you," she cries and Maddox and I pull her into a hug. We sit there until her tears dry up and she's able to compose herself. She finally pulls away from us and we drop our arms. "I'm so sorry you had to grow up so fast, honey. I wish I could go back and change things and maybe you wouldn't have been so closed off like you have been."

"I'm fine and the girls are good. They don't even really remember those times, Mom."

"You deserve all the happiness in the world, Maddox," she says and cups his cheek.

"Thank you, Mom," he says with a tight smile then places a hand on my knee. "I'm going to go and shower before dinner. I'll be quick."

He leaves us and I take in everything Susie has told me.

"Please don't hold what he did to his father against him." Susie looks over at me as I stare blankly at the wall. "He cares so much about those he loves and will do anything to keep them safe."

"I could never," I say. "What you all went through had to have been a terrifying experience. I'm sorry you had to endure it."

"Maddox told me earlier that your mother just passed away. I'm so very sorry for your loss. He explained what happened with their crash and the care facility they were put in."

"Thank you. Mom didn't deserve to suffer any longer. She wouldn't have wanted to."

She nods and holds onto my hand in comfort that both of us need at this moment.

"Maddox has been going through the motions of life since that night. He's never allowed himself to actually live until you," she says shocking me.

"How do you know?"

"Baseball was the only thing Maddox cared about growing up. If he had baseball he had everything. There was always a twinkle in his eye and you knew it was because of that sport. After that night, his twinkle died and part of my son did too. It wasn't until he told me about you that I saw and heard it in his voice. The way he looks at you when you're in the room is like the sun hitting a prism. He lives for you and only you."

Her words hit my chest and my heart double thumps. "I feel the same," I admit lowering my eyes to the floor.

"Then hear him out when he tells you the good, bad, and ugly of this lifestyle before you make any decisions. He'd turn the whole world upside down for you."

He'd even kill for you.

"I will."

"Good, now let's go see if dinner is ready. I've got some best friends coming over later that I haven't seen in a long time."

CHAPTER TWENTY-FOUR

Bishop

IT'S PITCH BLACK OUTSIDE WHEN I JUMP THE FENCE INTO THE backyard. The grass is high and there's clutter built up along the wooden panels. There are no dogs to alert someone of my presence so I take my time as I stalk toward the back door. It's late Friday night so everyone is out of the house except her.

Jessica McClain.

The woman who is so jealous of my wife that she was the one who got the ball rolling the lead to almost getting Piper killed.

The sound of rustling has me pause and snap my neck to the side of the house. I crouch down blending in with the darkness. My eyes are focused as I see another dark figure come from the side of the house from the street. I've got my blade out and ready to attack when I recognize the figure.

"What the hell are you doing here?" I sneer as I approach and grab his black long-sleeved shirt. We're dressed the same in black from the beanie on our heads down to our black combat boots.

"I'm not letting you go at this alone. We've never not been there for each other and we're not going to start now," Thomas grunts.

"I don't need backup," I seethe.

"Maybe not but I'm here for you just in case."

I huff through my nose knowing he's not going to leave. "Stay out of the way," I say then turn away from him as I make my way over to the window.

Inside, I can see that she lives in a messy space. There's crap everywhere in piles. I watch as Jessica comes from a back room toward the kitchen. She's wearing a robe and some slippers. Thomas and I move down to the next window to the right and find that it's unlocked. Easy as pie. Carefully, I lift the frame and maneuver my body into the dark room. My eyes are adjusted to the night and can see it belongs to a young female. I hear humming from the hall letting me know that she's coming back to her room.

"What's the plan? Home invasion?" Thomas breaks the silence just above a whisper.

I shake my head. That'd be too easy. I want to ruffle some feathers and draw some gossip just like they did with Piper. I want people to label them something they're not but also for them to suffer.

A door clicks and when I take a peek down the hall I see her bedroom door shut. Using years of training, I silently walk down the hall and the closer I get, the sound of the TV lets me know she'll never hear us coming. I've got everything I need in my back pocket to set this up. I open the door slowly and when she comes into view I make my move before she can register that her life is over. She's lying on the bed and when the door creaks her attention shifts from the TV to where I'm already advancing on her. She opens her mouth to scream but my hand stops any noises as I pin her to the bed.

"Hello, Jessica," I say as I peer down at her. I'm sure the look on my face terrifies her. She's struggling to get out of my hold but she's not going anywhere unless I want her to.

Thomas walks up to the bed and she sees him over my shoulder. He quickly takes a piece of heavy-duty tape from his pocket, tears a section off, and secures it over her mouth after pushing my hand away.

I've already cased her house. I know the layout and where she keeps her things so it's no surprise that her laptop is on the bedside table. I reach over and snag it as she starts to tremble. Little does she know it's too late to be afraid. Her fate was sealed the day she went to Jackie and tried to take revenge on my wife. Even if she didn't know the full extent of what was going to happen, actions have consequences. I just happen to be the reaper coming to collect.

"I want you to type this out," I tell her as I pull a piece of paper out of my pants pocket. She's shaking as her face floods with tears.

Thomas loses patience and grabs her hair lifting her to a sitting position. We have to be careful handling her because we don't want too many questions that don't add up with the scenario I've got planned out.

"Start typing," he demands.

Jessica starts to speak behind the tape but I just shake my head and point down at the paper in my hand. It takes a few minutes for her to comply but once she starts to type and she realizes what it says, she tries to move away from us and the bed. She doesn't even make it an inch before she's back in the same position.

"You're a real piece of work, Jessica," I say as Thomas takes the computer away from her lap and starts to type the rest of the note with his gloved hands. I could've typed it out to begin with but she needs to understand why all this is happening to her.

She's trying so hard to speak but I don't want to hear any words from her. Once Thomas is done with the note he places the laptop back on the bedside table. Carefully, I reach behind me in the back of my waistband and pull the plastic bag out that contains a shiny gun.

"I don't think you realize how much of a better place the world will be once you're gone," I tell her as she starts to struggle in my grip. "I'm going to remove the tape and if you scream or make loud noises I'm going to slit your throat then wait for your kids to get home and do the same to them," I threaten even though I'd never follow through with hurting an innocent child. "Nod your head if you understand."

She does and before I can, Thomas butts in and rips the tape off. Jessica whimpers but doesn't scream like I thought she would. I cut my eyes over to him but he's just glaring at her.

"Please, I'm so so-sorry for everything. I'll never do—"

I hold my hand up to stop her from telling more lies. A person like her can't help herself from creating drama. "You don't get to plead your case to me. I've read all about you and what you've done to not only my wife but the students who you've taught. They deserve better than some angry woman who blames the world for her own problems and takes it out on them. As a teacher, your job is to teach and nurture them into becoming our future but instead, you purposely beat their self-esteem down and pick on them every chance you get making their parents believe they are problem kids. A person like you should never be in charge of teaching our youth."

She tries to speak again but I'm done here. The longer we stay the more likely we'll get caught.

"You are doing the world a favor and Donald Tucker was so nice to let me borrow this heavy piece of equipment." I look down at the gun and then back at her. She starts to sob but I don't even have one ounce of sympathy in my body for a person like her.

A few minutes later, Thomas and I are making our way back to my SUV a few blocks away.

"I don't need a babysitter, Thomas. Next time I need your help, I'll call." I glare over at him as we walk along the dark sidewalk out of view from the streetlights.

"You aren't the only one who almost lost her, Ox," he says and it makes me stop abruptly. He stops and looks back at me. "I've never seen you so happy and full of life. She's the reason for that. I've known you a long time and when you first met her I knew she was going to change everything in your world. She has this infectious bright light around her that draws people in. She's the good that this world needs, what you need, and as your best friend and second in command I never want you to be without her. Piper is so special and she's your perfect match. I'm not going to let anything or anyone ever come between that. So, yes, I'll be by your side through all of these hunting missions."

Thomas has been with me throughout my time when I took over after Bobby and Arturo brought me into the fold when I graduated college. I value him as my second but also as a brother.

We start walking back, not saying anything. When I'm far enough away I take out my burner phone and make the call.

"Hello?" he answers on the second ring clearly being woken up.

"Heard a gunshot that need to be attended to."

I hear a series of curses and shuffling on the other line. "What am I walking into this time?" His voice is angry but I couldn't care less. He gets paid handsomely for his time so he's on the clock twenty-four-seven for when I need him.

"Sounded like a suicide to me." I tell him the address as we come up on our vehicle. "Make sure you run the serial number on the gun. Open an investigation and make that shit public. Check the laptop next to the bed. Pretty sure she left a note."

I hear a door closing and locking before he huffs, "On it."

The line goes dead and I remove the SIM card, tossing the phone in the dumpster by the car. Once we get in we head to the house. I use the hands-free audio in the car to make a call.

"Sir," he answers right away.

"Report," I say and listen.

"There is no movement; everything is the same as it was an hour ago," Clint says. He's in the security office at my house in the building on the far side of my property. Far enough away not to be noticeable but close enough where he and the other men can take action if something happened to my house where my wife sleeps.

"And Rob?"

"Cameras show he came home at ten and hasn't left. The team has the street and perimeter secure."

"Good." I push the button on the steering column ending the call. "You staying over tonight?"

Thomas has a room over the garage for when we have late

nights but since Piper and I started dating he's not been staying as often.

"Think the Mrs. would mind?"

"You know she wouldn't."

He nods then lays his head back against the headrest. My mind goes to my checklist and I mentally mark off tonight's name.

Only a handful more to go.

CHAPTER TWENTY-FIVE

Piper

THE WEEKEND WAS CRAZY AS FAMILIES ALL CAME OVER TO see Susie and welcome me into The Family. Susie labeled it a delayed wedding reception. I was able to meet Arturo's wife, Adele, and Gemma's adorable son, Dante. Bobby's wife, Mary, never left my side and she introduced me to her new daughter-in-law, Kendall, and her son, Wyatt. Her other daughter Gracie was out of town with some friends.

I'm walking out of the closet when my phone rings.

"Piper!" Belinda says before I can say a proper hello. "Did you hear the news?"

"No, what news?"

We've released two more blogs about school board members since my attack last week. I've been staying low hoping things won't get any crazier. I've been checking a few times a day but nothing has been said about Brad's death or about me being attacked. Maddox assured me that he has a team working on keeping that event out of the public.

"One of my PTA moms just called and told me that Jessica killed herself over the weekend. Left a note and everything." She says it so fast she has to catch her breath at the end.

"Oh my God! That's horrible." I feel my eyes bulge and take a seat at the end of the bed. My hand goes to cover my mouth when Maddox comes through the bedroom door.

"What's wrong, Piper?" he asks coming over and kneeling in front of me.

We haven't had time to sit down and talk since he told me about being head of his mafia family. The weekend was one big social gathering that never left us alone except right before bed and I was too tired to have such a heavy conversation.

"Ox is there? Put me on speaker phone, Piper," Belinda yells getting my attention.

He takes the phone from my hand and taps the screen. "I'm here Belinda. What's going on?"

"I was telling her that Jessica killed herself over the weekend. But that isn't all, the mom who told me about it also said that the school board is calling a special meeting tomorrow night and that Piper is the main topic."

"Do you think it's to give me my job back?" I ask, my mind still reeling from the news of Jessica.

"From the gossip, it's not, but I don't know," she informs. "Andy said that a large group of his friends and students from other schools are all going to the meeting to speak up for you."

"How do you know that?" Maddox asks.

"Apparently, one of the school board's daughters doesn't know how to read a room and popped off about it to her little minions. Now everyone is aware and are going up there."

"I can't even go and defend myself because the school's attorney, Mitch Connors, made it very clear at the meeting that I was not allowed to step foot on any school district property until this was resolved."

"What the fuck? What do you mean you aren't allowed to defend yourself?" Maddox growls.

"Did I not tell you that part?" He shakes his head. If it were possible steam would be coming out of his ears. My face falls. "I'm sorry, so much has happened I thought I covered that."

His body softens slightly and he rubs my knuckles with his thumb. "If they think they can bulldoze my wife and treat her like this they are going to have a hard time finding boosters to sponsor their sports and programs. Gemma alone funds three programs for the district," Maddox growls, his jaw ticking.

"WIFE?" I vaguely hear Belinda scream before I realize we are still on the phone with her.

"Oh, umm. It's kind of a long story but we got married last Wednesday." I feel my cheeks heat.

"The day after your mom passed?" Before I can answer the phone rings for a face-to-face. I press the accept and watch Maddox smirk while shaking his head. "Go somewhere away from him," she tries to quietly say.

"What, why?"

"Blink twice if you need help."

"Belinda!" I start to laugh as she does the same.

"This is wonderful news, honey. I hope you know that Joseph and I are so happy for you."

"Thank you," I say.

"And you tell him that if he doesn't allow us to have girls' nights, I'll spike his coffee with laxatives."

"No need to threaten my colon, Belinda," Maddox chimes in amused.

"Good, that's good. Well, I thought I'd give you that heads up about Jessica and the meeting. I'll be there and you can bet I'll be signed up to speak during the public comments."

"As will I," Maddox says. "Send me the details so that I can pass them on to others who donate."

"Okay. Call me later, Piper."

"I will," I say and we hang up.

Maddox tosses the phone on the bed and then sits back on his haunches.

"You don't have to go to that meeting—" I start to say.

"Like hell I'd miss it. They aren't going to get away with how they've treated you, Piper. No one deserves to be treated this way. The more I've looked into the situation the more I'm concerned you aren't the first one to endure this. You're just the first one to stand up to Goliath."

We sit there for a moment thinking.

"I feel bad for Jessica's family. I hope her children didn't find her," I finally say.

"I was coming to tell you about it. There was an article online. According to the report a neighbor called in hearing a gunshot and the police were sent out. Her kids didn't see anything," he tells me. "There was a note found and they are going to release it at a later date."

"I wonder if the school will help out with what her kids are going to need. Jessica never mentioned their father. Maybe Belinda can get the PTA to start a fund for them or something," I say trying to think of how hard this might be on them.

"You are too good for this world, babe." Maddox leans in and kisses my forehead. "I'll take care of it."

"Is your mom already up?" I ask as he rises to his feet and stretches out his hand for mine.

He shakes his head. "Apparently, her, Adele, and Mary are making up for all the years she's been away. I think I'm going to have to get a shipment for several cases of wine to be flown in to replenish my stock with their little gatherings. Adele and Mary didn't leave here until after three this morning."

I start to giggle. "They were a hoot last night. I can see them getting into some serious trouble if let out on the town according to some of their stories they were telling me last night."

"Ahhh," Maddox rubs his hand over his face, "you have no idea. Arturo and Bobby said the three of them were a handful back then."

We start to make our way down the staircase with my hand in his and I can't help but feel at home.

"You look very casual today; are you not heading to work?" My eyes roam over his dark jeans and a polo that stretches over his chest.

"I'm taking my wife out for the day." He gives me a smirk as we reach the kitchen.

"Oh, and where would that be, *husband?*"

I see a flicker of heat in his eyes as his tongue sweeps out and wets his lips. "I thought we might head over and pick up your wedding ring," he says as he pulls out my chair at the breakfast table. "Then I can show you where my office is and have you meet some important people with my business."

"Are you sure?" My hand automatically goes up around my neck where the bruises have finally faded.

He reaches across the table and grabs my left hand, his thumb rubbing across my empty ring finger. "I need you to wear my ring," he states. "And I want yours on mine."

"This is Nancy," Maddox introduces a woman in her mid to late fifties as we're seated behind his desk at his office. I rise from my chair and greet her. "Nancy handles all the businesses occupying my commercial buildings. She also loves to give my money away," he says with a laugh.

"It's nice to meet you, Mrs. Bishop. Congratulations on the wedding," she offers sincerely. Her voice sounds very familiar for some reason.

"Thank you so much," I say. "Have we met before?"

She gives a glance over to Maddox before returning to me. "I don't believe so, dear, but I hear we are going to get along wonderfully," she answers with a mischievous smile.

I've met several people involved on the banking side of Maddox's business. A lot have been the executives that run all the banks here and along the west coast.

"Oh, well, I'm not planning to—" I start to say but Thomas comes in with Mr. Saunders following close behind.

"I'll let you and Nancy meet up at a later time. I've got some things that need to be signed right away," Maddox interrupts sending Nancy out of her seat and out the door.

"Good afternoon, Mr. and Mrs. Bishop," Mr. Saunders greets me with a handshake and then Maddox. He then moves over to the large table by the window and starts laying out documents along the entire length.

"You were able to get everything prepared as we discussed?" Maddox asks standing next to his attorney while I take a seat in my chair over by his desk, not wanting to disrupt his meeting. Maybe I should go to the restroom and give them some privacy. Or maybe he is here about Brad?

"Piper, can you come over here and take a look at these?" Maddox asks holding his hand out. The one with a wide black Tungsten wedding band. There is just something so sexy about my man wearing a mark that belongs only to me. Maddox notices where my eyes are focused and chuckles. "I feel the same, cherry bomb," he says. His eyes lower and I feel a flutter in my stomach. The light hits my two-carat, double halo of diamonds. Maddox wanted a larger size but I refused to wear something so extravagant. The matching wedding band helps set off the sparkles that light up the room when a ray of sun shines on it.

Gracefully as I can, I walk over to the man, placing my hand in his as he pulls me in front of his body so his chest is pressed tight against my back.

"I've marked the tabs in pink for Mrs. Bishop and blue for you, sir. Just sign on all those and I'll have them filed on my way back to the office." Mr. Saunders gestures and holds out a pen for each of us. "If you can start on the first one down there then work your way to the other end we'll be finished in no time."

"What are we signing? Is this about the other night? Are the police still coming after you?" I shoot off questions in a panic.

Maddox wraps his strong arms around my middle and snuggles his face into my neck. My body immediately calms.

"The police are not going to be pursuing any legal recourse for the attack against you last week," Mr. Saunders states.

"Oh, that's so wonderful," I say twisting in Maddox's arms and squeezing him.

"But there is a matter I'd like to discuss with you," Mr. Saunders continues. "The family wanted to release a statement saying that Mr. Rollings passed away in a hunting accident. The wife is so distraught that the small children will suffer horribly if it were to be made public of Brad's actions that night. Mrs. Rollings understands if you aren't able to go along with it—"

My head tilts back and I look up towards Maddox. "What do you think?"

He smiles down at me. "I'm okay with it if you are, *wife.*"

"I'm willing not to speak of it," I say.

"Very good," Mr. Saunders agrees locking eyes with my husband. "Then all that's left is your signatures on these documents and I'll be on my way."

"All of these just to say that I won't run and spread the truth about a man who tried to kill me?"

"Piper, these are to put you on all my policies." Maddox turns me to face him.

"Policies?"

"Life insurance, bank accounts, things like that in the instance something should happen to me. I want to make sure you are taken care of," Maddox informs me.

"But I don't need all that—"

"I know you don't but it would give me peace of mind knowing that everything was taken care of for you. If we have children they will also be included in these documents. It's just a precaution."

My palms start to sweat. I hate the topic of other people's money.

"Maybe you should have everything put in your mom's or sister's names?" I suggest.

"I already have trusts for them. This is only for my wife." He leans down and kisses the tip of my nose. "Please do this for me."

I lean in and whisper, "Is this because you are mafia?"

The corner of his lip quirks up making him smirk. "This is because you are my wife and family and I want you to never have to worry about paying another bill in your life."

I just stare up at him trying to gather my thoughts. After a few moments, he rubs my arms then takes my hands in his.

"I wanted to speak with you about your dad," he says and pulls out a chair for me and then does the same for himself. "I have several smaller homes on our property and was thinking that we could move him into the one by the pond and garden. He'd have a full-time medical staff and doctor on property at all times. You could be close to him and see him every day and make sure the staff is doing things the way you want."

I pull in a breath. "I'd love that but the cost for private care is so much and insurance—"

"Won't be a problem," he assures. "I'm so sorry I didn't handle your mom's care better and that won't happen this time, I promise."

"But doesn't your mom want to come back and stay for a while? She was talking about staying on the property."

"There are several other places there for her to choose from. She is the one who designed the entire property when it was being built."

"Oh." My head is swimming with all that has happened today from ring shopping to hearing that Maddox won't be in trouble to the possibility that my dad could be close. "I think I'd like that."

"Okay." He smiles and nods. "We can set up interviews for staff and doctors and get everything settled this next week." I nod. "So can we sign these and then go celebrate?"

"I'd like that."

Thirty minutes later, Mr. Saunders is walking out the thick wooden doors with a briefcase full of documents with my name on them. I'm sitting down in the leather chair across from Maddox's desk as he shuts down his computer and locks away his files.

"Are we going to talk about the elephant in the room?" I ask.

"I guess it would depend on which elephant," he jokes but we both know we need to have this conversation.

"Let's start with the mafia one and then you can tell me all the others," I sass and interlock my fingers over my crossed legs.

His shoulders slump slightly like a teenager getting busted. "I was hoping we were just going to sweep it under the rug," he says as he walks around his desk and sits down beside me in the matching leather chair. Turning my chair and pulling it closer together we are now face to face and knee to knee.

"I think you know me better than that," I say and raise an eyebrow. "Why didn't you tell me sooner about your occupation and who you were? We could've had this talk months ago. Why hold off?"

"I wanted to tell you but the more you shared with me and the more I fell for you, I didn't think you felt the same. I wanted to make sure you were so hooked on me that leaving wasn't going to be an option. I honestly thought this was one-sided for a while. You were so independent, not needing anyone, so I thought I'd hold off until you were more comfortable around me."

"I can understand that, but once I told you I loved you that should've been the time to come clean. We can't have a marriage based on secrets and lies." He nods and I see a twitch in the corner of his right eye. "Is there anything else I should know about?"

He turns his head slightly away from me. "After I killed my father I swore no other person would suffer at the hands of a monster if I could help it." My heart cracks hearing the hurt he carries with what he had to do. He takes a deep breath, closes his eyes, and releases it before looking back at me. "I find people throughout the city who prey on the weak or vulnerable and stop them from doing it anymore."

The weight this man feels he has to take on because he lacked having that support growing up.

"Like Batman?" He shrugs but doesn't elaborate. "And you're sure these people deserve it?"

"I make sure of everything before I…confront them."

"And these people are like your father? They're all bad?"

He nods and I rub my mouth with my hand. He has a Batman complex. He feels the need to save people.

"Oliver didn't fall several months ago in the alley, Piper. He was jumped by several punks to intimidate him to sell the building. I found them and took care of the problem so they couldn't do that to another person."

I gasp and my hand comes up to my mouth covering it at the revelation. I thought something wasn't right about his story because he looked much worse than someone who had taken a simple fall, but I never questioned it out loud. How could someone target a helpless older man?

"What about laundering money?" I lean in and whisper scared someone might hear us.

"The room is soundproof and swept for listening devices, but to answer, yes, I launder the money for all the Families of the mafia. I'm very good at it and so is my team. That is something you'll never have to worry about touching you. We have things and people in place to make sure it never blows back on us."

"How can you be so sure?"

"Because we have politicians, police, and government officials all in our pockets. The world can speculate all they want but they'll never be able to pin us with anything." He must see the worry in my expression because he places both hands on either side of my face. "We are businessmen who have a lot of hands in many different pots."

"It just worries me—"

"I'd die before anything were to happen to you. You don't need to even think about that side of our lives." I nod and he leans further in to place a soft peck on my lips.

"No more secrets or lies moving forward, okay?"

"I'll tell you everything that you need to know," he agrees.

"Is there anything else you've kept from me that I need to know about now?"

He looks at me like he's thinking things over and weighing what to tell me. I don't know if I should be scared or worried.

"I set up the raffle for you to win the washer and dryer."

"What!" I screech then lean back in my chair and fold my arms over my chest. "I knew it sounded fishy when Rob—" I pause. "That little weasel was in on it too?" Maddox nods totally fine throwing him under the bus. "I can't believe it." I shake my head in disbelief. "Then—"

"Wait, there's more?" My eyes bulge and my head lurches forward flabbergasted.

"Just one more thing…I think," he says but I'm not convinced at this point. "I stole your car in the middle of the night and had a mechanic fix as much as he could in the few short hours we had."

"What the heck? When was this?"

"Right after I brought your purse up to the rehab facility after you left it behind at the sandwich shop when you rushed out," he informs me. "We'd just met."

I try to think back to a few months ago and remember Rob telling me he had a guy replace my tires for little to nothing. The guy also fixed the air conditioner and a few other things. Rob is going to be on my shitlist for the next few weeks for this.

"Anything else you want to share with the class?" I cross my legs bracing for the next one. "You seem to be on a roll."

He smirks at my sass and I try to school my face to not smile. I'd be laughing along with everyone too if it weren't me that this happened to. Or at least I'm trying not to but failing miserably.

"I think that's it, cherry bomb."

"You sure?" I cluck my tongue on the roof of my mouth but he shakes his head.

"Do you want your job back at the school?"

It takes me a minute to realize what he asked, but immediately shake my head. "I'd never feel comfortable being there. I love working with the kids but seeing how they treated me for speaking up, I'd never feel safe there."

"I can understand that," he says with a nod.

"I guess I can continue to help Oliver and Rob until I figure things out."

"Or," he pauses, "you could come and work with me?" He holds up a hand to stop me from talking. "You are amazing with numbers and the banking world would be like your playground. Nancy loves to give my money away to charities or such things so there is always room for you with her. Gemma has a foundation that helps kids in the district if you want to do something like that. She mainly works with the elementary kids but you could help the older ones. Look at the good you did for Rob. The Family gives millions of dollars every year to the district and it would be better spent if someone we knew was in charge of it."

I nod. Possibilities are popping up all over my brain. I've talked with Gemma a lot about her foundation and love the avenues she takes in giving back to the kids without the administrative leaders having a say in how the money is dished out.

"I think I might like that but also a little on the banking side," I bring my hands up and touch the top of my head feeling a little overwhelmed. "I don't know."

"You don't have to decide right this minute. Take some time to catch your breath. Let's make sure we get your mom's urn settled and then whatever you decide with your dad and then we can come back to this."

I nod. "Yeah, okay," I agree. "What about Rob?"

"What about him?"

"I want to make sure he's safe and never left out. I'm—we are his only family and I don't want him to feel like he isn't."

"We can put him in one of the apartments on the property or we can set him up somewhere else. I'd never want you to lose him or anyone else, babe."

"Do you think giving him my house is too much?"

Maddox thinks for a moment, his eyes show him coming up

with different scenarios like I always do. It's one of the many things we share.

"I think the responsible thing would be to draw up a contract and have him pay rent for an extended amount of time. He's more responsible than most people but he is still barely an adult and I think structure and having a goal would benefit him." He makes a lot of sense. "Don't get mad but I've upgraded his and your vehicle but I'm making him pay for the insurance and all future maintenance."

"Really? You don't—"

"I know I don't but I am and did. I can't have either one of you breaking down or stranded."

"I'm not going to win this battle, am I?"

"Not this one," he says.

"Experts say that the key to a happy marriage is compromise and to pick your battles."

"Sounds about right." He smiles knowing he's won this one.

"I won't always let you win, you know," I tut with my chin rising in a sassy way.

"I've always liked a challenge." He has a glimmer in his eye and it makes him even more handsome. It's a wonder some women hadn't already swept him up. "There are some things that I can't discuss with you because of business and I'd never want to put you in a situation where you'd have to lie, but I'll tell you everything else. I don't want you to feel like we can't be equal partners in this marriage. Having you by my side is something I never thought I'd get in life and I don't want to fuck it up."

"I love you," I blurt out. "I'm sure there are bad and ugly things that happen in this lifestyle. Hell, I feel like if you can love me with how messy my life is and not give up on me then I know I can do the same for you. I mean your issues are on a different scale but in the end, I know your heart is in the right place." I place my hand over his heart. "I know the man you are when you're with me and I don't see that ever changing."

Maddox stands pulling me up with him. "I'll love you until the very last beat of my heart and even then my love for you will continue," he promises then captures my lips with his. His hands dip down under my butt and he hauls me up to eye level. I wrap my arms around his neck and give in to my husband.

"As much as I'd love to christen my office, I want to take you out to dinner and then ravish you in our bed at home until tomorrow. And if we stay any longer, there is going to be a line of people wanting signatures that are never-ending. Let's get out of here, Mrs. Bishop."

We start towards the double doors when I think a little laughter is needed. "If we work together I'm going to need a new name plaque," I say.

"A new name plaque?" He looks so confused.

"Yeah, to fit on my matching desk next to yours." I pause as he waits for me to explain. "Like yours will say *Batman* and mine will be *Perfect Piper*." I try to hold a straight face but have to curl my lips inward to keep the laughter in.

"Perfect Piper?" He bursts out laughing and I stop holding mine in.

"What? I think it has a wonderful ring to it," I defend.

"More like *Batman* and *Pipsqueak*." Before I can reply he has me over his shoulder fireman style and is walking out the door as if it's normal for the boss to carry his wife around like this.

"Hey!" I try to sound offended but can't stop laughing even when he moves us through the office and down to the waiting car. Darren and Thomas both share a knowing smile as they hold the doors for us.

At least life isn't going to be boring.

CHAPTER TWENTY-SIX

Bishop

I'M SITTING IN THE BACK OF THE AUDITORIUM WAITING FOR the school board to start the meeting. The place is packed with parents and kids. Some have signs calling for Ms. Caldwell to be put back into the classroom. Some of the students are wearing mathematical clothes like Piper's dresses. I snap a few photos wanting Piper to see the impact she's had on these kids. Belinda is talking to several parents at the front as she passes out copies of documents against some of the school board members. The signup sheet to speak is long and I told Darren to record some of the students so that Piper could see all these students speaking up for her. Bobby is sitting on the opposite side of the room towards the back and Arturo is sitting opposite with me in the middle. When I mentioned the things Piper has had to endure over the last week they asked how they could help and when to be there. I'd told them I had it under control, but I knew they'd find a way to be here.

"Can you believe the public actually voted to have those fuckers be in charge of their kids?" Thomas says after he went and put my name on the list to speak. I'm trying to stay out of sight for now hoping the board doesn't recognize me just yet. They know I donate a shit ton of money to this district and it would piss me off if they spoke ill of my wife. I'm already itching to slit all their throats over what they've done to Piper but I need to come across calm and collected.

"Things are going to be run a little differently soon," I say and he nods knowing what's coming for them. We both are on the same fucking page as to what needs to happen to this lot.

"Mrs. Roberts, can you sign our poster?" I hear a kid ask who is standing in the aisle.

Piper's principal looks down at the student and at the poster of pictures of Piper and her students. "No, that would be inappropriate," she chides then walks past the kid.

"That fucking bitch," Thomas hisses under his breath. "Please tell me she's next on the list."

Oh, Jackie has some fun times coming soon to her for sure. I received a phone call yesterday morning from one of my bank executives, Katie, informing me that a Jackie Roberts had come into the bank and wanted to make a complaint against me. The bitch wanted to put in a complaint about *ME*. The fucking CEO of the bank. Katie went on to say that Mrs. Roberts assumed I was a lowly employee and was telling her that she worried that being associated with Ms. Caldwell put her account in jeopardy with security risks. She claimed that she worried since Ms. Caldwell and I 'are dating' that I'd expose and harm her because of some rumors she'd heard had started spreading around town. Katie being the professional that she is took down all Mrs. Roberts' information and said she'd get with her boss and have him give her a call. We have audio cameras on every square inch of all our banks, and I've watched the video so many times I could quote it verbatim. I've yet to call her back but I do think I might confront her on her way out tonight.

"Did you stop by and pick up the envelope from Katie?" I ask.

Thomas pats the upper part of his suit jacket. "Sure did."

The side door to the stage opens and a string of adults walk out across the stage to the tables and chairs set up to have the meeting. I recognize each and every one of them.

"Let's all take a seat and we will get this meeting underway," Ryan Jackson, the voted President of the board, announces. "First, let's all have a moment of silence for our friend and board member, Brad Rollings, who tragically passed away a few days ago."

"I heard he was mauled by a bear," the lady in front of us whispers to another lady seated beside her.

"They said it was gruesome and that the family had to have a closed casket," the other gossips.

Thomas snorts and I narrow my eyes to not draw any attention to us. Oh Brad, did have a gruesome death. I made sure every inch of his body was covered in pain and agony. I left no square inch of skin untouched. We'd made arrangements through his phone for his family to believe he went hunting and even pinned his location after I was done with him for them to find him. The abundant wildlife had their fill of him before anyone knew to go check on him though. With our connection in the medical examiner's office, all the documents show he was attacked by some type of large animal.

"Thank you all for coming tonight, we weren't expecting a group this size, and the sign-up page is full. We are here to discuss and move to vote on a teacher who is under investigation. I know the public would like to be heard before we make a motion and I would like to express that as a board we have the right to move all discussions to a closed meeting if this gets out of hand," Ryan states behind the microphone. "Let's start with the names from the list. With the list being so long we are reducing the time to only three for each person."

Belinda walks up with Ms. Irene and several students with posters and shirts championing for Piper.

"First and foremost, I'd like to say that every one of you sitting up there on the stage is garbage, and that goes for the administration all the way down to the principals and teachers who have allowed this to go on—"

"Mrs. Garcia, I'd like to say that under the advisement of our attorney, Mr. Connors, this meeting is being recorded. So everything that you say can be used if a legal matter comes up," Barry Carver, the Superintendent, pulls the mic up to has fat face.

I've learned a lot about him over the last few days after going over the file Davis sent me. Seems like Mr. Carver can't keep his little pecker in his pants when it comes to the other district employees. Davis was able to recover several email transactions where a former employee put in a complaint with his extracurricular activities but the board was able to make the situation go away.

"That sounds fantastic Mr. Carver. Are you, your administration, and the board members being held to the same accountability and standards?" When no one utters a sound she continues to lay into the school board and give the audience an outline of the findings and how Piper is being punished for bringing it to light. A timer sounds and Barry Carver motions to someone in the sound booth, turning off Belinda's mic.

"Thank you for your time, next," Barry calls out.

"None of the members are paying any attention," Thomas says under his breath.

"I bet they do when I get up there," I say as a student finishes up her plea to return Ms. Caldwell to her classroom.

Thirty minutes later, I'm ready to put a bullet into every member sitting up there on the stage. If it weren't for the kids and witnesses the meeting would already be over. Not one of them has paid any attention to the kids or parents coming up and speaking at the podium. All members have had their heads on their phones or are filling out paperwork or doing something other than being attentive. I hear my name called and watch as Arturo and Bobby both stand as I make my way to the podium. Ryan Jackson and Donald Tucker along with most of the board snap their necks up from their phones when they hear my name called. They know the large donations my businesses give to the foundation that disperses grants to all the schools.

"Mr. Bishop, we are honored to have you here," kiss-ass, Ryan, sugars his greeting. When he looks at the two other men standing next to me his eyes widen.

It's no secret to some who we are and what we do, especially if you are a part of the Mayor's or Governor's inner circle. The City Council and the school board know who we are and give a wide berth when they see us coming. When we need things done we make it happen and everyone's pockets get a little heavier for it.

"I must say how disappointed I am here tonight—"

"Mr. Bishop, I can assure you that tonight isn't our normal meeting. We've had a difficult employee—"

My fingers dig into the podium as I try to school my emotions. "My *wife*," I grit my teeth so hard I feel a pulse in my jaw, "is anything but difficult. In fact, after listening to the last thirty minutes, I'd gather she is the most loved *employee* this district has."

"Your wife?" Donald Tucker, who was voted as the Vice President of the board, stumbles over his words. He looks down at the papers in front of him. "Piper Caldwell is your wife?" He looks to his side at Ryan and his Adam's apple visibly bobs on a gulp. "We didn't realize—"

"I'm not here to listen to you. My business associates and I will be contacting The State of Education and the Governor's Office regarding an independent investigation conducted over this district. Donors have a right to know where exactly our money is going and to trust the district will be completely transparent about the funds. That also goes for the administration and how they are conducting themselves in their duties as educators." A loud applause rings around the room. "I've read all of the members' posts online about what they think of my wife and the accusations that are being fabricated about her. You think because you're a public official that you can't be held accountable for your misleading words, trying to make the situation seem more scandalous than it is. I'm here to tell you that all of that ends here tonight. One more derogatory, defamatory, word comes out of any of your mouths against my wife and there will be hell to pay." I narrow my eyes at each and every one of them. The room temp drops to bone chilling with the silence.

Mitch Connors, the district's attorney, is out of his seat on the front row and up the steps off to the side of the stage. He covers Ryan's microphone and speaks to him briefly.

"We are calling for the members to go to a closed meeting at once," Ryan says and all the members' chairs screech on the flooring as they jump up to head back through the door they came in from.

Voices start to bounce off the walls as people begin to speak to each other. Most are already on their feet and I spot Jackie. We lock eyes and I can tell the woman is trying to put on a brave face but she isn't fooling me.

"Do you need anything?" Bobby asks as he pats my shoulder. Both he and Arturo or dressed like me in three-piece suits. We definitely command a room.

I shake my head. "I've got this but thank you for coming here for support."

"Did you see that fucker, Ryan? Pretty sure he shit his pants." Arturo chuckles. "Luca is gonna be pissed he missed this."

"Wyatt too," Bobby says. "You tell our girl that we've got her back."

"I will," I say, thankful to have them treat Piper like part of the family.

"Adele keeps raving about her and is so happy to have Susie here for a while," Arturo comments.

"Mary wants all the women to have a weekend away from us." Bobby chuckles then frowns. "Last time they did a girls' trip they went to visit Susie and we got a call from the police department in New York."

"Why don't we set them up in one of our hotels instead? The last thing I need is to worry about my wife getting tossed into the drunk tank," Arturo says thoughtfully.

"It's gonna have to wait a while because I'm not letting my wife out of my sight for some time," I add. Too much has happened in the last week; I'm not willing to take my eyes off her.

Both men start to laugh. "Good luck with that, my boy."

The side door to the stage reopens and Barry Carver walks over to the first mic. "We have consulted with Mitch Connors, the District's attorney, on the investigation, and at this time we feel like the situation should remain private until further notice. There will be no voting on anything and with that, this meeting is adjourned." He doesn't waste any time and walks out the same way he came in.

"I guess that's it for the night," Bobby says.

"Plenty of time to have a quick drink before we head over and pick the wives up," Arturo says. "Besides, they stole Dante for the evening before she and Mary went to see Susie. Coming with us?"

I spot Jackie walking out the back of the auditorium. "No, I've got to have a quick word with someone then I'm heading home to Piper. She's been a nervous wreck all day because of this bullshit."

We walk out together with our teams in the background keeping watch. I see Thomas hovering in Jackie's direction.

"What's the plan?"

"Just going to have a friendly conversation," I say.

"Mrs. Roberts," I call out when I'm within three car lengths away. She turns and clutches her fake-ass pearls like I'm there to rob her. "Can I have a word?"

She looks around at all the people standing nearby. "Yes, of course, how can I help you?"

I leave several feet to separate us so I don't come across as too intimidating.

"I wanted to follow up with you about your complaint at the bank," I say. She tries to look confused but the bitch would never make it in Hollywood. "You went into the bank off of Fourth Street and spoke to one of the managers named Katie."

"Oh, yes, uh huh," she nods and stays quiet.

"Well, I just wanted you to know that being the CEO and owner of the bank you have nothing to worry about regarding your account. There hasn't been any security breach and I have all the proof to show that I've never searched or gained access to your account."

She starts to fidget. "I think there might have been a mistake. I'm not sure what the manager spoke to you about but I'm very close with Piper and her family. Her parents and I have been friends for decades. I was the one who got her the job in the district. In fact, I was at her high school graduation party and watched her grow up."

"Is that so?" I say.

"Mhmm, I've been her biggest supporter through the years helping where I can when her parents had that awful crash," she continues, and it churns my stomach.

"Yet you didn't call her to give your sympathies when her mother passed away last week? Or to congratulate her on her wedding?"

"The-the district made it very clear that I was not to have any contact with her until the investigation was over," she defends her lies and then crosses her arms over her chest.

My patience has run out and I've spent way more time with these assholes than necessary. Stepping closer I say, "Bullshit. I know every-fucking-thing that has happened and who was involved, Mrs. Roberts. I would suggest that you stop with the lies before your nose trips you where you walk." I bristle. Holding my hand up in the air I snap my fingers and Thomas comes out of nowhere, reaching into his suit jacket. Jackie takes a step back and puts her hands up in the air as if she's surrendering. "I suggest you pack your shit up and move elsewhere, Mrs. Roberts." I hold out the envelope Thomas hands over. "This is a letter from my attorney stating that you are no longer a banking member at any of my banks here in Las Vegas. You have until tomorrow to come by the bank and pick up a check with the balance in your accounts."

"What?" She looks affronted. "You can't do that."

"I. Most. Certainly. Can," I seethe.

"I-I—"

"There is not a bank within three hundred miles that is going to open an account for you and I have a feeling that your termination papers will be given to you by the end of the week. I suggest you start packing your shit and move to the East Coast or farther." I take another step towards her. "You are going to live a miserable life with the time you have left on this earth, Mrs. Roberts." She trembles and Thomas' hand on my shoulder makes me straighten to my full height. "Watch your back, Jackie."

I turn and Thomas and I walk away heading to where Darren has the car ready. I nod to a few parents and students and wave over to Belinda then hop in the car.

"I think that went well," Thomas says adjusting his holster.

"We have our work cut out for us," I say thinking how each and every one of those bastards are going to pay for what they've done to Piper.

"That's what makes the hunting so much fun." The glee in his voice should shock me but I know he is just as protective of Piper as I am.

"Where to, sir?" Darren asks from the front seat as he turns onto the main road.

"To my wife."

CHAPTER TWENTY-SEVEN

Piper

"AND THEN HE WAS LIKE, 'HEADS WILL ROLL IF Y'ALL CROSS me'—" Belinda deepens her voice trying to reenact the conversation along with over-exaggerated hand gestures.

"Maddox said that?" I ask her as we sit down at the sandwich shop for lunch. Maddox didn't mention *that* when he came home from the meeting a few nights ago.

"Well, not those words exactly but I think everyone in the room could read between the lines. And let me tell you his business associates were *hella* intimidating standing next to him," Belinda informs me as she takes a bite out of her sandwich.

It was my understanding that my husband was going to sit in the back of the auditorium quietly and then relay it all back to me. He never said he was going to go up and speak on my behalf. When he came home he was tense but said that the community really showed up for me. He showed me several clips of my students, former and current, who got up and spoke along with their parents. It made me so emotional hearing them speak and I felt so blessed to have made such an impact on their lives.

"I can't believe so many showed up," I say.

"Really? More wanted to sign up to speak but the old hag who's had way too many plastic surgeries cut the sheet off after the second page filled up. They cut everyone's speaking time down too."

"Old hag?"

"You know the one who just happened to come into all that money from a former employee. I bet if we were to deep dive into her and him we'd find an entirely new scandal to blog about."

I shake my head still wrapping my brain around things. We still haven't researched a few of the other board members. We'd need to ask for more record requests but I think after the meeting I'm going to step away from all of it now. The public knows most of the information and I'm hoping the state will start their investigation for the rest of it.

My union attorney called this morning and said that the school has decided to leave me on administrative leave until the end of my contract in June. I'll still receive my paycheck with all the benefits but was told that *having me at the school now would be a distraction to the children's learning*. I was also told that no action was going to be taken or any disciplinary recourse would show on my employment record for when I planned to apply at another school district. Whatever that means.

I have no plans to work as a school teacher again or at least not in the near future. Maddox has given me so many options and I think since I've got the opportunity to relax and take a breather for a minute I'd like to weigh those.

"You ladies good over here?" Rob comes over and asks after finishing with the last customer.

Belinda sits back in her chair. "I'm good, Rob, but let me ask you both something. Andy is wanting to work after school. Do y'all have an opening for him? He's learning that having a girlfriend can break his bank."

"Is he able to work weekends?" Rob asks before I can answer.

"Yes, except for Sunday mornings because of church," she replies.

"Tell him to come by and fill out an application and we'll take a look," Rob says but is interrupted as a few people come in to order.

I watch as Rob goes and takes the orders and handles business. He has come such a long way in the last few years and I feel like he is going to do so many good things in this world.

A few hours later I'm in the back office when Rob comes in. "How are things going?" he asks as he sits down across from my desk.

"Good. The numbers are strong and the profit is better than it was this time last year. I think talking with Oliver about expanding the catering side will benefit the business even more."

Just then Oliver and my husband, who is wearing my favorite dark gray suit with a black dress shirt, walk in.

"Hey," I greet. "Is everything alright?"

I watch as Rob gets up and ushers Oliver, who is still using a cane, over to the seat he was sitting in. I have a tick in my jaw when I think about someone wanting to hurt him.

"Everything is fine, dear." Oliver waves me off. "Mr. Bishop and I had an eventful lunch discussing business and we think we should share it with the two of you."

"Okay?" Rob answers confusion and worry tinging his tone.

"Well, I'm not getting any younger and I've been thinking about doing some traveling," Oliver starts to say.

"You're not selling the place are you?" Rob comes over to his side and crouches down. "We can do everything for you while you travel. Please don't sell the place. I love it here," he pleads and an ache in my chest forms at the thought of not being here anymore. "We can make this work—"

I look over to Maddox but his face gives nothing away. I can tell he's assessing our reactions.

"I'm sorry but I already have a buyer." Oliver places a frail hand on Robs.

Rob looks over at me. Our eyes are both stricken with sadness. "Pipe..." His voice catches.

Rob is a tough kid and has been through so much in his short eighteen years but he loves this place. This is where he found a home just like me.

"I'll sell my house and buy it from you, Oliver," I say standing up and going around the desk by Rob. I take his trembling hand in mine. "I'll need some time to work out all the details but I'll pay the amount you need."

"Oh, dear, I'm afraid the deal is almost done. I'm just waiting on a few signatures for it to be finalized," he says.

"That means there's still time for you to back out and let us do it," Rob pushes. "Please, Oliver, I'm begging you. Give us a chance."

"Mr. Bishop," Oliver turns to my husband, "do you have the documents?"

Maddox reaches into his suit jacket pocket and pulls out a manila envelope handing it over to Oliver. I feel Rob's shoulder sink. Oliver opens the envelope and pulls the papers out.

"The attorneys have already tabbed where to sign and date. I've got mine and Mr. Bishop's signature in the proper areas." Oliver holds them up for us to see but Rob looks away trying to hold his emotions in.

"Wait," I say when I catch the name at the bottom of the first page. I reach for the document and pull it out of his hand. On closer examination, shockwaves vibrate through my body. "What does this—"

Oliver reaches out and takes both mine and Rob's hands in his. "I'd never let this place go to anyone but one of you, dear," he says as tears form in the corner of his eyes. "This place will be in good hands with the two of you owning and running it for decades to come. You both are the reason it's been so successful these last years."

Rob breaks down hugging Oliver. I join in as we share this moment as a family. After a moment I break away and look over the papers. "Oliver, I'm going to need some time to figure out the funds—"

"Just sign on the tabs, honey," Oliver instructs.

"But I'll need to know how much to come up with," I say. I could sell the home or maybe refinancing it would be better.

"I have decided to just sign it over and I don't want to hear another word on it," he says leaving no room for argument. "You both need to sign on the tabs and then Mr. Bishop will send it over to the attorneys to file."

"Are you sure, Oliver?" I ask when he hands me a pen.

"With all my heart."

After signing and many hugs, Oliver goes home and Rob starts closing up the shop.

"Ready to go?" Maddox asks standing in the doorway.

"How long have you known about this?" I nod over to a copy of the business documents sitting on the desk as I grab my purse.

"He called me this morning after you left to have lunch," he says and places his strong hands on my hips mere inches from his body. I breathe in his cologne and it makes me dizzy. I love his manly smell.

"You didn't threaten him, did you?" I tease.

His fingers flex into my flesh sending a hot jolt to my core as he leans down towards me.

"It was all his idea, cherry bomb," he says, his lips centimeters from mine.

I close the distance and press my lips to his. He moves a hand up to the nape of my neck slanting my head to deepen the kiss.

"Yeah, I think we need to have some rules about no sexing in the office," I hear Rob say from behind Maddox's back.

I giggle and try to take a step back but Maddox holds me to his chest. "I can't wait to get you home and alone," he growls into my ear before turning us both around to face Rob. "You'll get used to it."

Rob shakes his head as he scrunches his face up. "She's like my big sister, dude."

"You got things covered like we discussed?"

"What are you guys discussing?" I ask curious about what they are up to.

"Everything is covered and I've got some help on standby with your guy if I need anything," Rob states both of them ignoring my question.

"Hello!" I wave out in front of them both. "I'm right here."

"Enjoy your time," Rob says finally looking over at me.

"What time?"

"He's talking about our honeymoon," Maddox says and I snap my neck to look up at him.

"Honeymoon?"

"Thought we'd enjoy some time away from here to relax. Your dad is doing well and Rob has this place under control," Maddox tells me.

"I-we—" I'm speechless. I can't remember the last time I took some time off to relax.

"Great, we leave tomorrow then," he says ushering me out and into the waiting car by the curb. Thomas and Darren are there waiting and watching the surroundings.

Now that I know Maddox is part of the mafia all the security makes sense. Before, I thought it was because he was just a wealthy man, but now I know that it's because he rules Vegas as one of the main men here. Do I still have reservations about all of that? Yes, it's a little hard to wrap my brain around with it all being so new to me. Do I ask questions? Yes, and he always gives me a straight answer. Does that change my love for him? Absolutely not.

"So, where are we going on this last-minute honeymoon?" I ask.

"To a private island where clothing isn't allowed," he says with a sly smile moving his hand up my thigh.

"You're incorrigible," I say.

"But you love me."

"I do love you," I say, and I mean it with everything in me.

"How much?"

"How much do I love you?" I repeat his question and he nods his head. "My love for you is like an exponential curve. It's unbounded."

EPILOGUE

10 Years Later

"**D**AD!" I HEAR ON THE OTHER SIDE OF THE PANTRY DOOR and freeze. "I'm ready to play catch!" the voice shouts out echoing off the walls of the house.

I've got Piper pressed up against the wall next to the canned goods with my dick out about to thrust into her warmth. She clamps a hand around her mouth to keep from giggling or making a sound. The tip of my cock is nestled right at her entrance. Saturdays are busy at the Bishop household. Between classmates' birthday parties and sports, we are always on the go and pulled in separate directions.

We hear the sound of cleats tapping against the flooring as he gets closer to us and Piper starts to push at my shoulders to put her down but I'm hopeful we'll be able to finish what I've started as long as my son steers clear of wanting a snack.

"Honey, are you needing something?" I hear my mom ask and sweat starts to form at my hairline. It's one thing to explain and lie to your kid when they find you in a compromising position, but it's another when you're caught by your own mom.

"Trying to find Dad," he says. He's so close that only the wooden door stands between us. I make a mental note to have the door installed with a lock on the inside. "We're supposed to go throw the ball around."

"Well, I don't think you'll find him in there, sweetheart. Did you check his office or he may already be out there waiting on you," Mom suggests.

He doesn't respond but the sound of his shoes tapping away from the door indicates he's leaving.

"That was a close one," Piper whispers then giggles. Her hands have moved to the nape of my neck playing with my hair.

Pressing my lips to hers, I silence her and sink her down an inch on my dick forcing a moan to leave her throat. My dick is already throbbing being encased in her heat. I push her down a little further when a loud rap against the door startles us. Piper gasps as my body straightens automatically on high alert causing my dick to impale her on my full length.

"You have about ten minutes before the girls wake from their nap. Darren's taking Maverick out to work on some fielding drills," Mom says as Piper buries her face in my neck. "Next time, try to keep your clothes from peeking out from under the door."

We hear her footsteps leaving the kitchen and my body relaxes slightly.

"I can't believe we just got caught by your mom," Piper mumbles.

"At least she didn't see us naked," I say and Piper shoves back looking at me square in the eye. The movement causes me to pull out a little and we both groan at the feeling. Not one to waste any time since we are on a time crunch, I shove back in. "You feel so good," I praise as I pump in and out of her wet channel. Bending my knees I position us at a different angle and hit the spot that drives her wild.

She moans spurring me on, "Mmm, yes, right there."

The faster I pump into her the louder she gets. Removing a hand at her hips I grab the back of her head and pull her face down into the base of my neck to help muffle her sounds. The last thing I need is for the security team to hear something and come investigate it or for one of the other kids to hear their mother getting railed by their dad.

Her legs tighten around my waist where I'm holding her up and I know she's about to come. I feel her juices drench my base and it makes my dick harder. I start to thrust without care racing toward the finish line when Piper sinks her teeth into my shoulder trying to stop her sob as she peaks. My body ignites hearing her noises and I flood her pussy with my seed. I continue to plunge into her drawing out her climax as I make sure every drop expels from my balls.

After a few moments, Piper lifts her head from my shoulder and kisses up my neck to my jawline before ending against my lips.

"I love you," she says with depleted energy.

"Love you too, cherry bomb."

We dress quickly with the few clothes we managed to sling off in our impromptu rendezvous. Coming out of the pantry we snag bottles of water then head out of the kitchen.

"I'll go see if Millie is ready." Piper breaks off and starts to head up the stairs. I stop her before she is out of reach catching her hand.

"We'll have our encore after the kids are down tonight," I say wiggling my eyebrows suggestively.

She laughs and shakes her head." Your mom is taking them for the evening. Her, Adele, and Mary are taking all the kids to some indoor play place."

This is news to me."Even better. Now we won't have to worry about being interrupted."

She leans down and gives me a quick peck on the lips before she hustles up the steps. I walk out toward the back of the house and find my son in the backyard playing baseball with Darren. He is throwing the ball high up in the air like a flyball as Maverick runs out and gets under it to catch it.

A lot has changed in the last ten years. Piper and I have three amazing kids. Maverick is eight and a sports enthusiast like his dad. He and I share a love for baseball and we are at every home game here in Vegas. I've coached all his teams and can't imagine doing anything else on a Thursday night. Mom thinks Maverick might be even better than I was when I played and I love that for him. I hope he sticks with it if he wants to pursue it through college.

"Did you see that, PawPaw!" Maverick yells out.

"That was a crazy good catch, buddy!" Darren cheers for him.

Another thing that's changed is my mom and Darren are happily married. To say I was shocked is an understatement. We'd had a really bad situation happen many years ago in Chicago leading to Darren taking a bullet to save Mom and Piper. Mom insisted on being the one to help with his recovery and feelings sparked between the two. I think they are perfect for each other and he fits right into the family with the kids and my twin sisters and their families.

"Daddy," I hear a sleepy little voice and turn to see my three year old, Morgan, just waking up from her nap. She's the only one we've had to put on a strict schedule for her nap times or she'd be awake at all hours of the night. She doesn't wake up well and likes to be cuddled the first ten minutes.

I bend down and sweep her up into my arms. She's got her favorite little stuffie in one hand as she lays her head full of red hair just like her mother's on my shoulder. I pat her back and sway. Piper reaches us and takes a seat under the covered porch with our youngest, Millie, attached to her breast. Millie just turned eight months and Piper is starting to wean her off the tit to a bottle of breast milk instead. Being the perv I am, I watch for a beat and try to control my body when my mind starts to think about what plans I have for those breasts when Mom and Darren take the kids for the night.

"Later, MadDog," Piper says reading my dirty thoughts.

"Dad!" my son calls out to me and I turn. "Ready?"

Darren is already making his way over and he takes Morgan, who goes willingly to her grandpa. I hear him ask if she wants to go and have a tea party as they walk back into the house. I shake my head chuckling thinking about what a ruthless man he used to be and how he'd rather spend his days playing tea parties and baseball now.

"Did you see me catch that ball earlier? Did ya?"

"I sure did. Looks like you've learned to read the ball real well, Son," I praise and I'll never take for granted the beaming response I receive of how much it means to him that I notice his hard work and effort. "Do you want to take some grounders or hit the batting cage?"

"Grounders!" he shouts then runs over to get in the ready position. I grab the bat and ball and we practice for a while.

"All right, boys!" Piper calls out. "Lunch is ready and it's getting too hot out there!"

"Oh, Mom, we're men. We're fine." Maverick sulks knowing our playtime has come to an end for now.

"After lunch, we can take a quick dip in the pool before y'all head out with Glammy and Pawpaw for the night," I offer. We could play for a straight twenty-four never taking a break and it still wouldn't be enough playtime for this kid.

"Yeah, cool," he agrees then takes off running for the house.

I clean up the balls and put away all the equipment before walk back up to the house. Piper is waiting there with a smile on her face. "You're so good with him," she comments. "I love watching him hang off your every word."

"Let's hope that bleeds into his wild teenage years," I joke thinking back to mine and all the hell I put Mom through.

"You're a good man, Maddox Bishop," she says then wraps her arms around my middle.

"For a woman who doesn't want any more kids you sure are trying to get impregnated again with that talk, Mrs. Bishop."

"Rob called and said they were up for camping out next weekend," she says ignoring my comment. "I think you boys will have fun fishing and peeing off the side of the boat."

Rob is now married with kids. His wife is a little older than him and had a son from a previous relationship who's the same age as Maverick. The boys are best friends and spend all their time together. He and his wife also have three more kids together. They fit right in with us. Five years ago, Piper signed over her stake in the business to him so that he could have full ownership. He has been thriving and his wife works just as hard keeping Oliver's dream alive.

Belinda and Joseph moved back to Texas after their youngest, Samuel, graduated high school. Both of their boys went to college there and since most of their family was already there they made the move. We still see them from time to time but it's getting harder as our kids get busier.

We've had a lot of losses along the way too. Piper's dad got sick with pneumonia six years ago and never recovered before he passed away. Not long after that, Ms. Irene took a fall hitting her head causing a brain bleed that led to a stroke. An undiagnosed aneurysm ruptured and she passed away. Piper was beside herself. She felt like she was the only one left of her family and it was hard on her emotionally. It's why there is such a big gap between our kids. She struggled for a while and it was hard to not be able to help her. But the entire Family rallied around her. Gemma and Kendall slept over in bed with her many nights along with Mom, Mary, and Adele. The men were here helping me navigate the best way to help her and I'll forever be grateful for that.

Piper now is more at home than working and I love it. She comes and helps Nancy give my money away every so often. My mom and Piper have built several women's shelters in and around Vegas over the last ten years. It's something that they share to make sure women and their kids have a space to go. They both have leaned on each other and have an unbreakable bond. Darren and Mom live here on the property to be close to their grandkids.

"Oh, and Rob also sent me a news article about Mitch Connors passing away," Piper says before checking her watch.

"Who?" I ask.

"It was the guy who was representing the school district all those years ago. You probably don't remember him. I'd forgotten all about it too until he just sent it to me." She shows me the article on her phone.

"Huh," I respond after reading that he died from some flesh-eating bacteria. "Sounds painful."

"It's crazy how long ago that time in our lives feels. Almost like it happened in another life."

"One you'll never have to be a part of ever again," I say and mean it.

Mitch was the last one on the list checked off of that situation and it felt good to relieve this world of all those bastards.

The government came in not long after that meeting and replaced everyone in the administration. A special election was called and new candidates were elected, Belinda being one of them, and she served on the board for many years until Samuel graduated. As of today Clark County has the best schools in the state of Nevada and their testing scores are one of the highest in the country.

Both Ryan Jackson and Donald Tucker, the President and Vice President of the board, were arrested for fraud and convicted on charges against the government. They both received twenty-five years in prison, which is the rest of their miserable lives being already in their late sixties when they were brought up on charges. The state wanted to make an example of them with the maximum sentence and it made national news. They receive weekly beatings reminding them who put them there.

Barry Carver, the Superintendent, was killed in a mugging in Chicago about a year after being fired. It later came out that he was forcing women to have sex with him if they wanted to advance their careers. What the papers and his family don't know is that he was castrated then his dick was sawed off and he was forced to choke on it before taking his last breath.

Rachelle Flores, who owned the after-school care along with Barry Carver, died in a house explosion. There was a gas leak on her block and luckily she was the only one on either side of her that was home at the time. Thank God for small mercies and all that. What the papers don't say is that she was the only passenger on a small aircraft that morning. It was being flown by remote control when it happened and she knew her end was coming all the way to the ground. Her remains were then transported and planted at her home before the house explosion.

And lastly, Jackie Roberts. She tucked tail not long after being fired from the district. She passed away in her sleep two years ago in Kansas. She didn't go untouched though. Every few months something happened to Jackie. It started with her tires being flat then moved to an expensive plumbing issue then to the air conditioning going out. She really never could catch a break. Her hair fell out when somehow Nair was mixed into her shampoo before she developed a horrible rash all over her body. The lady just couldn't live a normal boring life. As the years went on spooky things started happening around her house and noises started to mess with any type of peace she found in her life. Thomas and I had a field day with that. There is more than one way to skin a cat and I thought ending her life would be too easy for a woman like her. She did eventually pass away of natural causes according to the autopsy report we saw, but we sure made her life miserable until then.

"You ready to eat, babe?" Piper shakes me from my thoughts. "You okay?"

"Yeah, just thinking about some work things," I tell her.

"It's the weekend so banking and *Batman* have to wait until Monday," she chides then takes my hand and pulls me into the house toward the kitchen where our family is.

Ever since she found out that I help clean the streets of scum after what happened to Oliver she's very supportive. She doesn't know any details about what happens and who we pick but she sees the difference we are trying to make. Two months after she and Mom built the first shelter she brought me a list of names of who abused some of the women who stayed there. She likes to call it her Santa List. At first, I thought she was kidding but when she started explaining each of the women's situations, I could see how much it affected her. Thomas and I, along with our team, stay busy needless to say.

Right before we make it to the kitchen I snatch her around the waist and turn her to face me tickling her sides. I love this woman more than my own life and would do whatever necessary to keep her smiling and happy as she is right now.

"What?" she asks smiling up at me trying to swat me away.

"We fit together like coordinates on an axis."

Then I kiss the shit out of her and pour everything I have into it. We may not live a normal life like most people but we have a love that will be around for generations to come.

THE END

Thank you for reading *Bishop*! I hope you loved it and will leave a review.

This was a rollercoaster to write and I never thought this book was going to be finished. I stopped so many times thinking I was going to shelf it and move to something else. I'm glad I pushed through it, though. I knew Bishop was going to need his own book in the middle of writing *Hidden Queen*. To see what it was like being the Head of his family and all they went through. This completes the series of all The Families…for now! I'm ready to work on some different projects that have been swirling in my head for a while and might circle back to our favorite couples or their friends a little later.

Follow me along this journey for updates on the
current and next projects.

www.AmberAllee.com

Goodreads
www.goodreads.com/author/show/48624101.Amber_Allee

Facebook Page
www.facebook.com/AmberAlleeAuthor

Facebook Group
www.facebook.com/groups/655580198616583

Instagram
www.instagram.com/author.amberallee

TikTok
www.tiktok.com/@author.amberallee

ALSO BY AMBER ALLEE

Las Vegas Mafia Series

THE PRINCE

HIDDEN QUEEN

BISHOP

ACKNOWLEDGMENTS

Kevin, you once again prove what a rock you are to me with all the support and love. This process isn't always easy on our family and it takes me away from a lot of responsibilities that you pick up the slack for. So being forced to read romance drafts when you have a million other things on your plate truly shows me how much you love me.

Bryan, we've had so many ups and downs in our lives growing up, and I want you to know that you are the best brother a sister could ask for. We might not agree about some things, but I'd walk through fire for you. Love ya, Bub.

Mom and Dad, thank you for always supporting me and cheering me on. This last year we've been through a lot of medical journeys together and I'm so glad we've all come out on the other side. I love y'all and appreciate all the sacrifices you've made for me over the years.

Misti K, you are the best PA around! Thank you for handling all the behind the scenes so that I could write this book! I would be truly behind in everything if it wasn't for you and your organizational skills. Girl, you are killing it!

Kristen P, I know I say this every time but you are truly a miracle worker and I love you. (Is it possible to love someone you never met? LOL!) Thank you so much for taking time editing and making my thoughts look and sound pretty. You are my hero on this book for working so quickly and I hope one day we'll meet in person so I can give you the biggest hug. Thank you!

Stacey B, as always you make the insides look BEAUTIFUL! Thank you for working me in and being so patient.

Stacy G, thank you for creating this gorgeous cover. I love how you found the perfect Bishop and made a million changes to make it look just how I wanted!

To the Readers, thank you so much for continuing to support

me through this journey. Your reviews and kind messages fuel me to be a better writer.

To the Promoters and Influencers, thank you for getting my book out there and seen by the readers. You guys make such a difference for indie authors like me and I am so thankful for each and every one of you.

ABOUT THE AUTHOR

 Amber Allee is a brand-new author with her debut novel *The Prince* released in early 2024 and *Hidden Queen* in June 2024. She started writing in 2015 but finally pulled the trigger to publish recently. Amber loves to write about romance, drama, and suspense along with hot alpha heroes.

She lives in the great state of Texas in the same town she grew up in. She lives there with her husband and two kids. When she isn't writing, Amber can be found under blankets reading or playing games with her family. She loves to travel and shop. She is the lover of wearing animal print and everything bling!